Cha X
Champion, David
Nobody roots for Goliath
  : a Bomber Hanson $ 22.95
1st ed.

Nobody Roots for Goliath

Acknowledgements

For copious help and advice freely given—and, even better,
given free, I salute and proffer my gratitude
to the following attorneys:
Dan Bruton, North Carolina,
Torey Racines, Pennsylvania
and Jim Scharf, California.
If occasionally I have taken dramatic liberties with the laws and
customs of a state, it should not fault the impeccable legal
scholarship of these gentlemen.

—D.C.

Also by David Champion

The Snatch
The Mountain Massacres

Nobody Roots for Goliath

A Bomber Hanson Mystery

By David Champion

ALLEN A. KNOLL, PUBLISHERS
Santa Barbara, CA

copyright © 1996
First published in the U.S.A. by
Allen A. Knoll, Publishers
200 West Victoria Street
Santa Barbara, CA 93101

First Edition

Library of Congress Cataloging-in-Publication Data

Champion, David.
    Nobody roots for Goliath : a Bomber Hanson mystery / by David
Champion. -- 1st ed.
        p.   cm.
    ISBN 1-888310-44-8 (alk. paper)
    1. Products liability--Tobacco--California--Fiction. 2. Fathers
and sons--California--Fiction. 3. Lawyers--California--Fiction.
PS3553.H2649N63 1996
813'.54--dc20   96-3399
                                                                     CIP

Typeface is Caslon Old Face, 12 point
Printed on 60-pound Lakewood white, acid-free paper
Case bound with Kivar 9, Smyth sewn

Nobody roots for Goliath.

—Kareem Abdul-Jabbar
Very tall basketball player

1

She was driving so damn fast I didn't know what was going to give first, the engine mounts of the old pick-up or my liver.

It was probably nerves that gave her the lead foot on the gas. Her nerves. My nerves were already shot.

Carrie Zepf was her name, short for "Carol" she had told me. She was strongly built with dishwater blond hair that was sheered off above her shoulders, by one of her sisters from the look of it. She was old enough to vote, but way too young to drive. She had written the letter that got me into this death trap in the first place. It was a beguiling letter—poignant and engaging—about her blind father on his last legs from lung cancer and her institutionalized mother with twelve girls at home. I had pictured the sender as younger, less worldly—not someone who would pilot a hundred-year-old Ford pickup on these rutted-country dirt roads at a million miles an hour.

"Carrie!" I yelped, my hands braced on what was left of the dashboard. "If I don't get there alive, I guarantee we won't take the case."

"Sissy," she said, taking a corner so fast I was thrown against her. She giggled, "Not my fault your plane was late. Dinner be gettin' cold by now."

"I'm not hungry," I said.

"I am," she said.

My father had flipped out this time—sending me across the United States to look into the feasibility of taking a smoking case on a contingency. It was a loser for sure, and I was against it from the beginning.

It was a harebrained idea. Of course, that is not a sentiment I would have the nerve to express in Bomber's presence. I didn't say "Boo" to my father, Bomber Hanson, who claims to be the leading trial lawyer in the country—and he doesn't get much argument. Not many people have the nerve to say "Boo!" to Bomber Hanson, except a few judges who are appointed for life.

I am unable to explain how we arrived at the Zepf farm without any structural damage. My nervous system, I was sure, was irreparable. And when I saw the flock of hens in their Sunday-go-to-meeting dresses fly at me from every angle, I got a lump in my throat as big as that battered pick-up I was just stepping out of. And, believe me, the earth never felt better under my feet.

There weren't any spreads in *Architectural Digest* in store for the Zepf place. A two-story box with once-white painted shingles on the sides and a peaked roof on the top. The windows on the front made some geometric sense. Not so on the sides.

There was a barn out back, bigger than the house, and a nice expanse of land to go with it. Bomber's house in Angelton, California sat on about a half-acre. This looked to be about three times as much land. Chickens were in their own fenced area adjacent to the barn. The fields were barren for the winter, but a couple of cows roamed the frozen earth.

The girls were gathered around me as though I were some kind of pop-icon and I was disoriented at first.

"Come on, girls," Carrie said, "let's get the grub in the trough. I'm starvin'." The girls squealed and dispersed in a flash and I hauled my shaky carcass up the five steps to the porch and went in to be confronted by the potential plaintiff seated in his shot-to-hell, formerly stuffed chair, staring blankly ahead with eyes the color of curdled milk.

"He's here, Daddy," Carrie announced, "and we best be eatin' before we all faint dead away from starvin' to death."

"Mr. Hanson," he said putting out his hand, past the tubes of oxygen running to and from his nose. "Rich Zepf." I went over and shook his hand. He had the pasty pallor you get from sitting indoors.

From where I stood, I could take in the whole first floor of the house, which was festooned like the junior high school gymnasium for a Sadie Hawkins Day Dance. It didn't take a mathematical genius to calculate there were not enough chairs in the place to seat the entire family—all the chairs and two benches were pulled up to the table for the banquet.

The girls were scurrying in and out of the room setting food on the table. "I am real honored you came to see us—a important man like you is."

"It's not him," Carrie corrected him. "It's his kid."

"Oh," he said, and he wasn't happy. He finally gave way to a few bobs of his head, while I hastened to assure him I did all the advance work for Bomber—that's just the way it was. "If you were the President of the United States and needed Bomber, I'd be there first."

"I doubt that," he said.

"I don't blame you," I said. "I'd doubt it too. But it's true. I'm the gofer. I do the investigation on his cases. He *tries* the cases. Period!"

We were called to the table and Rich maneuvered the path with some skill. Carrie had mentioned in her letter Rich was blind, but I had had my doubts, as I did about most of her letter. I thought it could have been an elaborate ruse. Bomber thought it was genuine. Bomber was right—as usual.

The table was set with mismatched dishes, glasses, and odd flatware. In the center was a bunch of dried flowers. Crepe paper hung limply from the ceiling lamp over the table. The tablecloth seemed to be an old flannel bed sheet that had worn out in spots and was tailor-cut to fit the long rectangular board that sat atop two sawhorses to form this oversized dining room table. It started in the dining room all right, but had its run through that small room and finished the race in the living room where the last four diners were obliged to sit.

Not so the guest of honor. I was shown by little Lee, age ten, with a face as round as a full moon, to the honored place at the head of the table. There I found a placecard drawn in crayon

3

by a hand I judged to be in the range of the second or third grade. It said:

Mr. Hannsen

Gest of Oner

Beside it was drawn a happy face on a stickish body. The work of art was signed by Joyce. I smiled at the five year old with the stringy brown hair. She smiled back, showing teeth that could have benefited from orthodontia. But there was little chance they could afford that.

On my plate was a paper napkin with a similar smiling face and my name beneath it with the same charming spelling.

Mary handed me a menu that nine-year-old Skipper had made up. Her name was written on the bottom of the first page, which showed a crude picture of their house under the heading:

ZEPF RESTERANT

Opening the folding page, I came to the menu of the evening, in the same vein.

"We made the ice cream together," Mary, the three-year-old with deep dimples, told me. "I turned the handle," eleven-year-old Rita rolled her big brown eyes.

The temptation was great with so many kids to write Girl 1, Girl 2, etc., but they had knocked themselves out, so I went to the trouble of fitting the names to the girls. The feeling I got in their presence was like nothing I'd ever felt before. I had an older sister once, but she took herself out of the fray. Couldn't cope with her physical disabilities. I think that's when my stutter began—in my father's presence only. Unaccountably, I was the strong one in the face of that tragedy, and I must have felt so sorry for my father, who went to pieces, that I took on this affliction in his presence to reassure him he was still superior.

But the feeling here was of mom and apple pie, love and joy—the happy contentment you might get from looking at a Norman Rockwell holiday painting. Except the real mom was gone. But any number of the older girls seemed eager to fill that bill. Not to mention the younger ones.

"I'm Joyce," the five-year old said, "and this is Jodi. We're going to be your waitresses."

She and Jodi, seven and a half, served the courses with all the aplomb and wisdom of their age. And everything was *delicious*.

"Tod, I'm kinda interested," said the blind man. "Tell me straight out it's none of my business, but how did your father get that there name the 'Bomber?'"

"No secret," I said. "He was a bombardier in Korea. His buddies called him 'Bomber.' He was an impressionable kid and he liked it. 'Bomber' stuck, thanks to his using it all the time."

"He was a war hero, then?" Rich Zepf said.

"Ah, not exactly," I said. "That is a little more sensitive. His crew was on its way to their first target when they got the word to turn around, the war was over. So, he never actually dropped any bombs on anything. Except now in the court-room."

Miriam, tall, blond and fourteen, asked me, "Carrie wants to know, do you have a girlfriend?"

"No," I said, and the girls tittered while Carrie blushed.

"Carrie could be your girlfriend," Miriam said.

"Now you hush," Carrie said. "This is *so* embarrassing."

The younger girls squealed with delight. Little Joyce said, "I could be your girlfriend."

"Yes," I said, "good idea. You could all be my girl friends," and squeals and titters filled the air.

"Now girls," Rich said, "settle down. Mr. Tod here's our guest. You don't want to go making him feel discomfort-able."

The dessert was fantastic. The apples had been pre-served from their own trees, the milk and cream in the ice cream came from their cows, just as the chicken, potatoes, celery and onions in the pot pie and soup had been from their farm. As soon as I put my fork down after savoring the last bite, Carrie asked me if I wanted seconds. When I assured her I didn't, I noticed my waitresses' eyes light up. They had not had dessert, apparently pending my appetite.

While they cleared the dishes, Skipper told me that Jan, June and Miriam—teenagers all—had written a play for me. I asked for a moment alone with their father and they all scurried to the kitchen like homing pigeons, while Rich and I made our way back to the livingroom. I took a chair with me. The place wasn't set up for privacy, but the buzz of the kids in the kitchen obscured our conversation. Not that it mattered. I didn't think there would be much secrecy in this household.

When we were seated and Rich had put his oxygen tank on the small table beside him, I said, "I'm going to be brutally frank, Mr. Zepf. I hope that's all right."

He nodded. "What's not all right is you call me 'Mister'. We just folks 'round here. I like to be called Rich—maybe 'cause I ain't."

"Rich in spirit," I said. "This case you want to try against the tobacco company..."

"The girls' idea," he said. "I got no need for lots a money. I ain't gonna be 'roun' for it nohow. But the girls figger it'd give 'em a leg up, they wanna go out in the world. Least I can do for 'em."

"What do you know about tobacco cases?"

"Nothin'. Girls tell me. Send 'em to school, they read stuff, I guess, hear stuff."

"Did they tell you no one has ever won a smoking case?"

"I don't recall that, no."

"And it is not an easy thing fighting a tobacco company. They have billions of dollars. And they don't give up—they'll spend it all if they have to. Could drag on for years."

I went on like that, shooting all the discouraging arrows in my quiver and Rich Zepf just nodded his understanding and acceptance. When I ran down, he said, "Tell me somethin'? You givin' me all this bad-mouth talk, how come you come here?"

I was glad he couldn't see me blush. I tried to explain it to him. "Bomber is a fascinating man," I said, "if he doesn't

6

happen to be your father. He likes to play the irascible curmudgeon, but deep down there's some marshmallow there. Carrie's letter got to him. Then, too, he rises to the bait of a challenge like nobody's business. And there is nothing so challenging as a sure loser."

"Why is it a sure loser?"

"Goes back to the government labels," I said. "Government mandates certain wording. Bomber says it is insufficient warning. The package should simply say: 'Smoking kills you.' Juries so far have felt a smoker knows he is taking risks."

"But Bomber thinks he can win a sure loser?"

"He is intrigued with your case for a couple reasons. First you are blind and he thinks he can make a case that you couldn't read the label."

"True. Couldn't."

"And some things have come out about the T. S. Armstead Company, makers of your favorite brand. Seems they may have been adding nicotine to make the smokes more habit-forming. The company denies it, has all along, but Bomber feels like he could crack that."

"Do you?"

"I don't see how. You need a stool pigeon from the company and it has *never* happened."

"You still against the case?"

"I still think it's hopeless. Blind or not, I don't see how we could prove you never heard cigarettes could be dangerous—on the radio, from your family. Somewhere. And I think getting someone in the tobacco company to turn is a real long shot. And, you know, the company will set out to destroy you—your wife, your daughters if they have to. Can you take it?"

"I expec' so."

"And your wife—and the girls?"

"They's tough."

"Maybe not tough enough. A lot of people start these cases then give up when the going gets rough. Too much mental anguish, too little hope of a pot of gold at the end of the rainbow. Say," I said, "didn't you smoke *before* you were blind?"

"Nope."

"Never read a cigarette warning on the pack, in a magazine, on a billboard?"

"Didn't pay no attention."

"Carrie said you were a truck driver."

"Was."

"Never saw a billboard advertising cigarettes?"

"Sure."

"The warnings were on the billboards. You never read them?"

"Nah. Who *reads* that stuff?"

"Carrie said in the letter you had an accident while you were a truck driver. Something fell on you that made you blind."

He burst into raucous laughter. "God bless Carrie," he said.

"Isn't true?"

"'Course it's true," he said. "Only the two weren't connected." He sucked some oxygen then sat back, as though he were going to relax before his big effort. "I am what you would call a randy person. I ain't ashamed of it. I was made that way's all. I guess you look around this here house, you get a idea yourself 'bout it. An' I ain't ashamed none I gone to them bawdy houses in my time, 'fore I married 'course."

"How long before?"

"The night before," he said and I must have imagined that twinkle in his dead eyes. "In them days, I wuz somethin' of a drinker, you might say, and we gets into a scuffle there on the premises."

"We?"

"Me an' the cops."

"Where was this?"

"The bawdy house. Down by the river. Way they tells it, I was on the unruly side and you can't prove nothin' by me when I'm so heavy on the sauce. Way they tells it, I was a pretty strong hombre in my time, and then they's scared an' they's using the pianner for a shield with me on the other side. Well, dad-blame it if that there old roller pianner don't come over on me and I still got this crazy memory the thing was playing *Shine on Harvest Moon* when it fell and knocked me over just so. So I couldn't see no more."

I looked him in the eye and got the eerie feeling he was looking back. I put my hand on his forearm. "Rich," I said. "Think about this seriously. Do you want all this stuff dragged up again? Want them to call you a whoremonger, your wife a loony bird? The case could easily outlast you."

He waved his hand at me. It reminded me of one of Bomber's favorite gestures. "I done thought 'bout it. I was alone, no way I'd mess with 'em. But I got these girls see. You can count 'em, cousin, they's an even dozen an', man, I gotta tell you, I love's 'em more 'n anything an' that include my life itself. I ain't been able to do fer 'em like I'd like. Oh, I don't wants to spoil 'em or nothin'—no need to plant a hundert grand on 'em or nothin'—but jest like them rich folks does, they sends 'em off to college, gives 'em a leg up wid a house 'n car. You know, help 'em out a little. I can't do nothin'. So they dream up this hair brain scheme and I says what the hell, probably won't work, but what good am I to 'em otherwise? So you asking me, am I game? I *am* game. I'll fight it to my last breath, an' if that ain't good enough, I tried my best, I'll go easy to my grave. These is good girls, boy, and ain't nothin' in this world gonna be too good for 'em."

2

When they came back in the room, there was an excitement about the Zepf girls that was catching. I have, in my time, both performed and witnessed children's homemade plays and they are as deadly as anything known to man. Yet the high spirits of the kids put an edge of expectation on the visiting cynic.

Three-year-old Mary came to take me by the hand while Rita moved my chair next to the big stuffed chair that held her father. Two of the girls moved the rickety coffee table and chair off their "stage" and eleven-year-old Rita came into the room carrying a tablet and sat in the chair off to the side. The other players were "in the wings" in the kitchen.

Rita began to read:

"One day a tall and skinny white thing with brown insides came to a small house in the North. Her hat was red like fire."

Tall Miriam came into the room wearing a red hat and her whole body was wrapped in a sheet. I caught on in a minute: she was a four-foot cigarette.

Rita went on.

"In the white house there lived twelve girls and a mother and a father. The father liked the visitor because he couldn't see him. He was blind. But the girls and their mother didn't like the visitor. They were afraid of him. Nobody invited this tall white visitor with the brown insides, but he got very friendly with the father and he just couldn't get rid of him. Soon the father saw he couldn't live without the visitor." *Here June, dressed in her father's severely oversized clothes, hugged Miriam, our visiting cigarette.* "His girls were all unhappy because he was getting sick from the visitor, but he couldn't make him leave. The mother told the father if the visitor did not leave this house immediately, she would leave."

Skipper, dressed in one of her mother's old dresses—too long for her, with a black hat with the veil pulled down—shook her finger at the bundle-of-man's-clothes.

"The father pleaded with her. He too wanted to get rid of the visitor, but the visitor made himself more appealing all the time and the father was helpless. He got sicker and sicker and the mother left him and their twelve girls alone in the country.

"Those girls loved their father."

Here all the girls in the family paraded by June, dressed in her father's clothes, then circled her and patted her lovingly.

"But they didn't know how to save his life. The visitor was with him all the time now. He could not get him out of his house. The girls were very sad."

They all wiped their eyes and ad libbed—"What shall we do? What can we do? What will happen to us if this awful white stick takes our father from us?

"Then one day the oldest girl said, (*Carrie spoke*) 'I cannot sit around here and do nothing while this awful stranger destroys my beloved father. I am going to get someone to help us.'

"'But where?' her sisters wondered. It would take a very strong and handsome man to save them from all this trouble."

"I'm afraid it is hopeless," Skipper said. *They had begun to drift away from June in her father's clothes. She was left alone now, except for Miriam, the cigarette who never left Rich Zepf's side.*

"So the oldest daughter searched the whole country to find a tall, strong and handsome man who could save them from their troubles.

"And then one day…"

Carrie came on the scene twirling in delight, her arms crossed over her chest. "Oh, I've found him! I've found him!" *She swooned and threw her arms out and spun around again.* "He's in California."

"But how will you get him here?" Lee asked.

"I'm going to write him a letter," Carrie said.

"He'll never come," Lee said. *All the sisters echoed her and shook their heads pessimistically.*

"The girls had no faith. They thought their older sister was dreaming. No one would come all the way across the country to save their unimportant family," Rita read. "Boy, were they in for a surprise! The tall, strong and handsome man *did* come from California to save them!"

Now Jan burst on the scene, dressed as closely to me as she could with the stock at hand, and said, "I will save this little family. They may be unimportant in the world, but they are important enough for me to come all across this country for. Now visitor, it is time for you to go away from here and everywhere. It is high time you stop making people sick. We have had enough of you. Out! Out!" *And Jan chased Miriam in her sheet and red hat from the room. The other girls cheered.*

Rita wrapped it up: "The terrible visitor was chased from the house by our hero and, thanks to him, the girls' mother came home and they all lived happily ever after."

Rich and I applauded heartily and so did the girls, so proud of their accomplishment. I looked over at Rich and he had tears in his eyes. I was relieved to see I wasn't the only one.

All the players gathered around me and I felt like I had twelve girlfriends, so much attention did they pour on me.

"Will you help us?" "Please say you'll take our case, oh please." "Help us, please."

I had to tell them the decision would be made by the man who would have to try the case—and front a considerable amount of money in their behalf.

Carrie was on to me. Right away she asked, "What will you recommend?"

"I don't recommend with Bomber. Whenever I do, he seems to do the opposite."

"You didn't like our play?" Miriam asked.

"I loved your play," I assured them all. Then I bungled an explanation about how a major part of it had to do with what was best for their family and the toll it would take on everyone. Then also there was the toll it would take on Bomber and me. And the slight chance of winning. And in the off chance we would win, the likelihood of getting enough of a cash award to pay even our expenses. And finally, the crushing wealth and power of the tobacco companies made them, in my judgment, unstoppable.

When I said thank you and goodbye, I was surprised they seemed to maintain a refreshing, if naive, optimism. They all seemed to think they would see me again.

"So, what are the pluses?" Carrie wanted to know when she drove me to my hotel.

"Your family is delightful. That's a plus. Jury victories sometimes hinge on factors other than justice and facts and laws. They could just look at you darlings, shut their ears to the evidence and vote you a ton of money."

"You don't think they would, do you?"

I shook my head.

We had arrived in front of the hotel. Carrie was smiling. I had not dented her spirits either.

"Okay, soldier," she said, putting out her hand. I shook it and thanked her for her hospitality.

"No, thank you for coming," she said.

I got out of the pick-up which mercifully, she had driven at a friendlier rate of speed than on the trek from airport to her home.

"See you again," she said, and before I could protest or at least qualify that, she was gone, in a cloud and a roar.

I checked in and found my room by myself. A bell staff in Cedarberg seemed to be a daytime thing, and it was after eleven. I was anxious to flee this burg so I called Bomber at home. It was only about eight-thirty his time.

When he said, "Hello," I said, "Don't take the case."

"Why not?"

"It's hopeless," I said. "He won't live until you pick a jury. He's sucking oxygen now to stay alive."

"The kids cute?"

"Yeah, adorable." I couldn't lie about that.

"Look good in the front row—in the papers, on the telly—dressed in their Sunday-go-to-meetin' finest? Clean and down home and cute as a bug-in-a-rug?"

"Well, yeah, I g-g-guess so."

"So what's your hurry? Check out the town. Look in the store windows. Ride the bus. Get the flavor of the place. Hit a couple lawyers, the newspaper; see how the wind blows. Then we'll decide."

Sometimes, I don't know why I put up with him.

3

Next day I was on Madison Street checking out the town.

From my talks with the locals, I gathered Cedarberg had been industrial in the heyday of industry. They made big trucks here and the steel mills were nearby. The trucks have moved south, thanks to the southern hospitality of lower labor, land and tax costs, and the steel mills have fizzled, leaving behind cleaner air and unemployment. There were two colleges in town. One for fellas, one for femmes. They were sparking distance apart and accounted for countless good times, but not many marriages. They are co-ed now. More marriages.

The main drag is quite a contrast to the tourist's delight, Main Street in Angelton, CA. There, we have low-slung stucco shops with darling red tile roofs—California's version of old Mexico. Here in Cedarberg, PA, they have sturdy brick buildings from two- to five-stories high with niggardly windows displaying helter-skelter merchandise. The street reminded me of retail-in-retreat. It once housed some fairly tony shops and department stores, but now was given mostly to what they call "thrift shops." There was fast food too, and one of the four department stores was still plugging along, though the merchandise had a shabby look to it, as though it had been pawed over by a thousand grimy hands.

My morning appointment was at the august firm of Bortz, Hillegas, Stimmel and Klerx, located in the heart of Madison Street. The ante room was pleasant with imitation-leather burgundy chairs for resting your dogs while you waited for someone more important than you to sally forth.

The receptionist was a pleasant soul with prominent

cheeks, a hush of blush and her lipstick under control.

"Mr. Stimmel will be with you in a moment," she assured me.

And he was. I had barely time to leaf through the back half of the *New Yorker* magazine, which graced the table in front of the burgundy-vinyl chair as a reminder, no doubt, of the day when that was a magazine with pretensions to sophistication. Beside it, *Architectural Digest* lay inert.

Norman B. Stimmel had about him the heavy scent of ivy, but he greeted me (the antithesis of ivy) as a long-lost friend of the family, one who might surface now and then when he was in need of the replenishment of funds. On the way to his office, he introduced me to some of the other heavy hitters in the firm and I commented that he was the only one with his name in the title.

He had a ready smile and he used it. "Second generation," he said modestly. I guessed he was fiftyish, and if he took any exercise it was in a golf cart at the Cedarberg Country Club.

"So you're a California boy," he said seating himself behind his large, shiny wood desk. On the wall were his diplomas, which I glanced at. He wasn't Ivy League after all, but he did get up to New England for undergraduate school (Trinity College) and came home to Pennsylvania for law school at Dickenson. In those days, I later learned, Dickenson was not considered on par with the University of Pennsylvania Law School where Stimmel's father had gone. But I was willing to wager that while the elder Stimmel's nose for the law was superior to his son's, the old man couldn't hold a candle public relations-wise.

"Always wanted to go to California—take Horace's advice."

"Horace?"

"Horace Greeley—'Go west young man.'"

"Oh, yes."

"How do you like our fair city so far?"

"Fair," I said, thinking I was clever.

16

He frowned in disappointment. "I suppose we are lacking in that Hollywood glamour."

"I'm not from Hollywood." I said. "Over a hundred miles up the coast."

"Yes, well, we easterners are bound to think of California in terms of Hollywood or the Watts riots," he smiled. "So how are your earthquakes?" He asked the perennial question.

I gave him my stock answer. "Lots of fun."

He rolled his eyes. "I bet."

"Actually, I don't ever feel them. I read about them in the paper the next day, but I don't feel any more than I guess you do."

The expected skepticism crossed his lips and he got down to business. "So what can we help you with while you're in town?"

I gave him a quick background on Bomber.

"Of course," he said. "I know Bomber. We all do. I don't want to say we envy him because that flashy, hotshot style wouldn't work here. But you can't help envy a big winner like he is. So you're his son...." he trailed off, but his eyes stayed put, as if looking for some cure to the condition we shared. "So you know what it's like following the footsteps of the great. How do you find it?"

"I guess that part doesn't bother me. I don't have any aspirations to outshine him. I do investigation mostly—legwork. Never really wanted to be a lawyer."

"No?" He seemed surprised. "What then?"

"A composer."

"Is that so?" he said, but his thoughts were elsewhere.

"We will be looking for local counsel to represent us as *amicus curiae,* if we decide to take this case."

He nodded encouragingly. He was seeing a jump in the firm's billable hours. Not much work involved when you had an out-of-state firm trying a case. Very easy money. "What's the case?" he asked.

"Wrongful death," I said. I don't know why I started

that way. It wasn't accurate, though it told the story, I thought, engagingly. And from the state of his eyebrows, Norman B. Stimmel was engaged. Wrongful death connoted giant-industry-crushing-man-with-untold-future-earning-power.

"From what?" he asked.

"Cigarettes."

He deflated before my eyes. "Oh," he said. "Those are tough cases. Has anyone ever won one?"

"Not really."

"And you're going to try that *here*?"

I said we were thinking about it. And he told me why we shouldn't.

Norman Stimmel told me his firm would, of course, have to leave its options open. For if big tobacco came to town, they would likely seek out Bortz, Hillegas, Stimmel and Klerx first thing: and, of course, their billings would be potentially higher. He understood contingency work and the financial constraints attendant thereto...Sometimes Stimmel spoke like a legal document, and I formed the quick impression of him on the other side of the table, should Bomber take complete leave of his senses and take the case.

Tobacco companies bought respectability. They paid handsomely for it. In Cedarberg, Bortz, Hillegas, Stimmel and Klerx *was* respectability. You could tell from the magazines in the waiting room.

For my afternoon appointment, I went to the other end of the spectrum. It was Norman B. Stimmel who put me on to Easy Willie Adams, the antithesis of the big-firm boys. Easy Willie got the nickname because he took it easy. No one had ever seen him riled. He'd had a few wives who still spoke affectionately of him, but they finally just left him because, as Number Two put it, "He never wanted to *do* anything."

Easy Willie's office was not one to inspire confidence in a prospective client. Neither was Easy Willie.

It was a one-room office with a desk and a pair of file cabinets that I would have bet were empty. There was no secretary in evidence, and no desk for one.

"Have a seat," Easy Willie said, easily.

I looked at the only other chair in the place, haphazardly facing the desk, and had the sudden urge to ask him for a vacuum cleaner to suck off the grime. But I was trying to make a good impression, so I sat.

He had a bulbous nose, did Easy Willie. I've always wanted to use that adjective for a nose, and here was a guy who really had one—(And his face wouldn't launch any ships either).

The thin blue lines of his capillaries put me in mind of chickenwire, and there were enough holes in both cheeks for a golf course.

Easy Willie took it easy, but his hair was that of a worrier. It wasn't completely white, but it was on its way.

The most disconcerting thing about Easy Willie was he was smoking. A cigar. He didn't ask if it bothered me (it did) nor did he make any move to put it out in deference to his visitor. Deference was not a concept known to Attorney Adams.

"We might be doing this cigarette case," I said, looking uncertainly at his cigar. "...need local counsel..." But even as I was talking, I knew this would never work. Bomber would explode at just the sight of this laid-back bozo. "I didn't realize you were a smoker..."

He took a puff and blew the smoke overhead, as if to verify my astute observation.

"You think you could go against a tobacco company— being a smoker and all?"

He nodded. "I hate cigarettes."

"But you...smoke."

"Not paper," he said. "It's that burning paper that'll kill you. Cigars are good for you. George Burns lived over a hundred years, did't he? Slept with a cigar."

"He used to do better," I said.

Easy Willie stared at me and then let a grin betray his easy countenance. "You're okay, kid." he said. "So what's your beef?"

"No beef. Just scouting the area for lawyers to associate with. Your name came up."

He looked surprised. "Yeah? Where did you ask, the Midnight Mission?"

"No. Actually, Norman Stimmel mentioned you."

"Ah," he nodded knowingly. "'Mentioned' is a far cry from 'recommended.'"

"True," I said. "If we decide to come in here in a face-off against the tobacco company, we're going to be looking for someone who won't sell out."

Easy Willie nodded and took another puff. "You think I wouldn't sell out?"

I studied the rutted face. "I got a feeling you wouldn't."

He shook his head. "Wrong," he said. "Nobody in town'd sell out faster."

"I'm sorry to hear that." Actually I was rather pleased to have him hand me an excuse for not hiring him. I thought Stimmel sent me here as a joke. I could just see the trial with three retired judges and the mayor at the defense table and Easy Willie at ours. Putting on evidence would be a waste of time.

"Sorry to say it," Easy Willie said. "Just want to be up front with you. I've lived the last half of my life, easy, hoping someone would buy me." He shook his head and studied the lit end of his cigar. "Nobody."

"Maybe you're better off—sleeping at night and such."

"Maybe. But there are no worries on that score."

"Sleeping?"

"Selling out. I'd do it in a minute, there just aren't any buyers."

"So what's your take on a tobacco trial in this town?"

"Hopeless. I couldn't discourage you enough."

"Why's that?"

"This is a law-and-order town. We go by the book. Lot of Pennsylvania Dutch left. Responsible people. Someone falls in a hole here, they *might* go to a doctor—never a lawyer. Plaintiffs need inner cities where the prevailing mores are something-for-nothing. Here we kinda want to take responsibility for our own actions."

"What if a guy couldn't read the warning on the package?"

"Have to have his head in the ground not to hear all the talk—newspapers—TV."

"He's blind."

He sighed and pondered, pondered and sighed. "Radio," he said at last.

"But he wasn't smoking radios. It was cigarettes."

"Yeah." He looked at his file cabinets behind him, then back at the cigar and then put it between his unhappy lips. Finally he shook his head. "Tough town for that," he said.

"Judges be bought?"

"Everybody can be bought," he said. "What's a judge make? Eighty grand—maybe five grand a month after taxes. How many million would they have to pile on the table to turn a guy's head?"

"You got some crooked judges?"

"I'm not saying that. Just might be a temptation. Most of ours are pretty straight when you come down to it, and I'd even say, depending on who got the case, it would be impossible—and if it was tried, they'd be up for bribery in a flash."

He filled me in on his jaded view of the pitfalls and pratfalls we could look forward to if we came to town.

"Would you associate with Bomber?" I asked him.

He shook his head.

"You know Bomber?"

"Everyone knows Bomber Hanson—not personally, of course. No, I just don't see it in the cards. You want someone who'll boost your stock in the eyes of the locals. That's not me."

"Can you give me a card. Maybe we'll call you later."

Easy Willie Adams shook his head. "Fresh outa cards," he said.

On the way out, I said, "I notice you don't have your diplomas on the wall like the other lawyers."

"Yeah," he said laconically. "You probably also noticed I'm not like other lawyers."

"Yeah, well, did you go to law school?"

"'Fraid so," he said. "Not among my proudest achievements."

"Where did you go?"

"Little place outside of Boston," he said.

"Boston College?" I asked.

"Harvard," he said.

4

I could easily have predicted it. My strong objection to taking the cigarette case only spurred Bomber on. The more impossible I made it seem, the more eager he was to do it.

"But they're enormous," I protested. "They'll crush us."

"That may be so, kid," he said, "but just remember one thing: nobody roots for Goliath."

Then, he saddled me with a whole raft of assignments. These I began carrying out with my customary resentment.

I often wondered why he sought my advice if he was going to do the opposite anyway. Maybe he sought my advice just to *do* the opposite.

Among my assignments was the hiring of Easy Willie Adams, which proved not so easy, and advertising for, interviewing, and hiring a lawyer to do research and other dirty work. Bomber was anxious that Easy Willie not feel like he was being hired to do clerk work.

The three-line ad in the *Cedarberg Courier* for full-time legal assistant drew a flood of calls. I cut the field to three interviews.

Bomber let me rent a suite in the Hotel Madison for the interviews. It made me feel important. My first meeting was a Yalie about to end his stint as the law librarian for the bar association, a plum that paid him less than most janitors, but had the beauty of being part-time so you could do other work if you had any. Jason Kline didn't have any and I could see why. His personality was, to put it kindly, difficult. His credentials seemed impeccable and he was bright and quick, but he gave me the creeps.

After Jason, I saw Fred Bogart. He was, he said, the

man for the job. He was in his thirties, had worked for the steel mills—in an executive capacity, he hastened to assure me—and was "ready to get my feet wet lawyerwise. You won't regret hiring me. I'm a whiz on research."

Two minutes after he walked out, Shauna McKinley walked in. I talked to her for two-and-a-half hours and thought it was about thirty minutes.

She was not knock-out beautiful. But she had verve and energy and a penetrating stare that took the wind out of your sails.

The first thing you noticed was her forest of red hair, and if you tried to kink your hair for a hundred years, you couldn't get it that kinky.

She was in fine fettle physically, but she was not a poster-girl like Bonnie Doone, Bomber's secretary. But, she wasn't an airhead like Bonnie either.

She had a high, broad forehead, a battalion of freckles and was almost as tall as I was. She wore one of those dark granny dresses that covers everything—in her case out of modesty rather than necessity.

And we had *everything* in common. She played the flute, which would inspire me to write a whole batch of new music for flute and piano.

She had graduated from the University of Pennsylvania law school in the previous May and, in an act of astonishing daring, hung out her own shingle in a small office where five people shared a receptionist. She did her own typing and was getting lonely. She was only able to hold out thanks to a loan from her parents, and she was beginning to consider supplementing her income by waiting on tables at night. When I asked if our work would conflict with hers, she got a twinkle in her eye and said, "Not yet."

She explained her situation. "Things aren't exactly booming for lawyers locally these days. And this is a pretty provincial place. Even in this modern day, I'm only the fourth woman lawyer in the history of the county bar association."

"Did you ever consider moving to a city?" I asked her.

"Sure. But I live at home and my mom and dad would die if I left them. My brother was lost to the drug scene, we were devastated. He was such a lovable guy."

"What happened?"

"No self image, I guess. Can't say why. Nobody had unreasonable expectations for him or anything."

"Did you outshine him?"

Her nose moved as though she were trying to scratch it without using her hands. "Maybe a little," she admitted. "Someday I'll have to get the courage to move, but I'd have to have a job first."

"Did you have any offers from city firms?"

"Not really. I had some interviews, a little encouragement, but the brass ring was never extended."

"Do either of your parents smoke?"

"Mother does. Dad quit when Brad O.D.'d. Blamed himself for setting an example with the narcotic cigarettes."

"So you don't have any sympathy for or strong ties to the tobacco industry?"

"Absolutely not. I can't stand smoke. I just can't even be around it."

"So you could give your heart and soul to the cause?"

"And then some," she said.

I adored the way she talked; earnestly, intelligently, her eyes so alive and probing. She had the aura of honesty, decency and goodwill. I not only hired Shauna, I fell in love with her.

Of course, I didn't tell Bomber how I felt. When I told him I had hired our researcher, he asked, "What's his name?"

"Shauna McKinley," I said.

He paused for a moment. "Isn't that a girl's name? He's no pansy is he? I'm not keen on pansies, you know."

"He is a she," I cut him off before he got deeper into his Neanderthal prejudices.

"A she? Jesus Jenny Tod, a *she*! You hired a *girl* lawyer?"

"Woman," I corrected him.

"How old?"

"Twenty-five."

"Jesus Jenny, oh my God in heaven. I should have known you couldn't be trusted. Weren't there any men available? There must have been."

"I interviewed two b-b-boys." I said. "She was j-just so much b-b-better."

"Oh, my God!" Then he seemed to pause for reflection. "Say, you aren't sweet on her are you?"

"How could I be?" I lied. "I just met her."

"Well, get her started," he said with a sigh. "You got a place for her to work?"

"She agreed to keep her office and I agreed to pay her modest rent."

"Okay," he said. "See how she does for a couple weeks. Give her the lowdown," Bomber said. "Have her get all the cases. You can do that with computers now," he said, as though he were telling me something new. "Have her read them all, extract what might be helpful. See if she has an analytical mind. Geez," he muttered to himself, "a girl!"

"Woman," I corrected without a stutter.

"What's she look like?" he suddenly asked.

"No Bonnie," I decided to downplay.

"She an Amazon?"

"N-n-no."

"Nicks'll walk all over her."

I was glad to know he couldn't see me blushing.

"The Nicotine boys," he added, as though I'd miss the point. "They'll massacre her."

"But she's supposed to d-do r-r-research, not in-intimi-dation."

"Yeah, but we'll need her help with declarations, depositions, interviewing witnesses."

"Might be better," I said. "A gentle woman's t-touch."

"Get her going. File an injunction. She have a fax?"

"Yes."

"I'll fax her a list of projects. Cases first. You get her take on the judges. I expect with a case of this publicity value we'll get the top guy. What's he like—" he paused. "Don't tell me *he's* a she."

"There is one woman, "I said. "Out of seven."

I heard a soft groan on the wire. Bomber was a master of intimidation with other men, but his innate chivalry (or so he would have us believe) made him courtly to all but the coarsest women.

"Have her interview the family. Spend a lot of time with the smoker. Get all the details. You know the routine. Get her moving and you can come back. Then, after we plan the next step, you can sashay down to the Confederate States and see if we can find a crack in the facade. Someone to testify how they pump the habit-forming nicotine back in the cancer sticks after they washed it out. I'd love to have someone high up who's sick of the whole mess who will spill the beans on the outfit."

"Not easy," I said.

"But not impossible. Even the Mafia has cracks in it. The stools are eating away at them. Putting killers in jail for tax evasion is a joke. We find someone who says 'Yes, it was policy to keep those little cigs narcotic, keep the sales up, bottom line was more important that millions of casualties a year.' That's our man. *You* can win our case by finding him. Most of the investigation for this thing will go on in North Carolina; and you'll be there doing it."

I hung up the phone from Bomber and called Shauna. Her voice was low and not very musical, and yet it had an inexplicable quality that made me feel good.

We agreed to meet the next day for lunch. In the meantime, she would massage the computers to get the smoking cases.

Shauna and I had lunch in the basement of Cedarberg's lone surviving department store—an eatery which, in its heyday, was noted for its superb quality and giant portions, but was now noted only for its giant portions. Shauna took my breath away with her simplicity of dress and agility of mind.

Ordinarily, I was turned off by frizzy hair. I never took a second look at a redhead, and I don't think it was out of any fear of their legendary tempers. They just didn't appeal to me.

Shauna also revealed herself as a health-food nut— ordering the vegetarian sandwich festooned with bean sprouts, avocado and other tasteless foods of that ilk in a place noted for its brown-butter-drenched steamed clams and its ponderous, greasy burgers and fries.

I did want to impress her, but I drew the line at bean sprouts.

She impressed me instead by having called up the tobacco cases and culled the meaningful information from them already.

"Want to hear it?" she asked.

I laughed. "Geez, if you work this fast, you'll make us wonder why we need you full time."

She laughed too. "That's okay," she said. "I can slow down if I have too. But I don't think that will be necessary when you take on a tobacco company. Not the first hundred years, anyway."

The basement restaurant was called The Terrace and everything was done up in the store's signature colors of pink, baby blue, and lime green. The formica table tops were lime green; the walls, pink; the menus, baby blue; even the sugar crystals were a combination of the three colors.

Having no experience in business associations with the opposing sex, I had to check myself now and then to keep from responding like a date.

"As you know, the record for the plaintiff hasn't been good. The only case you could call a victory of sorts was *Cipollone v. Liggett Group Inc.*"

I loved the way she said "v" instead of versus, and even "Ink." I looked into her eyes. She was looking back.

"Rose Cipollone began smoking when she was sixteen and there was no warning label on the cigarette packs. She thought it was cool, glamorous and grown-up to smoke. She developed lung cancer years later and she and her husband Antonio filed suit against The Liggett Group, Inc., Philip Morris, Inc., and Lorrilard, makers of the cigarettes Rose Cipollone smoked.

"Before the trial started, there were ten reported district and appellate court rulings and Rose Cipollone died."

"Always better for the tobacco interests: the invalid plaintiff can't be seen by the jury."

"Exactly," Shauna said. "What shape is our plaintiff in?"

My heart was warmed by her saying "our." It denoted camaraderie. I shook my head, "If he lasts till the first day of the trial, it will be a miracle."

"Maybe this is none of my business," she said, "but is your boss in this for the long haul?"

"Oh, yes."

"He's alone, isn't he? There aren't a thousand plaintiffs and other lawyers in it with him?"

"No."

"You know, Rose Cipollone was awarded four-hundred-thousand dollars."

"Yes."

"But it cost two million to try the case."

"We know that," I said.

"And your boss can put out two million or more?"

"He can."

"And he's willing to?"

"Apparently."

"But how well do you know his financial situation?"

"Pretty well," I said. "He's my dad."

She blinked and fell back in the chair, then moved closer to me, leaning over her plate. "Bomber Hanson is your dad?" She was clearly more startled than impressed. "No way!"

I nodded, "Yes way." I hadn't bothered to tell her that little detail. I didn't want to prejudice her, I told myself. What I was more likely afraid of was a disappointing comparison. "Does it make a difference?"

"Well, *does* it?" she said. "The all-time great trial lawyer is your dad? Well, yeah. Wow!"

"So if you know Bomber's reputation, you must know he's good for the money."

"I guess I'm not up on those things, but I do know just because someone *can* pay doesn't mean they *will* pay. And one common thread runs through these cigarette cases—the tobacco giants wear the plaintiffs down—and out! Even in cases where the plaintiff is getting favorable rulings. It can take them fifteen years."

"Bomber might go faster," I said. "He likes to cut to the chase. His forte is courtroom theatrics. He knows he'll never wear down the tobacco interests with motions and legal gymnastics, so he wants to get to court as soon as he can."

"But won't the tobacco companies drag their feet?"

"Sure, as much as they can. But he's going to push it for the two-year limit now being offered."

"Why do you suppose those others gave up?"

"Don't know. I suspect everyone was out of money. Lawyers tied up their practices for years. It becomes all-consuming, and face it, no one has the resources of the tobacco companies," I said. "They sell a lot of those little death sticks. What were the issues in *Cipollone?*"

"Fourteen counts in the complaint. First, she developed bronchogenic carcinoma as a result of using the defendants' products for over forty years—pain and suffering, great economic hardship. Plaintiffs sought compensation under strict liability, negligence, breach of warranty, intentional tort and conspiracy," she said. "The big stumbling block in most of these cases seems to be The Federal Cigarette Advertising Act. The tobacco companies claim the federal government mandates what must be put on the package. Therefore, they not only don't have a duty to make the warnings stronger, they are forbidden to."

"Did that fly?"

"In many cases it did. In one of our own Pennsylvania

cases it didn't fly, but the plaintiff threw in the sponge anyway. There's a lot more but I haven't had time to read it all yet."

"Geez, how were you able to go through *that* much? I only hired you yesterday afternoon."

She smiled at the compliment. "What do you think Mr. Hanson wants to allege?" She stopped short, then put her hand to her mouth. "I just realized *you* are Mr. Hanson. Why didn't you ever mention you last name?"

"Something about shadows, I guess."

"Living in his?"

"Yeah." Then I explained about Mr. Hanson. "Nobody calls him that except people who don't know who he is. He *wants* to be called Bomber, if you can imagine."

She frowned. "I might have real trouble with that," she said. "I was brought up to respect my elders."

I changed the subject. "Do you know an attorney named Easy Willie?"

"Everybody knows who he is. I've never met him."

"What's his reputation?"

"A kook. Went to Harvard or Yale, didn't he? Supposed to be a bright guy, but never had the personality or salesmanship or whatever it takes to have a successful practice."

"Married?"

"Think he was once or twice. Don't know. He probably belongs in a firm doing grunt work, but he'd never do it, and no one would hire him. He may be a little hard to get along with— if a preposition at the end of a sentence is something up with which you are willing to put."

It was flashes like that that drew me to Shauna. I don't know if I would have been able to get my mind off her. I just never got around to trying.

Hiring Shauna McKinley had added a new dimension to my life. I wasn't so anxious to go back home to Angelton, CA anymore.

5

So naturally Bomber summoned me back to our Victorian office in Angelton to lengthen his shadow.

He had overnighted an injunction. When I got it, I stopped in on Shauna, gave her the injunction to file, and asked her to start drafting the complaint.

She glanced at the injunction. "Wow," she said. "Does he think there is any chance of getting the companies to stop producing cigarettes by judicial order?"

"Of course not, but that's Bomber. He likes to start with a bang. It could make the national news and start people thinking."

"Yeah," she said, "like why not? The things kill you, everybody knows it, so why not stop making them?"

"Get a rise out of the tobacco company anyway," I said. "Bomber wants you to work on the complaint. Get as many causes of action as you can dream up. Get the citations, and fax us your ideas or a rough draft. Bomber says if Cipollone had fourteen counts in her complaint, we want twenty-eight."

"But surely he knows you can't be that arbitrary," she said, logically.

"When you know Bomber better, you'll see. He loves to be arbitrary. He says people make decisions on juries as they do in life, and logically is way down the list."

"Oh, by the way," she said, "speaking of logic and other thought systems, I did some more reading last night." She paused, not eager to go on.

"And?"

"*Cipollone* was overturned at the appellate level. So there really are no victories."

"Bomber will like that," I reassured her. "Bomber likes to be first."

She smiled. That seemed to appeal to her too. "Good," she said.

"I'm off to the courthouse to file the injunction, then I'm off to the land of milk and honey," I said. "You ever been there?"

She shook her head.

"Want to go with me?"

"California? Do you mean it?"

"The courthouse," I said. "Show me around?"

"Oh," she said, her pretty jaw dropping. "Sure." She jumped to her feet, grabbed her coat and led the way.

The courthouse was two blocks and change from her office. "Rent is cheaper the further you get from the courthouse," she said. The building was gray with a white New England steeple, small window panes in larger, balanced windows. Inside there were high ceilings and creaking wooden floors.

We went first to the clerk's office where we filed the injunction through one Shauna McKinley, member-in-good-standing of the local bar.

The clerk, bespectacled and bored, stamped the paperwork like she might have in any number of Eastern European countries. I felt like Franz Kafka.

"Come on," Shauna said, "let me show you the courtroom where the case will probably be heard." She took me upstairs to a large room big enough to seat a good-sized church congregation.

"Pretty great, huh?" she said. An old judge with a black eye patch like Captain Hook was holding forth. "That's the president judge," Shauna whispered to me. "Judge Druckenmiller. Been at it too long. Never was a heavyweight legal scholar, but he has seniority and seems to be satisfied with motion court and other mundane matters."

"He assign the cases?" I asked after we left the large

courtroom with the empty seats.

"Yes."

"Is he liable to take ours himself?"

"I don't know. He sure wouldn't mind the notoriety, but I don't think he wants to work that hard."

"Those old courtrooms are great, aren't they?" I said.

"Yes, they don't make them that big anymore," she said. "In the old days, a court trial was an event that drew a lot of spectators."

"Sort of like a good hanging?"

"Next best," she said.

I was sorry to leave her, but I had a plane to catch. She offered to drive me to the airport, but I had my rental car. In front of her office, I took her hand in mine under the guise of shaking hands and we stood there for an eternity looking into each other's eyes. Some insignificant babble passed my lips, the precise nature of which I have blessedly forgotten.

I made my plane out of Cedarberg for Chicago with just minutes to spare.

In Chicago, I had an hour and a half to kill so I went to a bank of phones to call my mother (such a good son). I waited (interminably) for a free one.

Whenever I spoke to my mother, the first words out of her mouth were inevitably, "Find any nice girls yet?" or a variation thereof. It seemed to me the word "nice" was tepid gruel. It was almost as though, by settling for a merely "nice" girl, Mom had given up hope of me ever doing better than the minimum. It was a pessimism that I could not say was unfounded.

"Hi, Mom," I said when she answered.

"Tod! How nice of you to call—any nice girls in the Northeast?"

"I'm sure there must be," I said.

"Your father tells me you've hired a young girl to do research."

"Well, she's not *that* young, she's a lawyer."

"About your age?" I could see the twinkle in her eye as

clearly as if I were in the same room.

"No, she's younger. About twenty-five or so."

"But that's nothing these days, Tod. How *is* she?"

"Seems to be in good health."

"No, I mean what kind of person?"

"Seems nice."

"Tod, this nonchalance is maddening."

"Mom, she's an employee. How do you think Bomber would like it if I took a personal interest in an employee?"

"He'd love it! Especially a *lawyer*! That's someone he could talk to. You know that's practically all he can talk about: law, law, law."

I tried to conclude the conversation as noncommittally as I could. "We'll talk about it after I know her better," but I suspect Mom wasn't fooled.

I hung up the phone to make way for the next person waiting to reach out and touch someone. I felt good having talked about Shauna, however obliquely.

I drove across town from the Angelton airport, where I had left my little car, to my over-the-garage pad on the ocean. There, as I waited for a light on the main street, a gaggle of tourists crossed in front of me.

One of the most noticeable contrasts between Cedarberg, PA and Angelton, CA, in addition to the weather and architecture, was the tourists. I love tourists! They come to town with engaging awe. They spend money and a lot of guys who moan about tourists don't realize how much our delicate economy depends on these rubber-necked, camera-toting folk.

They exhibit a sense of wonder about something we take for granted—reminding us constantly it *is* wonderful. Sometimes they try to appear blasé about it, but even in that deceit there is wonder. If you actually *live* in a community that others can only visit, you have a leg up the ladder on them and it provides you with someone you may feel superior to.

I realize all that, and still I love 'em. They don't stray very much from the main street so it's hard to get annoyed on

Albert Avenue where our Victorian house *cum* office is. And that is where I presented myself next morning.

There, Bomber's impossible secretary, the inimitable Bonnie Doone, greeted me with, "Hi ya, Honey Cakes." Then she winked at me as an M.C. might do in a burlesque house, "Aren't you the sly one though?"

"What are you talking about?" I shouldn't have given her the satisfaction.

"Hiring a *femme fatale* for your assistant-plaything. Everyone here is quite excited."

I looked at her dumbfounded. I should have been prepared for it, but I wasn't. I doubted she had any inkling what *femme fatale* meant.

"Are your clothes getting tighter," I said, "or are you putting on weight?"

"The subject was Miss Shauna McKinley." She had her name—naturally, Bomber would have given it to her for the paychecks. "Any action yet?"

I could feel the blood flushing my face. Bonnie grinned at me and said, "Got a message for you," and she handed me one of her message sheets with the name Harrison Hinkle and a phone number.

"Who's this?" I asked.

She shrugged. "Asked for Bomber, but we both know better," she winked at me lasciviously. I had more than a sneaking suspicion she knew who Harrison Hinkle was, but I wasn't giving her the satisfaction of begging for the information.

I went into the broom closet I call home and placed the call. The receptionist answered with a string of names that sounded like an advertising agency.

I spent a merry time going up the chain of secretaries until I got someone willing to put the big shot on the phone. Tod Hanson, it seemed, wasn't lighting any fires on the East Coast. Bomber Hanson had been called, not Tod. "Sorry," I said, "if he wants to talk to Bomber, I'm as close as he'll get for now. I talk to everyone first." There was a lot of grumbling and mumbling in the background and I knew I was calling a guy who was *very* jealous of his own importance in the world. I get a precarious pleasure out of seeing and hearing these mega-shots worm and squirm when they are given the take-it-or-leave-it option of talking to a nobody. I always think I can tell a man's character by how he speaks to his inferiors in the pecking order. Harrison J. Hinkle was a cold fish, but he was almost cordial in his own deep-sea way.

"Mr. Hanson," he said with a voice that let you know up front he was no ambulance chaser. "I'm Harrison Hinkle and I'll be leading the defense team in *Zepf vs. Armstead*." He said it just like the waiter who says "Hi, I'm Jeffrey, I'll be your waiter this evening." He just happened to be coming to California, so he thought he'd like to drop by and chat with Bomber. "Maybe we can short-circuit the thing."

"How did you find out so fast?" I asked, frankly in awe.

He chuckled. "T. S. Armstead pays us a lot of money to be on top of things. Got a call from Norman Stimmel of Bortz, Hillegas, Stimmel and Klerx alerting us to the possibility of an action. Norman was good enough to keep an eye out for us. We'll be associating with them."

Harrison Hinkle had the voice of a confident cookie. He let me know he was used to talking to the chief counsel and I went into my normal dissembling about how Bomber was peculiar that way. I promised to attempt to set up a meeting, then call him back. News travels fast when you sue the big boys.

"When would you be available?" I asked.

"I'm open," he said.

When I broached the subject to Bomber, he guffawed. "Well, well, well, he's open is he?" Bomber said. "Let's let him cool his heels awhile then. Call him tomorrow and suggest Friday. Lot of traffic on Friday," he winked.

6

From the rear of Bonnie Doone's overgrown reception area, I could see the legal eagle who I could tell at a glance was the head counsel for T. S. Armstead, purveyors of fine tobacco.

When he came in the door, I got a better look.

"Harrison J. Hinkle for Bomber Hanson," he said, taking in his surroundings with disdain.

So this was the head of the pack of jackals responsible for three-million premature deaths a year. Harrison J. Hinkle was almost tall, with tight, curly hair that was almost black. Everything about him was almost-something. He was almost cheerful, almost friendly, his grin was almost crooked. He had won almost all of his cases—*all* that he tried for the tobacco companies. It would be our mission to change that perfect record for the tobacco industry into "almost."

I stepped out to meet him. I extended my friendly-shaking-hand and said, "I talked to you on the phone."

He shook the hand, being at a loss to avoid it, and gave me an almost-smile. "I'm here to see Bomber," he said, just to set the record straight that he didn't schlepp three-thousand miles to be shunted off on the junior varsity.

"Have a seat, Mr. Hinkle," Bonnie said, jumping up to give the visitor a look at her undeniable charms. She scurried off to Bomber's lair to announce our big-shot visiting fireman. I watched Hinkle's eyes glom onto Bonnie's bod and I was glad to see he had at least one human attribute.

So maybe Bonnie Doone did have a body that Michelangelo wouldn't have dared chisel because no one would have believed him. Maybe between her armpits, she was Venus sublime. And between the back of her knees and the small of her back, she was *Playboy* perfect, but between her ears, she was out to lunch.

Bonnie is office decoration. She is a lot cheaper than a Van Gogh and I suppose she can make her computer dance. Just don't try to talk to her about anything more intellectually refined than the Grateful Dead.

When Bonnie returned from the inner sanctum, she was flapping her wings like an excited bald eagle. "Bomber will see you now," she chirped.

Harrison J. Hinkle nodded and stood to move toward The Bomber's door. He flagged momentarily, as though he wasn't sure where to go.

"I'll show you," I said, and he looked like he feared another trick.

"That's all right," he said. "I can find it."

"Yeah," I said. "It's not as though we were one of those fancy Wall Street firms with a million offices," I pointed. "One door," I said.

He didn't seem to care for my input. When he was convinced I intended to brazenly participate in the meeting, he blanched and said, "I expect to be received alone by Mr.—ah—Bomber. This is to be a confidential meeting."

I smiled and nodded. "Fine with me," I said. "Why don't you tell him?"

He did, and Bomber waved him off with a guffaw. "Hinkle," he said with a booming heartiness I realized always spelled trouble, "the boy does all the work on these things, I'm just the figurehead. I am approaching the stage of life when the D. R. S. syndrome sets in."

"D. R. S.?" Harrison Hinkle said.

"You know what that is, of course."

"I'm afraid not."

"D. R. S. Don't Remember Stuff."

Bomber slapped the desk with his hand. Hinkle was mildly amused. "I don't want to have to repeat everything to the kid so, if you don't mind…"

"But I *do* mind. This was to be a private meeting."

"Well, if it's a private meeting you want—"

"I do."

"—That can be arranged," Bomber said and stood up. "I'll just leave you two to your private meeting."

Hinkle jumped to his feet as though staying alone with me would give him leprosy.

"Oh, come now," he said with what I'm sure he considered maximum forbearance. "All right, all right."

We all sat, I on the periphery—on the couch against the wall in my customary role of spectator—Harrison J. Hinkle, across the desk from Bomber.

Hinkle brought his gold cuff-linked wrists up from beside him and crossed his hands on this lap. An almost-smile crept to his lips. This was more like it. Just as he'd rehearsed it, one-on-one.

He began with small talk, admiring the overkill celebrity photos on the wall, telling Bomber how he had followed his career with admiration.

Finally, when Bomber had had his fill, he said, "You can cut to the chase, Hinkle, as the kids say."

"Oh,—they say that, do they? What does it mean?"

"Get on with it."

Harrison Hinkle seemed startled. "Oh, yes, well, I'm here to see if we can make a deal."

Bomber sighed like he did when I exasperated him. "Should have told us on the phone. Saved you the trip."

Hinkle raised an eyebrow. "I didn't *get* to talk to you on the phone."

"Tod speaks English," Bomber said.

"We don't offer settlements as a rule," Hinkle said. "Naturally we'd be plagued with suits from everyone whoever *looked* at a cigarette."

"Do you smoke, Mr. Hinkle?"

"I? No, I—why?"

"Why not?"

"Not because of any health scare," he said.

Bomber nodded the "baloney" nod.

"Naturally, when we saw you were connected with the case we…"

"Connected?" Bomber boomed. "I *am* the case."

"Yes, all right," Hinkle said. "I suppose you'll be associating with other plaintiffs."

"Why would I do that?"

Harrison Hinkle seemed surprised. "To pool your resources, of course."

"I don't do committee work."

"But these cases are prohibitively expensive for a solo practitioner."

You could tell Bomber liked the sound of that "solo practitioner" business. He smiled.

Harrison J. Hinkle chugged on. "You'll have to associate with Pennsylvania counsel."

Bomber nodded.

"We've already retained the firm of Bortz, Hillegas, Stimmel and Klerx, the most influential in the area."

Bomber looked at me, smiling and winking and making no attempt to hide it from Harrison Hinkle. "I'm sure you have," Bomber said.

"We are in the process of tying up the lesser firms now."

Bomber nodded again. "More power to you," he said.

"Who will you be retaining?"

"I don't know why that is something that should concern you. You say you've already tied up the most influential firm in town. Isn't it funny, Mr. Hinkle, how those influential boys are always so willing to sell out to you merchants of death?"

Harrison Hinkle bristled. "That was uncalled for, Mr. Hanson, and it's slanderous."

"Perhaps," Bomber said, "but you know the infallible defense against a charge of slander is truth."

"Mr. Hanson—I've come here in the spirit of cooperation."

"To get us to drop the case? Some cooperation."

"If we're going to be working together for a long time, we might as well be amiable."

"I've no objection to that. You start."

I don't know for sure what was going through Hinkle's mind at that moment, but if the look on his face was any indication, it wasn't pleasant.

Then, as though he had a sudden change of heart, the Bomber dropped his bomb. "We will be attempting to associate with an attorney who goes by the name 'Easy Willie'," he said.

Harrison Hinkle was startled stiff at first, then he relaxed and let out a guffaw. When he got control of himself, he said, "Well, at least you have a sense of humor, Mr. Hanson."

"I'm so glad you're pleased."

"No, that was a good one—Easy Willie! I suppose you're wondering how I know the reputation of Easy Willie?"

"No, not at all."

He told him anyway. "We have dossiers on every lawyer in the county. We leave no stone unturned. Easy Willie is as close as you can come to a derelict and still have a license," he said, then wrinkled his brow as though he were giving the matter deep thought. "Not that he uses his license much. He has hardly any cases at all—a few drunk and disorderlies. You know what they say?"

"No, what do they say?"

"It takes one to know one."

At first I didn't know what that meant. Then I realized he was calling Easy Willie drunk and disorderly.

"No match for Bortz, *et al*," Bomber said.

"Well, not in the same league, no," Hinkle said cagily.

"All the more embarrassing for you, Hinkle, when we skin you alive in court: you with the country club crowd at your table and us with—how did you put it?—a drunk and disorderly at ours. Should be a cakewalk for you."

You could tell Harrison Hinkle was bursting to put Bomber in his place, and though I've never seen it done, I thought Hinkle might make a respectable stab at it. But he didn't. His Southern good manners got the best of him. Then he smiled a Northern smile and let his eyes pointedly travel around the room. "How many lawyers do you have here?"

"Two."

"We have hundreds." He flashed that snaky smile at us again. "We'll have you for lunch."

Now it was Bomber's turn to trot out his soupy smile. "Confucius say, 'Man who has Bomber for lunch gets indigestion.'"

There was that almost-smile on Harrison Hinkle's face. He almost frowned with it, and I could tell he was considering changing his tactics. You couldn't be as successful as he was at butt-kissing the big-butts without having some sense of when a shifting of gears was called for.

Harrison Hinkle turned almost suave, or, depending how you looked at it, almost unctuous.

"Perhaps we should take a different view of the case. Another perspective," Hinkle said. "I like to look at the industry as a machine with tens of millions of drivers. One or two of those drivers get angry, get off the machine, it doesn't stop it. There are too many drivers left and they are on there because they want to be—and they resent anyone who wants to stop the machine."

Here Bomber got off my all-time favorite line. "I see your mouth moving, but I don't hear you saying anything."

Harrison Hinkle's face reddened. You could tell he was not used to being ridiculed.

"People smoke because they want to," he said. "We don't *make* them. We manufacture a product that fills a need. Some people smoke one or two cigarettes a day. Some even two or three a week. It doesn't hurt them. They *like* smoking. It gives their mundane lives a bit of pleasure."

"So you guys are actually performing a service?" Bomber said in that *faux* wonder way he had of gently needling.

"I think we are. I say *we* with the understanding I do

not make cigarettes myself. I'm an attorney representing the interests of the defendants."

"What would you say those interests were?" Bomber asked.

"Survival," he said, in a word. "We are being besieged from all quarters. We have been nothing but cooperative, and the hysteria machine is running at full bore. They are even panicking people about secondhand smoke. Utterly ridiculous, unless you are in a closet with it twenty-four hours day. The government says put a warning on the package, we put the warning."

"Why do they do that?"

"Politics."

"Politics?"

"Political pressure from the meddlers. Look at alcohol. Where are the warnings that too much alcohol may impair your driving and you may contribute to or be part of the twenty-plus thousand annual accidents caused by drunk driving? Where is the warning that drinking can lead to domestic violence? There is no study anywhere that links smoking with dangerous driving or domestic violence."

"Or athlete's feet either," Bomber added.

"Yes, we are easy targets for mockery, Mr. Bomber. But think about what you are doing. I don't think the causal links of smoking to disease are proven."

"Oh, really…" Bomber said in disdain.

"No, really. A lot of people smoke who do not die of lung cancer, heart disease, emphysema. Millions of women smoked while they were pregnant with no ill effects on the offspring. And no innocent people suffer because someone else smokes."

"You don't call losing a loved one prematurely cause for suffering?"

"There's no proof…"

"No proof, man? It's everywhere. You've got to be an illiterate ostrich to believe that."

"There are studies on both sides…"

"Horse feathers—"

Harrison Hinkle winced. "All right, I see you are fixed in your prejudices. I will say only one more thing: In our lifetime, I expect the continuing DNA research will prove these deaths you attribute to smoking are genetic in origin. People are living longer than ever, yet it is never long enough for the doomsayers. If a man smokes three packs of cigarettes a day and dies at sevent-five, what is to say how long he would have lived had he not smoked? Maybe he would have died at sixty of hypertension."

I'll say this for Harrison Hinkle, he played his best arguments like the pro he was. I had no trouble envisioning a jury going along with him—even with the incomparable Bomber head-to-head.

"Mr. Hinkle," Bomber said, "if you've come to scare me off, you couldn't have done better."

Hinkle seemed to relax his facial muscles, almost. "I thought we could come to some agreement," he said. "As I said, we don't settle these cases—no bargains—but in this instance, what with your national notoriety and all, we would be willing to make some accommodation to you and the family."

"I'm not for sale."

"No, no, certainly not. I wouldn't expect a man of your integrity to sell out, but life is compromise. We make a bad decision, we cut and run."

"This was not a bad decision."

"But it's going to tie you up for years. We have limitless resources. I'm not suggesting that money could ever touch your soul—but think about some other thing that catches your fancy. We could commission several symphonies from your son to be performed by the major symphonies of the world."

"He'd like that," Bomber said.

Wow, I thought, these guys do their homework.

"Good."

"But he's not the boss. He's not trying the case—I am,

and the proposition leaves me cold."

"Yes, of course, it was just an example. Now isn't there something along those lines that would appeal to you?"

Bomber seemed to screw up his face in serious concentration.

"Well...?" Hinkle said at last.

"Yes..." Bomber trailed off.

"Well.... What is it?"

"I would be willing to give up the case..."

"Yes, yes?"

"If you could bring back from the dead all the victims who suffered premature deaths from smoking."

"Oh." The balloon was punctured, the shoulders slumped. "I can see my time can be spent more profitably elsewhere," Harrison J. Hinkle said.

"That's an understatement," Bomber said. He liked to have the last word.

7

After we were at last free of the presence of Harrison J. Hinkle, Bomber started reeling off all kinds of legal filings he wanted me to make. It was a whole barrage of stuff that would never be granted, but might make some headlines.

"Think of the publicity we'll get in the Cedarberg rags—precondition the potential jurors."

"Maybe against us," I said. They were just more of Bomber's dramatic gestures. Surprisingly, he was usually right where the delusions and madness of crowds were concerned.

"They're going to bury us in motions to dismiss, to quash. We just want to give as good as we get."

"Since when do you want me to prepare the legal stuff?" I asked. Of course, I stammered in a sentence that long. I always do.

"So, have your broad do it," he said, referring to Attorney Shauna McKinley in Pennsylvania. Bomber was not only politically incorrect, he was politically impossible.

Bomber talked strategy and, when he did, he could talk far into the night. My usual investigating role was going to be somewhat altered since this was a civil case, not our usual criminal venue.

"You're going to have to hit North Carolina," he said. "Talk it up with the natives."

"What exactly are we looking for?"

"A mole would be ideal. A guy who wore a wire at one of those executive sessions where they talked about pumping more nicotine into the ciggys to make them *more* habit forming."

"Don't think we'll find that."

"We'll find something. You heard Harrison J. Hinkle.

'Gosh,' he'll say, 'we don't control how much people smoke. Doing a service'—all that baloney. And that hypertension *schtick*. That's good, you know. Everybody who smokes doesn't drop over at thirty-five. So our best shot is going to be the nicotine pumping. The calculated, callous, deliberate design to make the product which is inherently harmful and dangerous, addicting. That, my boy, is conspiracy to commit murder. We prove that, we may get some D.A.'s interested in indicting the whole shootin' match."

"That might be a stretch," I said.

He waved me off as though my mild protest were insignificant. "See what you can turn up," he said.

Then I argued with Bomber about using Easy Willie as our Pennsylvania associate. "Shauna has a license after all," I said. "What good could it possibly do us to tie up with that old reprobate? He would only give us a down-at-heel image."

"Exactly!" Bomber boomed. "Underdog! That's what we want."

"We have it with the p-pl-plaintiff," I argued inarticulately.

"And we square it with Easy Willie. Look—there are a couple things about Easy Willie we can't get from the girl alone. One is, Easy Willie goes way back in Cedarberg. He was a lawyer before Shiska was born."

"Shauna," I corrected him. "She's Irish."

"Easy Willie knows where the stuff is stashed. He knows the judges, the lawyers, the jurors. Cedarberg is the kind of burg where everyone knows everyone, if not personally, then by some connection—family, friends, work. We don't need him so much for what they will think of *us* because we have him, but what he *knows* about them—and he has zilch to lose by telling all. Besides, he is available—cheap. Full time."

"But you haven't even seen him. He's a mess. He will make a terrible impression. There must be others…"

"Like the country-club set?"

"Establishment—"

"Nicks'll tie 'em up, you know that. Besides, I don't want to work with the silk-suit crowd. They're *laissez-faire*, don't-rock-the-boat folk. But remember, boy, we're the *plaintiffs* this time. We need to embrace, or at least grasp, the far-out hippie mentality. The establishment is responsible for all our problems, and big tobacco is responsible for some three-million deaths a year and they continue to thrive through the sufferance of the establishment and the likes of Bortz, Stimmel and Porky Pig."

So, I piled up some more frequent-flier miles in the eastbound direction.

On my way to the hotel, I stopped in on the Zepf family to give them the good news.

The kids, from Carrie to Ginny, were all over me like flies on red meat. I should come out here more often, I told myself. It was an incredible ego boost. Then June invited me to dinner. I asked if I could bring my associate.

"Sure," she said, "bring him along."

I didn't have the heart to tell her, "him" was a "her."

Rich Zepf seemed to improve just hearing the news.

When I left the happy Zepfs, I went right to Shauna's office, about a ten-minute drive.

"Hi, Tod," she greeted me with her inimitable smile. I always felt warm and cozy in Shauna's presence.

"Hi," I said like a parrot and stared at her. She stared back, the smile staying with her. Somehow we broke it.

Shauna had a very plain office which I could fancify by calling "Spartan": white walls, a gray file cabinet, room for her modest desk, her chair, and two chairs facing it. Her red hair was like a sunset in front of all that white. The shared secretary was also the shared receptionist and her room was larger than Shauna's—like Bonnie Doone's reception area was larger than my room.

"How are you coming along?"

"Fine," she said. "Of course, there isn't much encouragement in the cases."

"I know. Bomber wants to push the inadequate warning scenario, and he wants me to start investigating in North Carolina on the angle of the company making cigs addicting by pumping more nicotine back than they took out."

"They *do* that?"

I nodded. "So we are led to believe. Industry denies it, of course, but I'm supposed to get the evidence to back it up. What happens, we think, is that during the manufacturing process they have to take all the nicotine out. So why don't they *leave* it out? They say, of course, no one would buy the things."

"I could live with that," she said.

It was such a joy to work with Shauna McKinley. I began to refer to her as my all-natural girl. She wore no makeup; didn't dye her hair; drank no booze, coffee or tea; didn't smoke or cuss; and wore simple, unsexy clothes that made her all the more sexy.

The first time I called her my all-natural girl, I apologized for not saying woman.

"I don't mind," she said. "That stuff is so overdone."

I sat facing her and told her about my safari to the West Coast, about Bomber's dreams and irrational expectations.

"That's how all great things begin," she said, "with irrationality."

"He'd like you to get the videos from the network—maybe an affiliate can give you one locally."

"Of what?"

"Oh, sorry, of the congressional hearings into the nicotine industry. He wants you to watch them. Not only to see what they say; the claims they make, those they refute; but also see if you detect any weakness in their ranks. See if you can find someone we can go after. A mole. Someone to feed us information."

"How will you do that?"

"If you can find someone who looks shaken in his professed belief that smoking is really good for you; I try to make contact—sub rosa. See what he really thinks."

"Can you *do* that?" she wondered. "I mean, can you

really get someone who is paid by big tobacco, just to talk to you like you were a favorite cousin?"

"Yeah, probably nephew in this case. To have any pull, he's going to have to be twice my age anyway."

"He? Could it be a she?" she asked.

"My guess is in the old South, where they make the cigs, a woman's place is on the other end of a mop," I said. "I almost forgot, our clients want us to come to dinner tonight."

"Oh?"

"Are you available? I mean, I know it's short notice and all—"

"I'm available."

"—but, I only found out last night."

"I said I'm available," she said.

"Actually, I asked them if you could come." I apologized.

"I'm glad you did."

"I thought it would be good for you to meet them A.S.A.P."

"Yes, me too."

"So, is it okay?"

"Okay."

"I could pick you up at your house," I think I was perspiring. I know *she* thought I was. "If that's okay."

"*Okay!*" she exclaimed. "Phew, do you always have this much trouble asking a girl for a date?"

My speech had escaped me momentarily. When I located it again, I muttered, "Sometimes more."

We both laughed, but hers was the more genuine.

After I left Shauna, I walked the block and a half to the offices of Easy Willie, attorney-at-law.

I was not surprised to find him in. Nor was I surprised to find him in the same dreamy pose I had found him in before. He still needed a shave. It was difficult for me to interpret the look he gave me. It could have been a "not-you-again" look. Then again, it might have been a struggle to remember where he had seen me before. It must have been the former because, when I introduced myself again, he nodded and said, "I remember you."

"May I sit down?" I asked.

"Why not?"

"Well, I…maybe you're too busy…"

"That's a good one," he said without smiling.

I sat. He looked at me through eyes that had seen more cares than they cared to.

"Bomber wants to hire you," I said, deciding Easy Willie was not the sort to be swayed by small talk.

"For what?"

"*Zepf vs. T. S. Armstead*. We need a local lawyer to associate with and you're his choice."

"Me," he said, not as a question but in amazement.

"Yes. I was, as you might imagine, opposed to the idea."

Easy Willie nodded.

"Of course, I have met you and he has not, but there is no reasoning with Bomber when his mind is made up." I paused only briefly before I launched my tactless salvo. "So what's your story, anyway?"

He gave me one of those who-wants-to-know looks, and we sat in silence for awhile. I broke it by giving him Bomber's offer.

"Very generous," he said, still reluctant to take the bait.

"And if we prevail—get a judgment—you'd get ten percent of whatever Bomber collects." His eyes widened in amazement, then narrowed in suspicion.

"What am I supposed to do for this windfall?"

"Give us the lay of the land in Cedarberg. Fill us in on the judges, the lawyers, the jurors. Give us a local presence."

His whitish tongue made its way surreptitiously around his lips. "Nice offer," he said, "but you really want someone else. A little classier."

"I hear you went to Harvard, Willie, any truth to that?"

"Maybe."

"Finished near the top of the class."

He shrugged.

"So tell me the rest of the story."

"Nothing to tell."

"Sure there is," I said. "Like, how is it a bright guy like you is sitting in this hole staring at the wall?"

"Pick and chose my cases," he said with a smirk.

I nodded doubtfully. "When's the last time you turned down a case?"

"Oh, must a been just the other…" he paused and pinched his brow as if reaching for a precise date. "Roughly twenty-five years ago."

"What was it?"

"Don't remember."

I didn't believe him. "So what have you been doing the last twenty-five?"

"Taking it easy. Trying to live up to my name."

"So what's your story, Easy Willie?"

"Story? What makes you think I have a story? Do you have a story?"

"Everybody's got a story."

"What's yours?"

"I asked you first."

Easy Willie sat there like a water cooler. Maybe if I went first, he would follow.

"Wanted to be a musician—composer, conductor—classical. Couldn't make a living. Took the easy way out. Do investigation for my father."

Easy Willie nodded. "Get a law degree?"

"Yeah, but not like you. I was close to the bottom—second last, actually. I just never found those cases that interesting; and the guy who finished last is making a fortune in personal-injury."

He nodded, and for Easy Willie, that always seemed an effort. "Thanks for sharing," he said, and I felt small.

"You?" I prodded.

"Nothing," he said, "just taking it easy."

"Any reason we shouldn't hire you?"

"I can't think of any reason you *should.*"

"Maybe the first question should be, do you want to work?"

"Been so long."

"Yeah."

"Maybe forgot how."

"Did you?"

"Don't want to work too hard, that's for sure."

I was beginning to weary. I was just about to report to Bomber, Easy Willie didn't want the job. I could see us burning a lot of rubber to get this lump in gear.

"Let me think about it," he said. "Tell you tomorrow."

When I left him, he seemed to be thinking. At least he wasn't doing anything else that might interfere with any thought processes he might possess in his bag of tricks. I could always hope tomorrow he would say no. Bomber may have thought that hiring Easy Willie would be a cute idea, but I was the one who would be stuck working with him and I was much less sanguine about it.

When I got back to the hotel, I called Bomber to tell him Easy Willie was playing hard to get.

"Don't worry," he boomed, "he'll come around."

I kept on my Ivy League uniform for my "dinner date."

I drove to the 17th Street address she gave me. The streets got more desirable in Cedarberg as the numbers went up. The town topped out about 28th Street, so I'd say the McKinleys were around the middle streetwise, but it was a modest brick half-house with a nice large porch which they had closed in with screens but no glass.

Shauna met me at the door. "You're right on time," she said.

Shauna was wearing a full white blouse buttoned to the neck and a dark plaid skirt with a big golden safety pin that looked like it was holding it together. The skirt went almost to the floor.

Then she whispered, "Mother wants to meet you, do you have a minute?"

"Sure," I said. I always managed to curry favor with girls' mothers, if not always with the girls themselves.

She led me into the dark living room. Even with the lights on, it was dreary.

Shauna's mother was seated with an open book on her lap. She wore a tan, silky shirt-dress with a blood-red cravat around her neck, as though she were expecting to go out herself.

"Mom, this is Tod."

She smiled broadly and extended her hand. I took it.

"My," she said, "you are a good-looking young man."

My throat clogged on that one. I finally managed a "Thanks."

The color of her hair (reddish) owed more to a bottle than to heredity. It was as though, on turning gray, she decided to match her daughter's color. She wore too much makeup and seemed a little fuzzy about things. There was a too-earnest smile on her face, and I got the ridiculous notion she was making a play for me.

Shauna saved me. "We have to run, Mom," she said. "They're expecting us."

"Have a nice time," Mom said, and I got the feeling she felt it would be at her expense if we did. "And drive carefully."

Shauna settled in the car as though we were old friends. I found myself making date talk.

"That's a cozy house."

"The dungeon, you mean?"

"Did you always live there?"

"No," Shauna said, with a strange drop in her voice. "I didn't."

"Where did you live before?"

"We had a real house farther out."

"Why did you move, to be closer to town?"

"No-o-o—my brothers were gone, it was pretty big for

just my parents. I don't think they thought I'd come home to roost."

"Where are your brothers?"

"One's in California, one's in Virginia," she frowned. "The other's in the ground—as I told you."

"What do they do?"

"One in California delivers bottled water, one in Virginia's a plumber."

"Wow," I said softly. "You're the star of the show."

"I guess."

"So you liked the other house better?"

"All of us did," she said. "Actually, we lost it."

"I'm sorry to hear that," I said. "How?"

"They mortgaged it so I could go to college and law school. Then my dad lost his job and they couldn't make the payments. Bank took it."

"I didn't meet your dad."

"He wasn't home."

"Where is he?"

"Girlfriend's place."

"Oh, sorry."

"Yeah, it's crummy."

"Your mother seemed nice."

"Well…she's a mom."

"Did you like your dad…growing up?"

"Oh, sure," she said and fell silent. Then she looked at me as though vetting my sensitivity. "Actually, I hated him."

"Why?"

"He never treated me like a daughter. I was like a mom. He leaned on me for psychological support."

"How old is he?"

"Seventy-five."

"Wow. So, he was about fifty when you were born. How old's your mom?"

"She was twenty-four years younger. Used to be his secretary. Second marriage."

"Do you think this girlfriend will be a third marriage?"

"I don't know."

"Hard on your mom?"

"She drinks. She's usually oblivious."

Some date talk, I thought. I was anxious to get back to talking business, but we had arrived at the Zepf place.

Squealing with laughter, as was their practice, the girls came tumbling out of the house and down the porch steps, like someone had knocked over a jar of marbles. But this time they stopped dead when they saw Shauna get out of the car.

"Oh, oh," the girls said when I intro'd them to Shauna. "We thought you were bringing another lawyer."

Shauna and I laughed. "But she *is* the lawyer."

"Oh, oh," there was a whispered conference among the older girls, a low-toned argument. Something seemed amiss, but I hoped it wasn't anger at me for not telling them Shauna was a woman.

Shauna was good with the kids, very unaffected. She met Rich and took his hand warmly and said, "Mr. Zepf, you are a hero in my eyes."

He chuckled and said, "And if my eyes were any good you'd be a hero in them too."

"I'm glad you can't see me blushing," she said.

"I'm not," he said, and laughed again to show her he wasn't hurt.

There were soft packages at Shauna's and my places at the table.

"What's this?" I asked.

"It's your present," Rita said. "Miriam and I made them. She sewed, I painted."

"Shall we open them now?"

"Maybe you should open yours first," Carrie said.

"Okay." I tore open my package. There was a navy-blue necktie with the international symbol for no smoking—a red circle with a red slash through a burning cigarette.

"Oh, wow, it's great!" I exclaimed, genuinely touched.

There was an awkward silence, which I decided to break. "May Shauna open hers now?"

The girls hung their heads. Rita mumbled, "I guess so."

Shauna opened her package with care, as though she planned to enshrine the wrapping paper. When she saw what it was, she squealed with delight, just as though she were one of the family.

The girls raised their eyes and looked from one to the other, confused, then surprised. "Do you...*like* it?" Jodi asked.

"Oh, I love it!" she said.

"We thought you were a boy," Miriam said bringing her hand to cover her face.

"I *love* ties. I can wear it like this," she said and opening the top button of her blouse she wrapped the tie around her neck like a cravat, with the no-smoking symbol showing, and the girls cheered and clapped in delight.

Much relieved, the Zepf girls threw themselves into another banquet for their guests.

This time we had mashed potatoes and fried chicken, with corn fritters and maple syrup for dessert.

They couldn't get over that Shauna, a girl like themselves, could be a lawyer.

"And you can too," I said. "If we win this case, you could all be lawyers."

"I don't want to be a lawyer," Skipper said. "I want to be a nurse."

"I want to be a movie star," Lee said.

"I'm going to have to go to North Carolina," I said, "to investigate the case. Shauna will be here, so if you have any questions or anything you can call her. If you want to talk to me, let her know and I'll call you. I'll be back in a little while and check in with you often."

"When's the Bomber coming?"

"He probably won't be here until we are ready to do depositions."

"What's that?" Barbara asked.

"That's when you question the other side's witnesses to see what they are going to say at trial."

"And they *tell* you what they are going to say?" Carrie asked.

"They're supposed to. If they lie to you, they can be arrested for perjury."

"Per what?" Jodi asked.

"Perjury—it's a word for lying under oath."

Shauna and I both loved the corn fritter dessert. Of course, the girls didn't want us to leave.

"We could put on the play for Shauna."

"Oh, that would be great," I said, "but we have to work tomorrow, and you have school."

We were no sooner in the car then Shauna said, "The oldest girl asked me if you were my boyfriend."

We both had an edgy laugh. "What did you tell her?"

"I said we were madly in love and expected to get married any day now."

"You didn't!"

"You don't think so?"

"Nooo—" Actually, I hoped she had.

She laughed. "I think it's cute."

"What is?"

"They all have this mad crush on you."

"Hard to understand, isn't it?"

"Oh, I don't know," she said.

8

I always envied guys who could romance a girl to ecstasy the first time out. I settled for "I had a very nice time" on her doorstep and "I'll see you tomorrow."

She put out her hand and I shook it. Then I felt foolish.

In the morning, I went for Easy Willie's answer—a half-hour early. His building had only four floors, but the elevator had an operator. He must have come with the building, for he was about eighty years old. Now there's a guy, I thought, who could tell some stories.

And, given that his communication came in short blasts, floor-to-floor, and likely emphasized the weather, the old guy might, I thought, be ripe for opening up.

I'd heard someone call him Frank. Frank was like a hothouse plant too long in the darkness. His complexion was as white as his hair, which flopped over his forehead like Carl Sandburg's had. Frank looked short on nourishment, bent and frail, but it was nothing that a good dose of sunlight wouldn't cure. If he'd hit a hundred pounds, it wasn't very hard.

As it turned out, he was easier to start talking than to stop. The only thing that stopped him was a call for the elevator. Then, when he returned, he picked up where he had left off.

"How long you been working this thing?" I asked, pointing to the archaic cage he called home.

"Hired the day the building opened up," he said.

"When was that?"

"Nineteen and thirty-four. It was a depression baby. Went through a lot of foreclosures and bankruptcies before it got off the ground. Only three tenants, them early years. One of 'em paid, maybe."

"Over sixty years on the job!" I said. "Wow. Any celebrations?"

"Nah. No one left from them days. I was seventeen years old when I started."

"I'll bet you could tell a thing or two about the tenants here."

"Oh, yeah."

"I just been to see Easy Willie," I said. "How long's he been here?"

"Imagine, let's see now—came in here late sixties, early seventies. Quite a man, that one."

"Yes? How so?"

"His name'n all. Takes it pretty easy now."

"Now? He wasn't always like that?"

He looked at me as though I had flipped out. "I should say not. I thought you knew him."

"Not really. I've been to see him," I said. "I'm from California," I said. "Tod Hanson."

"Oh—you the Bomber's kid?"

"How did you know that?"

"This's a small town, Tod. Take about five minutes word to get 'round here."

"Does Easy Willie do much business?"

"Not so's I can tell," he said. "Takes it easy. Oh, anybody get in trouble gots no money, they make the beeline for old Willie."

"How does he live?"

The old-timer shrugged with the lower half of his face. "His people had some money, I think—and then there was the settlement."

"Settlement?"

"Yeah. From Bortz, Hillegas and them."

"He in an accident?"

"Not really."

The buzzer rang, calling the elevator and its operator skyward. He returned with a woman of mid-years bundled up for the cold world, though the temperature in the building seemed about eighty-five and I had my coat over my arm.

He didn't miss a beat. "There was that business with the woman," he said, whetting my appetite, only to be called away again. He returned this time with an unhappy young man who raced to the street without a word as soon as the old timer opened the cage. The whole thing put me in mind of the zoo, with the old one acting as the keeper. It was in his power, after all, to open the cage door or not.

He started to tell me the tale of the young man, but I wasn't interested. "What was the business with the woman?"

"What?" He'd seemed to have forgotten.

"With Easy Willie?"

"Oh, with Bortz and them?" he asked. "Don't know I should be telling tales outa school," he said looking up to the second floor. "But shoot, ever'body knows it. You might as well too. Seems he came out that there Harvard School with his pants all hotted up like them young bucks liable to, ya know?"

I told him I knew.

"Lotta folks surprised Willie came back here to work, him being something of a star up there in Harvard and all. Expected he'd be in the Supreme Court or somethin'."

"Clerking?" I said.

"Not Willie," he said. "He wouldn't be no clerk for nobody. I say they expected he'd *be on* the Supreme Court."

I didn't correct him. People didn't just step out of law school onto *any* court.

"So he goes to work for the Bortz gang an' pretty soon he's a star there."

"Easy Willie?"

"He wasn't so easy in them days. Came in here plenty, visiting my lawyers an' such like. No one called him Easy—he was like a house a fur in them days. Used to take them there steps two at a time."

"So what happened?" I was anxious to move him along before another customer—maybe Easy Willie himself—

impressed him into service.

"Old man Bortz—he's dead now—and him had a run-in."

The hothouse plant seemed to be wilting in the telling. "Over a woman?"

"You might say, yes. Willie was a young stud too long cooped up with them law books, and them other fellas at Harvard. Not so many women in them days. So there's this here secretary at Bortz and them he takes a shine to. Old man Bortz's secretary it was, but Willie tells me later he thought nothing of it, see, because Bortz a married man an' all. Well, the feelings of this here secretary is pretty mutual for Willie and they's crazy in love. Only one thing she don't tell Willie is she's doin' old man Bortz on the side."

"He didn't know?"

"'Parently not. Lot's of 'em *did* over there, only no one bothered to tell Willie. There was some talk that was on purpose 'cause Willie was setting the place on fur an' a lot of them newer boys didn't take kindly to them shenanigans."

"And the girl didn't tell him?"

"Alcestis? 'Parently not. Guess she thought old man Bortz would go the way of all them philanderin' husbands— straight back to the missus."

"But he didn't?"

"Oh, yeah, he done gone back all right, just not soon enough." He stopped to reflect on something, licking his lips before going on that "Alcestis was a looker all right. The most shining black hair you ever seen right down to her butt. I mean that hair was so long it musta been a real chore for her not to sit on it all a time. And built real compact. Skin like milk."

I appreciated the digression into Alcestis' looks, but I was itching for pay dirt here. "What became of Willie?"

"Oh, that's the tragedy," he said, shaking his head. "Apparently Old Bortz an' Willie had words over the thing. I don't doubt Willie used some intemperant language with the old man—what old Bortz would see as lackin' the proper respect for his position of seniority and superiority. But Bortz weren't all he's mad at. He takes on after Alcestis for not sharing her secret with him. Now the situation in the respectable old firm takes a turn for the worst ever. Bortz can't abide his star no more an' rumor has it he buys Willie off. Next thing I know he's movin'..."

"In here?"

He nodded. "Apparently Alcestis had a bit of a Greek temper, and she got it off on Willie for walking out without a fight. Musta had it bad for him in spite of old Bortz."

"What did Willie say to that?"

"Don't know," Frank said. "Wasn't there."

"So the girl went back to the old man?"

"Not exactly. She come in here after Willie. They had some shoutin' matches up there you could hear all over the building. I mean it, fourth floor, basement even. Then just as sudden she's gone."

"Where?"

"For good. Musta had it real bad for Willie," Frank said as though he could still fell the loss. "She killed herself—gassed in her little car. Only she didn't have a garage where she was living. Turned out Bortz was paying for the love nest, but a garage was five dollars a month extry so she parked on the street."

"Where did she...?"

"When Willie's gone she let herself in his garage and done it there. Rumor has it she left him a note, but nobody's ever seen it 'cept Willie 'course."

"Oh," I said. I couldn't say much more. "What a story. So the fireball..." I started to say and Frank finished it.

"Became Easy Willie. Spends his time taking it easy. Don't know if he blames hisself or what. Don't think Bortz lost a lotta sleep. There was that hint of scandal for a while, then things got back to normal, except for Easy Willie, who ain't had a normal day since."

"Wasn't he married?"

"Yeah, couple times in there somewheres, but it never

stuck very long."

"Oh, man," I said, while a customer for Frank's services came in the front door, taking off his hat and unbuttoning his coat. I thanked Frank and bade him goodbye.

I ran over to Shauna's office to call Bomber before he left for the day. I saw no reason to keep our offer open to a guy with that load of emotional baggage.

Shauna gave me the oh-fella-you-are-welcome-here smile.

"May I use the phone?"

"Why not, you're paying for it," she said. "I had a good time last night."

"So did I," I said.

"Do you want privacy?" she asked.

"Not necessary, thanks," I said, without thinking. "Just heard about Easy Willie—his history."

"Oh?"

"Want to tell Bomber so I can withdraw our offer."

"I wondered—" she said, and stopped.

I dialed the big Bomber and little Bonnie answered, "Law offices, Bomber Hanson," in that way of making it sound like *she* was Bomber Hanson.

"Hi, Bonnie," I said. "He there?"

"Sweetheart!" she exclaimed, and I was glad Shauna couldn't hear it. I wasn't anxious to explain our airhead to her. "You've thawed out just in time. Much as I'd adore to chat with you all day, I've got real work to do. I'll put him on."

"How's it going, boy?" Bomber boomed.

"Not s-so good," I said. "I just g-got W-W-Willie's s-s-st-story." I was so excited I was spitting all over the place and I realized too late I hadn't prepared Shauna for my embarrassing affliction. I saw in her face the recognition of my terror and all the sympathy she could spare.

"We can't hire h-him."

"Why not?"

I told him the story as best I could while I humidified

Shauna's office with my spittle.

There was a silence when I finished and, for the first time, I realized the parallels between Easy Willie's girlfriend's suicide and my own sister's—Bomber's first born. Gale's was not over a specific man, but a lack of men she saw no hope of overcoming with her withered arm. I could not speak further.

Bomber rescued me. "Sometimes tragedy brings out miraculous things in the survivors," he said. "Hire him."

When I hung up the phone, I saw Shauna was looking at me curiously. She moved toward me and ran her finger around my lips. "Why do you stutter like that with your father?" she asked.

I started to tell her, then suddenly the words stopped coming.

She was kissing me.

*   *   *

It couldn't have been much after ten when I returned to Easy Willie's office. Frank, the elevator hothouse plant, told me he was not in yet. "Don't always come so early," he said.

I decided to wait upstairs. Frank had exhausted me. I cooled my heels for twenty minutes or so.

I was just about to cut and run when I saw Frank let Willie out of the elevator on the second floor of the G and G building on Madison Street. I nodded a tentative "Hello" and Easy Willie ignored it. Even his gait was easy. Like shambling. Seeing him on his feet for the first time, my first reaction was this was not a guy in whose way you wanted to get.

I stepped aside as he opened his door, took off his coat and hat and threw them on the chair I might have sat in. Moving to his own chair, he slowly seated himself and assumed his pose for the day—like an exiled guru who had just been asked the meaning of life.

I had decided to let him utter the first word today. Getting anything out of Easy Willie was like pulling teeth. I was tired of playing dentist.

"Well?" I finally prodded.

He heaved an exasperated sigh, as though preparatory to some announcement, then fell silent again.

I'd had it. I was tired of standing there looking at him and the chair he threw his coat on, but I knew I had to get his answer for Bomber. I took one of my Tod Hanson, Investigator cards out of my pocket and wrote on it my phone number at the hotel. "Here," I said, "in case anything comes to you that you can put in words." I threw the card on the desk in front of him as though I were an important man whose time he had wasted, then I turned to go.

When I put my hand on the shaky doorknob, I heard him clear his throat.

"I got conditions," he said.

When he had given me his modest demands, I grabbed Easy Willie's phone. He seemed startled.

"Don't worry, we'll pick up your phone bill," I said.

It was one of those phones with the numbers in the handset. I punched the appropriate ones.

"Hi ya, sugar plum," Bonnie said, after she knew who was on the phone.

"Bomber Hanson, please," I said. You could have made snowballs with my tone. "I'm here with Easy Willie Adams and he has some concerns."

"Give me a break!" Bonnie exhaled with, as was her practice, a minimum of forethought. An infant could have told I was in no mood for horsing around. "You trying to sound like Clarence Darrow or something? Come off it. It's me, honey-cakes, not some impressionable debutante."

"Bomber, please," I insisted.

"Soon as I get back from the little girls' room," she said, and I heard the abrupt click of the hold button. Just as I was thinking she wouldn't dare, Bomber came booming through the phone.

"Bomber Hanson," he gloried in saying his own name.

But what good was becoming an institution if you couldn't take some pleasure in it?

"I'm here with Easy Willie," I said. "He has some *caveats*. Shall I put him on?"

"You give 'em to me first, boy. Anything foreboding?"

"I don't think so."

"Rather you call me when you're alone. Talk freer."

"Thought you m-m-might like to t-talk to him your s-s-self."

I could see Easy Willie's eyes narrow at my selective affliction. I hoped *he* wasn't going to kiss me.

I told Bomber what Easy Willie had said, then asked our Pennsylvania associate if I had covered it. He nodded.

"No big deal," Bomber said. "If someone asks him why he smokes, he can always say the tobacco companies hooked him against his will. The rest of that stuff's routine. So put him on."

"He wants to talk to you," I said, handing Easy Willie the phone. He looked abashed.

"Hello," he said quietly into the phone.

I could hear Bomber's booming voice just as though it were going through one of Easy Willie's ears and out the other. "Welcome aboard," he said.

I noticed Easy Willie was forced by the sheer decibel level of Bomber's voice to hold the phone away from his ear, making it easier for both of us to hear.

"Thank you, sir," he said. It was strange to see Easy Willie awed. "What would you like me to do?"

"Give me the lay of the land back there. Maybe work on some motions and briefs. I expect the Nicks will try to nickel and dime us to death with petty motions. We have to answer them—you can help us there. We want to minimize their stalling tactics, of course—but the first thing is your feel for the case in that venue. Lay it out with Tod. Oh, and we have a court appearance. We'd like you to do that."

"Me?" Easy Willie seemed shocked. "Lot of people say I don't appear so well in court these days."

"Nonsense," Bomber boomed. "I have all the confidence in the world in you."

"But why?" Easy Willie asked almost meekly.

"Think about it," he said. "Check with Tod," Bomber said ringing off.

Easy Willie seemed energized when he replace the phone. He nodded his head toward the instrument. "Says you'll give me instructions."

"Only what comes from him. Remember, I'm just the messenger. Our court appearance for the injunction is a week from Friday. I think he wants you there."

"Injunction?"

"I'll give you a copy. Basically, it seeks to enjoin the tobacco company from making any more smokes, since they demonstrably kill people."

"He certainly doesn't expect…"

"No, no, he has no illusions. Just getting the ball rolling," I said. "Then I'd like you to give me the lowdown on the judges, on the Bortz firm, on the area in depth. Whatever you can tell us to make us feel at home."

"Well, for starters, the locals aren't keen on outsiders coming in."

"Not many locals are. That's why we have you and Shauna."

"Shauna?"

"Shauna McKinley. She's doing research. Do you know her?"

"No."

"You'll like her. Very intelligent. Competent."

"I don't know," he said. "I don't relate that well to women."

"She's non-threatening."

"It isn't the threatening I don't relate to."

"What is it then?"

Easy Willie clammed up. Changed the subject. "I notice you don't stutter when you talk to me. Only when talking to

69

your father. Why is that…?"

"I don't know," I said. "Maybe it's the same reason a bright guy like you sits in this hellhole all day and stares at the wall."

I left. He didn't kiss me.

9

Easy Willie was in charge of keeping me abreast of the enemy's movements. We had daily briefing sessions and every day seemed to bring more distressing news, enemywise.

Our Pennsylvania associate seemed to have made a transformation. He still took things kind of easy, but there was more of a forward thrust to him. Like he had at last found some purpose. He even spoke with a modicum of animation.

"Hannibal and his troops are thundering down the mountain and they are riding elephants," he said. We were in his office and he had hung up his overcoat, leaving me a clear chair to sit in. "They've not only locked up Bortz, Hillegas, they've just added two more firms to their stable: Schultz, Lictenwalner—Lictenwalner is our Mayor. He's extremely popular. Ran unopposed last two times out. He'll be at the defense table during the trial. Drawing some two-hundred an hour—a stiff wage for Gratz County. Backenstoe, Druckenmiller, and Peters is their latest coup. Peters is the brother-in-law of President Judge Druckenmiller, who was in the firm before he found his true calling belittling lawyers from the bench."

"Think he'll take the case himself?"

"That's a poser. He'd adore the publicity, but he's bone lazy. If he doesn't take it himself, he gets to pick the judge who gets it."

"Five judges in the county?" I asked.

He nodded.

"Any plaintiff's judges?"

He shook his head. "Not in this case."

I thought he might be being unduly pessimistic until he told me the rest of it.

"The other four: three guys and a gal. The one guy does the family stuff and wills and stuff. Another guy is strictly criminal cases. That leaves two other possibilities. One is Arlene Keller, bright as a whip, and Tony Stauffer, the whiz kid. He shines like the morning sun, is the opposite pole politically from President Judge Druckenmiller and Druck can't stand him. Not much chance of throwing him a plum like this. Druck would just die if he had to watch Stauffer shooting off his mouth on the six o'clock news every night."

"So it's Druckenmiller or the girl?"

"My guess—but wait, I'm not finished. Arlene Keller's family owns real estate up and down the county. Things haven't been so hot for their office buildings. We had a little recession. They have a couple doozies completely empty. Harrison J. Hinkle, Attorney-at-Law, at the behest of the T. S. Armstead Company, has just leased, for *two* years, the entire building on 5th Street—that's about thirty-thousand square feet—five stories. And it had been completely empty."

"Does she benefit directly?"

"Oh, not directly. They've seen to that."

"Could we challenge?"

"Waste of time."

"Change of venue?"

"They'll never go for it. Armstead is giving us a lesson in economics—tobacco economics. Farmers dependent on selling their sole crop to tobacco for their livelihoods, manufacturing hires zillions of people, whole towns are dependent on the uninterrupted production and distribution of those little killers. You could make a case that if you stopped cigarette sales the whole South would collapse."

"So what's *our* lesson?"

"They are moving into Cedarberg. Infiltrating Gratz County. They are putting under-employed people to work. They are taking two floors of a hotel that never rents more than a quarter of their rooms, and paying top dollar. The tap rooms are booming, so are the restaurants, and how many potential jurors do you think can remain untouched by Armstead's largess?"

"Bleak."

"And it's just begun. Anything they need, they buy here. Office furnishings, the most sophisticated computer set-up anyone around here has ever seen. They fly in experts from New York City because no one here is savvy enough for them, but you can bet the equipment is ordered through every computer store in the county."

"Bomber likes a challenge," I said weakly.

"He'll have it."

"If you had to pick the judge most likely favorable to our side, which would it be?"

"Arlene Keller," he said without any hesitation.

"The real estate connection?"

He nodded. "More chance of some objectivity. She's only been on the bench five or six years, not long enough to have developed that finely-honed arrogance that some of the old-timers fall so naturally into."

"Like the president judge?"

"Exactly," he said. "From what I know of your dad's courtroom style, he would drive Druck up the wall. He's a control freak and I don't expect that would wear too well with Bomber."

"Maybe not, but I've seen him wrap judges like that around his little finger."

"Not Druckenmiller. Especially not in this strange venue. We don't take kindly to outsiders here. Bunch of Puerto Ricans moved here from New York. Nobody talks to them. In two days Druck will have Bomber stigmatized as a piranha."

When I left Easy Willie, I felt like I needed a shot of optimism, so I dropped in on Shauna.

"I think I've found our man," she announced as soon as my foot was in the door.

"What man?"

"Our vulnerable tobacco titan."

"Oh? Who?"

"Here, let me show you," Shauna said, slipping a cassette into the VCR hooked up to the television she had brought from home. She punched the requisite buttons as I watched the delicate lines of her back move in slow motion. Then she dropped in a chair with such unconscious sensuality I gasped.

"What's wrong?" she asked.

"Nothing."

She had cued the tape to the start of the testimony before the House of Representative's committee investigating the tobacco industry. The witness was an overweight man whose pudgy face was that of the fat kid who was always bullied in the school yard—a face that suffered from sinus allergies and puffy eyes. He also blinked a lot which made me wonder if the cause of those fluttering eyes was more emotional than physical—like my stutter.

He raised his right hand, swore to tell the whole truth. The light-tan jacket of his suit hung open and, as if unconsciously, he buttoned it to cover his burgeoning middle. All the other players in this drama wore dark suits that not only gave them a more serious look, but were more slimming than the light colors. "Donald Cantwell Powell" was the answer to "State your full name for the records, please." Then, "You may be seated."

Don Powell unbuttoned the jacket again, as though sitting with that much midships restraint was out of the question, buttonwise.

The House committee members flanked the counsel and looked on with varying states of concentration, sometimes whispering to aides who sat behind them, sometimes talking among themselves, but always their faces were heavy with the *gravitas* of the situation, like the high school student council considering the ecological impact of a bonfire before the big game.

"What is your position at T. S. Armstead?"

"I'm vice-president in charge of production."

"The making of cigarettes? Is that what production is?"

"Yes."

Yes, he was a smoker, he said, and he took a lot of pleasure from it.

"Did you ever try to give up smoking?" he was asked by the young counsel for the committee, Sam Rose, one of those bright young men still close enough to his law school years to ape the professors who gloried in their mental superiority.

"Yes."

"Were you successful?"

"No," he said with those sad, beagle-dog eyes that hounded him in the clinches.

"Why not?"

"I missed it," he said. "I missed the pleasures of smoking. The great feeling I got inhaling."

"But if you liked smoking so much, why did you try to give it up?"

"I don't know. I suppose that was why I was not successful. I didn't really want to quit."

"But what made you try to quit?"

"My wife didn't like the smell of smoke around the house."

"She doesn't smoke?"

"No."

"Do you have any children?"

"I have two daughters."

"Do they smoke?"

"No."

"How old are they?"

"Twelve and fourteen."

"Would you want them to smoke?"

"Not at their age. It isn't legal."

"When they're old enough, would you encourage them to try smoking?"

"Encourage?"

"Yes."

"I don't believe so."

"Why not?"

"It is a matter of individual choice."

"But you get so much pleasure from it, wouldn't you want your daughters to experience that kind of pleasure?"

Shauna chimed in from her chair, "See how he made that question so suggestive? Sexual almost?"

"I think the pleasures of smoking are individual. Some people do not like smoking. Some love it."

"Do you know why that is?"

"No."

"Any speculation?"

"No."

"Body chemistry?"

"I'm not a chemist, or a doctor."

"You have read the studies linking cancer and heart disease, emphysema and other fatal diseases with smoking, have you not?"

"No."

"No?" The committee lawyer was incredulous. "Don't you think that knowledge would be essential to a man who is in charge of manufacturing cigarettes for the largest cigarette company in the world?"

"No."

"No?"

"No." Don Powell blinked.

"Why not?"

"You can get a study done to show anything."

"Oh? Could you get one done that showed smoking was good for you?"

"Certainly."

"Have you ever seen a report favorable to the tobacco industry?"

"Certainly."

"Oh? What was it?"

"Statistics that show certain cancers are less prevalent in smokers than non-smokers."

"Oh? What kind?"

"Colon cancer for example."

"*Colon* cancer?" The young attorney made an incredulous face. "You've studied colon cancer, but you haven't read any *lung* cancer studies?"

"No."

"Why not?"

"I'm not a doctor. I'm not a scientist."

"What are you?"

"I'm a businessman."

"And you are making a product that kills people, and you don't want to know anything about it?"

Don Powell just stared blankly ahead then, as if some signal flashed his nervous system, he began blinking.

Except for the blinking, I didn't see anything unusual about Don Powell's testimony. All the tobacco guys, I suspected, had used the same dodge. Didn't believe there was a link between their baby and premature death. Not proven. I was about to ask Shauna what she had in mind, when a young man on the TV screen appeared over Attorney Rose's shoulder and handed him a note. Sam Rose opened the folded paper and read the note, then glanced at the messenger and nodded. The messenger disappeared from the screen. Rose turned to the witness.

"You said your wife didn't like the smell of smoke, is that correct?"

Powell blinked and seemed to have trouble with the question. Then he croaked, "Yes."

"Is this your present wife you are talking about?"

"Yes."

"How long have you been married to her?"

"Six and a half months."

"So you were married before."

The witness nodded.

"Is that a yes?"

"Yes."

"How long was that marriage?"

"Eighteen years." The memory seemed to be affecting

the witness. It looked like he was stifling a sniffle.

You could see Sam Rose was building up to something. He was leaning forward and the tension tightened his vocal cords.

"Were you divorced?"

"No."

"Did she object to you smoking?"

Sniffle. "No."

"Did she, in fact, smoke herself?"

"Yes." His handkerchief came out and he wiped his nose quickly with it.

"How old was she when she died?" Rose asked.

Powell was staring again, not as though he couldn't remember her age, more like he couldn't remember anything.

"I'm sorry, Mr. Powell," Rose said, "is this difficult for you?"

The witness regarded his questioner through half-closed eyes, as though he had just awakened and found an unpleasant intruder in his room.

"Did you hear the question, Mr. Powell?"

"What was the question?"

"How old was your first wife when she died?"

He took a long draw on the expectant air in the committee room. "Forty-three...and two months," he said, trailing off into the land of blocked memories.

There wasn't a sound in the meeting room. Sam Rose lowered his voice.

"What did she die of?" he asked.

A pink tongue peeked through Powell's closed lips, and made a circle, then disappeared. "Cancer," he said, so you could hardly hear him.

"Cancer, you say?" Rose repeated. If I could think of a word besides "gloating" to describe how attorney Rose looked, I would gladly use it. "Would that have been *lung* cancer?"

Don Powell's face looked like it was about to implode. He nodded and started to say, "Yes," but got only as far as the

"Y" and it just stuck there. I thought the witness was going to have a nervous breakdown. Lawyer Rose smilied the smile of triumph.

"Creep!" Shauna said, and on the TV, the committee chairman called a recess.

10

For months, it was mostly motions. Your Honor this and Your Honor that. They call it motion court but that is a misnomer if there ever was one. There is no motion involved. The whole idea seems to be to stymie the process.

Bomber entrusted these court appearances to Easy Willie. That way, he could stay in his beloved Angelton, on the coast of central California as long as possible, while I wallowed in the frozen northland, keeping Easy Willie and Shauna defending against tobacco company motions. Mostly, Shauna did the legal research of cases to support our positions, Easy Willie wrote the briefs. Motions to quash, motions to dismiss. All kinds of contrarian motions.

The legal profession is so adversarial. Even the terminology is kind of an in-your-face language. A motion to quash, for example, is tantamount to saying I'm going to squash you. It is a language of animosity, the legal language, and it can't help but shape the characters and personalities of its practitioners.

Easy Willie seemed to be an exception. He seemed smart enough to foresee the damage and not let it take hold of him, though I did notice some signs of percolating adrenalin in him. I wondered how Shauna might change if she got into an active court practice.

To relieve the long, dreary nights of the Pennsylvania winter, Shauna and I got together to make music. We played duets: she on the flute, I on the piano. A lot of people play the flute well, getting all the notes just right. Shauna not only did that, but infused her playing with a musical passion that put her far above the crowd. It was a joy to play with her at her house. Her mother was an unobtrusive, but appreciative, audience. I look back on those times as moments of pure pleasure.

That evening in my hotel, I got a call from Carrie.

"I just wanted to offer to help you anyway I can. Jan and June could do something too. Whatever you want."

"That's very nice of you," I said, "and I'll let you know if we need anything. In the meantime, the best thing you can all do is keep your father alive and happy."

My next call was from the Bomber himself. "What's happening on the eastern front?" he wanted to know.

I brought him up to date and he said the words I had been dreading, though I knew they were inevitable, "Time to go South, young man."

I groaned.

"So talk to the guy—this Powell. He's vulnerable—*if* he'll talk to you. Be tricky at the company—find his home. Get an agency to get you all the dope—home address, phone—then close in. Our goal is a mole. Someone who can give us the inside scoop—how they *know* that nicotine is addictive, how they see to it there is enough in their death sticks to keep 'em puffin'. The North Carolina home of T. S. Armstead, purveyors of death and disease, is such a provincial, inbred town, I'm afraid we might be sorry if we used anyone local. Everyone's got a second cousin once-removed. You've got to do it yourself.

"Remember, their conceit is the whole South is dependent on them. The Virgin Mary couldn't be so pure. There've been a lot of cases for naught. What's going to bring home the bacon here is the mole. They never could get the Mafia until they got some stools and moles. Lot of wrist-slapping for tax-evasion went on, but now the big Dons are being put away for murder and real stuff. That's what we want—murder!"

After that conversation, I was plenty depressed. I looked out my tiny eastern window and saw the trees had been replenished with new leaves without my even being aware of it. Instead of snow and ice, we had rain and slush, then rain and mud. The thunderstorms, with their flashes of eerie lightening, took some getting used to. Scary at first, they became merely annoying. I always thought of these weather things in the context of Shauna and how you had to be strong to live in the East.

So, naturally, I was thinking about taking Shauna back with me to Angelton, California.

We were spending a lot of time together, working and playing. The months had flown by in her company and we had gone from the season we complain about the cold, to the season we complain about the heat.

She took me to the airport in her burgundy Chrysler product. Lee Iacocca was a product of this vicinity and a lot of people expressed loyalty to his products.

No turnpike or superhighways were involved in getting from downtown Cedarberg to the airport, but there were a bunch of lights. We were stopped at one and our easy conversation had suddenly stopped. "What are you thinking?" she asked.

"I've developed quite a case on you," I said.

The light changed. She moved the car slowly. The closer we got to the airport, the slower she drove. "It's mutual," she said. I don't know how my heart got in my throat, but I couldn't swallow it.

I reached over and she did too, our hands met and our fingers entwined. Such simple actions make for such delightful feelings.

"I wish you could go with me," I said.

"I do too," she said. "Can't I?"

"We could ask Bomber, but I know what he'd say—you have to do the lawyer work and I have to do the detective work. Can't do research for Pennsylvania in North Carolina, laws are different. Besides, I'd be distracted beyond any achievement. Maybe you could come for a visit."

"Oh, could I?" she said. "I'd like that!"

We seemed to be moving at about five miles and hour. "Hey," I said, "if you don't drive a little faster, I'll miss the plane."

"Promise?" she said.

We said goodbye at the curb in front of the airport entrance. "I'll call you everyday," I said.

"At least!" she said. She gave me a long and longing kiss. Finally, we broke it off and I jumped out of the car. I looked back at her and blew her a kiss. She mirrored the action and I ran inside—then, just before I was to turn out of sight, I looked back. She was still there, watching me and there were tears in her eyes. Shauna McKinley was not the kind of person you could picture crying. I waved at her, starting to sniffle myself. She waved back and I was gone.

As soon as I got off the plane in North Carolina, I went straight to a telephone and called Shauna.

She answered on the first ring.

"I think I love you," I said.

She purred. "Funny," she said, "I was just thinking the same about you."

It was four-thirty-something by the time I left the airport in my rental Ford. I had called T. S. Armstead to ascertain the location of Powell's office and that he was "in a meeting" there. I didn't leave my name. I got in the car instead and drove to T. S. Armstead headquarters.

I guess the South isn't a bad place if you happen to be an alligator. For my taste, it was a little hot and humid.

The town of Churchill Park was T. S. Armstead. There was no disguising it. Virtually everyone in town was employed by the company or was in some industry related to the company. There was no need to say T. S. Armstead, since everyone simply referred to it as "The Company."

I never understood why people built multi-story buildings in places where land was plentiful. But there the thing was, poking ten stories or so into the sky and casting its puny shadow on the parking lot which occupied about ten times the land the building did. And I didn't see anything aesthetically appealing about that parking lot *or* the building in the middle of it. Glass walls, flat sides—minimalist architecture I suppose, but if the number of cars was any indication, there were an awful lot of people inside.

I was looking for only one.

There was no guard at the entrance to the B-lot—I guess that was for the B-players in the enterprise—so I drove in there and parked as close as I could to the building, which was far. I walked toward the building and came to the A-lot, which did have a guard. And a fence around it. I saw a bunch of signs or standards reserving spaces for the big shots. I manuvered into position to see the names. With my Ivy League get-up on, I figured I looked like I belonged.

The third sign over said "Mr. Powell." Facing the sign was a maroon Caddy, the latest model. A quick scan of the lot showed the exec's bought American, and no one had the same color Caddy, though there were others—as well as Lincoln Town Cars, Mark IV's and a few Chrysler Imperials. But just to be safe, I scanned the numbers and letters on his license plate before sauntering back to my car.

At five o'clock on the money, the hordes poured out of the glass monolith and hurried to their cars with a uniform anticipation that I doubt was present when they entered the workplace in the morning.

I quickly visualized a traffic jam that could stymie my exit, so I drove out to the street while I still could. The street was wide, but stopping was prohibited. I could understand why when the cars began to pour out onto it.

I was afraid I would miss Powell's exit. Across the road from the lot there was a shopping center—a strip of stores really—and I found a place to park and spot the maroon Caddy when it decamped.

Not one of the A-lot parkers left with the crowd at five.

At five-thirty, the A- lot was still full, and I was getting hungry. I had hoarded a small pack of peanuts, "honey-roasted," from the plane but I knew eating them would make me thirsty. I didn't dare leave my post. It wasn't until around six that I saw the first car leave the A-lot. It was not vice-president in charge of manufacturing, Powell.

At ten of seven, I ate the peanuts. I was ponderously chewing the last few of them when I saw the rolly-polly, sad-sack go from the building to his car. The contrast between his exit and those of the B-players was marked. He seemed in no hurry to get home.

His mood carried over to his driving, so he was easy to follow. If he suspected someone was following him, he made no sign of it.

Naturally, just when I needed saliva to slake my thirst from the salty honey-roasteds, my mouth went dry.

I was a good block behind when he pulled into this colonial pastiche of a mansion that reminded me of those plantations in movies about the Old South. There were wide spaces between the houses, and those spaces were packed with privacy trees. This was definitely housing for the A-lot types.

His garage door opened automatically and the cavern swallowed his car. I pulled to the curb across the street, in front of another forest separating two mansions.

Rehearsing my speech, I made my way up the long walkway to the forest-green front door. The house sat on a small rise and it was a longer walk than I'd realized. I must have been a good ten feet from pay dirt, when I heard the shouting from within.

There was a man's deep, insouciant voice, which sounded like he was too tired to yell but was shouting nonetheless, as though out of some sense of duty. The real honest-to-God passion was coming from a voice in the female register. Her screaming was so violent I did not think I would have the courage to face her. My picture of her from her outraged voice was not pretty. A woman wrestler with stringy hair, a flat nose and a right upper-cut you would never forget.

I stood at the door, waiting for a lull before I knocked. The lull was not forthcoming. Finally, I retreated down the path, wondering what to do next.

I decided to walk up the street to give the Powells time to cool off. Of course, it was getting darker and I wasn't optimistic they would even open the door to me.

I took my time getting back to Vice-President Powell's house. All was quiet when I got back. Too quiet, I thought. I could just see me stumbling on the scene of a murder-suicide and trying to explain what I was doing here.

So now, weak with hunger, mouth dehydrated from anxiety, I gave the doorbell a macho punch.

I didn't have long enough to add to my paltry courage before the door opened. I was facing Don Powell. He had taken off his jacket and tie and was standing, shoeless in his suit pants and a ecru open-neck shirt. The circles under his eyes seemed to have been highlighted with a bluish mascara to match his eyes.

He looked me up and down as though he were trying to place me in the pantheon of door-to-door peddlers. Was it newspaper subscriptions (too well dressed), religion (always come in pairs), Fuller brushes (too late in the day)?

"Yes?" he said.

"Mr. Powell?"

"Yessss," more uncertain. The hucksters rarely knew your name.

"I'm Tod Hanson. I'm sorry to bother you at home so late, but I was wondering if I could have an appointment to talk to you sometime?"

"About what?"

"I am associated with Bomber Hanson, the lawyer." I could see him blink. "We represent Richard Zepf in an action—"

He raised his hand to cut me off. "Sorry," he said, and he actually *looked* sorry, "but you'll have to contact our customer service department during business hours."

"I was hoping to talk to you informally—"

"Sorry."

"—rather than subpoena you for a deposition."

"Afraid that won't be possible."

"Be done in private," I offered. "Speak freely. No stenographer. Just you and me."

He fixed me with his weariest gaze. There was a ton of hopelessness in that look, and I should have thought nothing would make him happier than to get it off his chest.

Wrong.

"I'm sorry," he said, and closed the door in my face.

11

I stopped at the first place I came to that even hinted of food. I had a ham and cheese on a roll the color and texture of marshmallow. The ham had a phosphorescent glow and the cheese stood alone. It wasn't much, but I stuffed my face anyway, after drinking a gallon of water.

Then I drove into town and checked into a motel called the Churchill Park Inn. It was a two-story concoction that harbored a desire to look like another plantation. Inside, it was motel basic.

I usually have trouble sleeping in a new bed, but I was so wrung out I fell right to sleep.

In the morning, I repeated the route I had taken the night before. Powell's electrically-activated garage door was closed. I drove to the end of the block, where I parked so I could see Don Powell come down the street.

It was a little after seven-thirty when I saw the maroon boat heading away from his house. His pace was somewhat quicker going to work than it had been coming home.

When he was out of sight, I turned back to park in front of the wooded area next to the Powell house.

It couldn't have been more than ten minutes when another Cadillac, this one green, floated down the driveway. By the time she was moving my way, I had started driving ahead of her. A glance in my rearview mirror told me I had made a mistake. The gorgeous creature driving must have been Powell's daughter. But there were others in the car—two *other* children. Then I remembered Powell had two daughters: fourteen and twelve, neither old enough to drive a car.

I thought I should return to the house to confront the wife, but I realized the Powells had only a two-car garage, and there was no other car in sight.

The looker pulled the car in front of the stately old red-brick school building and the twelve and fourteen year old got out. There was something in the exchange between the girls and their driver that didn't seem sisterly, but I couldn't put my finger on it.

The green Cadillac worked its way through the moving traffic in some haste. She got onto the freeway they call a highway back there, and in no more than a mile or so, she exited and drove into the parking lot of the sprawling shopping center. A rugged sign told you this was the Towne and Countre Shopping Center. I was immediately taken with their employment of the "e's". Upscale.

The lot was virtually empty. I didn't imagine the stores opened for an hour or two. But instead of parking near the buildings as one would expect from a family with an A-lot mentality, she parked along the perimeter fence, next to another lone car, a silver Lincoln. I didn't want to get too close, so I stopped my rental near a delivery truck where I could see what she was up to. My first thought when she jumped out of her car, locked it, then jumped into the adjacent car was she was making a drug buy. Maybe cigarettes didn't do it for her.

But then the car's rear lights went on and it began moving. I hadn't gotten a look at the driver, but I followed. They didn't drive far. At the next light, with no one between us, they embraced with a flurry of kisses that seemed, at the least, heart-felt and too long repressed.

It wasn't far to the motel. It was a nice enough place, but you didn't see any other Lincolns in the parking lot. I pulled into a gas station across the street and watched them go up the steps to a room on the far end of the second floor. The man looked maybe twenty years older than she; they moved with dispatch, but didn't evidence a lot of anxiety. My guess was this wasn't the first time—he was married and her mommy and step-daddy wouldn't like it if they knew. Neither would his wife. But domestic surveillance was not, thank goodness, my line.

As I drove back to the house, my mind seemed out of

gear. The closer I got to the southern mansion the more out of sync I seemed to be.

I parked in front this time, went up the walkway and rang the bell, much less certain of what I would find.

In (southern) time, the door opened and I found myself face-to-face with a black bulwark somewhat prettier than Mahalia Jackson, but not much thinner.

She seemed to think it was my place to speak first. I did. "Is Mrs. Powell in?"

She shook her head.

"When might you expect her back?"

"No telling," she said, with accent-free speech that could have come from an English professor at the university. "She took the children to school, then she's got some errands. May I tell her you called?"

I must have looked like a bozo. I felt like one. "What?—Oh—no thanks, I'll be in touch…"

I got back to the motel to find the silver Lincoln still in its place. I decided to do something that required more courage than I thought I had.

I went to the motel-room door and knocked as though I were the morality police.

There was no answer. I knocked again. Harder.

Nothing. "Mrs. Powell," I said, and I didn't whisper it either. Now I got a response. From a man who sounded like he was used to controlling things. "Who's there?"

"Security," I said. "I have a message for Mrs. Powell."

There were a few hushed words passed behind the door. "You must have the wrong room," he said.

"I could swear I saw her go in this room."

"Well," the big voice seemed to falter, "you didn't. Try next door."

"Okay, sorry. I hope I didn't wake you," I said to which he did not respond. "Oh, if you should see her, tell her she's wanted at home. Emergency," I added, and retreated down the balcony walkway, staying close to the wall so I couldn't be seen by the pair of eyes at the window.

I went down the steps at the street-end of the building, got into my car and headed back to the shopping center parking lot. There were more cars now and I could park with a row between my car and Mrs. Powell's.

It didn't take long for macho man to sweep into the parking lot and drop her off without a kiss or even a kind word that I could see. And then he sped away as though he were doing a qualifying heat for the Indy five-hundred.

I was almost unprepared for my good luck. I threw the car into gear, and was able to get to her just as she had unlocked the car and sat in the driver's seat.

I pulled my rental car up behind her Caddy and parked her in. I could see her woeful eyes looking at me in her rearview mirror.

I moved quickly to the driver's side of the car.

"What do you want?" she said. She hadn't lowered the window.

"Just to talk to you for a few minutes."

"How much?"

"Not long."

"No, how much money do you want?"

"Money? I don't want money. Just talk."

She looked at me as though I had insisted I was the tooth fairy.

"Look," I said. "I'm not going to move my car until you agree to talk to me for a few minutes."

"Who *are* you?"

"I'll tell you all that. I can shout at you through this window, or I can get in the car with you, or you can come inside and I'll buy you coffee. Up to you."

"I can call the police," she said, weakly.

"Sure. Let's go inside. I'll wait while you call them."

I saw she had a car phone, but I didn't mention it.

"I have an emergency at home," she said glancing up at me as though she were hoping there was no connection.

I shook my head. "I made that up," I said.

She wasn't surprised.

"We can talk at home if you like," I said. "Really, I have no interest in your private life."

"What do you want to talk about then?"

"Your husband."

"That's my private life," she said.

"His work," I said.

She looked up to me with eyes at once young and naive and yet with the hint of weariness of one who has seen forty years worth in half that time.

When she got out of the car, I was able to see her for the first time, up close, full on.

She had a body of such geometric perfection it could only have been designed by a computer. And no care had been taken to hide any of its subtle nooks and crannies. It was as though she belonged to the school of couture that held spray-paint as a legitimate apparel.

Her face, a trifle worse for the wear under the circumstances, was still under this train-load of stress. Her shining countenance of youthful vigor bespoke a lithe athleticism that must have left her competitors drowning in the streams of envy.

The whole of her garment was something knit, but I can't remember if it was pink, yellow, pale orange, or even baby blue. I was looking at texture, not color.

After she locked the door on her car, I pulled mine into the space left next to her by the fleeing lover.

Walking side-by-side with this beauty to the hub of the activity, I tried to imagine this gorgeous creature with that shrill screaming voice I had heard the night before at her house. I couldn't.

"By the way," I said, "I'm Tod Hanson."

She didn't say anything.

"Shall I call you Mrs. Powell?"

"Yeah, right," she said with the sarcasm only a twenty-four year old could muster.

12

We settled into a booth in a quiet corner of one of these eateries which seemed to drop from a self-contained module into one shopping center after the other throughout the country. The food you could imagine being brought in on the plate under Saran Wrap, ready to pop into the microwave.

Our selection of this particular eaterie did not hinge on its decor or its food but on its being virtually empty.

I ordered a doughnut and a glass of water.

Mrs. Powell, less daring, had the coffee—black.

It took some effort to focus my attention away from her person, and onto my topic.

"So what *do* you want?" she prodded me, obviously not convinced of my innocence.

I considered sliding into the heart of the thing obliquely, but I had her attention, there was no real need. "Your husband makes cigarettes," I said.

She nodded, wondering what that had to do with anything. "I hate them," she said, as though that put her on my side as well as the side of the gods.

"We are participating in an action for a man dying of lung cancer."

"You're a lawyer?" she said, as though she might have known.

"Yes—personally, I'm more of an investigator—working for a lawyer."

"Local?"

"No—California."

"Wow, heavy. Far from home."

"Yeah. The case is being tried in Pennsylvania."

"Also far," she said. "I'd sure like to go to California."

"Never been?"

She shook her head, the blonde tresses matted from her recent activity seemed to bounce back to life. "I'm a North Carolina girl: Born, bred and locked-in. So what could you possibly want with me?" She said that in mock innocence with a decidedly sexual undertone, I thought. Just my humble opinion, of course. I always wonder how much of this stuff girls know about boys. How much is deliberately titillating, how much innocent. Mrs. Powell didn't strike me as too innocent.

"It really is your husband I want to talk to."

"So talk to him."

"I tried. Last night."

"Oh, that was you?"

I nodded, locking in her eyes. She broke first.

"We had quite a battle last night."

"What about?"

"Oh, the usual."

"What's that?"

"You'd better get it from him."

"But I'm talking to *you*. He doesn't seem communicative."

"Not to me either. It's not personal."

"What is it?"

"His life—his work—his dead wife," this last she added with a touch of bitterness. "He's screwed up. I knew it when I married him. I thought I could help him out of it." She shook her head. "Hopeless."

"How long have you been married, Mrs. Powell?"

"Gina—'bout a year."

"Well, there's still time. A year may seem long at your age, but it isn't much in the scheme of things."

She shook her head. "No way," she said. "I'm going to marry Charles."

"The motel?"

She nodded.

"How soon?"

"Soon's he gets his divorce."

So that was it. Was she so naive, or didn't she care?

"He told his wife yet?"

She shook her head slowly. "Not yet. His wife is shaky psychologically. Has to be the right moment."

"Soon?"

She shrugged. "I know what you're thinking," she said, "but it isn't true."

I nodded. Why argue? I wanted her on my side.

"Your husband know?"

She stiffened, her eyes on me narrowed.

"No. You wouldn't tell him?"

"What good would that do me?"

She considered this and I thought we came to a mutual understanding that I had a powerful weapon which I would only shoot if she failed me.

"How did you meet your husband?'

"I was his secretary all the time his wife was dying."

"And you consoled him?"

"I tried."

Like she was consoling Charles now? I wondered, but I didn't ask.

"He took it hard?"

"Sure he did. Here he is in charge of making the things that killed her."

"And millions of others like her," I added.

"Yeah."

"You worked there too. Did that ever bother you?"

"Not really. You don't think about it much. It's a job—I had to work. Not many other places around here *to* work," she said. "I was typing letters and answering the phone. I was remote from the life-threatening stuff."

"Think so? You were secretary to the man who was in charge of making the things. That's not so remote. Like being secretary to Adolf Eichman and feeling remote from the gas chambers."

She looked at me a long moment, then looked away. "Yeah," she said. "Stupid! Well, I've made up my mind. I'm leaving Don. Charles or no, I can't take it any more."

"Take what?"

"The depression. You don't know what it's like living with a guy so depressed. The ghost of his wife is everywhere. He can't get away from her and neither can I."

"You'd think he'd be glad to talk to me. Get it off his chest."

"That's his problem. He doesn't get it out. Just mopes around," she said. "I see it all now. I was *so* naive. I was the rebound marriage. What do they say? Hope springs eternal in the human breast."

I am sorry to report that my eyes reflexively darted to her all-too-human breast. She saw it and smiled. Our secret.

"So every day he goes to work with this burden," she said.

"Was it easier being his secretary?"

"Than his wife, you mean? Much. There was a chance to get away from it. You know, we can all take sadness, but after a while you have to get away from it."

"And so there's Charles. Where did you find him?"

She tensed and looked at me with one of those is-that-any-of-your-business expressions, then she relaxed. "He's my therapist," she said wearily. Bomber was right. Women are much easier to talk to than the pseudo-macho sex.

"Isn't that illegal?" I asked, without thinking. I didn't want to rile her. She only showed me her wry smile, instead.

"So call the cops," she said, as though I might be doing her a favor.

I really couldn't blame the guy. How long could any red-blooded American boy looking at her for an hour a week or so keep his hands off Gina?

I had a wicked thought—I asked her anyway. "Was this one of your sessions?" I asked.

She nodded.

"Do you any good?"

"Sure—till you came along."

"You...pay for it?"

"Only an hour," she said. "He gives me lots of extra time. We'd have been there all day if you hadn't come along."

"But you only had to pay an hour?"

She nodded.

"Did you ever think about charging *him?*"

The smile of a pixie played on her lips. She wasn't insulted. "It's not what you think," she said. "He only charges for appearances—for an excuse for me to be gone, you know."

"Listen," I said, "I appreciate your candor with me. I really think I can offer your husband the help he needs."

"Oh, yeah?" she said skeptically. "And what's that?"

"The opportunity to atone for his wife's...murder."

"Murder?" she said. "Isn't that a little strong?"

"I don't think so," I said. "Apparently, he doesn't think so either."

"Hm," she considered. "How are you going to do this atoning?"

"Talk to him first. Give him the opportunity to cooperate."

"Cooperate?" she said, "With the enemy? You any idea how long he'd last in this town when they found out?"

"Could be a hero."

"Hero? Hah! For blowing the whistle on a one-company town? What do they say about better to be a live coward than a dead hero?"

"Well, surely no one would kill him."

She looked at me as though I were the biggest moron. "Oh no?"

"No."

"For about a hundred bucks they could do the job."

"And cover their tracks?" I asked, doubtfully.

"Are you kidding? *That* guy, the one who pulled the trigger, would be the hero around here."

"Okay," I said, "I give up. What's the solution?"

"*That's* the solution," she said.

"What is?"

"Give up."

"And then what? You don't really believe Charles is going to give up his wife, do you?"

Her gaze froze on my heretical lips for a moment, then thawed. "I guess not." She shrugged then, explaining more to herself than to me, said "Gets me out of the house."

"So you want to go on like you're going?"

"No, I told you. I'm leaving him before he destroys me."

"What about his two daughters?"

"They don't need me. He has the housekeeper, let him get them a chauffeur. That's all I am to them anyway." Then she seemed to have a foreign thought. "They smoke, you know."

"The girls?" I was shocked. I don't know why I should have been. Perhaps it was the way she said it. "Not the twelve year old?"

"Yes, the twelve year old. Not that unusual around here. Sales are down, we all have to do our bit."

"Do you?"

"No. It's a disgusting habit. I'm not interested in an early, painful death."

"Then help me get your husband to help us."

"I'm not interested in an early, painful death," she repeated.

"Does your husband know his daughters smoke?"

"Know it or face it? You can't hide smoking. Everything reeks: your breath, your clothes, anything you are near. But he doesn't face it. Couldn't, after what happened to their mother. Funny, he's in denial about that, but not about his job."

"Why doesn't he get another?"

"Job? Are you kidding? Doing what? He's forty-eight years old, worked in the tobacco industry all his life—nowhere else around here to utilize his talents. You want him to move to

California and start over?" She shook her head. "Not Don. And I don't see him flipping hamburgers."

"All right, just let me talk to him."

"I'm not stopping you."

"No, I mean, set it up."

"How?"

"Up to you. Tell him you ran into me at the motel."

"Very funny."

"Or the shopping center. We got to talking. No—he'll remember me. Just tell him the truth."

"About me?" She was alarmed.

"That might not be such a bad idea, but that's not what I meant. About me. I'm in town. I hounded you—came to the house, anything. All I want is a half-hour of his time: Anytime, anyplace. I'm at the Churchill Park Inn. Call me. You might look into it," I said. "It looks nicer than that flop house I followed you to."

She stared right through me. "We weren't looking for nice," she said. "We were looking for private."

"Wasn't that, either," I mentioned, to no great reception.

"Are we finished?"

"Are you with me?"

"I'll give it a try. Don't hold your breath though."

"Give me your phone number."

"What for?" she asked. "So you can hound me some more?"

"Would you rather have me at the front door?"

She gave me the number. "I guess we should leave here separately," she said, like a practiced infidel. "You never know who you'll run into."

"Okay," I said. "You first."

"Later," she said, and she jounced out of the place.

It was a wonderful view.

13

I called Gina Powell the next morning and she answered the phone on the first ring. I took that as a good sign.

I was wrong.

"I tried," she said. It's no go. Sorry."

"Hey, wait just a minute!" I snapped into the phone. "The choice wasn't yes or no, it was where and when."

"He won't do it," she said, working up some anger. "What do you want me to do about it? I *did* ask him."

"Don't ask, *tell!*"

"Yeah? Well, gimme a break. I'm in no position to do any telling here."

"Wrong!" I said. "Either *you* do the telling, or I do. Which will it be?"

"Blackmail?"

"Your husband is a murderer," I said, a little strongly for my taste. "He killed his first wife—you are an accomplice. What was it you were saying about blackmail?"

"You play tough," she said, more in surprise than anger. Tough, was apparently something she could understand. "Call me tomorrow," she said.

I parlayed my proximity to the telephone into three more calls. Shauna first—natch.

"Oh, hi, Tod, I'm so glad to hear from you," she said. "Is everything going well?"

"Maybe some progress tomorrow. You?"

"Just plugging away. Easy Willie keeps me jumping. I sure am learning a lot of law. I'm going to have every cigarette case memorized before you know it. But, you know what?"

"What?"

"I miss you."

"Me too."

"Where are you staying?"

I gave her the particulars.

"Is it nice?"

"It's okay. Nothing special."

"Describe it to me—I want to picture you there."

"Your average southern motel, I guess. White—blue shutters on the windows. Inside is a queen-sized bed, a formica desk and nightstand, and a TV set. Oh, and another chair. Kind of a reddish color."

"Can I come?"

"I'd love it."

"I'll be there tomorrow," she said.

"Tomorrow's a work day," I said, too rationally. "Besides I hope to be tied up with Mr. Powell."

"Will he testify?"

"I don't have anything yet."

"Keep me posted," she said, then gave me a rundown on the briefs she was working on, and some of the cases she found to support our view of things. If you aren't a lawyer, it's pretty dull stuff.

If you are a lawyer, it's not all that interesting either.

As soon as I hung up, I was sorry. Shauna was more up and enthusiastic than I'd ever heard her and I must have sounded like a wet blanket.

I almost called her back to dissemble, but I called Easy Willie instead.

He gave me the nitty-gritty legalwise, then said, "Old Judge Druckenmiller is hearing the motions. That doesn't mean he will assign himself the case. But it's a better bet," he said. "He seems to be getting into it. Sits here like a one-eyed Buddha, you can feel his delight in the power. He's never had a case this big. No one in the county has. Celebrity is creeping up on laziness in his weary soul."

"Not so good for our side?"

"Least of our worries," Easy Willie said. "Look at it this way. If he wants *real* power, who does he get it over—little us or the big tobacco cartel?"

"Good point."

"A jurist ruling for big tobacco will get lost in the law books as just more of the same. The courageous jurist who goes against them will make history."

"He have that much guts?"

"Probably not," he said, "but it's fun to think about."

"Judges in Pennsylvania don't mind making new law?"

"Don't have many opportunities like this," he said. There was a slight lull in the conversation, which he soon filled. "Oh, by the way," he said. "I had a visitor yesterday."

"Yeah? Who?"

"The enemy."

"Hinkle?"

"No, he's too big. One of his flunkies. Asked me what I was making with Bomber, said I could be a rich man. Told him I was satisfied with the side I was on. Said they didn't want me to change sides."

I don't know why I was so surprised. Everybody had been telling me they would do *any*thing.

"So how much?"

"How much what?"

"Will they pay you, and what do they want?"

"Information. They want to know what we have."

"They have discovery for that."

"'S what I told him."

"So what's the offer?"

"Wasn't specific. Let me know I could write the ticket." I could hear him breathing and it sounded unresolved.

"So?"

"I'm thinking about it."

"Just thinking? I remember before your telling me you'd sell out in a minute—'Wasn't anybody sell out faster' was, I believe, the way you put it."

"That's what I said, huh?"

"Uh hmm."

"That's 'cause no one wanted to buy me. You guys gave me something to sell," he said. "Puts a different slant on it."

"That's nice to hear," I said.

"Oh, I'm still considering," he said. "Pros and cons. Easy to rationalize I wouldn't be giving him anything he couldn't get legitimately. But I'll let you know. I wouldn't sell out without telling you."

I thought Easy Willie was pulling my leg. But I wasn't sure. I decided to bring the big boss Bomber in on it.

The airhead put me through with a minimum of harassment.

I gave Bomber the lowdown with a minimum of stuttering. He listened patiently without much browbeating.

"Not surprised," he said, when I finished the bribery recitation. "Next will be the threats. We have to watch out for wiretaps, too. Remember to move around so they can't keep up with you. You might check in somewhere else tonight. Use an alias. We have to always keep one jump ahead of the Nicks," he said. "How are you doing with our pigeon?

"Lot of resistance. Got t-tough with the wife. Calling again t-tomorrow."

"Don't let him fly," he said.

"Fly?"

"Get away. Say, why don't we let him fly?" he suddenly said. "A couple first-class tickets to Angelton on us. What do you think?"

I was always flattered on those few occasions when Bomber asked my opinion. Flattered and surprised. "Good idea," I said. "Probably won't go for it, but I'll p-p-put it to him."

"Good."

When I said goodbye, he added, "Remember: *Move*. The sooner the better."

I didn't feel like moving. It was dinnertime, so I drove a

little deeper into the heart of things and fed my hunger. I thought I would feel more like moving tomorrow—if you can ever really *feel like* moving.

Besides, check-out time was noon. They would probably charge me for another day. So I drove back to my motel, parked the car and considered asking at the desk if I could move out without penalty. I didn't see anyone at the desk, so I had all the excuse I needed to procrastinate.

When I got to my door, I was surprised to see the drapes were closed on my window. I had the distinct memory that I had left them open.

Then as I was about to put my key in the door, I heard a noise inside. It wasn't loud or distinctive, more like a rustle—the sounds of life you hear when you enter a house and realize someone is there.

I froze with that key about to scrape the lock—withdrew it and continued down the balcony, my heart having the heebe-geebes all the while. There were stairs at both ends of the balcony deck. I went down the ones at the far end, so I wouldn't have to go by the room again, got into my car and backed it out into the street. I am simply a contemporary investigator, not a swashbuckling cowboy. Confrontations were not my bag.

I stayed in my car and watched the door of my room. I wanted to make a quick getaway should that prove prudent, but I also wanted to see who came out of my room.

In only a few minutes my curtains opened, followed in seconds by a muscular man quietly letting himself out of my door. He was wearing a business suit, and I could not place him, but I could easily rule out the men I had any contact with in town. It wasn't Charles, Gina's lover; it wasn't the desk clerk, and it certainly wasn't Don Powell.

He must have been parked behind the building because I didn't see him get into his car. But I did see a car, driving at a healthy clip, turn away from me and speed down the street. I expect that was him. I considered briefly giving chase. Very briefly.

Instead, I parked my car on the motel lot and went into the office and pounded the dome-shaped bell that was on the counter for that purpose.

The lanky manager came toward me chewing unabashedly and I managed to apologize for interrupting his dinner.

"No mind," he said.

"Did someone come in here for a key to my room? I'm in twenty-nine."

"No," he said. "Nobody been in here for keys."

"Well, somebody's just been in my room."

"Beats me."

"Yeah, me too," I said. "Under the circumstances, I'm afraid I'm going to have to leave."

"'S no problem. Anytime 'fore noon's fine."

"I mean now."

"Well, now, that there's a problem. Gonna have to charge you for an extry day."

I shook my head. "With security like you have here, I don't think so. I am afraid for my safety."

"Not my fault," he said. "You got somebody after youse?"

"It's your fault if some stranger can just go in and out of my room—closed the curtain while he was in there," I said. "Any idea what he might have been doing?"

"No, sir."

"Happen often? People going in people's rooms?"

"Never happened while I was here."

"Well, I'd like you to check out the room before I go back in there."

"Hey wait just a minute. I ain't goin' in there if there's a bomb or something."

"All right, let's call the police."

"Oh—I don't—"

"Get the bomb squad out here."

"I don't think the owners want no police 'round here."

"Fine. Just get me my things out of there and I'll be on my way."

"I ain't movin' your things. I ain't no bellhop—this here's a motel, not a first-class hotel."

"You're telling me," I said, losing patience with this cracker. "Now, are you going up there or do I call the police and let them check it out?"

Making the decision caused him a deal of aggravation, but then I imagined any decision would have stressed him one way or the other. He finally decided, though he said it was against his better judgment (whatever *that* was) to investigate himself—if I went with him.

I accompanied him back up to my room and hung back as he tried to door—very gingerly. He got it open without anything exploding and went inside.

"Nothin' here," he said. "Musta imagined it."

I checked my stuff. It looked like it had been gone through, but I couldn't be sure. There was no telltale sign of it. If that was what he was doing, he did it neatly.

Then I realized what had happened.

"Well, thanks," I said. "Sorry again to disturb your dinner."

"Cold by now."

"I'll be moving out in a few minutes. I'll be down to pay my bill."

"Gotta charge you the extra day."

"Well, I'll make a police report then."

He looked at me as though I were crackers. Shook his head and said, "Suit yourself." Then he shambled out of the room and down the stairs to his cold dinner, which was probably not hot to start with.

As soon as he was gone, I closed the door and went to the telephone. I unscrewed the mouthpiece and there it was, that tiny testament to the electronic wizardry of man, the phone bug.

14

It made me angry to think that my father was right again.

I decided to step up with my new accommodations. Maybe the locks would be harder to pick. When the clerk asked me how long I would be staying I said not long. I registered under the name Art Ness.

In the morning, I called Gina Powell.

"Okay," she said. "I did it for you. I jeopardized my marriage. I hope you appreciate it."

"I do, thanks. I don't think I appreciate that goon you sent around last night."

"What goon?"

"To bug my phone."

"What are you talking about?"

"Come on, who else knew where I was, who I was, or why I was here?"

"Are you kidding? Everybody who had any interest in you knew all about you a half-hour after you checked in."

I didn't believe that. Perhaps there was some grain of truth there, but overall it had to be outrageous hyperbole.

"When can I see him?"

"He'll let you know."

"Wait a minute."

"No, you wait. You any idea the risk involved in just talking to you? It will be super-discreet—and he is promising absolutely nothing. Not even suggesting anything. There isn't the slightest hint of any kind of cooperation—he is only doing it to please me."

And I hope you'll do something in return to please him,

I thought.

"When shall I call again?"

"Give me your number," she said.

"Oh no," I said. "Sorry. Next time I might be hit over the head."

"Okay—all right. Call here every four hours—noon next. If I'm not here, Alice will pass on any info I have."

I decided to stay put for the four hours. I didn't want any more surprises. I spent the time orchestrating my next moves—as well as making some orchestration notes for the concerto for orchestra I was kicking around in my head. I could always tell how important I thought a case was by how much time I had for composing. This was the first thought I'd given my music since I arrived in Churchill Park, North Carolina, home of the T. S. Armstead Tobacco Company, makers of a whole slew of ciggy brands—some 283 by last count, each more sensually appealing than the last.

The time passed quickly, as they say it does when you are having fun.

I dialed Gina's number at twelve sharp. She picked it up on a half-ring, didn't say hello. "You're at the Sandspit Motel, sixteen hundred Bright Avenue. You are in room fourteen and registered under the name of Art Ness. Elliot's son, no doubt. Do you want the phone number?"

I gulped. "I have it… How did you…?"

"Nothing to it. And I haven't the slightest interest in the case. Imagine what you could do if you *had* an interest."

"Like bug my phone?"

"Piece of cake," she said. "Enough small talk. He will meet you at one o'clock sharp."

"His office?"

"Are you kidding? Dexter Park. You know where that is?"

"No."

She told me how to find it. "In the center there's a statue of Robert E. Lee—ever heard of him?"

"Sure, he was a third baseman somewhere, wasn't he?"

"That's the one. It is imperative you do not stop at the park if you are being followed. It's fairly remote out there, so park on some deserted street and see if anyone else does."

"Say," I said, "this is most impressive. Were you ever in this line of work yourself?"

"I'm just telling you what he told me. You'll see him walk by the statue within five minutes of one—unless he doesn't make it."

"Hey, wait."

"Be quiet," she said. "He's going to try, but they are more than a little skittish about him, what with his history and the house hearings in Washington."

I said I understood.

"If he walks down the path that Robert E. Lee is facing, you scram ASAP. That's all she wrote..."

"Wait a—"

"For today. He'll try again. If he walks on any of the other three paths, you follow him, pretty far behind. He'll stop when he feels he's safe, and you can talk to him. Ten minutes, max."

"Thanks," I said. "I appreciate—"

"You better. I used a lot of capital on this. Don't screw him up. He's a very good man."

Better than Charley? I wondered. But that was, as they say in court, extraneous.

"Oh," she added. "Take him a sandwich! Chicken-on-wheat."

I had just enough time to get in my car and start the diversionary tactics. I scanned the lot and didn't see anyone in a car. Then out on the street, I didn't see anyone I suspected. I drove along the main road in the wrong direction, ducked onto some side streets. I was convinced I was clear. I stopped at a deli on the main street, bought the lunch and drove on.

I followed all the instructions and was in the park, alone, at five of one, with a chicken-on-wheat and a beef-on-white. I thought I'd give him the choice. His wife looked more like a chicken eater than he did.

At a few minutes after one, I saw him approach the statue, with a newspaper folded under his arm. I didn't see anyone behind him. He stopped, looked around, and walked to the statue, where a mother and two preschool kids were climbing up on General Lee's foot.

If Powell walked the way the eyes were pointing, this woman had to be the tail, unless the kids were awfully precocious, because there was no one else in sight.

He walked down the side and I followed at about thirty paces. He sat on a bench and opened his newspaper. I sat next to him, placing my white paper bag between us.

"Chicken or beef?" I said.

"Beef," he said without hesitation.

"Funny, your wife thought the chicken would suit you more."

"Yeah," he snorted. "her all right. Chicken and fish. You don't get to look good as she does eating hamburgers."

I gave him the beef. "Thanks for coming," I said.

He looked at me with scorn and disdain, like he was trying to exorcise some old demon. "You're just a kid," he said. "Not much older than my wife."

"The operative word is *much*," I said. "How old are you?"

"I'm almost fifty." He turned back to feign reading his newspaper.

"Almost forty-nine or almost forty-two?"

"Forty-eight—and I look seventy."

"Oh, I don't know," I said, making an ineffectual argument.

"You'd never understand," he said. The demon wasn't leaving him.

"I realize that," I said. "Though I probably understand more than you realize. I shall not push the point. We are not talking penny-ante crime here, we are talking the crime of the century. Up to about three mil a year in deaths now, isn't it?"

He winced. I wasn't sure what could be said for Don Powell at this stage, but he was sensitive to the daily disaster he helped bring about.

"You are one of the most important industrial manufacturers in the world," I said, laying it on. He shifted only slightly. "I am just a kid lawyer doing legwork. But my father is Bomber Hanson and, if you've ever read a newspaper or looked at a TV news show, I don't have to tell you who *he* is."

He gave me a small nod.

"Bomber doesn't take cases to harass people. He's a big-picture man—and where is there a bigger picture?"

"Nowhere," he muttered in agreement.

"He wants me to offer you two first-class tickets to the coast. Limousines both ways from L.A. to Angelton. You pick the time and the duration. He'd like to have an hour or two with you, but he'll settle for half that."

"What do I have to do in return?"

"Just listen to his story."

He smirked. "Like one of those condos-in-the-Bahamas scams?"

"I wouldn't know about that," I said. "This is no scam."

"You mean, if I'm not convinced, I don't have any obligation?"

You'll be convinced, I thought, but I said, "That's right."

"Besides a free vacation," he said, "what's in it for me?"

"I don't know," I said. "A clearer conscience maybe." I was throwing darts I had not intended and they were hitting the target.

"And all I have to do is sell my lifelong friends down the river," Don Powell said.

"Bomber would probably prefer to look at it as saving lives."

His head bobbed as though it were Jell-O on springs.

"But before we put either one of you to the trouble, I am

obligated to get a few things straight. One thing always comes up hazy in discussions about cigarette manufacturing—at least to me. When you refine the tobacco, I understand you take all the nicotine out?"

He nodded. "Temporarily."

"Then you put it back?"

He nodded again.

"Do you sometimes put back more than you take out?"

He shrugged as though I had asked how the roast beef sandwich was. "It's possible."

"Why don't you just leave it out?"

"The taste," he said. "People don't like the taste."

"Isn't it the nicotine that makes the cigarettes addictive?"

"So they say."

"But you don't know? Is this another case of you not believing the studies because that's your employer's conceit, or do you genuinely not know?"

"I'm not a scientist." He started to say he was just a manufacturer, but I cut him off.

"And Eichman was a geneticist."

His cheek twitched. "Low blow," he said, but I didn't apologize.

"But is it so remote? You'd need a lot more gas chambers than the Nazis had to do the job you are doing."

"People smoke by choice," he said, trotting out the company wisdom. "Relaxes them. Like a drink of liquor. Booze will kill too, if you overdo it."

"So we have some three-million a year who smoke too much."

He started to nod, but he got only halfway.

"Well," I said, "it's up to you. We can call you as a friendly witness or subpoena you as a hostile witness. From my experience, when you are facing Bomber Hanson, you are much better off in the friendly category."

He stared straight ahead. No more pretense of reading the newspaper. "I'd be finished in this town," he said. "No question. No job, no reputation, no friends. Everything gone."

"You have anything put away?" I asked, being practical.

He gave a short laugh. "I have a good pension coming, unless I screw up. I've got a lot of company stock in options and bonuses."

"Sell it," I said.

"Not so easy," he said. "I'm an officer of the company. I have to report any substantial changes. I blow the whistle, what do you think happens to my stock?"

"Hard to outguess the stock market," I offered without much conviction.

"It won't make the stock go up," he told me.

"Do you have any other assets?"

"House."

"Is it clear?"

"No, there's a small mortgage. These places aren't worth what they are in California, you know. I have about two hundred equity in the house, I guess. Of course, if you *are* successful and it starts a chain reaction, the house won't be worth anything either."

"Sell it," I said. I was full of advice.

"Think anyone would wonder why?"

"Who has to know?"

It was that hopeless snort again. "In this town, a secret lasts about five minutes until everybody knows it."

I was going to ask if he knew his wife's secret, but I refrained.

"Think about it," I said.

"I'll think about it," he said.

"Fair enough," I said, putting out my hand for a shake. "Your wife has my number."

That smirk was on his lips again.

"Everybody has your number," he said, and I watched his back shamble out of the park.

15

On the way back from the park, I stopped at a gas station to use the phone. I felt like talking to Shauna.

"Hi, Shauna," I said. "I thought I'd take the phone company's advice and reach out and touch someone."

"I'm touched," she said.

"Touché," I said.

She seemed glad to hear from me, and I brought her up to date on my saga.

"Bummer," she said. "You can't make a move there without everyone knowing about it."

"That seems to be the case. I'm going to poke around here a little more, but if I can lock Powell in, I'll be heading back to see you."

"What about my trip to see you?"

"I'm a little skittish about it, aren't you?"

"Oh, I don't think anyone's interested in our personal lives."

I told her about the bug and having to move. "I'm calling you from a gas station just in case," I said.

"Geez, this is real cloak-and-dagger stuff. I thought it was just a lawsuit."

"Yeah, like a school yard tiff is World War II."

"Tod?"

"Hm?"

"I miss talking to you."

"So talk."

"I don't know. It's not the same on the phone."

"I'm at a gas station. No one's listening."

"You think mine could be bugged?"

"I doubt it—more likely here."

"My dad moved out," she said out of the blue, "finally moved in with his rich girlfriend."

"Oh. How are you taking it?"

"Hard," she said. "Mother especially." I thought I heard her sinuses kick up. "He said now that I had a good income, I could support Mom. He never did treat me like a daughter. Always leaning on me for something from the time I was six."

"I'm sorry," I said.

We talked some more about the case, then kissed the phone and hung up.

After dinner at a place I shall not return to if I don't want a stomach transplant, I called the Powells from another phone booth.

He answered. "I haven't decided yet," he said.

"Take your time," I said. "At three million a year that's only 8,200 a day. Like about twenty-five jumbo jets crashing every day."

"I've heard the statistics," he said.

"Then you know it's only six people a minute. When you reduce it to that, it doesn't seem so bad. Ten seconds each. But it's not like you know them all or anything."

He snorted in the phone. "You know what Stalin said."

"What?"

"Uncle Joe Stalin said one death is a tragedy. A million deaths is a statistic."

"And you believe that?"

"Believe it?" he said. "I've *experienced* it. But I'm a small cog in the machine. If I disappeared tomorrow, you think the tobacco industry would grind to a halt?"

"Guess not," I said. "While we are waiting for your decision, I'd like to interview some others in the company—people, hopefully, who would be forthcoming—honest with me. Could you give me the names of some likely ones?"

"No, I couldn't. Call personnel," and he hung up.

At that moment, I thought we had lost him.

Next morning, I called personnel. After a lot of fencing, they allowed as how I could come on out and they would try to put me on the right track. They were southern after all, and southern means hospitable.

The right track turned out to be customer relations. I protested that I was not a customer. The big cheese in that ubiquitous department was a woman who reminded me of my fifth-grade teacher, whose most memorable skill was to put me in my place.

Miss Jessup she claimed to be, and I saw no percentage in disputing that. Miss Jessup said, "Now, what was your question, Mr. Hanson?"

I went over the litany again, just as I had to everyone in the personnel department before her.

I trotted out the constitution and she played the vitality of the industry to the economy. We got nowhere.

"Would you like me to get court orders?" I asked. "Would that serve your purpose?"

"It would certainly not serve any purpose that I am aware of," she said, like my fifth-grade teacher, Miss Nye, at her peak.

The best I got out of her was she would query (that was what she said: "query") the personnel and, if anyone had any desire to speak to me, she would make a note of it and pass it on.

She was about as helpful as my fifth-grade teacher.

In my brief tenure inside the glass monolith that housed the brains behind the manufacture and sale of perhaps the most controversial product in the world, I couldn't help looking for demons. People with tails and horns who stood out as diabolical killers. Of course, they weren't there. They were just folks, out to make a living, and making and selling cigarettes was how one made a living in this neck of the woods.

When I got back to my room, I checked the mouthpiece of the phone. If they were bugging me, they'd changed the hardware. Then I called my ace—Gina Powell. She wasn't in and wasn't expected back until she brought the kids home from school.

The telephone directory yellow pages under Physicians and Surgeons, M.D.—Cancer, referred me to Physicians and Surgeons, M.D.—Oncology (Tumors).

I called the whole lot of them, alphabetically. It wasn't until I landed on a guy named Antonio Sciaparelli that I found one who would see me.

"Sure," he said, when I told him who I was and what I was after. "I'll see you after my office hours—come around five."

A little after three, I called Gina back.

"Sorry," she said. "No news yet."

"When?"

"Soon. I'm working on him."

I told her what else I wanted. The breath of exasperation came through the phone. "You don't let up, do you?"

"Neither does the enemy."

"Armstead? Yeah. Well, getting you names and numbers...that private stuff is way out of my line."

"But you know people," I said. "You used to work there."

"Okay, okay," she said. "I'll see if I can get you anything."

"I appreciate it, and I just want you to know I am holding fast to my part of the bargain."

We hung up to the sound of Gina Powell grunting.

At five sharp, after following the directions Dr. Sciaparelli gave me, I presented myself in his waiting room to a white-uniformed receptionist whose social life might have benefited from some weight loss.

"Mr. Hanson," she smiled. She had a sunny personality. What would we do without these compensations? "Doctor will see you in a few minutes. He's running a little late."

Was there ever a doctor who ran early? I wondered. I smiled, thanked her and sat down in the utilitarian waiting room on a vinyl chair not unlike the other boxy airport-vinyl chairs in the same room.

The magazines ran to health with a lot of dog-earred *Prevention*s among them. I wondered if, once you were seeing a cancer doctor, it might not be late for prevention. Like saying "Here's what you should have done."

The magic words "Doctor will see you now," came about twenty ("few") minutes later.

The Doc was a short, dark-complected man in his forties—forty-six if I could extrapolate correctly from the diplomas on the wall. They were from Wake Forrest and Johns Hopkins.

"It is good of you to see me," I said.

"Happy to—sit down, won't you?"

"Is there any foundation to the company's claims that a causal relationship between smoking and lung cancer has not been scientifically proven?" I began.

He shook his head. "Wishful thinking," he said. "If they'd look at the X-rays, seen half the black lungs I have—"

"What about their position these people might have died earlier of hypertension if it weren't for the saving graces of nicotine?"

"Pure speculation," he said. "Only the most spurious studies would back that up. That's not to say it could not be true, but we have no way of telling when a person *would* have died if he had lived differently. There are many activities we believe prolong life somewhat: healthy eating habits, exercise. Smoking isn't one of them."

He paused to glance out his window at what some referred to as the cigarette capital of the world. Green and peaceful, like a cemetery. He turned back to me.

"I won't be surprised if we discover through DNA studies that length of life is in most cases, hereditary. James Fixx, the man who helped make jogging so popular, died of a heart attack in his early fifties. Pritikin, of the fiber diet, lived only seventy years. William Howard Taft, obese as he was, lived longer than the fitness fanatic Theodore Roosevelt."

"In spite of all that, Doctor—"

"Oh, call me Tony."

"Okay, thanks. Are you convinced that smoking kills— prematurely?"

"You don't have to be a doctor, just look around you."

"I don't imagine your message is too popular around here."

He laughed. "Short, to the point. I'm not invited to speak at the Rotary Club, if that's what you mean."

"How did you wind up in this trade in this town?"

"I'm from here. I needed a specialty. What more appropriate?" he shrugged.

"Have attitudes about smoking changed a lot since you were growing up?"

"Oh my, yes. Hardly anybody gave it a second thought in those days. Now you get the feeling smokers are guiltily on the defensive."

"Even in *this* town?"

"Sure," he said. "There is still a lot of bravado about free choice in one's actions and all that. I can go along with a certain amount of that, but the ironic thing is, suicide is illegal."

"I wonder if you'd testify for us? You would be paid an expert fee, as well as expenses."

"Well, perhaps," he said. "But you can find a cancer specialist a lot closer to your trial."

"But maybe not as well spoken."

He smiled. You don't find many people who are not pleased by a compliment.

"And could you give me any names of people you know who work for Armstead who might be willing to at least talk to me?"

He frowned. "Might be tougher," he said. "Lot of self-congratulatory rationalization goes on at the company. Not hard to imagine why. Then there is the doctor-patient relationship. I'd have to ask their permission—"

"Fine," I said, and left him with my phone number and

my gratitude.

It was six-thirty when I left the doctor's office. On a hunch, I stopped at another gas station phone booth and called the Powell residence.

Gina answered the phone.

"I'm at a phone booth," I said. "Anything?"

"I'll put him on."

Don Powell came to the phone sounding like a man who had just won the lottery.

His first words were "I'll do it."

16

We arranged Powell's trip for the coming weekend.

What makes a man change his mind so dramatically? Certainly with Don Powell it had been boiling inside of him for a long time. His wife seemed to be motivated to sway him, and I came along to help that along; but ultimately, he had to make up his own mind. Gina and I provided the encouraging environment. Powell did the rest.

Next morning, with Doctor Sciaparelli's go-ahead, I headed for the hospital.

The Good Samaritan Hospital sat on a rise above a network of roads. It was built with dollars earned selling tobacco products, so it seemed fitting and proper that a large number of victims of those products occupied so many of the hospital rooms.

As with so many monuments built with ill-gotten gains, Good Samaritan Hospital was a first-cabin edifice. There was as much glass as on a New York City skyscraper and every room had a view. If you were positioned just right, you could see the T. S. Armstead headquarters in the distance. You could thank them for building such a beautiful hospital for you or curse them for putting you there, as the spirit moved you.

Ray Strong was the man I was looking for, and with little trouble I found him in his bed—wired for life, I thought. Tubes and wires were everywhere. It was not a sight to give you a lot of encouragement.

I introduced myself. "Can you talk?" I asked Ray Strong, who was a black man.

"Oh, yeah," he said with a hoarse, weary voice. "I can still talk, see and hear. That about the size of it, though. I'm about to cross over. What can I do you outa, my man?"

"Answer some questions," I said. "And promise to tell me when you've had enough. I can always come back."

He chuckled so the tubes rattled. "Wouldn't wait too long," he said. "Set awhile." He pointed to the metal chair next to his night table. I pulled the chair up to bedside.

I explained what Bomber was doing and how Dr. Sciaparelli had told me this dark and brooding bag of bones before me had some secrets he might be in a mood to part with.

"Well, I expect you know about that business of a few years ago," Ray said, closing his eyes for a moment as if to shut out the memory.

"What business?"

He opened his eyes and looked into mine, to see if I were pulling his leg.

"At The Company." He was dropping hints that didn't help me. The way he said, "The Company," I thought he was referring to the CIA.

"I'm afraid I don't know what you are referring to."

"The dead body, showing up there in the boiler room."

"Whose body?"

"Man with the goods. 'Bout to spill the beans."

"Spill the...?"

He nodded impatiently like I was a very slow pupil. "Had this case back then—only it didn't go nowhere. Not with him dead in the boiler room like that."

"He was suing the company?"

"No. He was the witness. Scuttlebutt was he was gonna tell about production an' all—how they makes them ciggys with a good jolt a extry nicotine to keep us fools puffin' 'em till we die. I wanta tell you Mr..."

"Tod."

"Mr. Tod, I's sceered o' dyin'. Anybody tells you they ain't sceered is lyin'."

"Did they catch the murderer?"

"Never said murder. He was a missing person is all."

He snorted, and I was afraid he would stop up those tubes.

"Missing, huh? Who brought him to you?"

"Security. Want me to cremate him."

"Then what?"

"I throws him in the furnace. Tells me I don't wanta go in there wid him I keeps my mouf shut."

"And you did?"

"Till now I did. I's goin' out, man. An' I's goin' wid a real bad conscience. I outa be tellin' this to a priest."

"You want me to get you one?"

He shook his head. "I ain't Catholic. Say, you ain't a Catholic?"

"Sorry."

"Ah well, I got it off my chest," he said, and settled back. Then he looked at me in a new light. "Say, you don't happen to have a cigarette on you, do you?"

"No, sorry," I said, and I was actually sorry I didn't. "So, the witness just disappeared?"

"Yep," he tried to snap his fingers but could generate no sound. "Like that," he said. "He's missing quite a spell when the company makes a nice settlement on his family. You know, he wasn't a old man. Had a pretty, young wife. Wonder what became of her. But one thing, she wasn't hurtin' for no money. Took care o' me same way. Real good. Never had no money worries. Retired me outa there on a generous pension."

"Nice," I said.

He nodded, not taking in my sarcasm. "Free cigarettes the rest of my life."

"How much did you smoke?"

"'Fore the, you know, cremation that, you know, I hadda do for them 'cause the furnace's my bailiwick, I smoked 'bout a pack a day." He stopped, not to remember, but to erase the memory. "Afterwards," he said with a wry twist to his lips, "why, you could say I smoked myself to death—goin' on four packs right off after that there cremation thing. Then I settled in around three."

"But you didn't have to buy them?"

"No, sir," he said. "They treated me real good."

I called Gina Powell from the phone booth on the first floor of the hospital.

"Okay," she said. "I called every name I knew for you. But none of them will talk to you, I did *all* I could. You get the company's approval, otherwise you're wasting your time."

Then I called Bomber. Bonnie answered. "Well, cuddles, you're starting to develop a southern accent you been down there so long." Of course, she said this with the broadest, most ridiculous southern accent. "Now you hurry home, ya' all hear? An' bring me some *gree-its*, honey-chile."

It was a relief to hear Bomber's booming voice. After I brought him up to snuff on Ray Strong, the welcome voice was supplanted by the unwelcome message: "I tell you boy, you can taste the pay dirt. Aim for the jugular."

"The jugular? How?"

"The president. What's his name? Something very common."

"Jones."

"That's it. That's where you get the results—at the top. Go get him."

"*Get* him? M-m-me? H-h-how?"

"With your wit and intellect, how else?"

"B-b-but…"

"You want me to send that girl instead? That…what's her name?"

"Shauna."

"Yeah."

"B-b-but I d-d-don't…" the stutter gripped me like a linebacker sacking a quarterback. "P-p-president's out-t-t-a my l-l-league."

"Not so," he said. "You're in the big leagues now."

"No."

"Then there's that guy who raided the company. What's his name?"

"Horowitz," I said. "Jerry Horowitz."

"See him."

"What for? He's just a m-m-money man."

"Exactly!" Bomber boomed. "And you try to activate that dead conscience of his. He must have had a conscience at some time. He had a mother didn't he?"

That didn't call for an answer.

"So be sure and tell these big cheeses we are going to subpoena them for the trial. Show their true stripes, unless they want to change them."

"Like the tiger," I said.

$$*\qquad*\qquad*$$

I couldn't have been more surprised when I called T. S. Armstead and asked for the president. I was put through, and he actually talked to me like we were old friends. Sure, he would be glad to see me: "My secretary will pencil you in," he said.

It was like good cop, bad cop, the contrast with Jones and my next call to Jerry Horowitz in New York. I didn't get past the ice maiden he hired to stonewall. She told me how terribly busy he was, hinting that any idiot would know better than to call and expect to actually *talk* to such an important man.

"As you wish," I said. "Please tell him then that we will be subpoenaing him for the trial in *Zepf vs. T. S. Armstead, et al*, and will also expect him to schlepp the hundred miles to Cedarberg, Pennsylvania for his deposition. If he has a change of heart, call this number,"—and I left her with Shauna's number.

The most fun of all came when I sat in Ed Jones' sumptuous office on the top floor of the glass tower. In the distance, you could see tobacco tenders in their fields on the one side and tobacco processing plants on the other. Tucked away in the corner of the view (for this was a fine, fair day) was the county seat of government, which said government was said never to be unfaithful to its tobacco heritage. Trying a tobacco case here would be the ultimate folly.

Ed ("Call me Ed," he said, when we were introduced by his hip, with-it secretary) Jones had paid his dues in sales the world over and got his lucrative position as one of the highest paid CEOs in the world by his folksy gift of gab.

"This is quite a spread you have here," I said, making no attempt to hide my awe. And I didn't even *feel* like adding he had done it on the backs of millions of nicotine stiffs.

His response was characteristic of the innate, ingrained sybarite. "Where is it written we should stint on the good life, eh?"

I smiled. He was obviously my pal. Besides, stinting on the good life was certainly in nothing I'd ever read, unless maybe that stuff about loving mercy and walking humbly with thy God and assorted other heresies about being rich in spirit and poor in goods. That was me; lots of spirit. When I compared Ed Jones' layout to my closet in Bomber's Victorian house/office in California, I almost asked him to break me into the tobacco game.

"Get you a drink?"

"No, thanks."

"Sure? We have everything. If I don't have your poison, I can get it here in minutes," and he snapped his fingers to show me just how easy that was. I was momentarily transported back to the hospital where Ray Strong tried to snap his fingers with less success.

We sat in a little grouping of couch and facing chairs over a coffee table the size of Rhode Island. It was friendly this way—no peering at me across his humbling desk.

There were a lot of sports mementos about, plaques on the walls with golden golf tees, pictures of President Jones and the big-time athletes he palled around with on the golf links.

On the table between us was a model of a medium-sized jet airplane. It was not a *company* plane. There were three or four others that were company planes. This was bought and was maintained by the company and flown by the company pilot,

Jones explained, but the plane was owned by Jones. It was in his contract.

"I like my perks," he grinned. "So," he said, getting down to business, "everyone treating you all right in our fair city?"

"Fine," I said. I decided against ruining the mood by carping about the wiretap.

"Anything you need to feel more comfortable, you let me know. Anything I can grant," he snapped his fingers again, "count on me."

"I would like to talk to some of the employees."

"Sure," he said. "Anybody you want. Anybody here not well-treated, I want to know about it."

"But isn't the issue not how *they* are treated by the company, but rather how the company treats the customers?"

"We give 'em what they want."

"Even if it kills them?"

"We can't make anyone smoke. We make the product, they have to want it to buy it. They don't buy, we're out of business."

"So it would be to your advantage to make the product addictive—assuming you could?"

"Addiction's in the person, not the product. We can't be responsible for our customers."

"Do you smoke, Mr. Jones?"

"Ed, Ed, call me Ed. Mr. Jones was my father."

That didn't answer the question, so I asked it again. "Do you smoke, Ed?"

"No, but I got plenty here—what's your preference?"

"No, no, I was just wondering how you could be in charge of making a product without using it."

"It's different than it was," he said. "T. S. Armstead is no longer a mom-and-pop business—out of the family completely. I'm sure they all smoked then. Now it's chips."

"Chips?"

"Money. We're in the business of making money. Keep

the smiles on those stockholder's faces. We react to public demand. If we found out this afternoon that people wanted to buy cigarettes made of dried dandelion, tomorrow we'd be raising dandelions. You want caffeine-free coffee, that's what you get. Supply and demand—a simple concept a third-grader can grasp."

He just carried on like he was a good ole boy and I was a cowboy. "So what's your case?" he asked. "Anything we can work out between us? Save a lot of unpleasantness up and down the line."

I shook my head curtly. "Bomber seems to want to try the case."

"So do my people," he said, shaking his head as though that were a bad idea. "Lawyers will be the end of us all, Tod, my boy. The end of civilization will not come with a bang or a whimper, but a motion to quash offered by an overpaid I.Q.-deficient attorney in a shiny silk suit." He sat back, the smile of pleasure showing at his rather neat characterization. "So who's your client?"

"Rich Zepf—a Pennsylvania Dutchman with twelve kids—all girls, actually."

"Is that so? Well, well, well, I suppose they'll be in the front row where all the jurors can see them. Yeah, all twelve dressed to the nines, velvet dresses, lace collars, ribbons in their hair. And Daddy is on his way out from lung cancer, that it?"

I nodded.

"Think if he lived, he'd find a cure for cancer?"

"He's found one already," I said. "Give up smoking."

"Yeah, that's a good one. You're all right in my book," he said. "But let me tell you something, just between us," he leaned toward me to emphasize the confidential nature of our talk. "You don't see the greats dropping over from lung cancer and stuff like that. As the immortal Leona Helmsley said about taxes, 'That's for the little people.'"

"Went to jail, didn't she?"

"Yeah, and she took to it like a duck to water. Leona is

one of the *big* people. She's a survivor. So, this Zepf guy smoke a lot?"

"Yes. Three, four packs a day."

"Phew. Why so much?"

"Addicted."

"Yeah? You addicted?"

"I don't smoke."

"I'm not addicted either. Why is that?"

"We don't smoke."

"Why don't we?"

"We're smart enough to know it's dangerous."

He gave a grudging twist to his lower lip. "*Could* be," he said. "You ever do any studying on the types of people in the world? You know the A-personalities and such? The compulsives?"

"Some."

"So don't you think this stuff is all genetically foreordained? I mean, certain people are born with a predisposition to hypertension—some can't live without cigarettes or something very much like them that could be worse. So maybe you have certain people who would die in their early thirties without cigarettes to calm them down. Instead, they get thirty, forty more years of life."

"The Surgeon General should be pinning medals on you."

"Not a bad idea. So how about a game of golf? Pop in my plane and head for one of the great courses in the country. Hell, the world. We could go to Scotland if you want to— Atlanta, Houston, Palm Springs, Pebble Beach, you name it. Nothing like a good game of golf in the great outdoors to clear your head and put it all in perspective."

"Sorry," I said. "I don't play golf."

"Seriously?" he asked, like I'd just informed him I was learning-impaired.

"Seriously," I confirmed.

"So you don't play golf, what *do* you do?" he asked me.

"I write music."

He looked at me perplexed, as though he didn't think that was much like playing golf. "Yeah? No kidding? Pop or rock or what?"

"Classical."

"Classical?"

"Like string quartets, sonatas, symphonies."

"I'll be damned," he said. "People still do that kinda stuff?"

"A few."

"I'll be damned."

We sat in silence for a moment while he was cogitating his next friendly play. "Your dad play golf?" he asked.

"No," I said, "sorry."

"Yeah well," he said, "just a thought. Maybe you'd like to go along sometime, drive the cart. I play with the biggest figures in the sports world." He named some pretty heavy hitters. "You might enjoy meeting them. They're on the payroll to jolly up the VIPs," he admitted guilelessly. I didn't see how you could spend thirty seconds with Ed Jones and not like him.

"Well, Tod, it was good of you to drop by," he said rising to dismiss me. But even in that classic maneuver, he left me feeling he was doing it for my benefit. He put out his hand and I was glad to shake it. "So, if we're going to face off in court, may the best man win," and he gave my hand a good pumping to go with it.

"Say," he said when he released my hand from his manly grip, "they got any great golf courses in that Cedarberg place?"

17

Ed Jones' secretary told me to make a list of people I wanted to see, but I didn't know names. So I called her and said I would just like to talk to as many people in manufacturing as I could.

"Oh, that's Don Powell's department. Why don't you call him direct?"

I got nervous. I didn't want to have any known contact with Powell and I was sure he would not appreciate my calling him at work.

"I'm a little shy about it," I said. "And I know they aren't going to be too thrilled talking to me——but if it came from *you*—you know, if the president is saying it's all right…"

"Sure," she said, "I understand." You didn't get to be the president's secretary unless you were as hip as he was. "I'll call you back. What's your number?"

She was so nice I almost gave it to her. "I'm going to be away from the phone for a while. May I call you back?"

"Certainly. Give me a half-hour."

A half-hour to set it up! Bomber was right. The results came from the top.

And I kept my word. I was away from my telephone—about six feet away. I was making some sketches in my music-staff lined notebook for my Churchill Park suite.

Forty minutes after I spoke to Jones' secretary, I called back. She had set it up.

"Come out tomorrow morning," she said. "Spend the day if you like. Talk to anyone. It's all set." And I could park in the A-lot.

I was getting to be family.

I spent the rest of the day on the telephone with Shauna, Bomber and Easy Willie. Willie told me we were kerbashing their arguments and they were about out of motions. So we might get a trial date for early next year. That would give us another six months to prepare, take depositions and do any other investigating we could. Easy Willie was up. He didn't mention selling out again.

That evening I called Don Powell from a phone booth and told him about my interviews.

"I know," he said. "I'd just as soon you didn't do them," he said. "I don't think you'll get anything from them. Nobody goes against the company. It's like the CIA and Mafia."

"But they are both experiencing some cracks—you never know. Anyway, I called you to ask how I should do it to make it least offensive to you?"

"Oh, I don't know. You can use the conference room on our floor."

"Think it's bugged?"

"Probably," he said. "Say—I just had an idea."

"What?"

"Interview me too. For the bug."

"Okay, I'll do you last. Okay?"

"Fine."

"See you tomorrow?"

"Yes."

Parking in the A-lot the next morning gave me a rush, but it was all uphill after that.

A more unproductive day I cannot imagine. The parade of satisfied employees of the T. S. Armstead company gave me all the symptoms of diabetes.

I suppose I should have predicted the response and saved the trouble. But I was, I told myself, hoping for one hold-out against the party line, which went something like this:

"Hey, I read about this health stuff, but I don't really know. I do know a lot of real old guys who've smoked all their lives. I know a couple women who tell me they don't *want* to get old. Rather get it over with before they need diapers. Suicide is illegal, smoking isn't. I need a job. This is a good one. They treat me right, pay well, *beaucoup* benefits. I *have* to work, you see. You get me a trust fund somewhere, we'll talk."

And I wasn't talking to anyone I thought stupid, duped or naive. They were all educated, well-spoken individuals, but there was not a witness in the busload.

After I exhausted the duds, I called in Don Powell.

"Thank you for coming, Mr. Powell."

"Glad to help."

"I must say all your employees seem to tow the party line."

"They're good people," he said. "They are happy here. It's a good place to work. The company treats them well. What did you expect them to say?"

"Well, for starters, I was hoping at least one of them would admit that you take out the nicotine in the curing process or refining process or whatever you call it, and then put more back in to make the cigarettes more addictive."

"Why, that's poppycock," he said.

We jousted a while longer. There were a few jabs, but no serious cuts.

After I left the A-lot to the salute of the guard at the entry/exit, I stopped at the first phone booth and called Shauna. It wasn't a business call, really, and our talk was mostly the cooing talk of love birds. I won't say she was often on my mind because that would be misleading. She was *always* on my mind.

Somewhere amid that personal stuff, she did manage to tell me I had a call from a lawyer who represented Jerry Horowitz. The attorney's name was William Shroyer and she gave me his number. This was a call I thought I should make from my room—on the hope that it *was* bugged. And even if it were not, I was fairly sure Mr. Shroyer would be recording the conversation.

When Shroyer's secretary intoned, "Who may I say is calling?" I pictured a dehydrated prune of a woman who suffered the effects of being suffocated each morning and evening on the overcrowded New York subways, a woman hardened with street-smarts, afraid to let down her guard and lapse casually into friendliness lest she be accused of inviting robbery, assault or rape.

I told her who was calling anyway.

"One moment," she said in tones that must have reverberated through the entire New York subway system.

William Shroyer on the line was a brand-new experience. I visualized him as the lawyer for Leona Helmsley, in addition to the all-time greedy corporate raider, Jerry Horowitz. Shroyer exuded, in the most simple sentences, that he was a man who didn't suffer little people gladly, and I never felt littler. Norm Stimmel, one of the kings of the legal profession in Cedarberg, wouldn't be fit to shine this man's shoes.

We did our share of verbal fencing—the upshot of which was we would subpoena the almighty Jerry Horowitz and he, through his attorney, would kick and scream, but we both realized he could run, but he couldn't hide.

*   *   *

I spent the weekend pouring through old newspapers for a mention of the murder Ray Strong told me about. Nothing. I asked the editor if he remembered anything, but he said he didn't. I asked him if this was the kind of town where something like that might be covered up: he said it was.

Sunday night I called Bomber to find out how it went with Don Powell.

"Fantastic!" Bomber said. "He's our *case*, boy!" Praise from Bomber was like manna from heaven. Monday I decided to share Bomber's appreciation with the Powells.

I dropped in on them at dinnertime.

I was greeted at the door by Gina Powell herself, and was astonished when, on seeing me, a huge smile lit up her face and she hugged me to her considerable bosom. "He's a new man," she whispered, "and it's thanks to you." Then she added a bonus: "I've even been able to give up my therapy."

"Oh, good," I said. "Is he home?"

"Sure is," she said, taking me by the hand into the living room decorated with colonial furniture. There was even an oil painting of a horse over the maplewood-framed fireplace.

Don Powell was reading the paper in a plaid-green wing chair.

"Look who's here, dear," Gina said.

"Well, Tod," Don Powell said, in a cheerier voice than I'd ever heard him use. He was actually smiling. He seemed genuinely glad to see me. "Nice to see you—can you join us for dinner? Alice does a mean pot roast."

"Roast chicken," Gina corrected him. "What do you say? We'd love to have you."

"Oh, no, thank you," I said. "I really came to say good-bye. I'm on my way back to Cedarberg. I just wanted to thank you for everything and tell you not to hesitate to call if you need anything." I left them Shauna's and Easy Willie's numbers.

"Bomber was quite excited with his discussions with you," I said to Don. "And Bomber is not a man who excites easi-ly."

Don nodded, reflectively. "I guess," he said, "it's an idea whose time has come."

"Bravo!" Gina said.

"He says you *are* our case."

Don's eyebrows went up.

"And because you are so important, he'd like to offer you a bodyguard."

"A bodyguard?" The idea startled him.

"It may not be necessary, but it's a precaution he'd be glad to pay for."

"You know this town, dear," Gina said. "You know how much the company has wrapped up in this thing. Maybe it's not such a bad idea."

"But...but, wouldn't that look ridiculous?" he argued.

"I mean, how would I explain, some guy following me around?"

"It could be done so discreetly even you wouldn't be aware of it," I said, believing it all the time. "We'll get an agency from out of town."

"Oh, do it, Don," Gina urged. "Just to be safe."

He frowned. "May I think about it?"

"Sure," I said. "Call me anytime. We would hire only the most reputable people—from out of town. No one here would need to know anything about it." From their looks, I could see how hollow that sounded. If I were orchestrating that, I would write a pianissimo roll on a high-pitched timpani.

"Wouldn't that be expensive?" practical Don asked.

"Apparently," I said, "Bomber thinks you are worth it."

*   *   *

I was met at the Cedarberg airport by the fabulous Shauna McKinley, who looked more radiant every time I saw her.

She brought me up to date on her activities as our legal researcher, as well as mother hen to the Zepf family.

"They are *so* poor," she said. "I went out there last night at dinnertime and you know what they were having?"

"Chicken," I said.

"Potatoes," she corrected me. "And that's all."

"That's a downer."

"My heart goes out to them. I wish I could do something for them," she said.

"You mean like if you were rich or something?"

"Yeah," she said.

"Speaking of rich, how's your mother getting along?"

"Terrible," she said. "She's in the hospital. Apparently she needs an operation for a hernia among other things. She's too young for Medicare and too proud to throw herself on the mercy of the county." She shook her head. "I don't know what I'm going to do."

"I think you should talk to your father about taking some responsibility."

"Yeah," she said. "Wouldn't that be nice…" she trailed off. "He's moved out. I'm pretty much it now, income-wise."

"How much *is* one of those operations?

"Thousands!"

Before long our conversation drifted to more pleasant things. Suffice it to say, I was not totally devastated Shauna's mother was in the hospital, because Shauna took me to her row house, where she made me a scrumptious dinner with candles and the whole bit. Afterwards, the unprecedented privacy afforded by the house provided an unprecedented opportunity for physical well-being.

Love, it has been said (and sung) is a many splendored thing.

I realized I could best express my feelings through a musical composition for flute and piano. I decided to call it *Suite: Love*.

18

In a case like *Zepf vs. T. S. Armstead*, you can go on for months, even years, without anything seeming to happen. Then all of a sudden things start to roll.

Civil cases had been taking way too long to come to trial. Some of that was due to lawyers positioning themselves for more advantageous settlements. In *Zepf vs. T. S. Armstead*, we spoke very little of settlement. Bomber was not a settling kind of guy (very unsettling actually). Bomber was more into drama than quick, big-buck, turnovers like the ambulance chasers were.

But recent laws have speeded things up a bit and now, a little over a year after our first contact, we were in the midst of depositions and on the brink of a trial which we expected to be calendared sometime in the late spring or early summer.

You could feel everyone perk up when Bomber came to town. He took a suite at the hotel where I was staying. We were careful not to make any sensitive phone calls and, in fact, Bomber got a kick out of having misleading conversations to throw off the eavesdroppers.

Bonnie Doone, Bomber's secretary, stayed in the office in Angelton, California to keep the home fires burning, like the good trooper she pretended to be. It was like house-sitting—the knack for which I was not stingy about granting the airhead.

Bomber had, as usual, a different slant on depositions— these question-and-answer sessions in a room with a witness, opposing counsel and court stenographer. While one school of thought held you wanted to ask everything, so there would be no surprises in court, Bomber liked surprises. Oh, he was well aware of the rule that you should never ask a question you don't know the answer to, but he realized that with a jury, psychology usually played the major role in their decisions.

Bomber's favorite use of the deposition was to make the witness feel he had been asked every question under the sun, to mislead him into thinking one area of testimony was especially important, then, at the trial, to switch gears and pound away on something the witness was not expecting. "The fluster factor" he called it.

Most trial lawyers were not above using the deposition process for its harassment value. When Jerry Horowitz strode into that little room with his personal attorney, William Shroyer, it was obvious the harassment tactic had already succeeded, big time.

Shroyer was a tall, spare, patrician kind of guy with an angular face and a nose worn sharp and thin by years of looking down it.

Jerry Horowitz was the perfect foil for him. Short, fit, looking like a street fighter in a Ralph Lauren suit, his eyes shifted at a rapid clip as though there might be another nickel hidden somewhere.

Harrison J. Hinkle brought up the rear and, if there was anything on his mind besides his escalating fees, his face didn't show it.

Render a powerful man powerless, for however brief a time, and you have put him adrift from his security blanket. He is seen for what he is, just another man whose obscene wealth will not keep him from a socked-in prostate or a flabby bladder.

This deposition lasted a day and a half, so obviously I won't give it verbatim. Bomber started low-key, as he often did, only to change to a storm trooper, then back peddle a bit to see how Horowitz would react to each nuance. One of my favorites was the pro bono exchange (from the transcript):

BOMBER:	Now, Mr. Horowitz, did you ever make a widget?
HOROWITZ:	I don't follow you.

BOMBER:	Yes, I notice. The goal should be for you to stay *with* me, not follow, but no matter…
SHROYER:	Now Mr. Hanson. That is uncalled for.
BOMBER:	As you wish.
SHROYER:	I think you should apologize to this witness.
BOMBER:	You're entitled to your opinion. Now, Mr. Horowitz, my question was, have you ever been involved in making a product?
HOROWITZ:	Well, I own T. S. Armstead. They make a lot of products.
BOMBER:	Cigarettes one of them?
HOROWITZ:	Yes. But they also make a myriad of other things, like baby food.
BOMBER:	I'm so pleased to hear that. They put any nicotine in the baby food?
HOROWITZ:	That's ridiculous.
BOMBER:	Just to start them young?
HOROWITZ:	Idiotic.
BOMBER:	I appreciate your frankness, Mr. Horowitz. Now the question is, do you know that they do *not* put nicotine in the baby food?
HOROWITZ:	They certainly do not.
BOMBER:	You know that personally?
HOROWITZ:	I'm sure of it.
BOMBER:	So you *do* know about the manufacturing processes at T. S. Armstead?
HOROWITZ:	I do not.
BOMBER:	But you just said you knew they didn't put nicotine in—
HOROWITZ:	I know *that*.
BOMBER:	Do they add sugar?
HOROWITZ:	To the cigarettes or baby food?

BOMBER:	Either one?
HOROWITZ:	I don't know. I have nothing to do with operating the company.
BOMBER:	What *do* you do?
HOROWITZ:	Provide capital.
BOMBER:	Just a provider, eh?
HOROWITZ:	You could say that.
BOMBER:	Of capital?
HOROWITZ:	Yes.
BOMBER:	Are you paid a fee for your services from your clients?
HOROWITZ:	Certainly.
BOMBER:	How much was that fee for the Armstead buyout?
HOROWITZ:	Seventy-five million.
BOMBER:	Have you ever had anything to do with manufacturing?
HOROWITZ:	No.
BOMBER:	With any company?
HOROWITZ:	No, my background is strictly banking.
BOMBER:	Bully for you.
SHROYER:	Mr. Hanson, please be professional.
BOMBER:	Like a capital provider, you mean?
SHROYER:	*Please.*
BOMBER:	Sorry, I'm more in the corporate raider mood.

The point was Bomber was succeeding in rattling Horowitz. Here was a mega-rich man who no one said "no" to, being ridiculed with impunity by the lawyer for a penniless blind man. It didn't sit well with him. But the more displeasure Horowitz and his attorney expressed, the deeper Bomber thrust the needle.

And, of course, in a deposition, Bomber could be even more outrageous than he could be in any courtroom, no matter how lenient or cowed the judge might be. You wouldn't think an almighty judge could be cowed by a lawyer, but I've seen it happen, and no one can make it happen like Bomber.

Here is an example of an exchange that was completely irrelevant to any of the court proceedings.

BOMBER:	How many companies do you own, Mr. Horowitz?
HOROWITZ:	Four, currently.
BOMBER:	You've had more?
HOROWITZ:	Certainly. I buy and sell.
BOMBER:	How many companies are there in the world?
HOROWITZ:	I've no idea.
BOMBER:	In the U.S.?
HOROWITZ:	I don't know.
BOMBER:	How many companies are listed on the New York Stock Exchange?
HOROWITZ:	Don't know.
BOMBER:	The American Stock Exchange?
HOROWITZ:	No.
BOMBER:	NASDAQ?
HOROWITZ:	Sorry.
BOMBER:	Mr. Horowitz, do you consider yourself a professional corporate raider?
HOROWITZ:	I consider myself a provider of investment capital.
BOMBER:	But not to create anything?
HOROWITZ:	Excuse me?
BOMBER:	You don't create products, do you?
HOROWITZ:	I buy companies that do.
BOMBER:	But your part of it—you have been adamant—has nothing to do with manufacturing anything to make the world a better place.
SHROYER:	Oh, Mr. Hanson, that is so loaded I'm surprised you were able to lift it off the

	ground.
BOMBER:	Well, did you "buy" as you term it, the T. S. Armstead Company to make the world a better place?
HOROWITZ:	No.
BOMBER:	Did you ever think you could have done that by buying the company then shutting down the cigarette manufacturing division?
HOROWITZ:	But that would cost billions!
SHROYER:	Wait a minute, don't answer that.
BOMBER:	He already has.
SHROYER:	No, he hasn't! That's not an answer. That's an off-guard comment—
BOMBER:	The best kind.
SHROYER:	Don't interrupt me when I'm talking.
BOMBER:	But you weren't saying anything.
SHROYER:	Mr. Hanson, you will return some semblance of dignity to these proceedings or I will pull my client right out of here.
BOMBER:	Then we'll simply get a court order to pull him right back.
SHROYER:	Oh, grow up.
BOMBER:	I'm afraid it's too late for that. All the grown-ups in this room seem to be on the side of the merchants of death. If that's your idea of maturity, I'm satisfied to be immature.
SHROYER:	This is getting ridiculous.
BOMBER:	Is there anything more ridiculous than cigarettes? And your client here has marshaled billions of dollars to buy a company that spits cash like a slot machine from selling the most addictive and lethal product on the market today,

	legal or il—.
SHROYER:	You're making a speech.
BOMBER:	How much did you pay for the T. S. Armstead Company, Mr. Horowitz?
HOROWITZ:	Nineteen point one.
BOMBER:	Nineteen point one what? Nineteen point-one thousand—nineteen-point-one million?
HOROWITZ:	Nineteen billion, one-hundred million.
BOMBER:	Killing people doesn't come cheap.
SHROYER:	That's enough, Mr. Hanson!
BOMBER:	No, no, think about it. At nineteen point one, it's costing you about 6,300 dollars for each person you kill. In the day of hundred-dollar hit men, that seems expensive. You might have done better with a hostile takeover of the Mafia. Death comes a lot cheaper there. Of course, that 6,300 amortizes. After ten years, it will only cost you around 630 bucks a corpse.
HINKLE:	Mr. Hanson, I fear I must step in here. I have been satisfied to let Mr. Shroyer ably fend for his client against your outrageous onslaughts and insults, but I'm here to tell you we will tolerate no more of it. And you know no judge in the country will ask us to prolong this abuse when we show him the transcript. I do understand you hail from the Wild-and Woolly West where a case may take years in court, and your outrageous behavior may seem cute, but it doesn't cut any ice here.
BOMBER:	On the exalted East Coast, you mean?
HINKLE:	If you are any indication, we certainly

are superior in our conduct, anyway. Now, either ask legitimate questions or we will adjourn. No more speeches.

BOMBER: Unless you make them?

That shut them up for a beat, so Bomber hit Horowitz again with how many companies, and he didn't know and Bomber asked a long series of questions that showed Mr. Gotrocks didn't seem to know much about the business world. He admitted he was interested in cash-rich companies. "The bottom line" was how he put it.

Finally, Bomber had asked Jerry Horowitz so many questions and badgered him so unmercifully about his lack of knowledge that Horowitz gave this delightful answer on the record:

HOROWITZ: Look Mr. Hanson, I'm not a do-gooder. I never claimed to be. I'm not an environmentalist, ecologist or a healthnut. I am a venture capitalist, pure and simple. I don't make things, I don't sell them, I buy companies that do. That's all I do.

BOMBER: And are you proud of it?

HOROWITZ: We have been very successful, yes.

BOMBER: At making money?

HOROWITZ: Yes.

You couldn't tell from these cold, transcript pages how flushed Jerry Horowitz's face was. How angry and rattled he was. But the next day we were paid a visit at Bomber's hotel suite that erased all doubt.

19

It was a visit from opposing counsel that most litigation attorneys would find supremely gratifying.

But Bomber was not *most* attorneys.

Pennsylvania had turned hot and humid and I was grateful for the air-conditioned hotel room, and Bomber's suite, to work in.

Sometimes I snuck down to the cocktail lounge before it opened to try out my sketches for *Suite: Love*. Shauna was never far from my thoughts, so the piece was taking on a romantic bent contrary to my usual dissonant, pulsing, multi-rhythmic work.

I was thinking of Shauna and humming the main motif of my *Suite: Love*, a lush melody that was passed back and forth between piano and flute. The instrument without the melody provided an accompaniment, which ran the gamut from placid to hectic. I was trying to catch the ups and downs of courtship.

Up in Bomber's suite I was still toying with one of these accompaniments while Bomber was reading some jury survey from Easy Willie. The phone rang. It was Harrison J. Hinkle in the lobby. He had not been to the hotel suite before, or I don't think he would have bothered to call.

I covered the phone mouthpiece (the underdog's hold button) and asked Bomber his pleasure.

He smiled the smile of the conquerer and gave me one of those the-matter-is-insignificant gestures, and I told Harrison he could come up—top floor, turn right, go to the end of the hall.

After I hung up, Bomber said, "They're crawling already."

It seemed only a moment later I opened the door to what I can only characterize as an almost dignified knock, and old curly top, Harrison J. Hinkle, stepped into the room. He let his eyes sweep the room and pursed his lips to express his disdain.

Bomber didn't get up. "Have a seat, Harrison," he said.

The way I remember Harrison J. Hinkle is as a guy you'd want on your side if you had an acrimonious divorce on your hands.

It was obvious Bomber didn't think that well of him. You can always tell by looking at him what he's thinking. The less he thought of an adversary, the more he was given to braggadocio.

Harrison sat. "That was quite a session we had yesterday," he said.

"Think so?" Bomber said. "I was only getting warmed up. I love to go into combat with a weasel."

Harrison J. Hinkle blanched. "I would not characterize Mr. Horowitz as a weasel," he said as though it were only fair to defend him. "He's one of the richest men in the world."

"I wouldn't doubt it," Bomber said. "And the remarkable thing is, he hasn't contributed the tiniest benefit to mankind."

"Yes, well, I'm not here to talk social science."

"How could you be?"

"You know, Bomber," Harrison said taking on something of a professional role, "you seem to go out of your way to aggravate people."

"Thank you," Bomber said. "Now before I aggravate you, why don't you tell me what you want?"

"What *I* want. On the contrary, I am here to find out what you want."

"Didn't we have this conversation in California?"

"Only in the broadest terms. I'm here for specifics. Ordinarily we would not consider an offer of settlement in a case of this nature."

"Not without seeing the pile of mincemeat I made out of Gotrocks."

I winced at that myself. Sometimes I wished my dad would have just a tad of humility. When I got the courage to broach that subject he thundered, "What? And be dishonest? Humility is arrogance," he said. "Unless you have something to be humble about." This, of course, was said with eyes squinting in my direction.

"Jerry Horowitz doesn't want to be bothered with this. I suggested a settlement might open the floodgates. He waved me off saying I could find the loophole—the man *is* blind—twelve kids—whatever."

"Bomber for the plaintiff," Bomber offered.

I winced again. Harrison ignored it. Then changed his mind. "We'd ask for an exclusionary clause—no future actions—"

Bomber chuckled. "Think I'd sign that?"

"Probably not. But hear my offer," Harrison said. "It's a million and a half—one million to the Rich Zepf plaintiffs, a half a mil to you."

"We—"

"Before you say anything," Harrison said, "You know that the highest jury award in one of these cases was four-hundred thousand to the widower of a man whose wife began smoking *before* the warnings were on the pack. And the appellate court threw that out so they got nothing. Plaintiff's lawyers went through around two million and they were finally left holding the bag."

"Tell me, Harrison," Bomber said, "did you make this offer to those appellate judges?"

Surprisingly, he did not seem insulted. He shook his head. "Didn't have to. Law's on our side."

"So why the offer?"

"I told you. Horowitz doesn't want the hassle."

"He'll get it with other attorneys."

A small, grudging smile pulled at Harrison's lips.

"Other attorneys are not the same. Well," he said, "think about it."

"I've thought about it."

Harrison put up his hand to forestall Bomber from making a hasty response. "You know, you are bound by law to disclose the offer to your principal."

"I'm aware of that. I can almost guarantee we will accept the offer."

"You *will?*" Harrison and I almost fell off our chairs. That was unlike anything I'd ever heard from Bomber. *Any* lawyer would make a counteroffer. The first offer was seldom the final one.

"I will—and I can almost guarantee Mr. Zepf will," he said, "if you will grant *our* one request."

"But…"

"No, I quite understand. You were prepared to go higher, but I think, monetarily, your offer is most satisfactory. Generous even. We don't need another million or two."

"Monetarily?" Harrison hesitated.

"Yes, means money," Bomber said, insulting him. "Money is great. You meet our conditions, we might even take less."

"Your *conditions*? What are they?"

"Stop making cigarettes."

Harrison Hinkle said that was ridiculous and I couldn't disagree, but Bomber liked those grand gestures. Hinkle said again Bomber was bound to make the offer to his principal and repeated it as though Bomber might not have heard the first time.

He heard. "And I'll thank you not to dictate my fees through your offers," he said.

"Well, it's standard here—one-third and two-thirds—I thought—"

"Don't think about my business."

Harrison nodded. "As you wish," he said, and left.

Bomber smiled broadly at the closed door. "They're

scared, me boy, and that was my first depo."

I couldn't argue with him.

"Get Zepf in here," he said.

"Oh," I said, "Mr. Z-Z-Zepf, I don't know. I m-m-mean, he doesn't m-move so easily."

"Well, if he's going to be up for a trial, he can come in here."

"Better we s-s-should go there."

"His place air-conditioned?"

I shook my head.

"You go there then. I have limits what I'll suffer for a client. Especially a contingency client. It's got to be a hundred and ten in the shade," he exaggerated.

"I'll c-c-call him," I said.

I picked up the phone and dialed. I got a recording. I hung up. "Looks like somebody's going to have to go out there."

"Why?"

"Their phone's disconnected."

You know who went. And the girls were so excited about going to see Bomber I didn't have the heart to tell them they would hardly all fit in the living room of his hotel suite. So they all piled in their pick-up truck and my car, Rich with the aid of a wheelchair, and we caravanned to town, down Madison Street and caught up on their news and mine. The phone had been disconnected, Miriam said, because they had forgotten to pay the bill. They expected to hook it back up real soon. No one contradicted her.

We parked in the garage behind the hotel. The girls in their farming jeans and overalls (I told them there was neither the need nor the time to change) got a big kick out of the hotel and riding the elevator to the top floor.

When we entered the room, I was surprised to see Shauna and Easy Willie in residence. I guessed Bomber wanted the whole crew for the momentous decision, which I thought uncharacteristically thoughtful of him. What was less thoughtful was we were quickly out of seats. But the girls were happy to sit on the floor.

Bomber got right to it without any opening pleasantries.

"We have been graced with an offer of settlement in our case against T. S. Armstead."

I looked around the room to catch the reactions. Easy Willie was impassive, Shauna seemed pleased, as did some of the older Zepf girls. Rich Zepf didn't show any reaction. It was as though either he was waiting for the nitty-gritty or he realized he wouldn't be around to spend it.

"The offer is for one million, five-hundred thousand dollars."

Now there was more animation from the audience. The girls were clapping, Shauna was ecstatic and Rich was smiling. Even Easy Willie seemed pleasantly surprised.

Bomber continued, "I am bound by the rules governing the behavior of lawyers to make you aware of the offer. Personally, I feel a moral obligation to tell you if we go to trial, we will ask for a lot more money than that, but there is a real chance that we will not win that much. No one ever has. You don't have to answer the offer right away, but I did want you to know about it so you could ponder what it means to you. And if you have any questions, now's the time—but first, I'll ask you all for your reactions. Shauna?"

"I'm overwhelmed. How did you get such a large offer so fast? They've *never* made an offer to *anyone*."

That could have been a smile on Bomber's lips. I couldn't be sure.

"Maybe we have them scared," he said. "What would you do?"

"Do?" she said. "Me? If someone offered me a million and a half, I'm very much afraid I'd take it."

"Easy Willie," Bomber turned his attention to the taciturn one. Easy Willie spoke slowly. "Economically," he said, "it's a good sign. *Too* good, perhaps. And if they offer one and a half to start, who knows how far you could take them. Four, five…?"

"Would you take it?"

Easy Willie pondered, then heaved a large sigh.

"Or would you ask for more?"

Easy Willie was breathing audibly, almost as though his lungs were giving him trouble. Perhaps it was nicotine withdrawal, because I suppose, in deference to the rest of us, he wasn't smoking.

"Or would you try the case?"

"The decision is not mine to make," Easy Willie said. "I'm afraid I'll pass."

Bomber turned to Rich, seated, wired and tubed in his wheelchair—a pole holding his oxygen. I was relieved Bomber didn't ask my opinion. I didn't want to stutter in front of the Zepfs, who were the only ones in the room that had not been treated to that display. "Rich," he said, "what do you think?"

"I think we are fortunate to have such a important lawyer on our case. The girls and I really 'preciate it."

Bomber waved his hand to dismiss the compliment. Carrie explained the gesture to her father.

"We don't know nothing about these things. That's a big number—more money 'n all of us could ever hope to see. And we could get by on a lot less. Fact is, we got a lot less now then we could get by on. Cain't say I ain't tempted. But I gotta ask you tell us what you think."

I could see a turn of admiration on Bomber's lips.

"The offer came after my deposition of the head honcho—a man who has devoted his life to piling dollar on dollar. A million and half sounds like a big pile of dollars to you, but believe me, it is a minuscule portion of the profit they make every day selling cigarettes. If you took a million-and-a-half dollars off their pile of profit for even a month, you would not see that anything was missing. We know that, they know that, and they know we know. Easy Willie is right, they would add to the pile if we asked them.

"Heretofore, they have not made offers because they feared the domino effect—make one, thousands more would be there with their hands out. And legitimately so, for theirs is a vile product. Lord, if the other manufacturing companies in the country got away with what T. S. Armstead gets away with, litigation lawyers would go out of business."

"Lot of people think that might not be so bad," Easy Willie said.

"And I'm one of them," Bomber said. "Now, the other side of this coin is our real motive in taking this case. Was it to make money, or was it to make a statement, or was it to teach the tobacco companies a lesson, or scare them, or what? I must tell you, my motive was not money. And if you're going to accomplish any of those other options, you will not do it with a million-and-a-half paltry dollars."

I noticed the girls to the woman, Shauna included, did not buy into the theorem that a million-and-a-half dollars was paltry. I could just imagine all of them speculating what they could do with those dollars Bomber characterized as "paltry."

"But I already told the opposing counsel, I would accept his offer on one condition..." Bomber paused and looked around the room. They were all on edge, but no one had the nerve to ask him what that was, so he told them.

"That condition was simply that they stop making cigarettes."

There was an uncomfortable shifting of bodies. Shauna spoke first.

"You're joking." It wasn't a question.

"Am I?" Bomber roared, and Shauna fell back in her seat as though she had taken a personal blow to her body, which, in a way, she had. "We all agreed to embark on this holy mission with a principled zeal. We can accept their offer or squeeze them for some more, but they will never feel it. And if we are to accomplish anything, they most surely must feel it."

"What would make them feel it?" Carrie asked.

"A jury award of a hundred-million dollars."

We all gasped ourselves to silence.

Again, Shauna was the one with the courage to speak

first. "What are the chances of that?"

Now Bomber was smiling. I was sure of it. "You never know what a jury will do," he said. "Especially with Bomber at the stick." He was making an illusion to flying an airplane—which he never did. He was a bombardier—almost.

"But a hundred mil—"

Bomber was no longer hiding his disdain for Shauna. Just my luck. He probably thought she was uppity for one so young and so…female. And I saw from Shauna's face I would have a lot of explaining to do. He had cut her sentence in midair with just his torrid look. But I remember thinking this was the downside of falling in love with someone who worked for your father.

Then Bomber's look-of-the-thousand-daggers faded, and he explained: "I'm sure if we accepted their offer—or three times as much—we would be obliged to sign a stipulation that swore us all to secrecy so no one would ever know they had given in. We would just blithely dismiss the lawsuit and nothing would appear in the papers or on the nightly news. In short, no one would know. A Pyrrhic victory. No blood. No pain. No gain. Except for the aforementioned pile of dollars."

"What if you refused that stipulation?" Shauna asked, emboldened again.

"They would withdraw the offer."

"Why?"

Bomber eyed her again with the daggers. I knew it was coming, but I was powerless to stop it or prepare Shauna. "Young lady," he said, not lifting his gaze from her lovely face, "I am a man of no little experience in these matters, and frankly, unused to being questioned by one so lately out of law school. I would be, I am bound to say, more comfortable if your questions had some grounding in knowledge or experience, or another one of those areas so lately out of fashion. Since you asked why, I shall tell you why. If they don't mind the unprecedented publicity about an adverse settlement, why not go for broke? Face it, we are trying a case everyone says is impossible. You are doing the law research. You know better than everybody that when all the appeals (quite costly, by the way) are done, no one has ever gotten a dime from a tobacco company. So what earthly reason would they have to trumpet this caving-in on the six-o'clock news? Nobody gives anything for nothing. Not you, not me, and especially not a tobacco company."

Bomber turned to face Rich Zepf, who was sitting quietly and listening intently.

"Rich. It's up to you. The offer is a million and a half. I'll gladly press them for more. We can most assuredly *get* more unless for some reason they have a sudden change of heart. Their counsel made the offer thusly—a million for you, a half million for me, claiming that was the local standard for legal fees. I thanked him to stay out of my business. The legal fees are between us. If you decide to take the offer, whatever it finally turns out to be, there will be no legal fee. You may have it all."

There was a stunned silence. I wondered if Shauna and Easy Willie were wondering about their percentage. I didn't have to wonder long. Shauna spoke up. "Excuse me, Mr…Bomber, but didn't you mention that if we won we would get a percentage?"

"Indeed I did. Nice of you to remind me in this company. You were to receive an extra award to thank you for the fine services you performed that helped bring about the victory. But a settlement is no victory, it's a capitulation."

"Is that fair?" she asked. I must admit I had not seen Shauna as so money-oriented before. Perhaps it was her mother's hernia and the foreclosure. I did want to tell her if we went to trial, her checks would continue—that's assuming she didn't alienate Bomber into firing her. My looks of warning were not acknowledged.

Bomber ignored her. "Mr. Zepf, what are your thoughts?"

Rich Zepf shifted in his seat. "We *did* want to teach them a lesson. Getting them to stop selling would be great, but I guess it isn't too realistic; and the Lord knows, we could use the money. But, I couldn't hear of you not taking your fee. You got expenses. Then there's your people's bonuses. And if the award don't make the news, we will have made oursells history—getting the first money from a tobacco manufacturer. I mean, what would our chances be at a trial?"

"Could go either way," Bomber said. "And that's not as equivocal as it sounds. That's optimism, because it implies that we *could* win. No one really has and we might have the edge because we have an important, reliable witness that will say the company *is* aware of the health risks and, within the company they don't dismiss the scientific findings like they do in public. And he will say that they knowingly add nicotine to the product to make them addictive—to sell more of the little killers."

"But won't they put on witnesses to refute that?" Shauna asked.

"Sure they will. They won't play dead. I'm just banking ours will be more believable—and I will be the better salesman. So, I guess, it comes down to a matter of faith. How much have you got, Mr. Zepf?"

Rich Zepf was frowning. I felt sorry for him. He obviously wanted to please Bomber—it was the only gratitude he could show—but the sound of the ready money—now, while he could still touch it, must have been sweet music to his ears.

"May I think about it, Bomber?" he asked. "I'd like to go over it with the girls."

"Certainly."

"You'll have your answer in twenty-four hours."

20

After the troops left, Bomber and I had a heart-to-heart.

"Jesus Jenny, Tod, where did you dig up Reds?"

I started to sputter about her qualifications, but he waved me off. "Yeah, yeah, I'm beginning to wonder if Bonnie isn't right."

"B-b-bonn—B-b-bonnie?"

"Yeah, she says you made the decision with the wrong organ."

Well, I was spitting all over the place on that one. What did Bonnie know? She had never even *seen* Shauna. Bonnie wouldn't know brains if they hit her in the face. How could she, she didn't have any herself. By the time I wound down, I could see that my immature outburst had amused Bomber. I wasn't amused.

Of course, I realized Bomber took perverse pleasure in playing Bonnie off against me. I once asked him if he ever worked the play in reverse and he said, "Why? She doesn't rise to the bait like you do."

The work day was almost over, but I decided to run down to Shauna's office to see if I could catch her to give her some friendly advice on getting along with Bomber. Perhaps Shauna, by virtue of her age, sex and profession, was more of a flaming feminist than I had realized.

Shauna was not in.

I was aching to see her, so I drove out to her house, but no one answered the door. I went back to my hotel room and added a section to my *Suite: Love.* I marked it agitato.

Even so, my thoughts turned to calamity. Does absence make the heart grown fonder? Not wanting to seem as eager as I was, I held off calling Shauna until the next morning at nine. She was not in the office, so I left a message for her to call me.

It was about ten-thirty and I had still not heard from Shauna when I began to wonder if she was deliberately avoiding me. Maybe she was put out about Bomber's treatment of her and maybe she held me responsible.

While I was considering the possibilities, Carrie Zepf came into Bomber's hotel-suite office. She looked as though she had not slept all night—which turned out to be the case.

Bomber eyed her curiously when she walked in and plopped herself in the hotel chair facing the desk where Bomber was reading some reports about Judge Druckenmiller.

He looked at me as though I might offer some explanation for this unannounced interruption—an aggravation Bonnie and I would shield him from in Angelton. I shrugged.

Carrie was in her work clothes—torn jeans and a pale yellow-plaid work shirt. The jeans were torn from wear, not as a fashion statement. She just sat there looking perplexed, but not saying anything or making eye contact.

I can usually tell what Bomber is thinking, and it was obvious dropping in on Bomber was not an act he found endearing.

Finally, she stirred, her face no less perplexed. "The thing is," she said, "we don't know. A million dollars is more money than we can even imagine."

"A million and a half," Bomber corrected her. "First offer."

"Yeah, well," Carrie said, "that we're sure, we aren't taking all of it, no matter what. You got expenses." Carrie waved her arm around the room. I was sure a hotel suite was more than the Zepfs could imagine, too.

It was a revelation watching this diamond-in the-rough in action. Short on opportunity, short on education, but long on what the locals called horse-sense, this teenager was acting quite grown-up. Yet there was no getting around the fact that she was still a child.

"That's most generous of you," Bomber said, "but I'm afraid that decision is not yours to make. I told you I will have none of the killer's hush-money. If you reject it, it will go back from whence it came."

Carrie seemed startled beyond her ability to verbalize her thoughts. "The thing is…I mean, there's Mom to consider for starters. She could come home an' all. I know you're against it, but—"

Bomber held up a hand. The traffic cop: "Wait—I'm *not* against it. The decision is rightly yours."

"But then how come you don't want any money?"

"I don't want *this* money. I would not feel I had earned it. It is nothing to them. It makes us disappear without a trace. No, you can increase your take fifty percent, just like that." Bomber started to snap his fingers, then seemed to get second thoughts and his hand dropped.

"Well, what about Shauna and them?"

"What about them?"

"Aren't they going to get some of that?"

Now I didn't have to speculate what Bomber was thinking as his torrid eyes bored into the poor child. I was thinking the same thing myself, but that didn't prevent me from feeling sorry for Carrie.

"My dear child," Bomber said at last, over the top with patronization for my taste, "the money will be yours. If you want to give it *all* to the redhead, or endow a cage for an alley cat at the zoo, that is entirely your prerogative."

"Up to you," I chimed in to save her the embarrassment of asking what "prerogative" meant.

Carrie was not stupid or dense. She could tell from Bomber's tone of voice how he felt about that. But her only response was a frown.

"So what did Reds tell you?" Bomber asked.

The Zepf messenger shook her head and looked at the floor.

Bomber stood up. He seemed to be wearing his elevator

shoes, not that they would have been necessary to cow the poor girl. It was painfully easy for him to get out of Carrie what he wanted. A few half-hearted denials, a fragment of "I'as not supposed to..." here, "She doesn't want..." there and before you know it she was sputtering Shauna's line. Bomber let her run-down.

"So she thinks you should take the money?"

Carrie nodded.

"And she bestirred herself to come to your house last night to tell you so?"

"She came out, yeah."

"And stayed all night?"

"We just got talking, yeah."

"And are you convinced?"

"Well," she hung her head again, "like I say, that's a lotta money for us."

"Yes it is. It's a lot for most people."

"And if you could just see your way clear to taking some of it..."

Bomber shook his head. "You mean that's all standing between you and grabbing the money?"

"Well...pretty much—you done the work, it's because of you we got the offer. An' we do want to see all them get a share."

Bomber was standing over her. She couldn't look at him. He punched the desk with his fist. "Enough!" he shouted. "I will not prolong this nonsense. If you want the money, you will have *all* of it. You will be free to give *all* of it to your beloved Shauna if that will please you. Now, *out*! I have work to do." I hustled Carrie out trying to smooth over the mental bruises Bomber sent her way. When I returned, Bomber turned his fury on me. "That redheaded bitch!" he spewed. "You find her and give her her walking papers."

"Me?"

"You hired her. I want her out of my sight before I open my eyes. Of all the unprofessional conduct—you can tell her

I'm giving serious thought to having her disbarred."

We had a hot argument and my stutter was completely out of control as I stoutly, if moistly, maintained he owed it to her to hear her side of it. It wasn't manly to precipitously dismiss someone without giving them their day in court.

"Hah!" he boomed. "She's out undermining the man who pays her. Sneaking around behind my back to fatten her purse. Get rid of her!" he shouted. "Today!"

"Not without hearing her side." I stood firm, my knees shaking all the while. I was feeling a combination of virility, independence, frustration, and vertigo.

I called Shauna's office from my room. I didn't want Bomber in the audience. She wasn't there.

I called her home. Groggily she answered on the twelfth ring.

"I have to see you," I said.

"Oh goody," she said, and I couldn't tell if she was being sarcastic.

"I'll be right over. Don't get up."

"Who's going to unlock the door?" she asked, then added the sexiest, "Mmmmmm?"

*   *   *

Her mother was still in the hospital, she explained as she opened the door. That should have made me wonder. Shauna looked so ravishing with her eyes laden with sleep, wearing a ridiculous granny night gown, my wondering mechanisms had clogged.

"Look, Shauna," I pleaded, "we have to talk."

"Mmmm," she purred, taking me by the hand to her bedroom upstairs. "Later."

The sheets were still warm and so was she. And I had to admit she had a point. Talking would have been superfluous.

Are liberated women better lovers? The proposition has my vote. Are redheads really more passionate? Do feminists take more initiative? I vote the straight party line.

Somehow we wound up at her kitchen table where she drank some cranberry juice and munched on some Wheat Thin crackers "baked, not fried" the box said. "Do people actually fry crackers?" I asked Shauna when I read that boast on the box.

But she didn't answer, just stared at me with those dreamy eyes of hers. For some reason, I thought her eyes were saying "hold the mayonnaise." or something like "you'll never need mayonnaise again"—I don't know why. There were no mayonnaise jars around or anything.

"Want a cracker?" Shauna said, waving the cracker box in my direction.

I thought I started in a low key. "Shauna," I said.

"Hm?

"You know you got Bomber all riled up?

"I did? How?"

"Going out to the Zepfs."

"Come on, Tod, be reasonable. Those people need help. *And* they need that money," she said. "Bomber sent them home with no guidance—I mean who does he think they are, a bunch of college-educated corporate executives? They need all the help they can get, so I gave them a little. If that's a sin, I'm a sinner, okay, but, I've got to tell you my sympathy is with that poor family, not with the powerful, famous, trial attorney."

"Well, put—"

"Who does he think he is, anyway, playing fast and loose with this poor, simple family's emotions? All very well for you to treat him like a god in California, but he's on different turf here. We're not high-flyers here, we're simple people who aren't ashamed to lend a helping hand to those in need. And the needy in this equation is not Bomber Hanson."

"That's quite eloquent, Shauna," I said, "but he *is* your employer, and as such, don't you think he's entitled to certain expectations from his employees?"

"Certain? What's certain?"

"That you don't intervene in a client's decision without

his approval. I know how you feel, but isn't that pretty basic?"

"Basic?"

"Even in compassionate Pennsylvania?"

"So what do you want me to do?"

"Talk to him. Admit your error. Eat humble pie."

"Why?"

"He wants to can you, is why."

"Can me? For being helpful?"

"Your idea of being helpful had a way of countermanding his wishes."

"His *wishes*! His *wishes*! My lord, Tod, what are his *wishes*? That this poor family who can't pay a phone bill and who eat potatoes morning, noon, and night turn their backs on a million dollars so he can grandstand in court for the TV? Is that the side of truth, beauty and goodness? Is that our justice and mercy? I'll tell you something, boy, you're living in that guy's shadow and he's a blowhard. The sooner you cut the cord, the sooner you'll obtain manhood—if it's not already too late."

"Wow—you're not holding anything back, are you?"

"Would you want me to? Bomber has enough yes-men around him. And if he wants to fool with these people's lives I'm not playing dead. Who does he think he is anyway, some god, who is really going to crush the tobacco companies? I mean, get real. We all know, Bomber included, that the chance of his winning the case is slim. The chance of his getting that much money for the Zepfs—after the endless appeals—is nil. Rich Zepf will be dead anyway. Rich will be poor." Her smile was as thin as last year's newspaper. "Dead, without the slightest satisfaction that his life came to something for his dozen daughters. Balance that against your father's ego. Because that's all it amounts to. This is a far better result for the Zepfs than anyone, the great, almighty Bomber included, could ever hope to gain for those poor saps."

"Zepfs," I corrected her.

"I know," she said. "The Zepfs are poor saps."

She seemed to have worn down, at least momentarily. I

started my defense of a man who would never consider a defense of him necessary. "Shauna, you have good instincts. I can't decide if your sympathy is an asset or a liability in a woman lawyer."

"I'm a lawyer," she corrected me, "who happens to be a woman."

"Yes, sure," I said, "but could there be some baggage there? Could this have something to do with why so many women leave the profession? All those lawyer jokes didn't invent themselves. Men *are* different than women. Maybe not tougher, but we are more immune to emotional breakdown. A woman sees a stray cat and she's right there with a saucer of milk. A man walks by and says, 'That's not my cat.' Your instincts for these people are good. I admit to some of them myself. But is there another way to look at this thing? Bomber is a showman, sure. Nobody is going to argue that—not even the man himself. But his showmanship is usually employed for the underdog. I can't imagine him taking General Motors for a client, no matter how worthy their cause. Bomber isn't trying to make headlines. And I don't deny he adores headlines. He is trying to serve a purpose. He has higher goals than we poor folks can understand. His offering to give the Zepfs his fee was not magnanimity, it was motivated by his genuine love and feeling for these people."

"Hah!"

"No, no. Think about it. He wants to try the case. He wants to make an example of the tobacco companies. He wants to accomplish something. It's a cause with him, it's not the money. He is saying, take *all* the money, if it's money you want. I don't want it—we'll have to deny victory taking it, but if you want it, I understand and I want you to have my share too. You need it more than I do."

"Wow, you're making him sound like a god."

"Well," I said, "he certainly wouldn't deny it."

"Okay," Shauna said yawning. "Now I'm going to shoo you out of here. I have to get some sleep—I had a good start, but something sidetracked me." She tapped my nose playfully with her finger. "I'll probably sleep through the Zepf's decision and that's okay. I spent the whole night out there trying to talk myself out of a job."

"Oh? Bomber thinks you were trying to talk yourself into your bonus."

"Well, he's wrong. I heard him say he wouldn't take his fee. Where would I expect to get a bonus from?"

"Carrie pleaded that he give you your share."

"She did, did she?" Shauna seemed pleased. "What did he say?"

"He said she could give it all to you, *he* wasn't taking any."

"If you say so."

"So how about that, Shauna," I said. "There's a test for you. If Bomber gave them his fee, would you accept your bonus from the Zepfs?"

"Silly boy," she said and kissed me on the nose. "Night, night. I'll be in the office around five if you need me."

"Thanks."

"Unless you are telling me not to go back to my office."

I stared at her a long time.

"Well?" she prodded.

"No, I think I'll let Bomber tell you that."

I left there without knowing what she meant by "Silly boy." Silly boy, yes; or silly boy, no?

21

I got back to Bomber's hotel suite on Madison Street just in time to field the call.

"Oh, yes, Mr. Hinkle." I said in my most bogus hail-fellow-well-met voice, so Bomber would know who was on the other end. The great man waved frantically, indicating he had no desire to talk to him.

"Well, he's tied up at the moment," I said into the phone. "May I help you with anything?"

There was the usual grumble of disappointment at being left with an underling.

"I was just trying to get a feel for our offer. Has it been presented?"

"Yes."

"And?"

"Still thinking," I said.

"Thinking?" Harrison said. "About what?"

"The offer, I guess. If Mr. Zepf decides to accept it, we won't keep it from you."

Bomber winked broadly and gave me the touché sign of the circled thumb and forefinger.

"Does he have a counteroffer?"

"Not yet." I said, "But I don't know...When you start so low..."

Bomber's eyebrows shot up in newfound respect.

"Listen," Harrison Hinkle said in the phone, "give us a break. We'll ask confidentiality, of course, but rumors will fly. The precedent will kill us. Do you think another mil would move him?"

"I'll ask," I said.

After we hung up, I said, "He upped it a million," and Bomber's face betrayed some admiration that was not underpinned with any words of praise. Instead he asked, "Did you can her?"

"No."

"What are you waiting for? Do it!"

"No."

"No?"

I put a question to him. "If Rich Zepf throws in the towel, do we go on?"

"Of course not."

"So why do we have to go out of our way to be unpleasant? She'd be finished anyway," I said. "But, Shauna aside, how many more millions do you think the poor Zepfs can turn down?"

"There's a principle here."

"Principles are for rich people," I said. "I have to tell you, if I were a Zepf, I'd have taken the money already."

"Especially with Reds out there promoting it," he said.

"Are you being fair to them? The girl, Carrie, came in here solicitous of everybody, not only Shauna, but you and me too."

"Agh—"

"And if it were *anyone* else in their predicament, it would have been 'give me' with no further ado."

I could hardly describe Bomber's look of stony silence.

"Okay, Bomber," I said, without thinking—and when I didn't think, I didn't stutter. "Three choices. One, you go to the Zepfs and make your pitch. Two—" but he had already pounded his fist on the table and I went to pieces inside. "I g-g-go and if they s-s-stick for t-t-trial, S-s-shauna st-st-stays. Three, they t-take the m-m-money, we all go."

"Am I to believe my ears?" he boomed. "My son and employee is telling me what to do about some skirt he mistakenly hired, a dish of cream that went sour? It makes me wonder just who is on which end of the paycheck."

He glared at me and I won't say I glared back, but I was breathing too hard to talk.

"Let me make myself clear here. If you want to keep your job, you do what I tell you. You, of course, may prefer to stick around and find a job here writing symphonies or something. Up to you." His eyes bored in on me and I left his room. I went to my room where I broke down like a second-grader whose feelings were hurt.

With some effort, I pulled myself almost together and headed for the Zepfs. If I did the job, maybe he would relent about Shauna.

Why did I take it? Don't think I didn't ask myself countless times. Sure he was insufferable at times, but he was also great. And I was perhaps the only person on earth who believed in him enough to go out and tell the Zepfs to hang in there. In spite of the bleak history of tobacco cases for plaintiffs, Bomber was not a loser. I did feel good about having Don Powell in our pocket. I was a skeptic as far as miracles were concerned, but I had seen Bomber bring off miracles and I was itching to see him do it again—if only to demonstrate to Shauna that there was more to life than easy money.

So it was back to the farm for the messenger of millions—me. It wasn't difficult to imagine what the poor Zepfs were thinking. What was more difficult to imagine was how to dissuade them from the easiest money they would ever hope to see.

We all have low spots where our emotions get the better of our judgment. I'm talking the Zepfs. I went out there to lend a hand (just as Shauna had). I invited them out to lunch, and you'd think I had offered a round trip to the moon the way they took on. The little ones got super-squirrelly.

Rich tried to beg off, but the girls wouldn't hear of it. They were so excited, he quickly caved in. I didn't dare ask when the last time they had been out to eat was, but by their behavior and expression of wonder in the simple family place I took them, it might have been never. For those six and under, I was sure of it. How, I wondered, had they ever learned to play waitress?

It was one of those cutsey places with a make-believe thatch roof and turrets and little cross-hatch windowpanes. It put me in mind of Knott's Berry Farm in Southern California, and the girls were in heaven.

Inside, the bare wood floors and rustic beamed ceilings assured the noise level would always be high. The tables were dark-oak planks and the chairs were just as hard. I always said you had to be strong to live in these rugged climates, and the restaurant chairs did nothing to make it easier.

I sat at one end of the oak slab—we put Rich at the head of the table, befitting the head of this unique family. Carrie was across from me and they sort of worked down in ages to the other end.

There was a lot of excitement with the menu and the pre-readers wanting to know what it said.

The waitress was in pleasant thrall of the kids. She was somewhere between voting age and menopause and was enormously fat, just bulging out of her white uniform dress. If her size made her self-conscious, there was no evidence of it. She had a name tag that proclaimed her "Norma," and she spoke with a Pennsylvania Dutch accent you could cut with a bulldozer, if you could drive it fast enough.

During the ceremonious ordering, which took perhaps three times the normal time, Norma displayed laudable patience. I had mixed feelings about a waitress going the extra mile. It always conspired to shame me into a larger tip which was an anathema to my penurious (by necessity, let us be fair) nature.

The ordering completed, Rich said, "What does Bomber want us to do?" Just asking the question seemed to lift a lead weight from his chest.

"He wants to go to trial," I answered brightly, my face lighting up like a pinball machine ("I thought you'd never ask."). My utter frankness was met with a stone-cold, deader'n-a-doornail silence. And it didn't take me long to realize my faux pas. I'm not *that* dense. So a little back peddling seemed in order.

"I wish I could tell you my father is only interested in your financial welfare, but he just isn't that kind of animal. I could give you some malarkey about him only wanting what is best for you, which for better or worse, is not true; and tell you the final decision is entirely up to you—which it is. But I have the feeling you wanted me to be honest about it."

Rich nodded once, as though he were not sure. "Your Shauna gave another take on it," he said.

"Yes, she's all compassion, and if compassion is your bag, there is no other decision but to take the money."

"It's a lot," Carrie said.

"Like winning the lottery," Barbara said.

"It is that," I agreed. "That and more," I said quietly.

"More?" Carrie was perplexed.

I dropped my face gravely. "T. S. Armstead just hiked their offer a million." There was a collective gasp around the table. My head continued to bob; I found I couldn't stop nodding. It was a poor substitute for finding the right words, but it was better than nothing. I could see, even in the littlest head, a doubling of all the dolls they had imagined they could buy, world cruises, big automobiles, designer dresses—who knew what the older girls imagined.

Rich spoke first. "Well, it looks like getting Bomber to take our case was the best thing we ever did."

The girls voiced their agreement.

Carrie said, "And it's all thanks to you."

Of course, I demurred, but they would have none of it.

"And," Rich said, "it also appears all we have to do to get more is say nothing."

That was going to be a difficult proposition to deny. I could see already I was in some pretty deep soup.

"Why does Bomber want to try the case?" Rich asked.

"To make his case about the evil of cigarettes. Probably also to show he can win when all the others lost."

"Do you think he can?"

"I've seen a lot of cases go his way I never thought would."

"Yeah, but what about this one?" Rich asked.

I found myself repeating all the arguments I had made to Shauna, but to a more receptive audience. I ended by adding what I had come to believe was my Mafia litany.

"For decades, the Feds seemed stymied by organized crime. The best they were able to achieve was a few convictions for income tax evasion. Then they suddenly got informers from within the ranks and things began to turn. Now jails are suddenly filling up with big-cheese mobsters."

One of the little girls got the giggles over "big cheese," and we all shared her amusement for a few moments.

"What's that got to do with us?" Carrie asked, bringing us back to earth.

"We have an insider we think will turn the case."

"You believe you can win?" Rich asked.

"I believe it. Bomber believes it."

"Shauna doesn't," Carrie said.

"So I've heard," I said. "But Shauna has never seen Bomber try a case."

"We haven't either," Rich reminded me.

"True," I said. "And no one denies the decision is two-and-a-half million."

"How much is the fee on that?" Carrie asked.

I shook my head.

"You mean he still won't take any fee—out of two-and-a-half million?"

I just kept shaking.

"And what about Shauna and the rest?"

I smiled. "If you're including me in that, we have all been paid up to our expectations."

"Not Shauna," Carrie said. "She says she was supposed to get a bonus if you won, and if we take the money it's same's winning."

"Does, does she?" I said. "Well, I guess Bomber couldn't pay out of his share if he doesn't take any. But you could always pay her. You would be getting Bomber's fees."

"We don't want his part."

I threw up my hands in that gesture of hopelessness.

When the food came, I was quietly appalled at the junk I saw set before the girls—burgers, fries, cokes, chips, all the worst. But I guess they deserved a celebration. I was unashamedly gratified to see how much they enjoyed it and thoughtfully refrained from further conversation while this stupendous treat was being ravished.

Then Rich Zepf got to the point. "What would you do if you were us?"

"I'd like to tell you I'd fight it out on principle. But as someone once said, principle is for the rich. I'm very much afraid I'd take the money and run, and as you can guess, that is not what I was sent here to say."

Rich smiled. All the girls' eyes were on me.

"But there are many answers. First, I would love to see Bomber try this case and bring big tobacco to its knees. Not easy, but if *anyone* could do it, Bomber could. And you must know their offering two-and-one-half million to you is *some* indication that they think so too. On the other level, if he wins you ten million and we get through two or three years of appeals, will that extra eight million change your lives that much? I don't think so. Then there is the other surprise factor of Shauna."

"Shauna? Why Shauna?" Carrie asked, probably intuiting that she had gotten her in trouble telling us about her visit.

"Bomber is quite angry she tried to talk you into the settlement."

"We asked for her opinion," Rich said.

"But she had an agenda. You shouldn't know about her bonus. That should not enter into your decision."

"But we *like* Shauna," said little Jodi.

"Yes," I said, "so do I. And that's the problem. Bomber told me to fire her."

"*Fire* her?"

"Yeah. And much as I like her, what she did—probably with the best intentions—was unprofessional conduct. So Bomber would be justified."

"So what did you tell Bomber?" Carrie asked, "when he told you to fire her, I mean."

"I said no."

A cheer went up from around the old oak table. I held up my hand. "That was a hollow victory," I said, "but he can do it himself. He doesn't like to, but he is not a man who got where he is by letting people go around him."

"But we needed her help. We're glad she talked to us." Jodi said. "What's that got to do with our decision, anyway?"

"I don't want her fired, so if you take the money that won't be necessary."

"Oh."

"Then the third level," I continued, my eyes taking in all the girls, "is the one of public awareness. The case will make the news. People will get stirred up, take sides—and they won't all be friendly to you. You might as well prepare for that. The company will defend itself with a viciousness you never imagined. They will seek to make fools of you. They'll drag your mom through the mud, they will belittle your father as a man who refuses to take responsibility for his own actions."

"So maybe that's not so good," Barbara said. They were all participating. It gave me a good feeling.

"Good *and* bad," I said. "If you take the money, no one will know anything. That's what would disappoint Bomber. He never dreamed the company would offer a settlement. They never have before, you know. He's a showman—and that may not be in your best interests. But he wouldn't have come all this way and invested all this money to have the tobacco company walk away with a payoff. That's not in his nature."

"But he refuses his part of the settlement," June said. "He could *pay* all his expenses."

"Yes, and have some left. Out of two-and-a-half million,

he'd get seven-hundred-fifty thou'. But that's just why he isn't taking it. He isn't doing this for the money, and this is his way of proving it. He *does* work for money sometimes. But, this is a case he *feels*. And when he really *feels* a case, there's no stopping him."

"Well," Rich said, "we all want to thank you for helping us out like this. I hope you won't get fired from talking to us."

I laughed. "No, I'm not trying to convince you to take the money. I'm trying to explain the options—and Bomber *knows* I'm here."

"But you said you'd take it, you wuz us," Miriam said.

"But he told us the other side, too," Carrie said.

"And lastly," I said. "One of the big reasons we took your case was because we were crazy about your family." I could see the older girls blushing, the younger ones were giggling. "Naturally, we thought you'd all be real assets in court—on the news at night—pictures of the Zepf girls, count'em cousin, looks like an even dozen. You might even get movie contracts."

Several of the girls unconsciously fussed with their hair and I realized I had said a very good thing.

We drove back to the Zepf's mini-farm and they left me with outlandish flattery, which all sounded to me like a swan song and I was disappointed, but not surprised. Rich said they would give us their decision in a day, but I was sure they had already decided.

22

Back at the hotel, Bomber was no more optimistic than I was. I decided to call from my room to check in with our ace witness to see if that would cheer the old man up.

It was a mistake.

"You!" Don Powell snapped at me in the phone. "Who is this goon you put on me?" he demanded up front.

"Excuse me?"

"This *goon*. He will not do! I can't even talk to him. It's like he's deaf and dumb."

"Talk to—"

"Well, hell yes, he's so obvious it's an embarrassment. I thought you said the guy would be unobtrusive. I tried to tell him that—just turns a deaf ear and snarls."

It hit me, not right away, but I finally caught on. "Don," I said, "That's not our man."

"Of course, it is. I *asked* for him."

"You *what*?"

"Asked for him. Things were getting weird around here. The goon is outside in his car," he said, his voice trembling. "I can see him from here."

"He's not ours."

"No? Then where, pray tell, *is* yours?"

"We don't have anyone. I didn't know you wan—"

"What do you mean, didn't know," he cut me off. "I called what's-her-face and told her I was getting uncomfortable."

"Shauna?"

"That's the number you gave me, wasn't it?"

"Yeeesss. What did she say?"

"Said she'd take care of it. Then this idiot shows up and he's all wrong."

It was all sinking in, and I was sinking with it.

"Did you, ah, tell her?"

"Damn right. Called her right away. Said she'd look into it."

"Oh—and—?"

"Nothing. He's still riding me." He sounded at the very end of his rope. "Called her again, no answer—got a machine."

"How long's that been?"

"Couple days maybe. Never called back."

"There must be some mistake," I said. "We will get you a man—today. He can watch both of you."

"They're on to me," he said into the phone in a half hoarse whisper. "It's all coming down."

"Listen," I tried to be reassuring, "try not to panic. The company must be in a panic. They offered two-and-a-half million to settle."

"They did?"

"Not the sign of robust confidence, is it? Neither is putting an obvious shadow on you."

"It's like he's here to intimidate me," he said. "There is definitely something weird going on—almost like they suspect something."

"How *could* they?" I asked, but I was afraid I knew the answer. "If they really wanted to catch you at something, the tail would be hidden. They're obviously trying to scare you."

"They're succeeding."

When I replaced the phone in its cradle, I did so gingerly, as though I didn't dare rock the airwaves. I sat there staring at the instrument wondering what to do next. Obviously, I had to call North Carolina and set up the guard. Simple enough, I had already laid the groundwork. One phone call is all, yet I couldn't move. All my feelings for Shauna bubbled in my throat and brought with them the taste of my lunch.

It *could not be*, I tried to convince myself. There is some giant misunderstanding here. I only wished I had the imagination to make up a logical explanation. I'd even be willing to sacrifice the logic.

Then I found myself wishing the Zepfs would take the money and run. That should forestall the need for any unpleasantness with Shauna. A wonderful old adage came to mind, "Never murder a person who is committing suicide." I don't know why that popped into my head, it didn't really apply, but the principle was the same.

I called the security company in North Carolina and they said they would have a man there within two hours. I made a mental note to call Powell at seven to make sure it had all worked.

When I got to Bomber's "headquarters," he was on the phone with Easy Willie. They were discussing the deposition schedule.

There was a rumble in the hallway and then a knock on Bomber's door. Bomber gave one of his gestures of terminal impatience at the interruption. I opened the door to the whole Zepf clan, and they were all smiling.

It was an old saw at law that if the jury didn't look at you on their way back from deliberation, you were finished. The Zepfs couldn't take their eyes off us.

The girls wheeled their father in front of the desk facing Bomber. Each stood around him with the happy face of expectancy.

"We have come to offer you a deal," Rich began.

Bomber's face soured immediately. "I don't make deals," he said.

Mother always wished she could get someone to give Bomber tact lessons.

But the Zepfs were too full of excitement to be discouraged.

"We talked this thing ragged, all baker's dozen of us. And what we come up with is something we hope'll make ever'body happy—'cause we just think you all coming into our lives is the best thing ever happened to us."

Now, after a recitation like that from a blind man in a wheelchair, a man dying of lung cancer who is obviously about to turn his back on two-and-a-half-million bucks you'd think there wouldn't be a dry eye in the house. Mine weren't dry, but the big guy behind the desk was staring at Rich Zepf with such ferocity I was glad Rich couldn't see him.

"So we decided you was right 'bout making a stand. That's what we wanted in the first place. Oh, we know we might not come out of it with a penny, but we'll stick with you whatever you say."

"At last," Bomber said, "someone is showing some sense."

"There is one thing we'd like to ask," Rich said.

"Oh?" It was not a neutral "Oh?" more a where-do-you-think-you-get-off-at? "Oh."

"The girls got kinda fond of Shauna an' all—"

I saw Bomber tense. He knew what was coming.

"So, we all thought you could try the case like you want, if you don't fire her. She was only trying to help us out."

Bomber turned the color of raw liver. I thought all the vessels in his face were going to blow their blood simultaneously.

For a while, their faces seemed to square off on each other, Rich like he was trying to place Bomber in the darkness, Bomber like he could cut through Rich's blindness.

"Let me tell you something, sir," Bomber said. "In all my career I have never countenanced a client telling me how to run my business; who to hire, who to keep, who to fire, what arguments to make, what witnesses to depose."

Rich and the girls were rapidly getting the picture.

"I'm afraid my staff is beyond the bounds of your say in the matter."

Rich was brokenhearted. He seemed to shrink to half his size. Not knowing Bomber, he had severely misjudged him. He probably visualized his being so ecstatic at the decision, he would gladly grant their request. Of course, they didn't know the whole story on Shauna—but, then, neither did Bomber.

"Could you," Rich spoke as a humbler supplicant now, "at least…consider it?"

"In the context of your moral blackmail, you mean?" Bomber was rumbling just like the land did near the epicenter of an earthquake, and I didn't want to be anywhere near him for the tremors and aftershocks. I hastily suggested I escort the Zepfs back to their truck and we could all sleep on it.

Bomber shot me one of his mind-your-own-business-kid looks, but I was busy heading the squirrels into the corridor and onto the elevator with my extravagant, if somewhat nervous, praise for their courageous decision.

When I got back to Bomber's "headquarters," I told him about Don Powell—and no sooner had I got the last word out my mouth than Bomber said, "The bitch!"

When he insisted again that I fire her, I said "No." So he said, "All right, then bring her here and I'll do it."

"When would—"

"Now!"

I stopped back in my room to exercise the plumbing, and the phone rang. I snapped it up—just knowing it would be Shauna.

"Hi, Tod, it's your mother calling," she said as she always did on the phone, as though I wouldn't recognize her voice.

"Hi, Mom," I said.

"How's that romance going back there?"

"I'm just going to see her now," I said, truthfully.

"Oh, good," she enthused. "I won't keep you. Is your father doing all right?"

"Fine form," I said.

"Good—well, I'll call again—and Tod?"

"Yes?"

"If you have any announcements to make, you'll tell me won't you?"

"You'll be the first to know," I said.

"Oh, good," she said.

I sucked up what little courage I could, and made a bee-line for Shauna's office. She wasn't there and the shared receptionist didn't really seem to know when she would be back. Shauna's door was not locked, so I went in and rifled the place—with maximum dignity—and found no clues to anything. I packed up all the files she had on our case and took them with me. I had been a fixture around there, and the receptionist wasn't even looking when I went out with the armload of folders and envelopes. I dumped the stash at my hotel room and walked on down to the garage—got the rental car and drove to that row house I thought so fondly of as a love nest.

Nobody answered the door. I must have knocked obnoxiously because the door next door opened—only about four feet away in this row of doors, windows and front porches.

Shauna's neighbor spoke to me from inside the closed screen door. I backed up so I could see her. She wore a faded print dress that fit her like a sack of potatoes.

"Ain't home," she said. "Gone away."

"You know where?"

She shook her head. This was not a woman anyone would look at twice. I wondered what she had heard through the common wall. "Went with plenty suitcases though. Must be nice to go on a holiday like that."

"When did they leave?"

"'S mornin'," she said shaking her head in frank disapproval. "Took a taxi when they got a perfectly good car in the garage."

I thanked her and drove back to the hotel to share the news with Bomber.

He nodded, fatalistically. "Thanks for sharing," he said, and I felt smaller than usual. He may have muttered something about Bonnie Doone being right about the organ I used for my hiring, but I ignored it.

"Is there any point in trying to find her?"

"Damage control?" he snarled. "I'm afraid it's *out* of

control. The only reason I can think of to locate the redheaded wench is to put her pea-brain in a jar of formaldehyde."

I winced at that, but I noted he had dropped the decibel level from bitch to wench.

Bomber seemed willing to forget her and move on. And move on we did with a hectic two weeks of depositions of the enemy-witness list, including President Ed Jones, who aw-shucksed his way through his grilling like he hadn't a care in the world. Bomber, I must say, went very easy on him. I imagined he was feeling his way with him for the trial, and there is nothing so futile and so counterproductive to a jury than to turn on the histrionics to a guy who doesn't take the bait.

After he'd finished with President Jones, Bomber turned to me, and looked me square in the eye with that look I had learned to dread. "I've got this terrible intuition, boy. We've been hit in the face with too many pies from the redheaded wench. Call Powell up. Tell him under no circumstances open the door to any redheads. Tell him to lay low, take a vacation, call in sick, until we can get his testimony."

"You don't think they'd k-k-kill him, do you?"

Bomber got one of his deep-thinking looks, like he was battling in his mind to try and rid it of unpleasant thoughts.

"Don't you?" he asked through a golden-arched eyebrow.

I did.

23

The birds loved the cute white cupola on top of the courthouse. Pedestrians were advised to give it a wide berth when the winged creatures were in residence.

Inside, there were corridors you could drive a Mack truck through, and a regal staircase at the end of the hall which took you up to the courtrooms. Number one, being the closest to the head of the stairs, was a barn of a room with honest-to-God oak slab benches like an upscale church. It was the courtroom built for a large audience, long before television usurped the entertainment attraction of a court case and a good hanging.

On the walls around the courtroom were oil paintings of the judges who formerly sat, as they say, in these hallowed halls. The artistry was as pedestrian as you might expect when the contracts were let to the local low bidders.

The Zepfs, bless their hearts, swallowed their pride and subverted their wishes to those of the great Bomber. They stood tall in my book, when they turned their backs on two-and-a-half million bucks and subjected themselves to the rigors of a court trial. Offhand, I couldn't think of anyone else in my acquaintance who would have had the guts to make that decision.

The thing about trying a case in Pennsylvania was they had all this old stuff and these quaint customs. They had what they called a court crier, who before every session whacked a gavel on a hunk of granite at the foot of the judge's bench.

Judge Druckenmiller made his entrance with a stern countenance.

"All rise!" the crier cried, and we rose.

"Oyez! Oyez! Oyez! All manner of persons having anything to do before the Honorable Judge Fritz Druckenmiller, Judge of the Court of Common Pleas, Gratz County,

Pennsylvania, let them come forward and be heard. God save the Commonwealth and this honorable court."

Another whack with the gavel.

"Please be seated."

The guy was a very old party, but his voice was strong. Judge Druckenmiller took a load off his feet with the aid of a high-backed chair that immediately dropped back on his impact. He remained in that position for a few reflective moments, then leaned forward to do battle.

All the parties-at-interest, as they say, were piled into the courtroom to await the pleasure of Judge Druckenmiller.

"I'm assigning the case to myself," Judge Druckenmiller announced from the bench, the sentence giving him the opportunity to use two personal pronouns, his favorite kind of words.

Judge Druckenmiller was a large man, more in width than height. His friends called him big, his enemies called him fat. We were all so hoping we might be included in the former category.

His round, pudgy face was highlighted with the shiny black patch over his right eye. He could have lived without it. Could he have thought it made him look distinguished? Black *was* a slimming color, after all, but there just wasn't enough of it. Even in his black robe, Judge Druckenmiller looked like the Goodyear blimp.

The judge's personality had been honed on years of self-righteous Sunday school teaching. Some years ago, when he had won the partisan race for judge of the Court of Common Pleas of Gratz County, he was fresh off a lackluster spin as district attorney. He had defeated the incumbent who had a reputation for being a hard drinker and a soft-hearted womanizer.

God got a good workout in that campaign. Druck made a lot of speeches in churches invoking the almighty, peppered with his admonitions against drunkenness and whoring. And his wife went door to door suggesting Druck's opponent didn't have the moral stature to be a judge. Never mind that he was twice the lawyer Druck was and four times the judge he would become, the innuendo and slander took its toll. The real jurist went down to defeat while Druck ascended to the bench, which was about the only thing he could ascend to without getting winded. Thenceforth to be addressed a "Your Honor."

We gleaned this perspective, of course, from our resident sage, Easy Willie. Bomber discussed the judge for hours with him, including Easy Willie's detailed advice, drawn from years of observation and an accumulation of just plain lawyer gossip.

After all that time and scholarly analysis, Bomber concluded that what was called for was a generous dose of butt-kissing. And he could perform that feat along with the best of them. What he was less adept at was camouflaging the cynicism and sarcasm he felt when down on his knees to one he thought was an inferior being.

I was looking forward to the combat. It could hardly help but be amusing.

"Both sides ready?" We said we were. It had been a long haul.

Judge Druckenmiller intoned the fateful words, "Impanel the jury." It always reminded me of impaling. Impale the jury, I thought. We don't use all these fancy sayings in California.

"Your Honor, if I could have a moment, please," Bomber said, "before the jury panel comes in?"

"Yes, Mr. Hanson."

"I should like to identify the people at the defendant's table for the record."

"All right—would you gentlemen state your names and association please."

"Earl Lictenwalner," the casually friendly one said. "I'm mayor of Cedarberg and local counsel for T. S. Armstead." He seemed rather proud of himself.

Next old tall-dark-and handsome stood up in an eight-hundred dollar suit. "Jonathan R. Peters," he said, "local counsel for T. S. Armstead." He sat down.

"Could I have the name of his firm?" Bomber asked

Judge Druckenmiller.

The judge nodded. Peters stood back up. "Backenstoe, Druckenmiller, and Peters," he said with a coy smile on his lips, then he sat.

"Your Honor, correct me please, if I am wrong, but doesn't the Druckenmiller in Mr. Peters' firm name refer to you?"

"I no longer practice law there," he said.

"But they kept your name?"

"Apparently so," he said. "No law against it. They seem to think it helps. But it could work the other way, too." There could have been a tiny smile on his lips.

Harrison J. Hinkle stood. "Your Honor, we will have no need to identify Mr. Peters' law firm in these proceedings, if that's what Mr. Hanson is worried about. I'm sure keeping Your Honor's name was just a matter of convenience to keep from having to change the stationery."

"Is that so?" Bomber asked. "Stationery, huh? You don't suppose they see any benefit from having the president judge of the county in the firm name?"

"Are you asking me to excuse myself from the case?" the judge asked, looking hard at Bomber.

"No, Your Honor, but I would not mind if Mr. Peters disappeared from the counsel table—for the sake of the impression it might make on the jury."

"You have county counsel at your table," Hinkle said.

"Not a law partner of the judge's."

Hinkle shrugged. "You could have. Why don't you hire Mr. Backenstoe?"

"Oh, really," Bomber said. "You don't have any ethical compunctions about a firm representing opposite interests?"

"Well, you could have tried to hire him earlier. We will have others at the table from time to time and I may as well mention them now." And he did, including spit-polished Norm Stimmel from from Bortz, Hillegas, Stimmel, and Klerx.

"Any objections?" Judge Druckenmiller asked.

"Your Honor, I have no desire to interfere with Mr.

Hinkle's battalion of lawyers. If I had a case as weak as his, I'd want an army to prop me up too. The question I have is, with so many lawyers on his payroll, why is it necessary to showcase the ever-popular mayor of the town along with a law partner of the judge at the counsel table? Why not use Mr. Stimmel, or any number of the men and women he mentioned?"

"Is counsel for the plaintiff suggesting he should be in a position to dictate how we try our case?" Harrison Hinkle asked the judge.

"Certainly not," Bomber answered. "I wouldn't have the least idea how to defend such a hopeless case. So if you are looking for help from me, Mr. Hinkle, I'm afraid it won't be forthcoming."

"I will appreciate that," Hinkle said.

"But I would be seriously remiss in my client's behalf if I didn't strenuously object to the political and moral blackmail we have represented at defendant's table."

"Blackmail?"

"Certainly! What else? You don't need to put a sign on Mr. Peters for these small-town jurors to know they were law partners. And the ever-popular mayor? Come on."

"So what are you suggesting?" Judge Druckenmiller asked Bomber.

"I'm asking that they be removed from the counsel table and be barred from any visible association with the defense. If their advice and counsel, and whatever other services they might give are deemed vital, or even important to the defense, I have not the slightest objection to their being employed along with the millions of other lawyers in the service of the tobacco industry. The judge will still know which side of the fence his law partner is on, but at least the jury won't know."

"Mr. Hinkle?" Judge Druckenmiller looked at the defense attorney.

"Your Honor, this is a tempest in a teapot if I ever saw one."

"Good," Bomber interrupted, "then banish them."

"Let me finish," Hinkle said. "The defendant has a

right to counsel of his choice. Mr. Hanson is nitpicking. I might even be moved to say his are stalling tactics."

"Stalling!" Bomber was appalled at the inference. "Get those ringers out of here and you'll see who is stalling."

"Your Honor," Harrison Hinkle said, "He's being tedious, and we've just begun. If anyone should be objecting to grandstanding showmanship, it should be I. He has the plaintiff at his table with an oxygen tank."

"He needs it to live," Bomber said.

"Maybe…"

"Thanks to your client's lethal products. Modern science is doing all it can to foil the quick death you boys peddle."

"Gentlemen!" Druckenmiller said impatiently.

"And that's not to mention the cute-as-a-bug-in-a-rug girls he has filling the front benches. Let's ban them while we're at it."

"The plaintiff and his family?" Bomber asked with that counterfeit incredulity he was so good at.

"If you want to talk about blackmail. *There's* emotional blackmail."

"I'm glad to know you see it as such," Bomber said. "It's high time big tobacco recognizes the emotional impact they have on all these poor people whom they addict to their weeds."

"Gentlemen, no more." Druckenmiller said. "Certainly we are not going to bar the plaintiff and his family from the courtroom."

"Thank you, Your Honor," Bomber said.

"As for defendant's counsel, I don't see how I can legally limit them in their appearances. I will, however, instruct the jury at the first opportunity that they are not to be influenced by it, and I will so charge them at the end of the trial."

"May I note an exception for the record," Bomber said.

"Noted," Judge Druckenmiller said. Not, I thought, happily.

Instructing the jury thusly was tantamount to reminding them which side of the case these community leaders were on. I expected Bomber to use his they-ganged-up-on-us spiel when we wrapped it all up.

Then Harrison Hinkle petitioned the court to ban the media and prohibit any of the principals from talking to them during the trial.

When you see what a circus some trials become, thanks to a voracious media, it's hard to argue against what seems to be a reasonable position.

Bomber, of course, did argue. Bomber loved circuses. He thrived on them and he trotted out the Constitution, free speech, freedom of access, of information, the works. It was one of the reasons he took the case. And the Zepfs were so photogenic.

A judge is always on the spot with the media. First, he or she wants good press and doesn't want to aggravate its lords and ladies. Second, it is a rare person who can shun the limelight. We've all harbored ambitions to be movie stars at one time or another, I suspect. Especially in this trade.

Well, the Buddha surprised me. He ruled for Hinkle. The best we would get would be silent pictures of the darling Zepfs on the courthouse steps. But Bomber would make the most of that and see that they all, Rich included, were arranged to their best advantage for entrances and exits. And we all were together. No sense wasting these photo opportunities on the plaintiff alone.

"All right gentlemen," Judge Druckenmiller said. "Are we ready to impanel the jury?"

"Ready, Your Honor," Hinkle said.

"Yes," Bomber said. And before you knew it, a whole flock of jurors poured into the room as if off the conveyor belt at one of those mega-chicken farms.

For jurors, we wanted types that favored a government to more or less control what we did to ourselves, from driving unsafe cars and motorcycles without helmets, to what we chose to put in our bodies, like fatty meats and sugar and salt-laced instant foods. And cigarettes. We didn't want libertarians who didn't want anybody telling anybody what to do. We wanted jurors who felt not everyone could take care of themselves, not everyone could be responsible for all their actions, and what was a big brother for, if not to look out for his helpless siblings.

Perhaps, the most elusive juror was the one who smoked. We certainly didn't want any juror that thought cigarettes were perfectly safe, or that death from them was merely a matter of individual body make-up. Or who believed anyone could quit smoking if they only wanted to.

We also didn't want anyone who disbelieved the preponderance of scientific evidence that claimed smoking *caused* cancer and a host of other killing diseases. There was a case in Oklahoma where the judge excluded from the jury anyone who believed those scientific studies, which had the effect of barring from the jury anyone who was honest and intelligent.

Harrison Hinkle put up the same battle here. Prejudicial, he called it—preconceived opinions detrimental to objective deliberation. Buddha, bless his heart, didn't buy it.

It was precisely on the night of that first day of trial that the bomb was dropped—on the Bomber himself, on the Zepfs, on Easy Willie, on me, and on everyone we hold dear.

It was a though Bomber had been expecting it all along. "Reds just dropped the other shoe," he said.

I argued this could not be her doing—she didn't have that kind of power.

He only nodded his head the way he does when he doesn't agree with you. "Her footprints all over the place," he said. "You think it would have happened without her? Where did they get the information he was testifying? He wasn't on our list, you know."

I couldn't disagree. Gina had called all hysterical, and I couldn't blame her. The cops had arrested her husband at work for embezzlement. The only lawyers he knew were company lawyers, and the one she had gotten out of the phonebook, who didn't seem to know what he was doing.

Bomber volunteered my services.

24

My heels were ice cold by the time I was permitted an audience with the district attorney of Benson County, North Carolina. It had given me time to concentrate on forgetting Shauna. I knew I had to get over her, I just didn't know how.

The office exuded southern charm, as did the secretary when she told me how busy the district attorney was—certainly I could wait, she just didn't want me to be inconvenienced at all.

The D. A. was a guy my age, but I could tell he wouldn't be D. A. long. Ambition flared from his broad nostrils. He had all the attributes of a man who could shoot up the political ladder in a flash: he was tall, good looking with an ingratiating manner—and bland. He was a guy who studiously combed his hair to make it look windblown—like he was always on the go. I could see him as a golfing buddy of Ed Jones.

And in this job, he got an unerring sense of where the bodies were buried—knowledge that could come in handy in this milieu.

He stuck out his hand. "Tim Emmons," he said, "glad to meet you, Mr. Hanson. Sit down, sit down," he waved me generously into a chair on the visiting side of the stadium-sized desk he had. I really felt like I was in the bleachers at one of those prime sporting events—and the hard-to-get tickets had been furnished by generous Tim Emmons himself.

"Don Powell," I said as I slipped into the plush velveteen upholstered chair.

He sat in his high-backed throne that reminded me of something from the minute I walked into the room—then I realized—it was a leather-covered swivel job like Judge Druckenmiller had. A judgeship could well be the next stop for

D.A. Emmons but my guess was he'd find that too confining. Governor would be more like it, and his chair wouldn't be out of place there either.

"Ah yes," he said, "Don Powell. So very sad. Company was as good as they could be to him, but," he threw apart his hands to show me just how hopeless the situation was—"apparently it wasn't enough."

"I know Don Powell," I said. "I can tell you categorically he did not embezzle so much as a nickel."

He nodded like you do when you think you know better. "What is your interest in Don Powell, anyway? You're a California lawyer aren't you?"

I admitted that was true, and told him my interest was privileged.

He laughed; it was a good-old-boy laugh with the blonde head tilting back and the body quaking just enough to prove he wasn't faking it. "That's a good one," he said. "You think there's anyone in this town doesn't know what you are trying to do to our town?"

"Do to you?"

"Rob us of our livelihoods."

"You mean if we win our case the county will do without a district attorney?"

"Not hardly. Crime'd be way up, I expect—nobody being able to earn a living."

"That have something to do with why Don Powell is in jail?"

"We don't know why he took the money, but it isn't hard to speculate."

"Speculate," I said.

The big hands went apart again. *I* speculated he had played basketball and could hold one basketball in each hand. "Trying to get a nice nest egg before he turns on the company," he said. "Makes sense."

I shook my head.

He spread his hands. "Lot of evidence," he said. "Air-tight as they come."

"How so?"

"It's been in all the papers."

"All? I haven't seen it."

"Well, all around here anyway. It was a simple enough scam. He set-up dummy vendors—sent through requisitions, dumped the money in his account."

"He sign the checks?"

He shook his head. "Controller signs all the checks for the company. Powell requested them."

"How?"

"Verbally."

"That's okay?" I said, shocked.

"Not for just anyone, but he *was* the head of manufacturing. A key player."

"You will, of course, release him in custody to testify at our trial, should we need him?"

"Oh, yes, there was some question of that," he said, "but then we noticed he was not scheduled to be called, so that was a relief."

"Not scheduled?"

"He wasn't on your witness list, apparently."

There it was—naturally! Bomber's ploy had backfired. But they must have known he was to testify for us or they wouldn't have framed him. How could they have known? Only one person, I'm afraid, could have told them.

"Are you acquainted with a young woman named Shauna McKinley?" I asked the D.A.

He seemed to ponder the name.

"She was redheaded on last sighting."

"I can't say that I am," he said. "Should I be?"

"I hope not," I mumbled. "Do you think you could get me in to see Don Powell?"

"Why certainly," he said, and it sounded so easy. I had already spent a day trying to break into prison to see him—I had been rebuffed at every turn, and I told him.

"Ah," he said, as though there were nothing to it. "Should have come to me first."

"I did."

"Oh?"

I nodded. "Wouldn't let me in. You were tied up in court, in meetings, away from your desk, out for the day. Just depended who you spoke to what the excuse was."

"Oh, I'm sorry," he said. "Sometimes they are *too* protective. Here," he said, and scrawled something on a piece of his official stationery. He handed it to me. It read:

> Please admit Tod Hanson, attorney
> -at-law to visit Prisoner Don Powell.
> (Signed), Tim Emmons

More than that I didn't need. I thanked him and gave him my back.

Driving out to the prison, I looked in every car for Shauna. No luck.

My note worked wonders, and in minutes I was seated in the visitor's cell facing our star witness.

I will never feel comfortable inside of a jail as long as I live. I don't care where it is, what size it is, what government entity runs it—it's the clanking of the metal doors and the smell of disinfectant they all seemed to have in common. I wonder if every visitor shares my fear that once inside they might not let me out?

"How are you holding up?" I asked Don Powell.

"You want to look at the bright side," he said, "I lost five pounds already."

"Well, good," I said, "I guess."

"'I guess' is right. What this place needs is a good food riot."

"You going to start one?"

"Tempted," he said.

"So what happened?" I asked, letting him tell it without

me grilling him.

"Caught me flatfooted," he said, startling me.

"You mean you did it? Stole the money?"

"Of course not, but I should have known *something* would happen. Gina is furious, but I tell her it could have been worse. They could have fitted me with a pair of cement shoes. This way I figure, I'll be out when the case is over."

"But, we're not going to take this lying down."

He shook his head. "Won't matter, they won't budge. It's so neat and perfect. Only needs one perjury to bring it off. Controller swears I requested the checks, then I deposited them in my account. Well, I know nothing about it until the cops come to my office, handcuff me and haul me off to the slammer. I had no *idea* what was going on, and that's where I was stupid."

"You did say something funny was going on," I reminded him, "when you asked for the bodyguard."

"Yeah. Maybe I did have a sixth sense about it," he said. "I just didn't act on it."

I asked about his lawyer and he said he was incompetent. "All the competent ones have done or do work for Armstead, so they are conflicted out of taking my case."

Then he surprised me. "Why don't you handle it?"

"I'm no trial lawyer—nothing more than an investigator really."

"What are you talking about?" he said. "You have a license, don't you?"

"Not in North Carolina."

"Nor in Pennsylvania either, but apparently there are ways around that."

I had to admit there were, but I didn't give up my protest.

"Just remember," he said, "you got me into this. Who better to get me out?"

"But the deck is stacked," I protested.

"Unstack it," he said. He was starting to sound like Bomber.

25

I interviewed a bunch of lawyers to represent Don Powell and what he said was true. Those few who the company didn't have their tentacles into did not seem to be too swift.

I did find a guy who I thought was smart enough, he just seemed to lack ambition. Shades of Easy Willie. Then I thought, why not? Easy Willie could do it. Let him associate with Easy Freddie down here in North Carolina and put a feather in his cap.

That night I called Bomber and he went for it. They had already seated five jurors and he thought another day and a half would do it.

"Easy Willie's been invaluable," Bomber said, which I took as a slam, since I had opposed his hiring. Next to my choice, the hiring of Shauna, Easy Willie turned out to be a star. I thought my suggesting him for the job in Churchill Park, North Carolina would put me on the side of the angels.

I was back in Cedarberg in time for the start of the testimony. I briefed Easy Willie on the situation with Don Powell and wished him good luck. He seemed pleased to be going to work in a place where they didn't know his history.

Bomber and I were at the plaintiff's table beside Rich Zepf with his oxygen rig. The girls were sitting in the front row of the audience on our side of the aisle. The younger ones' legs were dangling and they kicked them gently back and forth like they were swinging slowly—a luxury they had not often experienced.

Bomber had instructed them to wear their best dresses or pants outfits, but to wear the same ones every day. It wouldn't take long for the jurors to catch on to how hard a go life was when you were poor and had twelve kids. Sure, there could have been some birth control soreheads in the jury box, but that question was moot. The deed was done. And when you looked at a bunch of adorable kids, only the hardest heart could cry for birth control.

At the table to our left, facing the judge's bench, sat Harrison J. Hinkle, looking especially neatly turned out this morning. You see a lot of guys driving who have removed their suit jackets to keep them from getting rumpled. Hinkle looked like he did that not only with his jacket but his pants too—and probably his underwear. I looked at my father beside me—a symphony in contrast. Mother said he was colorblind and that's why he couldn't dress himself in a harmonious fashion. She instructed me to help make him more Ivy League like I was, but it was pretty hopeless. Today it was a brown jacket and blue pants. The tie had a purple cast to it. All that was redeeming in the outfit was the white shirt. All that saved me from despair was the realization that tomorrow would probably be worse.

Bomber's outfits seemed less outlandish in California where there were many casual dressers, even spilling over to the staid legal profession. But in this neck of Penn's woods, they still played dress-up in court and Bomber looked, well, funny.

"Can't be bothered, boy," is what he said. "Darrow wore suspenders," he added, as though that had the slightest connection. But I knew there was more to it. Bomber was a guy who not only could be bothered, but would be bothered about the tiniest detail. I expect the erratic dressing was to attract attention and to seem more down to earth—as most jurors were—than the Fancy Dans of the opposition.

With Harrison Hinkle were the ubiquitous and ever-popular mayor whose function seemed to be to smile at the jury, and Judge Druckenmiller's law partner whose function seemed to be to smile at the judge.

The guys who did the work, the young, eager, clerkish fellows, sat in a row of chairs with their backs to the railing that set the players off from the audience. They bounced back and forth like a truckload of agitated chickens, delivering notes, taking instructions in a great, distracting flurry of activity.

It didn't take long to realize we were going against real heavyweights this time. Some of the guys that had been thrown at us looked more like actors playing suave lawyers than lawyers themselves. And they talked like they had memorized their lines by rote, then added suitable gestures and facial expressions to them. Some of the gestures weren't that polished. And the actors seemed to have been typecast—chosen more for their looks than their acting ability.

Not Harrison J. Hinkle. He has been honed in a machine shop to zero tolerance and spit polished. And he was no dummy. When you had billions of dollars, you could buy brains. You could buy *anything*. They bought Shauna, didn't they? Miss Morality, Miss Ethics, and they bought her. Easy Willie warned us he would sell out, then told us they offered. Why wasn't I smart enough to realize if they went for him they would go for Shauna? Research, I thought, couldn't be that vulnerable. I kept wanting to believe they had blackmailed her somehow—or there was some other factor more palatable to a judgmental society than filthy lucre.

I looked from God's gift to tonsorial perfection, Harrison J. Hinkle, to Rich Zepf who sat on my right with his oxygen tank on the table. Usually the principal for each side sat in the middle. Rich needed the extra room for his paraphernalia.

Bomber seemed pleased with the jury. All women would have been ideal, but we had seven of them. Women, we reasoned, especially of the older generation which had a way of making up jury panels, had a way of sympathizing with the underdog. It was all that compassion build in their genetic make-up.

"We could have a couple clinkers," was the way Bomber put it, "but it's a civil case, so we only need ten votes."

"But with our s-s-star wit-t-tness in jail…," I began, taking charge of the wet-blanket department.

"Overcome it," he said, "or better still, turn it to our

advantage. Trouble is, the latter will take more time, and I'm just about to ask for it."

"Your Honor," Harrison J. Hinkle spoke, ever so carefully, "I would like to make a request concerning the plaintiff's demeanor. I notice his oxygen tank is placed on the table in front of him. In order that he not unduly influence the jurors, I respectfully request the tank be put out of sight—perhaps on the floor."

"Can that be done, Mr. Hanson?" Judge Druckenmiller asked.

"Can that be done?" Bomber put on his incredulous show. "The man *needs* oxygen to live. We can pull the plug if you like. I'm sure Mr. Hinkle would like him to commit suicide."

"That's a little extreme," Hinkle said, "and uncalled for."

"It is somewhat distracting," the judge agreed.

"As is the beloved mayor smiling at the jury," Bomber added, "but I'm told we must live with that."

"That's just his nature," Harrison Hinkle said. "He's a politician."

"It's hard to tell a man not to smile," Judge Druckenmiller said. This came from a man who smiled rarely and when he did, you had to be alert or you would miss it.

"Perhaps so, but in my mind this case is not a smiling matter. A man's life has been ruined and is about to end because this company has addicted him to a lethal product."

"He addicted *himself*," Hinkle muttered.

"And here sits mayor what's-his-name smiling to beat the band as though he were in a Saint Paddy's day parade."

"Mr. Hanson," Judge Druckenmiller spoke, "is there any medical reason the tank cannot be stowed beneath the table?"

"I don't know that. I'm not his doctor."

"Could you find out?"

"I suppose I could, if we could have a recess."

"Oh, just ask the man himself," Harrison Hinkle said.

"He certainly knows."

"Ask him," Judge Druckenmiller said.

Bomber gave a short nod, then returned to the table and leaned over to whisper in Rich's ear. "Any reason you can think of the oxygen has to be in view?—before you answer, think hard. Any excuse to see it will do."

"Wish I could," Rich Zepf whispered back.

"Okay—at least we have the tubes. And every once in a while you can fiddle with the tank on the floor, okay?"

Zepf smiled. Bomber might make it a smiling matter after all.

"And by the way, I notice the tubes going into your nose are clear plastic. Why is that?"

"So they won't be so noticeable."

"Well, lets get some that *are* more noticeable. Can you?"

"Try."

"Atta boy," Bomber said aloud, patting Rich Zepf on the shoulder, then made a show of putting the tank on the floor and appearing to have great difficulty. Finally, he put it in Rich's lap—then turned to the judge.

"Your Honor, the tubes don't seem long enough to reach the floor."

"Can you get longer tubes?"

"We will try to do that tomorrow, assuming there is no detriment to the patient."

"Detriment?"

"Yes—if traveling a greater distance inhibits the oxygen flow or something. I'm not a doctor. He has agreed to hold it on his lap today until it gets too onerous. Unless the defendant's counsel would rather recess."

"No," Harrison said. "Let's get on with it. Just keep the tank out of sight, please."

"Are we ready for the jury, counsel?" Judge Druckenmiller asked.

"If I could have a moment, please?" Bomber asked.

The bulk behind the bench nodded, but not happily.

Bomber told it to the judge—standing beside Harrison Hinkle in front of Buddha's bench.

"Your Honor, the most dastardly act of my long, and if I may say, honored legal career has just befallen us. A witness crucial to our case, the one who would set our case apart from all the other tobacco cases, has been insidiously incarcerated at the behest of the company in the company town which is owned lock, stock and barrel by the same company fighting for its life in this case."

"Who is the witness?" Druckenmiller asked.

"Don Powell, Your Honor, head of manufacturing for the T. S. Armstead Company, the defendants in this case."

"But that's preposterous, Your Honor," Harrison J. Hinkle said. "This alleged witness's name is nowhere to be found on the witness list."

The half-Buddha squinted out of half a pair of eyes, then consulted some papers on his desk, rifling back and forth until he found the right page. "That appears to be the case, Mr. Hanson."

"We just got him to agree to testify—long after we made the list."

"Did you amend the list?" Harrison asked. "If you did, I didn't see it."

"You know the rules?" the judge asked.

"I stand corrected," Bomber said. "I was just about to hand him the amended list. I have it at counsel table. This is the dirtiest trick I've ever experienced."

I could have been wrong, but I thought Harrison Hinkle was smirking in our direction—out of sight of the one-eyed judge, of course.

"Your Honor, I respectfully request you issue a writ so this man may come up here to testify. He was going to blow this case to the heavens so they trumped up these charges against him. Desperate corporations will stop at nothing."

Harrison Hinkle interjected, "The charges were *not* trumped up, I can assure you."

"Baloney!" Bomber said.

The judge waved the argument off with his hand. "Save your arguments for the jury. If this witness is important to your case, submit to me your arguments and I will issue a writ *ad testifcondom*."

It wasn't much, but it kept some hope alive.

"Now gentlemen," Judge Druckenmiller said, "are we ready for the jury?"

Harrison Hinkle said he was, eyeing the oxygen tank in Rich Zepf's lap. I had to say this for Zepf, he was a real trouper, because while the tank was in his lap, it was not totally invisible. And from time to time it seemed to me he bobbed it up and down as though joggling a toddler on his lap.

As the jury filed in I could see Cedarberg's beloved mayor earning his money, smiling away and even now and then nodding in happy recognition of a juror.

The jurors themselves were a sturdy, upright-looking bunch. They seemed to be taking their job more seriously than the mayor.

When the jury was seated, Judge Druckenmiller looked at Bomber, "Do you have an opening statement, Mr. Hanson?"

"Yes, Your Honor." Bomber stood and strode over to the jury box, placing himself between the jurors and smiling Mayor Lictenwalner. And as he did so, he allowed himself the luxury of a small smile.

"Ladies and gentlemen of the jury, I salute you for your service here. This will be a complex trial and your attention to the details will be greatly appreciated.

"This is a case of responsibility.

"The plaintiff in this case, Mr. Rich Zepf, has been smoking the product of the defendant the T. S. Armstead Company for twenty-some years. He is a blind man, and unable to read warning labels on the package. This we will establish with his testimony that will include his confession that cigarettes have addicted him to the point where he was smoking four packs a day. You will be able to observe the plaintiff every day during this trial—God willing—and you can see he can only breathe with the aid of oxygen—which we will try and keep as unobtrusive as we can during this trial.

"We will not be seeing the defendant during this trial. T. S. Armstead Company is a multi-billion-dollar corporation headquartered in North Carolina where their product is manufactured.

"The plaintiff is visible, the defendant invisible."

"Your Honor," Harrison said, "he's making argument."

"Yes, Mr. Hanson, please confine your remarks to what you intend to show by the evidence."

"I stand corrected!" he said with a new majesty. Bingo, the first I-stand-corrected for the jury. Jurors, he knew, loved humble pie.

"In addition to the testimony of Rich Zepf about his addiction, which has rendered him virtually helpless, we will show that T. S. Armstead was aware nicotine, a primary element of tobacco, was and is addictive. We will show that the company was and is aware the use of their product causes lung cancer, heart disease, emphysema and a host of other chronic ailments.

"We will also show that not only did the Armstead Company have knowledge that the nicotine in tobacco was addictive, but they *added* the same dastardly ingredient to their lethal product in the hope of making more sales to their victims."

"Your Honor!"

"Yes, Mr. Hanson—"

"I stand corrected," Bomber said and didn't miss a beat. "Then we will hear from research scientists who will tell you there are certain personality types who are virtually helpless to combat the addictive power of nicotine. And finally, we will show you good people that the warnings the company puts on the cigarette package are woefully inaccurate and misleading. They say smoking *can* cause birth defects, they should say, smoking *does* cause birth defects. They say cigarette smoke contains carbon monoxide, but so does automobile exhaust. Why don't they call a spade a spade and say, 'Warning: smoking cigarettes will kill you.'"

Bomber nodded at the jurors one by one, passing his eyes over the panel as he concluded.

"I thank you again for your service here. You have the opportunity to right a great wrong. Not many people are so fortunate in their lifetime"—and then he sat down.

I could see Harrison Hinkle was ticked off and on the verge of another objection. Instead he decided to give a terse opening statement when Judge Druckenmiller recognized him for the purpose.

"Ladies and gentlemen of the jury, I don't generally give statements to the jury before I open my own portion of a case. This case is different. Today we are being sued by a particularly sympathetic plaintiff and an able attorney who will attempt with every trick in his considerable bag to dissuade you from the facts of the case which are these: T. S. Armstead manufactures cigarettes to meet the demands of the public. These are for cigarettes with nicotine in them. T. S. Armstead is a legitimate company operating within all the laws of the land. There are some studies that purport to make tobacco look bad. We also have contradictory studies, serious scientific research which proves that smoking has benefits to many people, not the least of these is the reduction of hypertension which could lead to premature death.

"I don't have to insult your intelligence with a long and detailed disputation of his outlandish and sweeping statement that our label should say cigarettes kill you.

"We will demonstrate unequivocally that is not so. Some people drink themselves to death, some also, we will admit, smoke too much, and that sometimes causes diseases which later might prove fatal. But we all know people who smoke responsibly and live to ripe old ages. George Burns smoked all the time. Loved it as life itself. He said people die young from eating too much, and I'm inclined to agree. If Mr. Hanson has his way, we may be labeling food packages, Warning: eating will kill you.

"We all die, that's just a fact of life. Blaming it on one

thing or the other isn't going to change anything.

"We will further vigorously dispute Mr. Hanson's claim that we add nicotine to our product to make it more addictive.

"Finally, I ask you to pay particular attention to the *facts* in evidence. Mr. Hanson is a very able advocate, world famous, but he is also something of a magician who can fool you into believing the pea is under the wrong shell. Don't be fooled by his shell game. Keep your eyes on the facts and the evidence.

"Thank you."

"Very well," Judge Druckenmiller said. "You may call your first witness, Mr. Hanson."

"Thank you, Your Honor. The plaintiff calls Dr. Lawrence Woodring."

26

With Dr. Woodring, Bomber began to build his case step-by-step, first establishing expert opinion on the causal relationship between smoking and disease and fatality. Dr. Woodring cited study after study, including five of his own, that led him to the conclusion that smoking definitely causes lung cancer in people not otherwise thought prone to get it.

On cross-examination, Hinkle tore away at that assumption. And so it went for the rest of the day, Bomber produced experts to damn the tobacco industry, and Hinkle tore into them as though his life depended on it. In a way, I guess it did.

Hinkle offered to stipulate what Bomber's experts would say, but Bomber would have none of it. Experts, as seasoned as his were at testifying, made a far better impression on the jury than the reading of some dispassionate judge who is being careful not to weight his words for one side or the other.

The next morning, the Zepfs' pictures appeared on page one of the local paper. It was a carefully posed shot—carefully posed to look candid—of the twelve adorable Zepf girls holding hands and cautiously leading their blind father down the courthouse steps hugging his oxygen tank while Bomber looked on, his eyes tearing. The rest of the staff was deliberately out of camera range. Bomber liked to make it appear he was taking on the world, solo.

From time to time, these PR gems would appear in papers around the world, as well as on local and network television. The jurors were naturally admonished not to look at any papers or television, but most of these jurors looked at little else. At least, they would promise themselves not to be swayed by it.

Good luck!

On balance, we were pleased with our experts' testimony. We had, I think, demonstrated conclusive links between smoking and cancer, heart disease, emphysema, and some other maladies, as well as solid links between nicotine and addiction. We even got several experts to testify to their studies that showed nicotine to be the most addictive substance known to man.

The night after our third day of trial, under Bomber's instructions, I telephoned Easy Willie in Churchill Park, North Carolina.

He answered on the first ring. Those motel rooms are small.

"They really did a job on this guy Powell," he said. "The evidence is overwhelming and very convincing."

"But false?" I added, hopefully.

"He says it's phony as a seventeen-dollar bill," he said, "but that's not how it's going to look. I think I can give it a good go defending him, but so far I don't see any way to win it without breaking the D.A.'s witnesses, and their stories are pretty pat."

"The controller and the secretary?"

"Yeah."

"They set him up?"

"I imagine so, but how do we prove it? He's innocent until proven guilty and all that, but they've stacked the deck to put *us* in the position of breaking one of their witnesses."

"Not easy."

"Not when you consider they owe their livelihood to the company. Controller goes way back," Easy Willie said. "Rose through the ranks. Lot of gratitude there. The secretary is newer, but you can bet they've already made it worth her while. Not to mention their usual persuasion about the whole economy of the South—with the northerners conspiring to bring them to their knees—as though the Civil War wasn't enough."

"Find out all you can about them both, will you?"

"Sure."

"You think they really want to try him, or is it just a scare?"

"My feeling is—this is in my gut—not scientific—that they just want to hold him until your case is over. Rather not perjure the employees if they can help it."

"Think the employees would balk?"

"Doubt it," he said. "Apparently our Shauna tipped them."

I groaned. "So she sold out and you didn't," I said.

"Yeah, life plays funny tricks."

"What do you think she got?"

"Anything she wanted," he said.

"Yeah. I guess she needed the money." I could think of no way to put off the key question any longer. "Willie," I said, "do you think there is any chance he did it?"

"Embezzled? Powell? Why not?"

I felt that one all the way down.

"Understand, he's very convincing about his innocence, but go to any jail, you'll get the same. The company has a very persuasive set of witnesses. The controller is rock solid. The secretary lays it on pretty strong. They say the motive was overwhelming. Powell agreed to testify for Bomber, he knew that would finish him with the company, he cashed in what stock options he could—apparently they have some restrictions on how much you can cash in in a year—and after he testifies, they will block him from getting his pension and the stock."

"They can do that?"

"All the employees sign an agreement not to do anything detrimental to the company under penalty of losing everything—pension, stock options, health plan—the works. So their theory is, he helped himself to his own retirement fund. The money *did* go into his personal account."

"Did *he* put it there?" I asked.

"He says not. Secretary says he made the deposit himself."

"Any way to check it?"

"Not really. It's all on microfilm. No fingerprints."

"How about handwriting?"

"I'm trying to check. The bank doesn't seem too forth-coming. I suspect they are owned by the tobacco company, but that's a guarded secret too. The published stuff lists a bunch of blinds. When I ask, I get stonewalled."

"Okay," I said, "Go to it. And, Willie?"

"Yeah?"

"If you should run into Shauna down there, tell her to call home, will you?"

*　　　*　　　*

We made our formal request for extradition of Don Powell to testify for the plaintiff in *Zepf vs. T. S. Armstead Company*. It was denied. They feared flight, they said.

"How do you expect him to 'fly'?" Bomber asked the governor on the phone, "He'd have two deputies and hand-cuffs."

"Look here, Bomber," the governor said. "The D.A. over there in Benson County tells me it's a risk, I don't have inti-mate knowledge of these small things; I'd never get anything done around here. I'm sure you can appreciate that. I pretty much rely on the local authorities."

"So, if I get approval from the D.A., you'll go along with it?"

"I don't see why not."

Bomber hung up. "Hopeless," he muttered. "The whole state is run like a high-school clique."

The next morning before the jury came in, we petitioned Judge Druckenmiller to to videotape Don Powell's testimony in jail. Harrison Hinkle tried to pump up a weak argument, but Druckenmiller didn't go for it. Court would be in recess on Friday should we need to travel to North Carolina to take Don Powell's testimony in jail.

It was always fun for me to see how the jurors looked different every day because they changed clothes. It gave the jury box a changing dynamic the way the colors played off against one another.

"Plaintiff calls Mrs. Rich Zepf to the stand," Bomber said.

Nadine Zepf swept into the courtroom with her attendant, the burliest bruiser Bomber could find, dressed in the whites of an asylum orderly. She came not with the wary, tentative gestures one would expect from an inmate, one who had perhaps forgotten what it was like to venture out into the cruel world. She came instead as a conquering hero returned to liberate the feckless from their thrall.

She didn't look so crazy, except for the eyes: they were sunken and hollow as empty slop troughs. She wore the simple cotton-print frock she had worn when she checked herself into the institution. It bespoke, Bomber said, a woman who was poor but proud.

On seeing their mother come down the center aisle of the large, packed, courtroom, the Zepf children's eyes sparkled happily. The older girls had to restrain the younger ones from leaving their seats to run to her.

When Mother Zepf reached the front row where her twelve children sat, she paused and reached out her hand, and the kids broke loose to grab it one by one, kissing it, pressing it to their cheeks and foreheads. The entire display took only a few seconds, but its impression on the jury was eternal.

The burly attendant separated Mrs. Zepf from her children, and hustled her inside the low gate to the battlefield.

When she was administered the oath, "Do you promise to tell the truth, the whole truth, and nothing but the truth so help you God?" she snapped her head and said, "You bet your life!"

There was a titter in the courtroom.

"Where do you currently reside, Mrs. Zepf?" Bomber began questioning the witness.

"Out in Bitnerville," she said with aplomb, "in the insane asylum."

"Do you consider yourself insane?"

"Sure," she said with a wry smile. Then she added after a careful pause, "I don't know anybody who isn't."

There was an outburst of merriment from the spectators and Judge Druckenmiller angrily gavelled out a bullet sound that reverberated through the courtroom. It shot down the merriment.

Harrison Hinkle called for a sidebar conference.

"Your Honor, really, I've heard Mr. Hanson is a master at sideshow tactics, but using an insane woman to bolster his case is, well, simply insane. Now, I can see she is an engaging woman, but she certainly has nothing to contribute to the plaintiff's case."

"How do you know?" Bomber asked.

"Well, how could she? If she's insane, any testimony she has to give will only confuse the jury. In any case, I would ask for an instruction to the jury to weigh her evidence as that of an insane woman."

"Let her speak," Bomber said. "Then the jury can decide who's insane."

"She *is* the plaintiff's wife," Judge Druckenmiller agreed. "Let's hear what she has to say. I'm sure the jury can ferret out any insanity they hear."

Bomber stationed himself at the corner of the jury box so the jury could focus on Mrs. Zepf across the way.

"How did you come to reside in Bitnerville?" he asked.

"I went out there and told them I couldn't take it no more."

"What couldn't you take?"

"Nothing, I couldn't take nothing. I'd just had my twelfth kid and I felt like jumping out the window. My husband was dying of smoking, he was blind, we was poor and he couldn't work no more, he was spitting blood, he couldn't breathe, my world was coming to an end."

"Did you make arrangements to take care of your children?"

"The girls take care of 'em."

"Your daughters?"

"Yep. They better mothers than I any day. Younger," she said, to explain, "more spunk."

"Now, Mrs. Zepf," Bomber said, "how long have you lived with your husband?"

She seemed to count with the help of the ceiling. "Must be goin' on 'bout twenty years."

"Do you know when your husband started smoking?"

"When he had his accident."

"What accident was that?"

"Piano fell on him."

"All right, Mrs. Zepf, do you recall when, in relation to his accident, your husband started smoking?"

"Right away."

"He was blind when he started smoking?"

"Yes."

"So, he couldn't read the warnings on the packs?"

"He couldn't read nothin'."

"How did he get the cigarettes?"

"I bought 'em."

"Did you read the labels?"

"My reading's not too good," she said.

"Did you know what the warning label said?"

"Not really."

"How much school did you have, Mrs. Zepf?"

"Two years—"

"Two years is all? You only finished the second grade?"

She shook her head. "Two years in first grade. I didn't take to school too good."

"All right, in all those years that you were buying cigarettes for your husband, did anyone read the warning label to you?"

"Nobody read me nothin'."

"Did you ever try to get your husband, the plaintiff Rich Zepf, to give up cigarettes?"

"Not in the beginning."

"Did you try later?"

"When he's startin' to vomit blood an' be wheezin' like a worn-out bull. I mean he's grabbin' for air like he ain't gonna live another minute."

"Frighten you, did it?"

"Scared the bejesus outta me."

"Did you take him to a doctor?"

"Yep—a couple."

"What did they say?"

"Told him to stop smoking?"

"Did he?"

She tightened her lips and shook her head.

"No?"

"No."

"Do you know why not?"

"Objection!" Harrison Hinkle put some moxie into it. Like a fast baller turning on the heat. "How could she know what went on in another person's head?"

Mrs. Zepf turned to the red-faced defense attorney. "Oh, I expec's I know all right, what goes on in his head. Is married to him 'bout twenty-some years."

The audience enjoyed that. Their pleasure was not lost on Nadine Zepf.

Judge Druckenmiller said, "Rephrase the question, Mr. Hanson."

"Did your husband ever tell you why he didn't stop smoking?"

"Said he couldn't. It was too late. Like he was squeezed in a vise and ever'time he tried to get free, it just tightened on him."

"You said you bought cigarettes for him. How often did you buy them?"

"He smoked pret' near four packs a day. Sometimes more, sometimes a little less. So I musta bought 'bout three cartons ever' week."

"How much did they cost?"

"In the beginning 'bout two dollars a carton—now it's like twenty dollars."

"Where did you get the money for the cigarettes?"

"Didn't have money. Got what we could sellin' farm stuff. Seemed like whatever we had went to cigarettes."

"Did you mind that?"

"'Course I minded."

"But you kept buying the cigarettes?"

"Yeah, I didn't know no better," she said. "What would you do? You live with a man who's had this terrible tragedy—a man you come to love, I guess, and it's the only pleasure he has in the world, so you give up some o' your own wants. That's easy. Cigarettes and making babies 'bout all was left to him and I couldn't deny him neither."

"Is there any relationship between your husband's smoking and your going to the asylum in Bitnerville?"

"'Course they is."

"What is the relationship?"

"The relationship is I couldn't take it no more. Seein' my husband bein' eaten away by them cigarettes. I couldn't get him to stop. I didn't have the heart at first. Then I seen what it done to him, I tried my damnedest but it was too late. He was already all eaten up with that there smoke. I 'specs even if he did stop, the damage's done. It was just plum too late. I couldn't take it no more, havin' another baby, bein' dirt poor and him bein' eaten up with that there cancer."

"Do you miss your family?"

"'Course I misses 'em."

"Would you like to go back?"

"Yeah," she said, looking longingly at her girls in the front row, licking her lips at the prospect, "when I'm ready."

"When will that be?"

"We gets some money so he can get regular doctor care. So we can pay our old doctor bills. When I can hold my head up an' do my job's a real wife an' mother. That's when I'm goin' back."

"One more question, Mrs. Zepf. Do you think an award of money from the tobacco company to your family would be justified?"

"You bet your life," she said, as she had when she promised to tell the truth at the beginning of her testimony. "It is *necessary* to show them scum they just can't go on makin' them things that kills people—them *cigarettes*," she pronounced the word with special distaste, "takin' loved ones from they families with painful cruel deaths. Paying is the *least* they should do. They should close 'em down for good!"

Bomber gazed at Mrs. Zepf with admiration, and he let the impact of her words settle in with the jury before he quietly said, "You may cross-examine."

*   *   *

Judge Druckenmiller decided we needed a recess before Harrison Hinkle cross-examined Nadine Zepf. I wondered if it wasn't because Bomber had usurped his prerogative in saying, "You may cross-examine."

The Zepf kids were taking the trial like real troupers. None of them gave me the feeling they didn't want to be there—or that they were bored.

As the audience started to exit, Carrie came up to me and asked, "Have you heard from Shauna?"

I shook my head.

"Don't you even know where she is?"

I shook my head again. I guess I didn't trust my voice.

"I sure like her," she said.

"I did too."

"It's too bad what happened. But I guess if she disappeared we can't hear her side of it."

I agreed and quickly extricated myself from Carrie's company. I didn't want any untoward displays of emotion to slip out. This required a trip to the restroom and some cold water to my face. I returned to the hallway to find Bomber huddled with Nadine Zepf. Her kids were clustered around her, touching anywhere they could reach.

The tipstaff called us back into the courtroom and

Nadine Zepf took the stand again.

"You understand you are still under oath?" Judge Druckenmiller said, as though he were talking to a child.

"Don't matter none," Nadine said from the witness chair. "I tell the truth anyway—period!"

Judge Druckenmiller pressed her. "So you *do* understand?"

She nodded.

"Answer audibly, please."

"Auto blee?" she said.

"Put it in words," he said. "Say yes or no."

"Yes or no."

Judge Druckenmiller frowned. Harrison Hinkle seemed to have been momentarily derailed.

"Your Honor," he pleaded, "I think there must be serious doubt about the witness's competence."

"I said I tells only the truth anyways."

"Yes, but you understand you took an oath," Judge Druckenmiller said patiently. "Yes or no?"

"Yes."

"And that oath is still good. You are still bound by it."

"I don't need no oath to tell the truth!"

Judge Druckenmiller was clearly exasperated now. "Clerk," he said, "administer the oath again."

And she took it and answered, "You bet your life!" again.

Harrison Hinkle approached her with his oiliest smile. "Gingerly" was the word that came to my mind. It was like he knew she was a time bomb that could blow up in his face anytime.

The smile disappeared and he frowned, as though receiving a poor assessment of his chances. Then the smile flashed again. Harrison Hinkle could turn his smile off and on like a spigot. But he didn't say anything.

Bomber leaned over and whispered in my ear, "He's pulling these shenanigans to try and make her act crazy for the jury."

"They don't need much more than that oath business," I whispered back.

He shook his head. "That was golden," he said, and I didn't argue because I didn't understand.

"Do you have a question for the witness, Mr. Hinkle," Judge Druckenmiller asked, "or shall we excuse her?"

"No—yes," he said. "I have a few questions."

"Then ask them," the judge said.

"Ah… Yes… Mrs. Zepf, do you remember me visiting you at the, ah, your institution?"

"The nut house?" she said. "Never forget it as long as I live."

"Ah… Yes. Now, then, Mrs. Zepf."

"Which is it?" she interrupted him.

"Excuse me?" He was off guard.

"Which is it? Now or then?"

"I'm sorry if I confused you Mrs. Zepf, but I'm afraid *I* must ask the questions and *you* must answer them."

"Then ask one," she said, and I noticed Judge Druckenmiller's frigid lips turn up in a quasi-smile.

"Mrs. Zepf," he continued, trying to regain his footing, "this institution you live at…"

"The funny farm?"

"What kind of people live there?"

"Nice people."

"I mean, do they have anything in common?"

"They're all nice," she said.

"Mentally, could you characterize them mentally?"

"No, I couldn't."

"You could not? Would it be fair to make certain assumptions about people in mental institutions?"

"It's not good to make assumptions."

"Would it be fair to say that people who are locked up in insane asylums are insane?" Nothing was working so he was trying the frontal approach.

"Surely not," she said. "Half the people there are saner

than you."

There was a titter from the audience and Hinkle bounced his head in a maybe-so motion.

"Go get 'em," Bomber whispered under his breath, but naturally, not so far under he couldn't be heard by the jury and half the courtroom.

"Could you say that the people in your asylum have a different take on reality?"

"Than who?"

"Well, me for instance," he said.

"I seen your take on reality, mister, and you can have it," she said.

The laughter said things were not going well for Harrison Hinkle and the defense.

"Stop being cute, Mrs. Zepf, we are all onto your cute game. You have defrauded and continue to defraud your country's government out of the price of room and board so you can live the life of luxury and all you have to do in return is act a little crazy once in awhile. Isn't that right, Mrs. Zepf? You are a fraud and a welfare cheat and now you are conspiring with your husband to cheat and defraud a tobacco company so he can get rich on escaping responsibility for his own actions. Isn't that right Mrs. Zepf?"

"That's crazy," she said.

"No further questions."

Court was adjourned until Monday, when Bomber would put the plaintiff, Rich Zepf, on the stand. Now we were on our way to North Carolina to our star witness, who was slipping through our fingers at a depressing rate.

27

Bomber and I powwowed strategy on our way down south in the airplane. Ordinarily, Bomber flew first class and I flew coach, even if we were on the same plane and on an official work-related trip. He didn't want to spoil me, he said.

This was my first first class and it was a nice gesture on Bomber's part. I was away from home, had lost the girl, toiling on a case that was rapidly turning into a lost cause. All the good things that happened in the courtroom could easily be washed away by the absence of any proof that the tobacco companies and T. S. Armstead in particular, deliberately altered their product to make it addictive.

Easy Willie met us at the plane to drive us right to the jail so we could talk to Don Powell before the taping which was scheduled for the next day.

"How's it look to you?" Bomber asked when he slipped into the back seat where he could stretch out after signaling me to the front.

Easy Willie shook his head. "Not good," he said. "Both sides are convincing. Someone is psychotic." Willie started the car and we melded into the traffic.

"We do this video of his testimony," Bomber asked, "he's going to be convincing?"

"Oh, absolutely."

"Good."

"But, so's the other side."

"We'll just have to shake them up a bit," Bomber said. "What kind of people are they? The accusers. What kind of impression do they make?"

"The controller—Karl Eldridge—throws you off a little. He's colorless enough to be a big-numbers man, but he has that doctrinaire edge to him. I could almost see him marching in black boots, and not only with the state troopers of which he was one. Came up through the ranks—would do anything for the company."

"So he was a state trooper? How did he make the switch?"

"Started in security."

"Any hint of scandal?"

"Not so far. Lot of Armstead security boys started with the state troopers. You ever see one of those guys? Take themselves pretty seriously. Lot of speed traps, lot of revenue."

"Keep digging," Bomber said, "we're liable to find out he got his job when he stopped the president of Armstead for drunk driving with a naked bimbo passed out in the back seat."

I turned to face Bomber. "You want me to l-l-look into it?"

There was a silence as though Bomber had forgotten I did the investigative work. I shouldn't have been jealous of his thinking of Easy Willie in this regard, but I think I was.

"Yeah," Bomber said, finally, "sure. Look into it while you're here." The implication was Easy Willie could pick up the slack when I returned to Cedarberg.

"What about the skirt?" insensitive Bomber asked.

"Felicity Wilkins? Replaced Gina, Powell's wife, as his secretary. It's a good job—secretary to a department head."

"Like her boss?"

"Claims to."

To get inside the jail we had to be cleared by a bunch of guards whose day would have been happier if they had never seen us. Southern hospitality stops at the jailhouse door.

When we were all settled in the conference room, we all looked for bugs. We couldn't find any, but that was no sign they didn't exist.

We only cooled our heels about twenty-five minutes until they brought Don Powell in, handcuffed and in leg chains

219

like he was an axe murderer.

"You feel this man is a threat to anybody?" Bomber asked the guard, a young man with a commanding collection of zits.

"Only work here, Mister," he answered. "I don't make the rules."

He did have the grace to unlock the handcuffs. They seemed to be into humiliation, big time. Don Powell had a smirk on his face, but his attitude seemed resigned. "I should have known," he said, shaking his head. He said it often during our conference.

We started with some minor pleasantries, which social graces were an anathema to Bomber who thought small talk a sign of low-grade intelligence. Easy Willie wasn't so hot at it either, so I had *some* function.

"You think this place is bugged?" Bomber asked Don Powell.

"Probably," Powell said. "Though it could hardly make a difference. I have nothing to hide. I was framed, pure and simple. I know it and they know it. And it's for no other reason than to discredit me; to keep me from going up there and testifying. There won't be any trial. When your case is over, I'll be out of here."

Bomber frowned. "I hope your optimism is warranted."

"I should have known," Powell said. "As soon as I agreed to testify, I was doomed."

"How did they find out?"

"It had to be the girl," he said. "What was her name?"

"Shauna McKinley," Bomber supplied, after looking to me for help I wasn't about to give.

"Yeah. As soon as I called her for a guard, I had one on me. From *them*! She never even told you I called."

Then Bomber jump-started a new topic, "What was your relationship to your secretary?"

"She was my secretary," he shrugged. "There was no romance, if that's what you're suggesting."

"Where did she come from?"

"She's a local girl. College-educated. Bright, personable."

"Beautiful?"

"That might be a stretch."

"Sensitive about her looks?"

"I wouldn't know."

"Any reason for her to be?"

"Girls can always find reasons to be sensitive about their looks."

"Well, was she fat?" Bomber asked.

"She thought she had a weight problem, I guess."

"Did she?"

He shrugged.

"Was she in dire need of money?"

"Isn't everybody?"

"I mean, large sums. Did she have a boyfriend who was a gambler, for instance?"

"I don't even know if she had a boyfriend."

Bomber threw me a glance that said check it out. "Where did she work before she came to you?"

"In the company. She worked her way up the secretarial ladder, I guess," he said.

"Did you have any reservations?"

"She was well-qualified," he said. "Maybe if I had been doing it all, I would have discriminated against her weight, but I had a new, beautiful wife and I thought, so what? And even at my level, there is a sense of wanting to please the company. They think someone is right for you, you don't rock the boat."

"And how did she work out?" Bomber asked.

"Fine."

"Nothing ever made you wonder what made her tick?"

"No," he laughed. "What makes anyone tick?" he asked. "Their ticker, I suppose," and he laughed again.

"Do you know anything about her family life?"

"No. Lives with her mother, I believe."

Sounded like Shauna to me. "Was her mother in good health?" I asked.

"Far's I know. She wasn't very old—Felicity is in her twenties somewhere. Her mother, I expect, is in her forties."

"Hear anything about a father?"

"No, except that he was gone."

"Dead?"

"No, missing from the action."

"Can you think of any reason she'd want to frame you?"

"No," he said. "Of course, the company is good to its employees. Many of them would do *any*thing for the company."

"Was Eldridge, the controller, one of those?"

Don Powell nodded. "There's a guy they treated like a king."

"How so?"

"Promoting him way beyond his ability."

"He's not a good controller?"

"They fixed it so it doesn't matter. He's got a nice title, his name in gold leaf on the door, a secretary and a check stamping machine with his very own signature on it."

"Important to him?"

"Very."

"How long did it take him to climb the ladder?"

"I don't know, maybe fifteen years."

"What other services might he perform around there?"

"I don't know, but he's where the money is."

"Think he'd diddle with the accounts?"

"He diddled with mine."

"Touché."

The powers that make the rules decided we'd had enough time. Bomber balked. "I need time to prepare my client for his testimony tomorrow."

The guard, another jackboot, shook his head. "Orders," he said simply.

"Look, we waited twenty-five minutes for you to bring him. I don't imagine there was any great demand on his time

222

that conflicted. At least give me that twenty-five minutes."

"No can do" was his reply.

"When can I see him again?"

"Ask the boss man," he said.

Don Powell was more forlorn once the handcuffs were clamped back on his wrists.

"Keep your chin up," Bomber said. "Just tell the truth and you'll be out of this."

Powell smiled in reply. The smile seemed to lack a certain optimism.

On the way out, Bomber raised Cain with his bombast about the Constitution, the Bill of Rights, habeas corpus and a host of other legalisms designed to befuddle the constabulary. Through it all, he kept them on the defensive until they agreed to let him come back for another session that night.

Outside, we all seemed to breathe easier. Jails are not friendly places. I decided to start my investigation into Felicity Wilkins and Eldridge with Gina Powell, the witness's wife.

When we checked into our hotel room, I made the call. She was frosty, but agreed it would be nice for her to get out of the house.

Gina started unloading on me as soon as she opened the door. I listened patiently to her sarcastic barbs, her frustration and her anger. When she ran out of steam, I said, "Okay, the thing is now, what's the best way to handle it?" Then something occurred to me. "You aren't back in therapy, are you?"

"No, I am not," she snapped. "I am behind my husband one-hundred percent."

When she settled down, she told me some fascinating things. It all led up to my leaving the premises with the current annual report of the T. S. Armstead Company which contained a picture of the controller, Karl Eldridge.

28

The next morning, we met Harrison Hinkle at the prison entrance. He introduced us to two shiny young lawyers from the Armstead Company's stable. They must have been about my age, though they seemed younger. Probably lived more protected lives. I don't know why Hinkle needed them—maybe to even the score with Bomber, Easy Willie, and me.

In the conference room where we met the day before, the camera man was already set up and the sound woman with him was fiddling with dials trying to get the right levels.

Calling it "a conference room" was a nice conceit of the southern prison industry, but I had never liked the sound of "holding tank," either.

Anyway, we were going to be pretty tightly packed in this "conference room." I counted eight of us already, and we expected two more, the prisoner and a guard. I prayed for the air conditioning to hold up.

Don Powell was brought in by the very same guard who'd produced him the day before; the one who didn't make the rules. So when Bomber asked him to remove the handcuffs and leg chains, we got a reprise of the young man's status as a non-contributing intellect.

"You took off the cuffs yesterday," Bomber said.

"I don't make the rules," the guard reminded us.

"You don't mean you expect to have the witness in hand-cuffs and leg chains for the taping of his testimony. They don't require that in court."

The guard shrugged. "This isn't court."

"All right," Bomber said, "let me talk to the boss again." Bomber looked at Hinkle. "You behind this?"

"No."

"You have any objection to him looking like a human being for his testimony?"

"As the man said, I don't make the rules."

"So you don't object if we take off the chains and put him in a business suit?"

"Whatever the warden wants," Harrison Hinkle said, as though he were indifferent to something that had been pre-arranged to his liking.

There was a hubbub with Bomber going to plead his case emotionally with the warden who asked him why he was making so much fuss. "He *is* in jail you know."

"Yes, and I also know he shouldn't be. He's not a criminal, he's a victim of a sinister plot."

The warden smirked, as if to say, "They all say that."

A compromise was reached. They would (magnanimously) remove the handcuffs, but the leg chains would stay though they wouldn't photograph them. And, unfortunately, they could not locate his civilian clothes, so Bomber offered to send me for them but Harrison Hinkle objected to the delay. "It's not as though he's wearing stripes or anything," he said.

"He is the vice-president in charge of manufacturing for the rich and powerful T. S. Armstead Company and you have him dressed like a tobacco farmer."

"*Was,*" said Harrison Hinkle. "His connection to the company today is *less* than a tobacco farmer."

I'll say this for Harrison Hinkle, he knew how to get you mad.

Bomber gave in, and whenever Bomber gave in, I knew there was something up his sleeve. This time, it was the sympathy card and he would play it to the jury—all the more effective if he could prove his accusers false.

We had just begun the questions, after killing about an hour on the appearance of the witness and the other formalities, when I discovered there was no air conditioning in the room. The sun was working on our outside wall and the fan that worked through the central system seemed inadequate to the nine bodies in the small room. (The guard had had the grace to step outside. He knew better than to stay in the room with nine 98.6-degree bodies).

It wasn't long until the perspiration began to show on Don Powell's face, making him look like a nervous, evasive witness. Fortunately, his answers were still firm.

After the background questions which established Powell's history with the company, his vast knowledge of cigarette manufacturing procedures and processes, and his access to the highest councils of the company, Bomber got down to business.

"Mr. Powell, may we speak for a moment of the ways the cigarettes are made? Take us through the process, will you?"

"The tobacco leaves are grown by the tobacco farmer."

"There are many farms, I take it? A lot of tobacco farmers?"

"Oh yes, hundreds."

"Does your department purchase the tobacco leaves?"

"No, purchasing does that. Our responsibility begins when the tobacco arrives at the plant."

"What happens then?"

"We cure the leaf, and remove the nicotine for this process."

"So, at this point, you could put the tobacco into cigarettes without nicotine?"

"Yes."

"Has that ever been tried?"

"Only in tests."

"What kind of tests?"

"We had test groups of smokers. We gave them various brands of cigarettes already on the market, as well as cigarettes made from nicotineless tobacco. They were not marked, but numbered. And each person's were numbered differently so there could be no collusion or influence between the brands."

"Now when you say brands, you are talking about cigarettes that are already on the market?"

"Yes."

"Yours—that is, those manufactured by T. S. Armstead?"

"Yes."

"As well as other manufacturers'?"

"Yes."

"And do these have varying levels of nicotine in them?"

"Yes."

"How does that come about? Do different tobacco leaves have different amounts of nicotine?"

"Yes. But we take it out. The amount of nicotine in a cigarette depends on how much we put back in in the manufacturing process."

"And how do you decide how much to put back in?"

"We use these test groups. We let them smoke various brands with various levels of nicotine and ask for their preferences."

"Based on what?"

"Taste mostly. Smoothness is another word we use."

"And what do these tests show?"

"The preponderance of evidence shows most smokers prefer the cigarettes with the highest nicotine content."

"How does the cigarette with no nicotine fare in the studies?"

"It doesn't. No one likes it. No one said they would buy it. In a later stage, we explain it has no nicotine and is, therefore, considered less habit forming, and a few respondents claim they might buy it on that basis."

"Enough to make manufacturing them economically feasible?"

"No."

"Now when you come to the point in manufacturing where you say you add nicotine, do you ever add less than you took out?"

"Rarely."

"But it has happened?"

"Yes."

"Under what conditions?"

"Usually it is a marketing decision. We have over two-hundred different brands, and some of them we have advertised with less nicotine, less tar, what have you. I make them how they tell me to make them."

"Do they ever ask for your opinion on how much nicotine to put in them?"

"No."

"Do you ever put more nicotine in the cigarettes you manufacture than you took out of the tobacco during processing?"

"Yes."

"Often?"

"Almost always."

"What percentage of the time would you estimate you put more nicotine in than you originally took out of the tobacco you use to manufacture cigarettes?"

"Ninety-eight."

"Where do you get the extra nicotine?"

"From other tobacco."

"You use some tobacco leaves just for the nicotine content?"

"Yes."

Here Bomber moved between the witness and the camera, took out his handkerchief and wiped his face, then made a great show of taking off his jacket and tie saying, "Sure is hot in here." Then he rolled up his sleeves. He looked at Easy Willie and me and we followed suit, and I felt a lot better for it. While Bomber blocked the camera from Don Powell, the witness wiped his own face so he looked somewhat fresher as Bomber went on.

"You said you estimate in ninety-eight percent of the cigarettes you manufacture you *add* nicotine to the product?"

"Yes."

"You have no say about how much nicotine you put in cigarettes?"

"No."

"Who does, do you know?"

"I get my orders from the executive vice-president."

"Who is over him in the corporate structure?"

"The president and chairman of the board."

"Have you ever been in meetings with any of these people—the president, the chairman of the board, and or the executive vice-president, when the levels of nicotine have been discussed?"

"Yes."

"Can you capsulize those discussions?"

"Nicotine sells cigarettes. We are in business to make money."

"Why does nicotine sell cigarettes?"

"It improves the taste for most people, and then too, it is addictive."

"Could you explain that?"

"Our studies show that the nicotine in cigarettes is what hooks people, what keeps them coming back for more."

"Even when they have lung cancer?"

"Sometimes."

"Why is that?"

"We have studied that also. Those studies show that at that point they are so close to death, they don't care, or more predominantly, those who want to cling to what life they have left find they simply cannot break the habit."

"And the Armstead Company is aware of this?"

"Certainly, we made many of the studies."

"Are these people you mentioned, the president and chairman of the board, and executive vice-president, aware of studies that show the links between smoking and cancer, emphysema, heart disease and others?"

"Yes."

"You've been in meetings where it was discussed?"

"Yes."

"Have you formed any impressions of the stance these executives take on these studies, both in private and in public?"

"Yes. In public, they deny it. In private, they search for ways to work around it."

"Have you ever seen any of those three executives smoking?"

"No."

"Do you smoke?"

"No."

"Did you ever?"

"Yes."

"Why did you stop?"

Don Powell's eyes glazed. He looked away from Bomber for the first time. "My wife died...of smoking. I..."

Bomber paused as though considering further questions. Then he said, "Let's take a fifteen minute break. It's so damn hot in here I'm about to pass out."

Hinkle made a feeble attempt to argue, but Bomber said everyone would be grateful if he got to use the bathroom.

It's always hard to argue with a break. When we got outside, Bomber asked the guard to bring the witness out so we could confer with him. He said he'd have to ask the boss about that.

"Maybe you can double leg chain him," Bomber suggested, and the guard didn't like that.

"Listen, mister, I don't care who you are, you don't get smartass with me."

"I stand corrected," Bomber said without a thought.

We went out to the receiving room where the warden's offices were and it was a lot cooler. It felt like real air conditioning.

Easy Willie said, "He's a good witness."

"Yeah," Bomber said. "Of course, cross-examination is the real test."

"How much longer will you take?" Easy Willie asked.

"I'm finished."

"Really?" Willie seemed surprised.

"Imagine I'll do some redirect, but he's said it all. Short, sweet, to the point and devastating. I don't see any percentage in prolonging it with him sweating like a pig in there."

"You're going to let Hinkle go into Powell's wife's death?"

"If he has the guts."

"He'll have the guts. Another reason for Don Powell to be irrationally angry with his employer."

"Maybe."

"And what about his being in jail? You going to let Hinkle run with that?"

Bomber nodded. "I know what you're saying—you should get all the bad stuff out yourself so it doesn't look like you're hiding anything."

"Well, yeah."

"And I usually agree. But this time I'm going to let the enemy have a monopoly on the personal dirt. I have a feeling I can make it work to our advantage."

I could see from Easy Willie's face he thought that was a miracle beyond Bomber's considerable skills.

The guard came through the door with Don Powell—who had again been handcuffed. He brought him over to us, then stepped back a respectable distance to offer us a modicum of privacy.

Bomber didn't feel he needed it. Harrison Hinkle and his troops were in with the warden at the epicenter of the air conditioning. "Don, my boy, you have been a splendid witness. I don't know how you could have been better. So I'm going to throw you to the wolves now—are you up for it?"

Don's tongue circled his lips and he nodded, not with a lot of conviction to my mind.

"Usually I'd ask you more questions. Open the door to some stuff he will try to nail you on. This time, I think we got what we wanted. All his questions are going to be off the point.

231

He's going to try to score points on your wife and jail—just as we talked about last night. Look him in the eye, stay steady at the helm, answer firmly and honestly, and don't volunteer anything. Maybe Hinkle will cut it short. He's got to be as hot as the rest of us. But did you notice? None of them took off their jackets."

"Yeah," Don Powell shook his head. "I'm not disappointed they didn't let me wear a business suit."

"Is it always that hot in there?" I asked him.

"I don't know, I don't get to go in there often. Never with nine people," he smiled ruefully. "It's that hot in the cells."

"Yeah, well, it's gonna be our job to get you out of that cell."

Harrison Hinkle and his polished sidekicks came out of the warden's office, indicative, I suppose, of their being on the side of goodness and justice.

"Time to hit it," Hinkle said as though he had just learned a cool new colloquialism.

We filed back into the sweat box like wooden soldiers.

If anyone noticed Bomber had not gone to the bathroom, no one mentioned it.

29

It was obvious Harrison Hinkle for the defense did not expect to be called upon so quickly. When Bomber said, "You may cross-examine," he got only a dumbfounded look. He knew Bomber realized all the must-do's that had been left out.

Ordinarily the plaintiff could afford to take chances with videotaped witnesses. If it didn't work out, you just didn't show the tape to the jury. We could afford no such luxury. Don Powell was virtually our case.

Harrison was frowning; Bomber was smiling.

"You might have had the courtesy to tell me you were through before the break," Hinkle said.

"Oh, I'm far from through, Mr. Hinkle, as you shall see when I get up to bat again. I'm just letting you try a few licks in the meantime."

"You could have told me," he grumbled.

"I had to confer with our witness first. Then when I decided, you weren't around. Hobnobbing with the warden I believe…in the air conditioning."

Hinkle was startled. He would later argue strenuously to cut out this exchange on the tape and Bomber would argue just as strenuously that Hinkle had instigated it, but Judge Druckenmiller would side with Hinkle on that one. "That," Hinkle said, "is the beauty of taped witnesses. You can cut out the objectionable stuff."

"It's so artificial," Bomber said. "Ruins the dramatic flow, kills the spontaneity." And those were things Bomber counted on more than most lawyers.

Hinkle didn't waste much time on small talk. "Mr. Powell, your counsel neglected to have you explain why we are videotaping your testimony. Where are we today, will you tell the jury?"

"The Churchill Park jail in North Carolina."

"Is one of the participants here an inmate?"

"Yes."

"Who?"

"I am."

"What crime have you been accused of?"

"Embezzlement."

"The illegal appropriation of funds from your company to your personal bank account?"

"That's the accusation."

"And it was backed up by an arrest warrant, is that correct?"

"Yes."

"And now you are being held pending trial, is that correct?"

"So I am told."

"All right, I'll accept that. Did you attempt to make bail?"

"Yes."

"What was the result?"

"It was denied."

"Do you know why?"

"First, all my assets were frozen. Then the district attorney convinced the judge there was a high risk of flight," Don Powell said—then added with a crooked smile, "southern justice."

"Excuse me, what did you say?"

"Southern justice."

"What do you mean by that?"

"A system of justice that suits the needs of the establishment."

"Couldn't you say that for northern justice as well—or eastern or western?"

"Pure justice is justice that is just—fair, equitable, reasonable. Southern justice is situation justice—as in this case. It serves the interests of T. S. Armstead to keep me from testifying in the *Zepf* case, so they arrest me without bail. Like they only do for murder."

"But you are testifying now, are you not?"

Don Powell smiled and made one of those if-you-say-so gestures with his face. Hinkle repeated the question.

"I was not permitted to travel to Pennsylvania to testify at court."

"But this tape may be shown to the jury, you are aware of that?"

"Yes."

"So you are, in effect, testifying, is that not correct?"

"I don't think it's the same, no."

"Well, perhaps if the jury sees this tape, they can decide whether or not you are testifying. Now, I'd like to ask you a few questions about the crime you are accused of committing. You said the charge was embezzlement, is that correct?"

"Yes."

"Money from the T. S. Armstead Company showed up in your personal bank account?"

"I have no knowledge of that," Powell said. "I certainly didn't put it there."

"The police say you did."

"Well, I didn't."

"Do you know how it got there, if you didn't put it there? Did your wife have access to your account?"

"Yes, but not to the money. My secretary put it in my bank account."

"At your instruction?"

"Absolutely not. I knew nothing about it."

So far, Don Powell was doing well and Bomber's gamble had seemed to be paying off—the truth of the unpleasantness coming out at the hands of the enemy.

"You are married, Mr. Powell?"

"Yes."

"Is this your first wife?"

"No."

"How many wives have you had?"

"Two."

"What happened to the first wife?"

"She died." The memory of her was working on Powell's features. Like he had developed a sudden tic in his check.

"What was the cause of her death?"

"Lung cancer."

"Did she smoke?"

"Yes."

"Did you blame her death on cigarettes?"

"I still do," he said, bravely.

"Do you hold T. S. Armstead responsible for your first wife's death?"

"No."

"No?"

"I hold myself responsible."

"Why is that?" Harrison Hinkle asked. His work here could be characterized as smooth but aggressive. His posture and demeanor were almost rigid while his voice took an accusative, even argumentative edge.

"Because I made the cigarettes that killed her."

"You made them? With your own hands?"

"I was in charge of manufacturing."

"For T. S. Armstead?"

"Yes."

"And the brand she smoked was made by Armstead?"

"By me." Reliving this was not conducive to our witness's well-being.

"It made you mad, didn't it? Losing you wife like that?"

"I was devastated."

"Made you mad at the company who made the cigarettes she smoked?"

"Made me mad at myself."

"Not the Armstead Company?"

"No."

"Come now, not a little bit?"

"That's enough, counselor," Bomber said. "He's answered your question patiently many times."

"Well, that's an exaggeration," Hinkle said, "but I'll move on."

"Thank goodness," Bomber muttered.

"Mr. Powell, when did you agree to testify in this case?"

"I don't remember the date. It was some time ago."

"Would a week ago be about right?"

"No. More like two, three months."

"Did you tell anyone at T. S. Armstead of your decision?"

"No."

"Why not?"

"I don't know. It didn't occur to me."

"It didn't occur to you?" Hinkle's eyebrow went up. It was a facial expression denoting severe doubt that he had honed to a fine art. "How long have you worked for the T. S. Armstead Company?"

"Twenty-five years or so," he said.

"Does the word 'loyalty' mean anything to you?"

Bomber cut in. "That's a ridiculous question."

Hinkle flared. "Don't you tell *me* my questions are ridiculous."

"I just did."

They went at it for a while and Easy Willie had to calm them down. Maybe judges do have their place.

Back in the groove, Hinkle asked the witness, "Is the reason you didn't tell your superiors—or anybody—at the T. S. Armstead Company of your plans to testify possibly connected with your fear you would lose your job?"

"Possibly," Don Powell said.

"Did you like your job?"

"Before my wife died, yes."

"Not after?"

"Not so much, no."

"What changed your opinion?"

"I began to think of myself as an instrument of premature death and I didn't like that."

"So you looked for a way to get back at the company." Don Powell made no answer. "So, didn't you?"

"Was that a question?'

"Yes."

"No, I didn't look for a way to get back at the company. I never *blamed* the company, I blamed *myself.*"

"Then why did you embezzle the money?"

"I never embezzled any money. I never took a dime from anyone that wasn't mine. Never, ever."

"That's a nice self-serving pronouncement, Mr. Powell, but the facts show otherwise."

"Oh man," Bomber said, "objection. Now *you* are giving self-serving testimony."

"I am not—I'm—"

"Yes, you *are*. There are no facts as you say, there isn't even any evidence to support your flimsy contention that anybody took any money. On the contrary. *All* the evidence on the record to date is Mr. Powell's stout denial of the accusations *you* have made here. Now, let's move on or I'll end this travesty."

"There will be facts aplenty when the time comes," Hinkle said.

Hinkle calmed down and Bomber followed. "We'll see," Bomber said.

"Now Mr. Powell, are you going to sit there and deny that your decision to testify had anything to do with your first wife's death?"

"The question is in two parts," Don Powell said. "First, I *am* going to sit here because my ankles are chained together."

It was an ice breaker. There was a low mummer of appreciative, if guarded laughter. We almost felt cool in that moment.

"Second," Powell continued, "I don't deny that my wife's death from smoking the product I was in charge of making changed my outlook as a person and as an employee. I don't deny her death helped me make up my mind to tell the truth."

Harrison Hinkle switched subjects. He started to go after Powell on the meetings he had with his superiors and how he could have misunderstood, misinterpreted or forgotten what was said. Powell didn't budge. Then he turned to the addition of the nicotine.

"Every person connected with decision-making at the Armstead Company denies that more nicotine is put in the tobacco than is taken out. You stand alone with that accusation. Are you the only one who thinks there is extra nicotine added—the only one in the industry?"

"Certainly not. Everyone in a position to know, knows."

Hinkle fired his salvos, Powell ducked them admirably. Finally, Hinkle had unloaded all his innuendo, trying to paint Powell as an embittered man who wantonly and willfully tried to destroy the company that had been so good to him over all those years. He was, Hinkle would have the jury believe, a man who turned on his best friend, all because of a simple misunderstanding.

On redirect examination, Bomber attempted to set the record straight.

"Mr. Powell," he began, "are you guilty of the crime of embezzlement for which you are incarcerated here?"

"No sir, I am not."

"What is the name of your last secretary?"

"Felicity Wilkins."

"Did she have access to your personal bank account?"

"Yes."

"Why?"

"She deposited my paychecks in my personal account."

"How did she come to work for you?"

"The company sent her."

"She was not *your* choice?"

"No. I could have rejected her."

"Then what would have happened?"

"They would have kept sending people for me to interview until I accepted someone."

"All these applicants already worked for the company?"

"Yes."

"And even though you were a vice-president in charge of a division, you couldn't choose your own secretary?"

Hinkle objected to the wording and Bomber agreed to change it to, "You had to choose between people already employed by the company. Why was that?"

"They hired from within—they vetted people for security reasons."

"Why security? Are there competitive secrets?"

"The secrets the company wants to keep are those I am telling today."

"And those are?"

"That we knowingly add nicotine to cigarettes to make them more addictive—to make more money, and that all the executives are perfectly well aware of the real and documented dangers of smoking."

Bomber turned, as though he was finished, then as if an afterthought, turned back.

"By the way, Mr. Powell, do you know who your secretary, Felicity Wilkins, worked for in the company right before she came to work for you?"

"Yes."

"Who was that?"

"That was—Karl Eldridge, the controller."

"The other person who accuses you of embezzlement?"

"Yes."

"No further questions."

30

Our next hurdle was going to be the two Armstead employees that were going to say Don Powell was a crook—an embezzler. I saw one chance to neutralize that damning testimony, and Bomber agreed we should not leave any stone unturned. Of course, turning this stone was not going to be a cinch.

I found Ray Strong where I had found him before. He was watching the television that hung from the ceiling on the wall opposite his bed. As soon as he saw me come in with the Armstead annual report under my arm, he broke into a smile and turned all his attention onto me.

By then, the smile was the biggest thing about him. But wasted as he was, he still had that indomitable spirit. It would have taken a tougher guy than I not to love this sprite. Just imagining the life he had could put you in a funk, considering all the baggage that went with being black in the South while he was growing up. (And I'm not suggesting it would have been easier in the North. I wasn't around for the Civil War and I wouldn't be interested in participating in another one).

But through it all, Ray Strong had remained strong and cheerful and grateful to the company that had screwed up his life and was now killing him.

"Mr. Tod, it's so nice of you to come back to see me again."

"Yes," I said, "but I can't take any credit for altruism this time. It's business."

"What business?"

"You remember you told me about the body—the cremation, remember?"

The smile left his face. "Remember? I wish I could forget."

"Would you recognize those people if I showed you some pictures?"

"I don't need no pictures," he said. "I know who it was."

I was startled. "Didn't you tell me you didn't remember?"

"Yeah, maybe. I'm closer to the end now. Less skeered. But that's a night I wisht I could forget," he shook his head.

"Who was it?"

"It's such a long time ago. They was probably just messengers for higher ups. We all do what we have to to get by. Take me. I was a real strong person, don't you think I'da refused to burn that body in my incinerator? You think I'm proud of not going to the law?" He shook his head as the sadness shook his decaying body. "So you asking this black pot to call the kettle black." He shook his head again.

"I understand," I said, taking out the book. "The thing is, we got another man's life at stake here. He is in the process of being ruined by the same cast of characters that dispatched that body and ruined your life. Now the last thing I want to do is point a finger at the wrong guy. So with your permission, I'm going to show you a picture and if he is *not* the person who brought you the body and ordered you to cremate it, I hope you sound off—*That's not him* loud and clear—so we don't incriminate the wrong guy, okay?"

He was thinking—as if trying to pull out of all those instructions the fallacy that would somehow cook him. I guess he never found it because he nodded, silently, and I showed him the picture.

He closed his eyes, and turned his head, but didn't utter a sound.

After that moment of silence, I patted him on the shoulder with a small part of the affection I felt. He opened his eyes. I sat on the edge of his bed. The television was still cackling from on high.

"I'm going to ask you a favor, Ray," I said gently. "It is too much to ask, really, and I don't think your doctor would approve. He's here in the hospital now on an emergency and if it's not too late when he finishes, he'll drop in. If not tonight, tomorrow. You can talk it over with him. The dangers, risks and all."

"What can a poor soul like me do as a favor to anyone?" he asked. "I gots one foot in the grave an' the other on a banana peel, like they says."

"Ever been to Pennsylvania?"

"Pennsylvania?" he screwed up that slight, angelic face. "Sounds like I heard o' that place, but I ain't ne'er been outta North Carolina."

"Want to go?"

His eyes shot up in what I can only describe as a gleeful suspicion. "What I gotta do?"

"Go with me and tell your story. The one you just told me."

There was a twinkle in his eye when he said, "I ain't said nothin'."

"Yeah, well, I expect you could put it in words if you wanted."

"There's the problem, friend. You want me to talk at this here case you got against my company."

I nodded.

He shook his head. "Too late," he said. "I'm coming apart at the seams. I go that far to that there Pennsylvania, I be a grease spot 'fore I gets there."

I turned on all my charming, persuasive powers, trying to lean, subtly, on how this was his big chance to make a difference.

"I don't see how I'd ever make a difference," he said. "Not now anyways."

"Testify. We got a chance to make a difference."

He seemed to be thinking about it—the muscles left on either side of his brain seemed to be pumping. "Like to help out," he said finally, "but they been awful good to me."

I patted him on the shoulder again. I couldn't fault him.

All I could do was tell him not to close his mind to it.

*   *   *

On Monday morning, we were back in court in Cedarberg.

Rich Zepf moved slowly to the witness chair—a raised platform walled off from the courtroom beside the judge's bench. With him he carried his oxygen tank. He set it on the low wall in front of him. Harrison Hinkle rose and asked for a conference at sidebar. We all knew what was coming but Bomber let them stretch it out. When he heard the complaint, Bomber slapped his forehead and said, "Sorry—didn't remind him," and turned to Rich and whispered so all could hear, "Put the oxygen tank on the floor."

The clerk asked Rich to rise to take the oath. He bent over and picked up the oxygen tank.

"Don't let them see it," Bomber said urgently in his stage whisper. Rich made a good show of trying to hide it behind his back while freeing the right hand for placement on the Bible that was presented to him. Rather Rich held out his hand, palm down and the clerk placed the Bible under Rich's hand. To accomplish this hiding the oxygen tank on the chair behind him, Rich had to stand at an oblique angle between the chair and the clerk.

Bomber had instructed Rich Zepf to exaggerate his blindness, beef up his groping motions, move slower.

The oath accomplished, Rich turned carefully and made a blind-man show of reaching for the tank and missing on the first few tries. Finally he connected and made a further show of trying, unsuccessfully, to hide the tank on his way to sitting down. It all came off just the way Bomber had rehearsed it.

After Rich's ballet, Bomber took him through his paces: his accident causing his blindness, his smoking.

Bomber pretty well established, through Rich, the plaintiff, that he didn't know cigarettes could put you in the fix he was in. He'd tried to stop smoking, but he couldn't. He felt he was taking food from his babies' mouths, but he just couldn't kick the habit. His doctor told him his lung cancer was caused by his smoking, and still he couldn't stop.

"What are the other symptoms of your lung cancer, besides having trouble breathing?"

"Spit blood."

"You spit blood?"

"Yes, sir."

"Often?"

"Too often."

"Objection."

"Yes, Mr. Hanson, be precise please."

"Well, Mr. Zepf, can you tell us how often you spit blood?"

"Too often."

Nervous laughter rippled through the courtroom.

"Once a year, twice a week—can you give us an approximate idea?"

"Sometimes onc't, twic't a day, sometimes more."

"Up to what—four times a day?"

"Gets really bad, go up to six or eight, I reckon."

"All right, Mr. Zepf—your wife left home some time ago did she not?"

"Yes, sir."

"Would you like her to come back?"

"I reckon we all would."

"Do you know why she left home?"

"Well, she was feelin' poorly—lot of—oh, what's that word they use so much nowadays—you know the one that means you're all fahuddled?"

"Stress?"

"That's the one. Lotta stress, all the kids, me smokin' my lungs out and not bein' able to work none. It was just like we was too poor to afford a mom in the house."

Bomber let a lot of areas for cross-examination go, as he

had with Don Powell in North Carolina. During the morning break, Bomber told me, "Zepf's a rock solid witness. Poor, blind, gentle, the father of twelve adorable girls who sit and gaze at him worshipfully. That's got to tug on those jurors' hearts more than the damn mayor smiling at them from the defense table and not doing another damn thing. So far, the sympathy's with us—I hope Zepf stays calm and Hinkle blows."

Then we got our first surprise from the defense. Instead of the oily and sometimes abrasive outsider from New York asking Zepf the questions on cross-examination, old Earl Lictenwalner, the beloved mayor of Cedarberg stood up to finally contribute his talents to earn his keep.

It was a good ploy. Every once in a while, a trace of an accent owing its origins to the communities across the east river from Manhattan Island slipped through Harrison Hinkle's lips. This could work mischief on the Pennsylvania Dutch jurors in juxtaposition with a guy like Rich Zepf who talked country. And couldn't see. And breathed through tubes coming out his nose.

So the defense came up with the mayor who had very little trouble affecting a country accent himself. He was Will Rogers with a Dutch accent.

Zepf kept his cool. I didn't realize it when the questions began, but Bomber had given Rich Zepf a nice little escape valve, should his interrogator start to get on his nerves.

I decided Rich Zepf might have had a strange advantage being blind: He would not have to see the mayor while he seemed to be looking at him. Had he seen him, he might have burst out laughing at his brazen attempt to be a folksy pal. But Lictenwalner wasn't stupid and he went at the blind man gingerly, asking his questions in reasonable and friendly tones.

"Now, Mr. Zepf, this is your old mayor talking at you. I'm not going to ask if you voted for me or not because I want to be your frien' either way. Fershtay?"

Easy Willie told us that was a Pennsylvania Dutch word for understand.

Rich nodded and said, "I don't at all mind telling you, I

never voted for you to be my mayor."

Good old Lictenwalner seemed crestfallen. He was the kind of guy who needed everyone's love. "I'm sorry to hear that," he said.

"And I never would vote for you."

"Well, it's a free country."

"A-men." There was something in Rich's tone that threw us off at the plaintiff's table. He wasn't angry, he wasn't terribly serious, he was sort of light-heartedly mocking.

"I guess I won't ask you why you didn't vote for me."

"Glad to tell you anyway…"

Judge Druckenmiller was frowning at the mayor and looking to Bomber for an objection. Bomber was smiling blithely.

"I'd never vote for you because I don't vote in Cedarberg—I live outside…" The courtroom had a good laugh, and though it seemed to be at Lictenwalner's expense, he seemed relieved it wasn't worse.

The mayor was everyone's favorite uncle, smiling to beat the band at Rich as though he didn't know he couldn't see him. Then I thought that smile was permanently cemented in place on his face. So many election campaigns, speeches, church picnics grubbing for votes, had put that smile there permanently, and I doubted there was an undertaker in the state who would be able to wipe it off.

Smiley started in on a reprise of how and why Rich began smoking.

"Now you said, I believe, on your direct-examination that lots of people smoked and you didn't think about any dangers. How did you know people smoked?"

"I seen 'em."

"But you's blind."

"Wasn't always."

"But since you started smoking?

"I could smell it. I could smell smoke anytime we went anywhere. I could smell it on people's clothes, I could even smell it on mail we got."

"Is that so?"

"When you can't see, your other senses develop way more'n normal."

"You indicated you had difficulty stopping smoking, is that correct?"

"Yes, sir."

"Can you tell ole Earl how that was?"

"How it was?"

"What you did to stop, and how was it, it didn't work?"

"You smoke, ole Earl?"

"No, sir, I don't."

"You're a lucky man."

"Your Honor," Hinkle interrupted the flow. "The witness is asking questions. Please instruct him in his duty to give answers only."

Judge Druckenmiller smiled. "Sounds like you did it yourself." Hinkle sat down. I think he was blushing.

"Tell us what was the hardest part?"

"I suppose, you don't smoke you can't understand. There's a feeling of well-being comes over you when you draw that smoke deep into your lungs. I mean, it feels like it just go plumb to your toes an' then rushes right back up to you head like it was on a roller coaster. I mean, it gets inside you total. You feel it ever' where an' when you finish with that good feeling, you miss it right away like the most powerful drug in the world. An' if'n you blind, why ever'thing is hundert times more powerful. Like them other senses becomes more important."

"So you like to smoke?"

"I *love* it," he said. "I can't live without it."

"So you would say cigarettes gave you much pleasure in your lifetime?"

"Pleasure and pain."

"What kind of pain did you get?"

Rich dropped his jaw. "I'm dyin', man. I'm forty-four years old an' I'm finished. I got a dozen darlin' daughters an' I'm leavin' 'em. I burned up my insides with your smoke."

The mayor made a grand what-me? gesture with both hands against his chest. "Why me?"

"You workin' for them killers, ain't you?"

"Do you know people who smoke who are in their eighties?"

"It'll get 'em sooner 'r later."

"How did you go about trying to quit smoking? Did you join any groups?"

"No."

"Take any therapy?"

"No."

"Try to substitute chewing gum?"

"Yeah—that didn't do notin'."

And the questions continued with the major trying to show the witness didn't really try to stop smoking. There were many opportunities, he said, and he availed himself of none of them. Why was that?

"Couldn't afford to pay," he said.

"But you don't have to pay more than the cigarettes cost for some of the programs."

"Couldn't do it. I was hooked, man, don't you understand? It was like they say, nicotine is the *most* addictive thing in the world, and when I tried to stop, I like to went crazy from the pain and anxiety. I just could not stop. I ain't proud of it, that's just the way it is."

Then good ole Mayor Lictenwalner asked Rich some questions about his meager income, with an eye to establishing his loss of income at about zero. If the jury was going to consider damages, it would be good for them to know Rich Zepf was not a financial heavyweight and the income his family would be deprived of at his death was as close to zilch as it was possible to be.

There were other questions calculated to show Rich Zepf was a weakling—a spineless no-account who never would have amounted to anything and who was trying desperately at the last moments of his life to make up for his unrelieved string of failures.

That was the moment Rich Zepf chose to have a coughing fit and spit blood all over the place. It projected out over the low wall of the witness box onto the table of the court reporter. It splattered on Rich's own shirt and Bomber was on his feet to comfort the witness in his most solicitous pose.

Judge Druckenmiller called a recess and excused the jury. Harrison Hinkle was livid. He asked for a conference with the judge. The tipstaff was taking Rich to the bathroom, his children looked horrified and Hinkle was storming.

"That smacks very much of a grandstand act to me," he said.

"Don't be stupid," Bomber countered. "The man is dying of lung cancer, thanks to your employer, and it's too dirty for you to look at."

"I'm not arguing that, I'm saying this display with the blood and all that showmanship was a play for the jury's sympathy."

Judge Druckenmiller looked down on Hinkle. "Really?" he said "You believe that was faked?"

"I do. I know Bomber Hanson's reputation and this kind of flimflam is right up his alley."

"Up my what?" Bomber said. When Hinkle looked afret, Bomber added, "I didn't hear you."

"Alley."

"Alley? My alley? What's my alley?"

"Never mind. I ask you to inquire of the witness under penalty of perjury if that was put on."

"Put on, man? Spitting blood for entertainment? Is that what they do in the Bronx or wherever you practice law?"

"Your Honor, I've had this clown up to here," Harrison Hinkle said, holding his nose. "Will you admonish the jury at least not to be swayed by what could very well be theatrics."

"And while you're at it, Your Honor," Bomber said, "mention the same goes for the smiley mayor. That's real grandstanding having him ask this witness the questions."

"Gentlemen, enough!"

"Tell you what," Bomber said to Hinkle, not heeding the judge's admonition. "Why don't you ask the witness if he faked it? He's under oath."

Judge Druckenmiller turned a hand palm up, as though he thought that was a reasonable solution.

Bomber knew Hinkle would never ask such a question in front of the jury. It would most certainly backfire. It was a no-winner, and Bomber knew it when he concocted the scene. I can't imagine anyone bringing it off better than Rich Zepf had.

The questioning continued, but Rich Zepf was not asked if his spitting blood was an act. The mayor wound down, leaving lots of innuendo here and there, but not scoring any real points.

Bomber asked a few clarifying questions and let Rich step down, which he did with dignity, aplomb, and his oxygen tank in front of him. No one complained the tank was visible.

None of the juror's eyes were on the smiling mayor. They were watching, I thought with respectful sympathy, Rich Zepf slowly and carefully take his seat.

"The plaintiff calls Edward Jones," Bomber said, and Harrison Hinkle hit the ceiling.

31

I'll say this for old Harrison J. Hinkle, Attorney-at-Law, he did his level best to keep his two biggest clients, Jones and Horowitz, off the witness stand and out of the clutches of the great Bomber.

The judge ruled against him, as I expect any judge would have done, but Hinkle wouldn't let up. I suppose he was trying to make a record to show President Jones and Bigbucks Horowitz. When Judge Druckenmiller finally closed Hinkle down, Bomber came back to our table. "Oh brother," he said, "now look who's grandstanding and that I'm-a-high-priced-New York-lawyer schtick isn't winning any points with the judge."

Bomber had Jones declared a hostile witness after his taking of the oath. The big, amiable man smiled and shook his head in that aw-shucks way of his, and he volunteered, "I'm not hostile to anyone."

Everybody warmed to him instantly.

Bomber laid the groundwork, getting Jones's background, profession, tenure, then asked, "And what are your duties at the company?"

"Oh, I guess you could say I'm a figurehead mostly. I schlepp around the countryside shaking hands, making speeches, playing golf."

"You played some golf in Cedarberg didn't you?"

"Yeah, if you want to call it playing. You have a very tough course here," he said looking at the jurors individually. "I didn't do so hot." The jurors smiled. You *had* to love this guy. There probably wasn't one juror who played golf, but they had their civic pride and he had flattered it.

"I noticed in the papers you were playing with some pretty famous sports figures. Do you pay them to play with you?"

He smiled. "I'd have to pay *any*body to play with me. Why not get the best?"

"How much do you pay that football player to play golf with you?"

"I don't know the details," he said waving a friendly hand. "He gets a yearly salary."

"To play golf with you?"

"He does PR—shows up at stuff. Plays golf, whatever."

"Is that what you call 'imaging'?" Bomber asked. "Giving your company a kind of athletic and fit image?"

"Yeah, I guess."

"Does he smoke?"

"I never asked him."

"Have you ever seen him smoke?"

"I don't remember if I have."

"Do you smoke?"

"No, sir."

"Why not?"

"Just never got the habit, I guess." Then that round, cherubic face beamed. "I got nothing against it."

"Do you have any health fears that might keep you from smoking?"

"Nah, that stuff's a bunch of baloney."

"Baloney? Will you look at the plaintiff please?"

"Where is he?"

Bomber moved over to stand behind Rich Zepf. Jones peered at him, then looked up at Bomber as if to say, "So?"

"This is Mr. Rich Zepf, father of these twelve lovely girls here. He's forty-four-years old. Mr. Zepf contracted lung cancer smoking four packs of your product every day."

"That's a lot of cigarettes," he said. "I imagine if you ate that much Swiss cheese you'd have trouble too."

"Do you have any studies to show Swiss cheese is additive, Mr. Jones?"

"I'm sure I could find one. They got studies to show anything."

"Are you aware of the studies that show cigarette smoking is addictive, and that smoking causes cancer, heart disease, emphysema?"

"I've heard of them."

"You haven't read them?"

"Nah."

"Why not?"

"That's not my thing."

"What is your *thing,* Mr. Jones?"

"Selling product, keeping up the image of the company, not scaring people to death."

"Are there others in your company who do deal with the studies?"

"Oh, yeah, and they make studies of their own."

"That show smoking is good for you?"

"In some cases, yes they do."

"What are some of the good ones?"

"Well, as I said, that's not my area of expertise. I'm a salesman."

"And isn't one of the vital attributes for a salesman product knowledge?"

"Sure."

"And do you feel you can achieve that requisite knowledge turning a blind eye to all the scientific research that continues to show smoking is not only dangerous, but lethal?"

"I don't buy that."

"Based on what?"

"I don't think it's been proven."

Bomber got his astonished look again. He waved his hand at Rich Zepf. "No? What more proof do you need?"

"Objection!"

"Sustained."

"Mr. Jones, you are aware people are dying of lung cancer?"

"Sure. And of colon cancer, pneumonia; we all die of something."

"Mr. Jones, please limit your answers to the questions. If

I want more information from you, I'll ask for it. You are an engaging man and I'm sure it would be pleasurable to chat with you sometime, but we are limited here to an investigation into your product that causes death."

"Your Honor," Hinkle pleaded.

"Yes, Mr. Hanson," Judge Druckenmiller said. "Don't lecture the witness."

"I stand corrected," Bomber said, with this short bow. Then Bomber, through arduous questioning, attempted to fathom Jones's compensation package—amid requisite objections from Harrison Hinkle. In addition to the gift of the jet airplane, Ed Jones took home a million in base salary and a nice passel of stock options.

Bomber was examining a report that the government conveniently required of public corporations. "Now it says the bonus is tied into the stock price and the profit of the company. Last year your bonus was about two-and-a-half million and change, it looks like," said Bomber, squinting at the fine print. "That seem about right?"

Jones shrugged. "I couldn't argue," he said.

"So the more cigarettes you sell, the more money you make personally, isn't that right, Mr. Jones?"

His hand started to move in front of him. "Everybody benefits when the company benefits."

"Did Mr. Zepf benefit?"

"I would have to say he did," Jones said. "We have to please our customers to be successful. People like to smoke or we wouldn't be in business. Wherever I go in this country, there are always people thanking me for making cigarettes."

"In the cancer wards?"

"*Ob*-jection!"

"Perhaps a bit inflammatory," Judge Druckenmiller said.

"You bet," Bomber said. "Their lungs are on fire!"

"Your Honor!"

"Mr. Hanson, please—no more of that."

"I stand corrected."

Before Bomber had finished with the Prexy of T. S. Armstead, he had elicited the information that the company's profit last year was over five billion. But Jones continued to deny that he ever gave anyone orders to add nicotine to the product to increase addiction.

"Any taste concessions we make are at the behest of our customers. We have to sell what they want or we'd be out of business."

"Mr. Jones, are you aware there is a considerable market in this country for cocaine?"

"Yes."

"Would you supply *them* with what they wanted under the guise of staying in business?"

"No, no. That's illegal."

"Why is it illegal?"

"Because its destructive, I guess."

"And what of the numerous studies that show cigarette smoking is destructive?"

He shook his head. "That hasn't been proven to my satisfaction."

"Yet you say you haven't read the studies."

"The studies, no. But I've read about them."

"Then what is it you don't believe?"

"They don't address the underlying issues of personality and heredity."

"Oh, but there *are* studies that do just that."

"I never analyzed it."

"Mr. Jones, you are giving us the impression here you are one laid-back dude…"

"Yeah, well I'm just really a figurehead, like I told you."

"You know anything about advertising?"

"I know we do it," he said with a twinkle in his eye. It got a laugh, and he was pleased. Making people happy was obviously his bag.

"Who makes the decision to target the kids with your ads?"

"Objection," Hinkle said. "Assumes facts not in evidence."

"Sustained."

"Do you target children to sell cigarettes?"

"Certainly not. Selling cigarettes to children is illegal."

"Why is that?"

"I don't know. I don't make the laws."

"Would you say it is because smoking is harmful to children?"

"I couldn't say."

"Do you not believe it is harmful?"

"Lot of people doing it."

There was more fencing with the president and C.E.O. of the T. S. Armstead company, but he was a man sublimely secure in his prejudices and even the great Bomber could not shake him. It would have been nice for us if he had admitted they added nicotine to make the product more addictive, or that they knew the studies linking smoking to terminal diseases were accurate, or that yes, they did study hypertense third graders to ascertain if they would be good candidates for smokers. But Bomber seemed satisfied some points had been made.

Harrison Hinkle declined the opportunity to question Jones, trying to make it look, I suppose, that none of the things he'd said to Bomber were important enough to bother with. Maybe too, he didn't want to risk alienating or disappointing the head man of the company that employed him and his firm full time, defending these burgeoning law suits.

"The plaintiff calls Mr. Jerry Horowitz," Bomber said, but Judge Druckenmiller wanted a recess.

*   *   *

Jerry Horowitz on the stand was a dream come true for Bomber. The "venture capitalist" was haughty, impatient, imperious, and sometimes downright nasty to Bomber and his questions. And to watch Bomber handle him was an education in itself. The meaner Horowitz became, the nicer Bomber was, until finally he was talking in a gently hushed voice I don't think I'd ever heard him use, in or out of court.

What we seemed to have established with Jerry Horowitz was that it was an astonishingly lucrative business, and it had become so big and so successful, with so many people dependent on it for their livelihood that the God of the Almighty Dollar had ascended to the heavens leaving a vacuum of morality here below. And they could afford any monetary award any jury could imagine.

It was no surprise to us that Harrison Hinkle said, "No questions," when Bomber was finished with Jerry Horowitz. Hinkle was relieved to get him off the stand.

Then it was time for our movie. Don Powell made a good impression, we had decided, when we screened the questioning, and now it was time for the jury to decide.

I watched the jury all the time they were watching the video. I wish I could say I divined what they thought, but they were a pretty impassive lot—and how could they have been anything else, with so many of us staring at them (the mayor was the official starer for the defense—I couldn't see if the smile was still pasted on his face because his back was to me).

After the film played itself out, Bomber made a big show of announcing, "The plaintiff rests, Your Honor."

Harrison Hinkle immediately made his motion to dismiss, claiming we had not proven our case, and Judge Druckenmiller immediately denied it.

After lunch, Hinkle opened his case with a short, but devastating speech.

"Ladies and gentlemen, you have had an opportunity to hear the plaintiff's version of the case and now it is the defendant's turn. We simply plan to refute everything they have claimed from their proposition that smoking kills you, to their strange insistence that nicotine is *added* to tobacco that already has it. And that this evil substance, by nefarious design, hooks and addicts people irreversibly. Well, this is nonsense, as you all know. We all know lots of people who stopped smoking. We will introduce studies to back up this claim, as well as other studies showing how smoking can be beneficial to certain types of people—those who are hypertense, those who have weight problems, those whose social life is boosted by conformity. Smoking is a pleasurable activity for many people. It is a *legal* activity. Manufacturing and selling cigarettes is legal, as we shall show. We are required by law to put certain warnings on all cigarette packaging and advertisements. This we do. We will also perform the sad duty of destroying the absurd testimony of this desperate former employee of T. S. Armstead, Mr. Don Powell. (He pronounced our star witness's name with a sneer). We will show he was simply an embezzler who was caught with his hand in the cookie jar. A man desperate to steal is a man desperate to counterpunch, which he has attempted to do in the film you have just seen. We will call two witnesses who will testify how they caught him embezzling. You then will make up your own minds about who are the honest, reliable witnesses. The defense calls Dr. Gerard Steinmetz."

Harrison Hinkle took him through his paces gently and the doctor showed he was a well-schooled, experienced witness—well worth whatever they were paying him—by his demeanor: serious, succinct and salesman-like. He had done a study, he said, showing the incidence of death from colon cancer was lower in smokers than in non-smokers.

Dr. Gerard Steinmetz was a tall, angular, slightly-stooped man who seemed to lean into the questions before he delivered his answers. It was time to cross-examine.

"Now, Dr. Steinmetz," Bomber began, "you *are* a doctor are you not? Mr. Hinkle referred to you as 'doctor.'"

"Yes."

"But he neglected to get your specialty. Are you an M.D.?"

"Ph.D."

"In micro-biology was it?"

"No. I am a specialist in diseases."

"Very good," Bomber said. "You did mention that under direct examination—would you mind telling us what your Ph.D. degree was in?"

"Physical Education."

Bomber got the hoped-for gasp in the courtroom. He looked at the witness as if he had just heard him say he was Alice in Wonderland. "You mean you are doing these studies and trying to pass them off as scientifically sophisticated?"

"Objection!" Hinkle said on his feet. "Mr. Hanson is editorializing, and there's no direct evidence for his accusations."

"Sustained," said the Buddha.

"No direct," Bomber muttered. "I stand corrected," he said aloud. "Now Mr.—ah, doctor—I was just trying to understand what a Ph.D. in Physical Education entailed. Is it shooting basketball hoops, kicking a football or what?"

"Oh no, it's *academic* work," he said with a measure of pride.

"I hope you're not angry at these questions?"

"No."

"Ordinarily, your attorney would get *all* your qualifications on the record."

"Objection."

"Sustained. You know better, Mr. Hanson."

"I stand corrected." Whenever Bomber said this, I always felt I was experiencing the peak of his showmanship. "Now Mr.—ah, doctor—"

"Your Honor," Hinkle was up again. "Mr. Hanson continually calls the witness 'Mr.' then corrects himself. This transparent belittling ploy is obviously a blatant attempt to minimize the witness's accomplishment, and I would thank you to ask Mr. Hanson to address the witness as doctor."

"Yes, Mr. Hanson," Judge Druckenmiller intoned solemnly.

"Simply a slip of the tongue," Bomber explained, but I doubt that anyone believed him. "A Ph.D. in Physical

Education certainly entitles a man to be called doctor, just as a Ph.D. in Nuclear Physics would—or Micro-biology perhaps. People with medical credentials who do academic studies—"

"Your Honor!" Hinkle demanded.

Druckenmiller squinted out of his remaining eye. "Yes, Mr. Hanson. No speeches, please."

"It was a grievous mistake and I abjectly apologize for it," Bomber said. Then turning to the witness, he said, "Please accept my apologies Mr.—ah, there I did it again. Doctor. *Doctor.* Doctor! I'll get it yet."

That called for a sidebar conference with the judge. "Look, Mr. Hanson, where you come from, your brand of showmanship may be tolerated, but it won't fly in *my* courtroom, and I don't want to hear any more of it. You have made your point about the man's qualifications, now move on to some real questions. Question the report in evidence if you want to. That's the testimony on the record."

"I stand corrected," Bomber said.

"Yes, well," Druckenmiller said. "I've heard *that* before. I'm serious. I don't want to hear any more of it. Sarcasm may have its place. It is not here, in any case."

I don't know if Druckenmiller was aware of his pun. I don't think so. Too bad, it might have contributed to humanizing him.

Bomber had no trouble showing up this charlatan. The research was flimsy, the results were tampered with and the good *doctor* used the most unscientific of methods. But for a measly hundred thousand, a figure Bomber squeezed out of his nemesis, the tobacco company got yet another "scientific study" showing the remarkable salubrious effects smoking could have.

After Dr. Steinmetz stepped down, somewhat shaken, Harrison Hinkle was quick to offer for stipulation his other experts. He had four more. Bomber would not stipulate to any of them.

"No, thank you," he said. "I'm sure you put your best foot forward with *Doctor* Steinmetz, and I'd be most anxious to cross-examine your string of charlatans."

"But I'm only suggesting you stipulate to what they will say, not to the truth of it."

"I'll stipulate to anyone who says smoking will kill you. Anything else, I want the jury to hear it from their own mouths. Look in their eyes. Weigh their souls."

Harrison Hinkle asked for a recess to contemplate putting on his "experts" and Judge Druckenmiller granted it.

32

Attorney Harrison Hinkle opted to put on the stand only one of the four experts he had scheduled. His selection was Ida Inman, a woman who would catch every eye in the house as she slithered sensuously to the witness chair. She had tobacco-colored hair that fell well below her shoulders and bobbed when she did. Her skirt was well-fitted and did nothing to inhibit any other bobbing.

Once she was settled into the witness chair, I was a little annoyed that she brought Shauna back into my thoughts. Court had been the one place I had been able to escape her spell.

Dr. Ida Inman began to speak to the glories of cigarette smoking as an antidote for hypertension, a promoter of weight loss and thus an enhancer of self-image. She was, she explained, the person who got the idea to track third graders who were hypertense to see if they smoked later in life and how they fared if they did or didn't. She emphasized, under Harrison Hinkle's expert questioning, there was no thought of using the study to sell cigarettes by targeting third graders, hypertense individuals or anyone else.

When it was Bomber's turn, you could see the witness dig her pretty red fingernails into the arms of the witness chair. She had been warned to expect the worst.

Bomber stood up slowly, didn't move from the plaintiff's table and asked gently, but incredulously: "I have only one question, Dr. Inman. Do you actually believe the things you said?"

She sputtered. Her mouth started to open, then shut. She ran her hand through the tobacco hair, her lips began to form a word, then gave up. Finally she cleared her throat and put what force she had left in the words: "Yes, I do."

But it didn't come out as convincingly as she meant it to, and Bomber just stared at her as though listening to a fruit cake popping candied cherries.

Then came our case crushers in tandem. Karl Eldridge, controller of T. S. Armstead was sworn in. He would be followed by Don Powell's secretary, Felicity Wilkins.

You could easily tell Karl had been a state trooper. He still had the posture of one striding toward your driver's side window, and as you slid it down, asking to see your driver's license. And it would never have seemed routine with Karl. His actions always carried with them the dead weight of the world, and with Karl leaning in your car window nothing would seem as serious, not war or peace or the super bowl.

Often shorter guys like Karl seem taller because of their ramrod posture. Karl just seemed like a short guy trying to look tall.

There was no leaning into the questions with Karl Eldridge, no twiddling with his hair and it was moral rectitude he tried to pass off with that posture.

Harrison Hinkle, advocate for the defense, put him gingerly through his paces, getting out the background of his discovery. Karl Eldridge was not an endearing witness, he was too stiff for that, but he was far worse for our side. He was believable. And the story he told was devastating.

He made no pretense about his importance, rather cleverly underplayed it. "My signature is in the check signing machine so it does most of the work," he said on the witness stand.

"Do you see every check that goes out?" Harrison Hinkle asked.

"Oh no. There are thousands a day. I try to spot glance at them, but I do see every one over ten-thousand dollars."

"Why is that?"

"The company requires two signatures, originals, on checks over ten-thousand dollars."

"You mean they must be hand-signed?"

"Yes."

"What do you do when you see a check that doesn't seem legitimate to you?"

"Question it. Check the paperwork. The work orders, purchase orders, check requisitions. Call the originating party to verify it."

"Now, directing you attention to your official duties last month, did you see anything in the checks that were presented for your signature that seemed unusual?"

"I did."

"Tell the jury what that was, if you please."

"I found a check for the purchase of tobacco from a supplier I didn't recognize. The amount was just under one-hundred-thousand dollars—ninety-eight-something, as I recall."

"Would $98,317.95 be that amount?"

"I think so."

Here, Harrison Hinkle offered the check made out to Country Tobacco Co-op as a defense exhibit.

Then he offered a paycheck made out to Don Powell as another exhibit. "Checking the deposit information on the back of these two checks, do you see any similiarities?"

"Yes, they were both deposited into Don Powell's personal account."

"So the check was deposited?"

"Yes."

"With your signature on it?"

"Yes."

"Why did you sign it?"

"I called Don Powell and he assured me the company was a new supplier and we got a great price, and he wanted to deliver it personally to cement relations for future business."

"And you signed and sent the check to Mr. Powell?"

"Yes."

"All right, did you get any more checks made out to

Country Tobacco Co-op?"

"Yes, sir, I did."

"The amount?"

"About the same."

"Would $99,207.15 be correct?"

Harrison Hinkle showed the witness the check and made it another exhibit. "Did you sign this check?"

"No, sir."

"Why not?"

"Because I had just gotten the other canceled check and I noticed it went into Mr. Powell's personal account."

"How did you happen to notice that?"

"I check all the endorsements on large checks."

"Those over ten thousand?"

"Yes. I wanted to see how this company endorsed it. You are always wary of fraud and theft on these larger checks."

"And that fear was well-founded this time?"

"Yes, sir, it was."

With that, he recited the facts of the arrest—telling his superior what happened, and that had ended his involvement, until today.

Bomber rose to cross-examine.

"Company treat you all right, Mr. Eldridge?"

"I never worked anywhere better."

"You worked for the State Troopers before you went to T. S. Armstead?"

"That's correct."

"How did you happen to make the change?"

"They were looking for security people, and I applied and got the job."

"How many others applied at the same time?"

"That, I do not know."

"How did you find out about the opening?"

"I just heard about it."

"From whom?"

"I don't remember."

"Was it advertised in the paper?"

"I do not know."

"You didn't see an ad at any rate?"

"I did not."

"Someone told you about the job opening?"

"Yes, sir."

"But you can't remember who?"

"I cannot."

"Can you try to remember something about this person—anything at all?"

"No, I cannot."

"Was it a man or a woman?"

"A man."

"So we've already narrowed the field to about half the population; good," Bomber said. "Now, was it a minor? A man under eighteen, say?"

"No."

"Over sixty-five or seventy?"

"No."

"Bald?"

"No."

"Taller than you are?"

"I couldn't honestly say. It goes back many years."

"Have you ever been in a barroom?"

"Yes, I have."

"Do you drink?"

"Socially."

"Ever been drunk?"

"No, sir. I always keep my drinking under control."

"Good for you. Now, in your work for the State Troopers, you did a lot of highway patrolling, I believe you said."

"Yes, sir."

"Did you stop drunk drivers?"

"Yes, sir."

"Do you remember the last person you stopped before

you got your job offer at T. S. Armstead Company?"

"Your Honor, I really must object," Harrison Hinkle said after lifting himself wearily to his feet. "I'm afraid we are so far afield now. I would hope we could get back on the track."

"Yes," Judge Druckenmiller said. "I don't see the relevance here, counselor. Aren't you working on the integrity of your witness?"

"Yes, through this witness. He is the one who has attempted to destroy Mr. Powell's integrity. I think his bears looking into."

"Well, I will allow it, but get to it."

"Very well," Bomber said bowing to Buddha, then turning to Karl Eldridge. "Isn't it true that you stopped an officer of the T. S. Armstead Company and he was quite drunk, flunked all your tests and you took him in to the police station where he offered you a job at a much higher salary than the state was paying you, in exchange for dropping the charges against him?"

"That's not true." Karl Eldridge answered while Bomber tried to stare him down.

"Then who did tell you about the job?"

"I don't remember."

"Come now, Mr. Eldridge, an important move like that—"

"Objection," Hinkle said. "Asked and answered."

"Sustained."

"Now, Mr. Eldridge, you testified for Mr. Hinkle that your first job in the company was in security. And that entailed patrolling the building to keep it secure, looking for intruders, potential criminals, detaining suspects where you had evidence of crimes. Is that right?"

"Yes, sir."

"Did you make any arrests for crimes?"

"Yes, we had some robberies, some theft of property among the employees. Attempted rape. Battery."

"And did you catch the perpetrators?"

"In most cases, yes, sir."

"Do you remember crimes for which you did not catch the perpetrator?"

"I'm sure there were some, but I cannot recall the specifics at this point in time."

"Did you investigate—during your time as a security guard, any murders at the company?"

"No, sir."

"Were there, to your knowledge, any murders committed?"

"No, sir."

"Does the name Nick Underwood mean anything to you?"

The witness considered the name for a few moments. "I cannot say that it does."

"Ray Strong?"

"No."

"Both worked for Armstead when you started."

Eldridge shook his head.

"Mr. Underwood disappeared, was never heard from again. Wouldn't that have been a security case?"

"I cannot say. It was not my case if it was a case. Missing persons are police work."

"But you remember nothing about it?"

"Nothing."

"Never heard the name?"

"Your Honor, this is all irrelevant. He has been asked, he has answered, and yet Mr. Hanson keeps plowing the same ground."

"In search of the truth, counselor," Bomber said.

"I'm inclined to agree with Mr. Hinkle," Judge Druckenmiller said. "Please move on to something else, Mr. Hanson."

"As you wish. Mr. Eldridge, you said you had a conversation with Mr. Powell about his check—the first check for ninety-eight-something thousand—before you deposited it. Is that correct?"

"Yes, sir."

"Was that in person or on the telephone?"

"Telephone."

"Do you remember when?"

"No—the day I got it, I think."

"Would that be the date on the check?"

"Could be, or it could be the next day."

"You don't remember which?"

"No."

"But that would have been the twelfth or thirteenth of last month, is that correct?"

"If the check is dated the twelfth."

"It is. What time of day would it have been?"

"I don't know."

"Anytime?"

"Yes."

"Do you get checks dated the twelfth on the eleventh?"

"No."

"Are they on your desk when you come in in the morning?"

"Sometimes. It just depends when they run them."

"What hours do they print checks?"

"Around the clock."

"But you don't remember if this one was on your desk, or brought to you later?"

"Sorry, I don't."

"Do you remember if there were others with it?"

"I don't think so, but I couldn't be sure."

"So your testimony is sometime the twelfth or thirteenth you called Don Powell and asked about this check."

"Yes."

"But you don't remember when?"

"No."

"Who answered the phone?"

"Felicity."

"Felicity?"

"His secretary."

"You were acquainted with her?"

"Yes."

"On a first-name basis?"

"She used to work for me."

"Did you have a personal relationship, also?"

"Objection."

"I think it's very relevant."

"He may answer," Judge Druckenmiller said.

"I would say I try to have personal relationships with everyone in my department."

"What do your personal relationships entail?"

"Oh, talking to them about their lives, their families, dreams and such."

"Ever entail intimacy?"

"Not physical, no."

"Never?"

"Never!" He seemed adamant.

"But you knew Mr. Powell's secretary Felicity because she had been your secretary?"

"Yes."

"Right before she moved to him?"

"Yes. I was sorry to lose her."

"Why didn't you keep her?"

"Personnel wanted to promote her. She got more salary, working for a more important man. I didn't want to stop that." Did the witness betray any jealousy with that "more important man" stuff? I hoped the jury thought so.

"Did you have any say in the matter?"

"Not really."

"Did you encourage her to move?"

"I didn't discourage it."

"Will you answer the question please?"

"Did I encourage her? I don't remember. I hope I did, because it was better for her."

"But you don't remember?"

"No, sir."

"You seem to have a very selective memory. Mr. Eldridge."

"*Objection*! Strike that."

"Yes," Judge Druckenmiller agreed. "You know better."

"I stand corrected. So Felicity answered the phone. Did you discuss the check with her?"

"No."

"At no time?"

"Not that I recall."

"Think, please."

"I don't know why I would have."

"I don't either. The question was, did you?"

"Not that I recall."

"Did you talk to her then about her hopes and dreams?"

"I did not. She was no longer working for me. I asked to speak to Mr. Powell. She put him on and that was that."

"And what did you say to him?"

"I asked about the new vendor. He said it was legitimate. They were offering top product at a good competitive price."

"So you signed it?"

"Yes."

"With no more doubt?"

"I didn't have any doubt, no."

"Mr. Powell was a man of integrity."

"As far as I knew, yes."

"Felicity didn't give you any reason to believe otherwise?"

"No, sir. She was no longer my secretary."

"So you said. Did you call again when you found the check had been deposited to his personal account?"

"No, I did not."

"Why not?"

"I did not know what I could say."

"How about, 'Did *you* deposit this check to your

account?' or perhaps, 'Could this have been a mistake?'"

"Well, I didn't. This was beyond my job description. I went to my boss with it."

"Who is that?"

"The executive vice-president—Evan Keller."

"And what did he say?"

"Not much. He was shocked, of course, but he said he would take care of it. And that's the last I've had to do with it until today."

"They arrested Don Powell, didn't they?"

"So I've heard."

"Put him in jail."

"I understand."

"And you said you respected him as a man of integrity."

"Before that, yes."

"And Felicity did not give you cause to waver in that respect in any way?"

"She did not."

"Then why, in the name of goodness and brotherhood, justice and mercy, didn't you call him to ask if *he* put that check in his personal account?"

"Who else would do it?"

"Now you're asking the questions. I can think of many people who could have, now that you asked."

Harrison Hinkle started to get up but Judge Druckenmiller beat him to the crack of his gavel. "You're not testifying, Mr. Hanson."

"I stand corrected," Bomber said. "No further questions."

"Call Felicity Wilkins," Harrison Hinkle said.

33

Felicity Wilkins was a woman who carried with her the burden of the arithmetic mean.

She was not tall nor thin, but had a regal air that somehow seemed bogus. She fell somewhere near the middle of a mass of nine or ten kids born to a couple with a small tobacco farm. Sharecroppers, they used to call them, because they didn't own the farm, they just worked it and shared the profits when there were any. Every now and then, the federal government had paid them *not* to plant tobacco, and those were good years for the Wilkinses.

Felicity might have been stouter, had she not been a smoker. Smoking was a matter of patriotism for her. All her family was economically tied to the tobacco industry in one way or the other, and they all smoked. And not one of them ever felt any pain from it. The Wilkinses, among others, were convinced that the smoking scare was a Yankee plot to bring the South to its knees the second time.

Some witnesses were impervious to being rattled even by the great Bomber. Either because they were telling the truth and were secure in that knowledge, or because they believed so strongly in the importance of what they were saying they couldn't let go.

Felicity was a calm, reassuring witness. She answered the questions carefully in a well-modulated voice which was just strong enough to be heard without straining.

"You didn't want to testify here, did you?" Hinkle asked her.

"No, sir, I didn't," she said.

"Will you tell the jury why not?"

"Because I like my boss. I can't bear to see him in this trouble," she fought back a torrent of tears. "He's such a nice man."

"He was a good boss?"

"*Very!*"

"Did you agree to testify back when the embezzlement was discovered?"

She shook her head and the hairs of her blond pageboy wafted side to side like a stage curtain pulled closed in a hurry, perhaps on a disastrous production. I only wished for a little disaster in Felicity's performance. So far it was flawless.

She told a tale that dovetailed perfectly with the tale told by her former boss, Karl Eldridge. Too perfectly for my taste. I didn't envy Bomber trying to poke holes in her story.

Felicity had a partial smile on her face when Bomber came toward her. "Miss Wilkins—you *aren't* married, are you?"

"No."

"Ever been?"

"No."

"Mind if I call you Miss—or would you prefer Mizzz." The way Bomber drew the later out left no doubt which he preferred.

"No, that's okay. It doesn't matter."

"Thank you. Now Miss Wilkins, you said Mr. Powell was a wonderful boss, is that correct?"

"Oh, yes."

"You worked for Mr. Eldridge before Mr. Powell, correct?"

"Yes."

"Was he a good boss?

"Oh, yes."

"So, you like all your bosses?"

"Well, I wouldn't go that far. But these two were great."

"If you had a choice—all other things like salary, hours, office environment were equal, which man would you rather work for?"

She shook her head as if bewildered. "Oh, I really couldn't say, they were both great."

"Can you characterize the differences between them?"

"Well, I guess Mr. Eldridge I worked for longer and I got to know him better personally. Mr. Powell is very pleasant, but it was pretty much business with him."

"Mr. Eldridge took you for coffee and things?"

"Yes."

"And talked about your dreams and things?"

"Yes."

"Mr. Powell didn't get that personal?"

"Nooo." She seemed unsure of this answer, as though it might not have been the right thing to say.

"Exactly how personal did Mr. Eldridge get?" Bomber asked. "Was there any physical intimacy?"

"Oh, no!" she answered quickly. Too quickly.

"Is that an idea you have never entertained?"

"Not with my boss, no."

"Why is that?"

"He was married."

"Had he not been married would you have considered physical intimacy with Mr. Eldridge?"

"Only if *we* were married."

"How long did you work for Mr. Powell?"

"About six months, I guess—before he was arrested."

"In that time, did you do any personal chores for him?"

"Oh, no, he never asked for anything personal."

"Who deposited his paychecks?"

"I did that."

"You don't consider that personal?"

"No, I didn't," she said. "That was to do with business—his pay from the company."

"To his personal bank account?"

"Yes, well, if that was personal, I did it."

"And how did you do it—what were the steps?"

"Well, when his check came in the interoffice mail, I

would endorse it for deposit only to his account number, and fill in his deposit slips and mail it to the bank—they gave us envelopes."

"Where did you get the deposit slips?"

"Mr. Powell gave them to me at first. When I needed more, the bank sent them."

"How did you fill the slips out—with pencil, pen, what?"

"I typed them."

"Typed them? Isn't that a lot of trouble?"

"No. My handwriting isn't so good. I don't want them getting the wrong numbers because they cannot read my writing, so I typed them."

"On your typewriter at the office?"

"Yes."

"Can other people use it?"

"Sure, it's not locked or anything."

"Did you ever see anyone else use your typewriter?"

"Just the time I saw Mr. Powell using it."

"Could you tell us about that? How was he typing? Was it one finger at a time, or did it look like he was good at it—using the touch system?"

"I didn't see that. I wasn't close enough and he was finished in such a hurry."

"Did Mr. Powell ever ask you to deposit any checks in his personal account, other than his paychecks?"

"No."

"Did you write checks on his account?"

"Oh, no."

"Ever see his bank statements?"

"No, they went to his home, I believe."

"How do you know that?"

"Well, that's true, I don't. They didn't come to the office that I know of—and I got the mail first, but I don't know for sure, you're right."

"Were you in love with Mr. Eldridge, Miss Wilkins?"

Bomber shot at her out of the blue, hoping to catch her off guard.

"Gosh, no," she said flushing slightly, but the jury would excuse that because of the suddenness of Bomber's thrust. "We were friends is all."

"Did he ask you to deposit the ninety-eight-thousand-dollar check made out to Country Tobacco Co-op?"

"Did who ask me?"

"Either one of them?"

"No."

"Then why did you ask *who?*"

"I don't know. I think you're trying to confuse me."

"I'm not trying to confuse you, Miss Wilkins," Bomber said, but, of course, he was trying to do just that and not having a good time of it, either.

Bomber did not so much finish with Miss Felicity Wilkins as a witness, as give up on her. At the end of the day, we went out to a very glum dinner together.

Without having to say it, we all communicated our feelings that we were doomed. Bomber spoke of hope. "Somewhere in that pair, there must be an Achilles heel."

I told him what it was. I had to apologize for not telling it sooner, but I didn't really see what good it would have done. Ray Strong wouldn't tell his story—the company had been too good to him.

"Remember me telling you about Ray Strong?"

"Who?"

"The guy in the hospital—was a janitor."

"Oh, the black guy? Yeah, what about him?"

"I showed him Karl Eldridge's picture. He identified him as being the guy who brought him the dead body of the missing Armstead executive."

"Brought him a body? What for?"

"To put in the furnace."

Bomber's hand came down on the table like a meteorite. "Jesus Jenny, Tod, why didn't you *tell* me about this?"

"Thought it was hopeless. The guy is bedridden—the company picks up the tab. He is very grateful to them."

"Hell, we could support him."

"Without making it look like we had bribed a witness?"

"Yeah, well, *they're* bribing him."

"He was on their their dole before we had a case."

"But this is golden, Tod. There has to be a way."

"I shook my head. "Too f-f-frail to trav-vel."

"Another video," Bomber said, the steamroller was in motion.

"I don't think he'll d-do it."

"Well, get him on the horn. Give him the motherhood, country, duty pitch. We are being lied into a defeat here that is going to be very hard to take. He's our ace. Tell him."

"Will the judge let it in?"

"Sure. Impeaches their witness. Said he had nothing to do with that guy. What was his name? The disappearance. He knew nothing, remember—*falsus in uno, falsus in omnibus*," Bomber said. It was one of his favorite Latin legalisms—false in one thing, false in all things. A tenet at law that allowed a jury to assume that everything a witness says is false if they catch him in one lie.

With a little more coaxing—strong arming would be more accurate—I went to the phone to call Dr. Sciaparelli. I told his answering service it was an emergency and he took the call.

"Doctor," I began with all the heartiness I could fake, "how *are* you?"

"Not so good," he said. "Lost a patient last night, one of my favorites—more than a patient, he was—a real friend."

He didn't have to tell me who he was talking about.

The next morning in court, Bomber told the tale to Judge Druckenmiller and asked permission for me to testify to what Ray Strong had told me. Hinkle objected so strenuously he got red in the face.

"Blatant hearsay," he stormed. Lucky for him the jury was not in place because it didn't look like he would be able to bring these emotions under control. "And from one of the plaintiff's own lawyers—his *son* yet! Absolutely *un*believable!"

Judge Druckenmiller looked me in the eyes with his open eye. "Tell me what transpired with this man, this Ray, ah, Strong."

I gave him all the background, my trips to visit him, his story about the cremation. When I got to that point, Hinkle cranked up his emotions again and said, "The hallucinations of a deranged and dying man. What stock could you put in such a fantasy?"

"Please, Mr. Hinkle," Judge Druckenmiller said. "Let him finish, then *I'll* decide."

"When I heard the defense witness used to be in security at Armstead, I had a hunch. I got from Gina Powell, our witness's wife, a copy of the annual report with Eldridge's picture in it. I took it to Ray Strong in the hospital, told him I had a picture and I wanted him to tell me if this was one of the security men for Armstead who brought him the body to put in the furnace."

"This is pre*pos*terous!" Hinkle shouted. "There are over a hundred security people there, all with impeccable credentials. This is a new low in trying to destroy the company."

"Please, Mr. Hinkle, calm down, will you? Go on, Mr. Hanson."

"He didn't want to look for fear it might be the right man. Frankly, I suspect he knew who he was. You don't forget an incident like that."

"Did he identify him?" The judge seemed in a mood to cut to the chase.

"I tried to be tactful—to respect his wishes, so I said, 'I'm going to show you this picture, and if it is of an innocent man—if this is not the man who brought you the body it is your duty as a human being to tell me this man is innocent. To be fair and just to this man *and* the company, you must say, *"That is not the man!"* loud and clear.' I showed him the picture, and he said nothing."

"Ah ha!" Harrison Hinkle said. "You expect to use silence as hearsay evidence? No way, Jose."

"It does seem a little tenuous, Mr. Hanson. It is a very tricky proposition to start with. But him saying nothing can be construed in so many ways. Maybe he refused to look because he didn't want to cooperate. Maybe his eyesight was shot and he didn't want to admit it. Or maybe it was so poor he couldn't make out the features."

Bomber got into the fray. "And maybe the reason he didn't want to voice his knowledge was he was terrified. He'd participated in cremating a body which, even in North Carolina has to be against the law, that didn't make him feel secure, I'm sure. And if they could do *that*, murder an executive that displeased them, what would they do to a lowly janitor?"

"Fantasy! Pure fantasy!" Harrison Hinkle stormed. "Bomber Hanson is well known for these fantastic diversions, and, sure enough, here is another one."

"Well, hold your horses there, partner," Bomber said. "Bomber Hanson may well have an undeserved reputation for diversions but you aren't paying attention here. This is *Tod* Hanson talking. I never met Ray Strong."

"Tod, Bomber, what's the difference?"

There was a lot of difference, I wanted to tell him, but surely he could figure that out on his own.

Judge Druckenmiller decided he would give us the rest of the day to cite case law in our behalf. He dismissed the jury and told us to be back in the morning with our best ammunition.

Easy Willie went to work in Shauna's department but he was no slouch at case law. I tried to pitch in, but I wasn't much good at it. And Bomber spent the day, as he characterized it, looking for a miracle.

Next morning, we presented our cases. None of us were too surprised that Judge Druckenmiller ruled for the defense. We just watched our case drop out from under us. I'd seen Bomber pull out some pretty weak cases with his jury oratory, but this time we were stretching.

Bomber asked for a recess until Monday so we could go back to North Carolina to video rebuttal testimony from Don Powell. Harrison Hinkle objected, of course.

"Well then, get him up here like a human being," Bomber shot out. "Our case has been irreparably damaged with this charade of your defendants, locking him up on a trumped-up charge and not letting him appear in court. Put him up on the witness stand where everyone can judge him, compare him to that storm trooper who is accusing him, or shut up and make us all schlepp back to North Carolina like going to hell in a hand basket. The man has been irreversibly maligned. We are certainly entitled to hear from him on rebuttal. And don't be surprised if we slap you with a lawsuit for false arrest, defamation of character and slander."

Buddha granted our request.

But we were not a trio of happy campers who made the flight to Churchill Park, North Carolina. Doom was in the air, gloom was in our bones. What could Don Powell really say that would pull this thing out? Their two witnesses had been too firm. Impeaching Karl Eldridge now seemed an impossible dream.

We went through the motions anyway. Don Powell roundly denied, and persuasively so, that he ever deposited any check while Felicity worked for him, or ever used the typewriter. "*Never!*" he said. "I don't even know how to use it. I don't think I could get the paper in the thing."

Of course, we all believed him, but we all know the defense could, and probably would, come up with as many witnesses as they wanted to swear they had seen him use the typewriter—all with synchronized watches if need be.

Powell also swore he never heard of Country Tobacco Co-op, never asked anyone to make up a check to them, and when shown the typed requisition, he said he never saw it before.

What's more, Karl Eldridge never talked to him about that check or any other.

We believed him, and I wouldn't have been surprised if Harrison Hinkle believed him. He did not seem too involved in cross-examining Powell. Harrison Hinkle was acting like a man who knew he had the case won. He had put on *two* believable witnesses to our one. Corroboration was potent.

On our way back to Cedarberg, Bomber confessed that he hadn't expected more than we got, but we had to do it. "Who knows, maybe the jurors will believe Powell. Karl Eldridge is pretty hard cheese and the girl is almost too-too. You know that stuff about nothing physical unless she were married."

"Maybe we should do some more digging."

"Could," Bomber agreed, halfheartedly. "Let's suppose we turn up Polaroids of Karl Eldridge in bed with Felicity Wilkins. What would we have? A motive for blackmailing Don Powell?"

"No," Easy Willie said, "we would have proven them both liars."

"Yeah, but easily explained away by Hinkle," Bomber said. "A blushing young flower of southern womanhood, frightened for her reputation. A harmless white lie in the scheme of things. Maybe we could blast 'em, but maybe it would backfire."

We were served something on the plane. I wasn't sure what: chicken, pork, veal, turkey—something that color with a faint flavor that was interchangeable.

Easy Willie and Bomber had the sense not to eat it. I am still at the age where it is very difficult not to eat free food.

When we arrived back at the hotel, I declined the invitation to join Bomber and Easy Willie for dinner. I was in no mood for further depressing camaraderie. I went to my room instead and pulled out the score for *Suite: Love* from the dresser drawer and began to tinker with it. I wondered if I would ever see Shauna McKinley again. I wasn't sure I wanted to, understand, I just wondered if I would. She was, I congratulated myself falsely, pretty well out of my system.

The operative words there were "pretty well" which

actually meant she wasn't out of my system at all. I just wasn't admitting it. I could not get out of my mind the certainty that Shauna was not that kind of girl. Something had befallen her that was not her fault.

Just as I was entertaining this fantasy, the phone rang. I just knew it was my mother asking me how I was getting along with my new girlfriend. So I was pretty glum when I said, "Hello."

"Tod," the voice said, and it was so small and unsure I wasn't sure who it was.

"Yesss?" I said, half expecting to be pitched to buy the local paper.

"Do you hate me?" she asked. And then I knew who it was.

34

I wouldn't mind sharing my emotions on hearing Shauna's still, small voice, but I have not yet been able to sort them out. There was joy, but also anger; hope, but also despair. But by the time our voices parted, she had made us an offer we were in no position to refuse.

I went right Bomber's room to tell him in person. I met him in the hallway. He had a toothpick in his mouth. "What's up?" he said. He could tell from the look on my face something was exciting me.

I signaled him away from the door. I didn't want to share my news with any possible electronic devices. After I looked up and down the hall which ran the length of the building, I whispered, "Shauna called."

"The bitch," he muttered. "I hope you told her to drop dead."

"No. I didn't."

"Well, you should have."

"No, I shouldn't have," I said, then I told him what she offered to do. And I did it without stuttering. At least that's the way I remember it.

He changed his tune in a hurry. I could see through his eyes all the gears whirling and meshing in his brain—the transformation of good news to strategy. Instantly, he was in a world of his own, anxious to get to his room to get it all down on paper. I don't think he realized I was with him at that point. Feeling the conversation needed a conclusion, I said, "Well, good night. I'll s-s-see you tom-m-morrow."

He didn't respond.

Back in my room, I couldn't sleep, so I took another

look at *Suite: Love* which was still out on the desk. I had some ideas for softening revisions. Maybe even a kind of triumphal march which I could now imagine.

I must have dozed off with the strains of my *Suite* running through my head at about three-thirty in the morning, only to wake up humming at about five, at the thought of Shauna flying back to town.

We were all in court a few minutes before nine. The girls were sitting in the front row and Rich was sitting at our plaintiff's table, tucking his oxygen tank out of sight. The Zepf family looked down. Perhaps it was my imagination, but they seemed to reflect the mood of their attorneys, which should not be that surprising. Of course, we tried to hide our discouragement from them, never discussing it with them, but somehow those things seep through, even to the youngest child.

I stopped at their row and put on my quarter-moon smile. "Girls, you look like a million bucks. You want to look like ten million, stick some smiles on your beautiful faces. Come on now, that's it. We're going to have some real good news for you."

Rich was turned to face us, and as the girls's faces lit up, so did his. This kind of thing *is* contagious, even to a blind man.

Bomber asked the judge for a conference before the jury came in. Buddha seemed a little weary this morning. "What is it?" he asked, as though he thought this aggravation was about over.

"With your permission, Your Honor, we would like to wrap up our case."

"Good. You *have* my permission."

"We would like your permission to show the video we made of Don Powell in rebuttal…"

"Any problem with that Mr. Hinkle?"

"No, Your Honor." Hinkle was a man who knew he had the case in the bag. You could tell he had programmed himself to magnanimity from here on.

"Very well," the judge said, as though that were the end

of it. "We'll call the jury then—"

"Oh, Your Honor—"

"Yes."

"There *is* one more thing."

"What is it?"

"A witness in rebuttal."

"A new witness?"

"Yes, Your Honor."

"Who is it?"

"Shauna McKinley," Bomber said, and I saw Harrison Hinkle's face drop right to the floor. He started to sputter his objections. He was so tongue-tied you'd have thought it was me talking. The Buddha calmed him down.

"What will her rebuttal be?" Judge Druckenmiller asked Bomber.

"Shauna McKinley will testify that, while she worked for me on this case, she was bribed by a defense attorney to feed them information, which she did. The timing will be shown by her testimony to coincide with the arrest of Don Powell and the bogus deposit to his account."

"This is preposterous," Harrison Hinkle said.

"Yes, isn't it?" Bomber said, with all his bravura restored.

"Do you have a copy of the bribery check?"

"We will have," Bomber said. "I'm expecting it today. Tomorrow at the latest."

"Where is she now?" Judge Druckenmiller asked.

"On her way here."

"From where?"

"Your Honor, I would respectfully request not to have to answer that because of the sensitive nature of her testimony."

"You mean you fear for her safety?"

"Yes, sir, I do."

"This is *so* outrageous," Harrison Hinkle sputtered. "I can assure you, Your Honor, I had nothing to do with any bribery, nor did any of my team. And I can also assure you that

T. S. Armstead Company never issued a check for bribery. How foolish can you be?"

"Quite right," Bomber said, "The money was wired to a bank account she set up."

"Well, that is not from the company," Hinkle answered the judge. "No connection."

"No? Well, it certainly was sweet of someone to give my legal researcher a million dollars."

"A mil—" Hinkle choked on the word and Buddha frowned.

"I think I'd like to hear this testimony," Judge Druckenmiller said.

"But, Your Honor," Hinkle complained, "this is a ruse, pure and simple. I wouldn't put it past the plaintiff to make all this up to muddy the waters. They are desperate. Everything has gone against them, so Bomber tells the girl to disappear, make up some cockamamie story and set up some bank account."

"And have the transfer clear?" Bomber asked.

"Your Honor, I want time to examine this witness *in camera*. This is highly inflammatory, misleading testimony and I was not apprised until right now that he was planning to put her on the stand with this fantasy."

"We didn't know until last night Miss McKinley would testify, Your Honor," Bomber said.

"It is completely irrelevant to this lawsuit, Your Honor," Hinkle said. "And totally fraudulent."

"You will have a chance to cross-examine her," Druckenmiller said. "We will hear the witness. When do you expect her, Mr. Hanson?"

"I would like to schedule her for first thing tomorrow morning, if I may, Your Honor. I don't expect her in until late this afternoon."

"Any objection, Mr. Hinkle?"

"I've already made my objection," he said glumly, "and I'd like to note an exception from your ruling on the record."

"So noted. Well, I'm sure the jury won't mind the afternoon off. Call them please, tipstaff."

The jury came in and the video was shown. It took up the rest of the morning. As near as any of us could tell, the jury did not seem moved by our witness and his sincere denials. It seemed their minds were already made up.

They did smile when the judge excused them until the following morning. It was getting hot in Cedarberg, Pennsylvania, and this glorious old courthouse was not air conditioned. We were upstairs and heat rises.

As an extra precaution, Bomber had Shauna fly to the Philadelphia airport, a couple hours from Cedarberg. I wimped out on going to get her. I felt I had been betrayed, big-time, and maybe she could partially redeem herself with her testimony, but I would wait and see. So Easy Willie went for her and, with him, two burly armed guards. Bomber wasn't risking a hair on her head. We feared the enemy might camp out at the little Cedarberg airport, but thought they probably wouldn't think to cover any of the others.

The guards were to stay with Shauna until the case concluded. Bomber got her a room at the hotel, though I protested. I was convinced that it was a lot safer than stashing her somewhere else, guards or no. The problem was I was fighting with myself to keep myself from running to her. Not going to the airport was the first step. There were about eleven others.

Shauna was due in Philadelphia at about five. She would be back at the hotel at seven at the earliest. At five, I went across the street to Sachs Department Store (no relation to Saks) and headed for their basement restaurant, where they served food, the portions of which were ideal for burying your sorrows.

At six-thirty, I was back in my room posted at the window, a hidden but anxious look-out. It wasn't until almost half-past seven that the car rolled up and the two armed huskies popped out and cased the environs like they were advance men for the president. Then Easy Willie stood out and looked both ways—and then I saw her, but briefly, as she was whisked in the front door. I got mainly a glance at the red, foamy, top of her head and then she was gone. She would be under the same roof as I was, and in a few minutes Bomber would be drilling her on her testimony and I would be going crazy in my room, trying to stay away from her.

Easy Willie followed the entourage into the hotel with Shauna's suitcase. It didn't look from that lone piece of luggage that she planned to stay very long.

I tried to work on my *Suite: Love*. I thought it would be germane to add a haunting melody or two. But I couldn't even hum a melody, let along write one in my suite.

Somehow the sun went down and the room went dark without my knowing it.

A century or two later, I had a strange feeling like I was being tugged in the direction of the bed. Naturally, I thought it was Shauna tugging me and just as naturally, I realized she wasn't. I got myself over there and lay down on the spread. I didn't seem to have the gumption to take my clothes off.

Still another century later, the phone rang. It wasn't like Bomber to call me so late unless he needed something I could provide. "Hello," I grumbled.

"Hi, Tod," Shauna said.

"Oh, hi," I said like a zombie talking to his nemesis.

"I don't blame you for not coming to see me," Shauna said. "Shall I come to see you?"

My knuckles turned to icicles I squeezed the phone so hard.

"What room are you in?"

"I... I... I don't, ah, re-mem-ber."

There was a silence and I thought I heard a sniffle. "That's okay," she said. "I deserve it. I just want you to know I'm doing this for you."

"For *me*?"

"For you. I'm burning all my bridges, but I'm not asking for thanks or gratitude or anything like that. I'll explain it all on the witness stand, okay?"

"Okay," I said. I had to say something.

"I really screwed up this time," Shauna said. "But I don't deserve sympathy—if I were you, I would have probably hung up the phone. But I'm so glad you didn't. Well, I'm in room seven-twelve, if you want to see me. It has two beds."

"Thanks," I said, because I didn't know what else to say. It came out a lot snider than I planned.

"And, Tod—"

"Yeah?"

"Whatever happens," there was a short, rhythmic intake of breaths, "I love you." She had the grace to hang up the phone on that note so she couldn't hear this almost-grown man break into tears.

I wasn't cognizant of much the rest of that night except I don't think I ever got that infernal sobbing under control. It gave me a good excuse to hold fast to my vow not to see her until she testified in court.

35

There was a buzz in the courtroom as we entered. The Zepfs were all in place and smiling more than the mayor was—for the first time.

It was a remarkable thing that we never once had to wait for the Zepfs to come to court. Twelve kids, some of them virtual babies, a father debilitated, lugging around an iron lung, and never were they late. Now it was as though the word had spread through Gratz County like a brush fire and everyone knew something big and exciting was about to happen.

To celebrate the occasion, I wore the no-smoking tie the girls had made for me—with the international symbol of the red circle and slash over a smoking cigarette. The girls squealed in delight when they saw it.

The guards were still with Shauna and, when Bomber called her to the witness stand, they came in on either side of her, eyes working the crowd like the Secret Service.

The first thing I noticed about Shauna was her hair seemed to have gotten bushier. It seemed to frizz out even beyond her broad shoulders and almost dwarfed the rest of her. Then I saw it: she was wearing the same no-smoking tie as a cravat. A great sob welled up in my throat and I had to avert my face from everyone to keep from blubbering like a baby.

They escorted her to the low railing that separated the playing field from the spectators. The younger Zepf girls reached out to touch Shauna as she passed. A deep smile creased her face, but the guards hustled her through the low railing. There she was the sheriff's responsibility. But our free-lancers sat in the chairs on the low railing and kept their eyes on the crowd.

Shauna looked straight at me all the time she was moving and, of course, I lost my breath. I was frankly fighting to hold back those tears of joy I felt at seeing her look so lovely.

She was tanned, as you would expect someone who has been laying on the beach in the Caribbean after a two-week cruise. She wore a white shirt dress that set off her red hair like whipped strawberries on top of a scoop of vanilla ice cream.

She looked strong as she raised her right hand and took the oath. And when she sat down, she looked vulnerable.

When a witness is good and believable, Bomber often lets them run with their story. Shauna got through the preliminaries of how I hired her (and, of course, she looked right at me with those devastating eyes). I'm sure everyone in the place thought she was making a terrible play for me because every time she had a moment between questions, she would give me those sheep-dog eyes. I couldn't stand it. I stared back at her once or twice, but usually I just dropped my eyes to the table.

"I was working in my one-small-room office one day, when I received a surprise visit from Norman Stimmel of the area's largest, and many say, most prestigious law firm Bortz, Hillegas, Stimmel and Klerx. Mr. Stimmel is a partner in the firm and I had never spoken to him in my life. I would never have had the nerve. I am intimidated by important people."

(Harrison Hinkle would later ask her if she wasn't intimidated by Bomber and she admitted she was. "If I hadn't been hired by his charming son, Tod, I don't know how I would have ever gotten the job," Shauna said.) She was playing the delicate flower with panache.

"Out of the blue," Shauna went on, "if you can call suddenly appearing in my office out of the blue, he asked me to go to lunch with him at the country club. I'd never been to the country club. So my heart started fluttering and all I could say was 'When?'

"'How about right now?'" he asked me and I was floored. He quickly said another day would be fine if I was busy. Well, I wasn't busy but something didn't seem right. So, I asked him, 'Isn't this a conflict of interest or something, us being on opposite sides of the case?'

"He chuckled and said 'Nonsense. We won't even discuss the case. In Cedarberg, we go to lunch with the judges. This is a close community—you'll find that after you've practiced here for awhile.'

"So, I went with him. I still can't believe it. I had this feeling all the time it wasn't right. Maybe he wouldn't talk about the case—then wouldn't it be more like a date? And he was *married*. None of this would have happened if I had followed my instincts," Shauna said looking glum—in my direction. "But a young lawyer just starting out in a closed town being invited by arguably the most important attorney in town—well, it just made me light-headed.

"And the country club! It was so spacious and grand, and all the important people were there and Mr. Stimmel knew them all, introduced me to them as a young lawyer with a bright future and after he did that three or four times, I got to hoping that they wouldn't always say that about me—that I had a bright future.

"The food was really good. I had something with crab and papaya that I loved. While I was eating it, Mr. Stimmel tells me he has been watching my work for Bomber Hanson and he is most impressed. I almost fell off the chair. To think that anyone would notice my work was astonishing to me, let alone the leading lawyer in the county. That was simply making my head spin.

"Then he said, 'We are looking for a woman associate for Bortz, Hillegas, Stimmel, and Klerx, with an eye to a partnership, of course—six, seven years maybe. I have let my feelings be known that you would be the ideal candidate. Bright, articulate, cultured, charming, and on top of it all, a gifted lawyer.'"

Shauna smiled ruefully. "I wonder if he memorized all those adjectives before he came. I have a lot of questions about the whole thing in retrospect, like he probably surprised me with that last-minute invitation because if I'd had a little time to think about it, I wouldn't have gone.

"'I wouldn't expect an answer so suddenly,' he said. 'Think about it. You'd start at sixty-K a year with full benefits, a month's vacation and a generous pension plan.' Sixty-thousand! I hadn't earned that much my entire time as a lawyer. I kept thinking something wasn't right here. He should not be making this offer while the case was going on. But the mention of sixty thou' blinded me to those niceties."

Bomber stood up, "Miss McKinley, were you under any financial pressure at the time of Mr. Hinkle's offer?"

"Was I?! Oh, my." And she told the tale of her father and mother. She managed a few discreet tears during the recitation.

"Were there any other discussions of money at that country club lunch?" Bomber asked.

"Yes, there were."

"Would you tell us what they were, please?"

"Mr. Stimmel asked me if you were paying me well. I said I was happy with my salary."

"You weren't getting sixty thousand a year from me, were you?" Bomber asked.

"No. So he asked me if I ever needed extra money. 'Who doesn't?' I said. Then I told him about my father leaving us with the mortgage we couldn't pay and mom's illness and all and he said he thought he might be able to help me with that. He might be able to get me a signing bonus like the baseball players got, he said. I don't know much about baseball, so he explained it to me—about how these players who are in demand can get millions of dollars extra to come to a team. He said this could be like that."

"What did you say?"

"I laughed and said, I didn't think there would be any bidding war going on for my services, and he said, 'Don't be too sure.' Well, that was like cold water in my face. I couldn't tell what he was saying. I was *so* naive. The next thing I knew, he was talking about astronomical figures, like a million dollars, and my head is spinning and he says not many lawyers around here clear that much in a lifetime. Of course, he had my attention and I seemed to be agreeing with everything he said. All the time, I knew deep down something was wrong. He still hadn't asked me to do anything besides going to work for him after the case was over. Then he was talking about me going to the Grand Cayman Islands where I could open an account and money could be wired there and I wouldn't have to pay taxes on it. He would save our little row house from foreclosure, sell it and put the money in the same account. He would arrange for the best doctors to operate on mother and she could recuperate with me in the Grand Cayman Islands."

"Did you ask him what he wanted you to do in return for a million dollars?"

"Finally, I got the courage."

"What did he say?"

"He waved his hand as though that was so trifling it wasn't worth bothering about. Then he said if I had any interest, someone would contact me about the details of this gift. That's all he ever made it seem like—like it was a gift or a signing bonus or something."

"Didn't you know better?"

"Of course, I did. In my heart, I knew this was crazy—but getting my mother out of her medical and financial mess was weighing so heavily on me that thinking about a solution was such a relief—even if it was as logical as winning the lottery."

"Did someone come to you about this million dollar 'gift'?"

"Yes—next day—because, of course, I told Mr. Stimmel I was interested. Who wouldn't be, the way it was presented? Anyway, this guy came to see me and asks to go for a walk. I like walking, so we get out on the street and he says his name is Dick, and he doesn't give me a last name or tell me where he is from—but he is here because of my lunch with a local attorney, he says. Then he tells me confidentially that generous offers of settlement are going to be made to the Zepfs. He expects I feel, as he does, that it would be in their best interests to take the money. Mr. Zepf wasn't getting any younger, he said half-factitiously, or any stronger, and until they could win an award and go through all the appeals they would go through, they would certainly do better taking this tax-free windfall. I asked him how much they would offer, but he said he didn't know but it would be generous."

"That sound good to you?"

"Did it! By now, I am walking on air. I could certainly in good conscience encourage the Zepfs to take the money. 'But what if they refuse?' I asked.

"I could keep the money, he said, as long as I shared certain other information with him."

"What was that?"

"That turned out to be our case."

"And did you?"

She nodded and a handkerchief came up to her eyes.

"I'm sorry Miss McKinley—does that mean yes? You have to speak audibly for the record."

"Yes," Shauna croaked like a frog with laryngitis.

"And did you tell this person about Don Powell, our star witness?"

She didn't answer right away. She looked at me again as though she thought I might provide her with the preferred answer. And then her features seemed to melt as though the weight of her betrayal was tearing at her flesh and she broke down just after she had used her hoarse frog voice again to croak, "Yes."

She composed herself barely to provide the corroborating details—the betrayal took place only two days before the bogus check was placed in Don Powell's personal bank account. It took only a glance at the jury to see the worm had turned and they were with us again.

Then, what I had quietly dreaded was upon us, Judge Druckenmiller called for a break. I could hardly avoid Shauna any longer.

The jury left first. I could have run out to the men's room, but I couldn't stoop to that cowardice. As she stepped down from the stand, twelve squealing Zepf girls ran up to hug her as though she were Elvis Presley returned from the grave. They circled Shauna so completely I got only a glimpse of her eyes. They were still on me. This time I didn't look away. It didn't take long for the girls to catch on and release Shauna from their clutches. We stared for a moment into each other's eyes. Then, as if on cue, started toward each other. When we met, we stopped and stared some more. When we finally hugged, we clung to each other as though we might drown if we let go. Soon there was a cheer from the Zepf girls and Rich, still at our plaintiff's table.

Shauna spoke first. "Maybe we shouldn't be seen this way," she said.

We shouldn't, I agreed, but neither of us let go. Finally she said, "After I'm finished, will you talk to me? Just for a few minutes?"

"Yes," I said, but I didn't know exactly what I was feeling.

After the break, Harrison Hinkle had his go at Shauna. She had composed herself and stood so admirably at his belittling onslaught. She didn't break down once, even though he called her a spy, a traitor, a turncoat, a liar and everything else he had in his bag of tricks. "You realize you are admitting to taking a bribe?" he stormed.

"In a way. Of course, it was presented as simply a payment for information."

"You could be disbarred," he said, "lose your license to practice law. Do you realize that?"

"I do."

"Tell the truth for once in your life…"

Bomber was on his feet. "Your Honor, I'm sure the jury is delighting in Mr. Hinkle's desperation performance. I know we at the plaintiff's table are happy…"

"He's making a speech."

"Forgive me," Bomber said. "My speech is prompted by yours. Don't you tell our witness about truth—your side has no corner on it. I don't think they'd know the truth if they fell on it."

"Gentlemen," Druckenmiller banged the gavel. "Enough."

Hinkle turned back to Shauna. "You've made the whole thing up to try and save a sinking case."

She didn't answer.

"Answer me!" Hinkle demanded.

"Then ask a question," Bomber boomed.

"Didn't you?"

"Didn't I what?"

"Make all this up…?"

"Absolutely not. Where would I get a million dollars, if not from you?"

"Me?" Hinkle panicked. "Me? Not from *me*! You didn't get it from me!"

"Your side."

"You have no proof of that."

Bomber said, "Is that a question, counselor? Why don't you ask her what proof she has? I'm sure she'll tell you."

Bang! The gavel. "Mr. Hanson, please address your objections to me."

"Sorry, Your Honor, Mr. Hinkle seems to be at his wits end—or half of that—so he's making incriminating, false, statements instead of asking questions, and I object to it."

"Yes, sustained, just ask questions, Mr. Hinkle."

"I stand corrected," Harrison Hinkle said with a huge smirk on his face. I thought he had been waiting throughout the entire trial for that parody. Bomber took it right. He smiled from ear to ear.

"You must hate yourself, Miss—"

"Objection!"

"Do you hate yourself, Miss Shauna McKinley, for

these despicable acts?"

"What was despicable, Mr. Hinkle? Turning on the Zepfs, or turning on you?"

"Your Honor," he bleated. "That is non-responsive."

"Well, your question wasn't that clear."

He rephrased. She admitted she felt badly, that was why she came forward, to atone for her grievous wrong.

They pulled and pushed, parried and thrusted, danced around, but finally Shauna got the best of it—maybe because she was so composed about it—maybe because every time Hinkle tried to tar her with the evil of the transaction it seemed to stick to *him.*

We had a quiet lunch, just Shauna and me. She was very self-effacing. Said she would never live down her selfish mistake. She made the clean breast for my sake. "Because you're the finest person I have ever known." It took me awhile to gulp that one down. But she had no expectations "about us." She knew her betrayal could not be forgiven.

I argued, of course, and she said. "See what I mean about you being the finest person? I don't even deserve to be eating with you. You may forgive me, and I'll bet you would, but I can't forgive myself."

"Try."

"I have."

"But I think we're going to win, thanks to you—and the ironic thing is, I don't think we would have won without you. Even surprising them with Don Powell. They'd just put ten guys on to deny it."

"Strength in numbers?"

"Sometimes. But this, it was so darn dramatic. It really caught their attention—right between the eyes. I really think, if we win, it's *you* that won it."

"By selling out?" she shook her head. It was not an idea she was willing to entertain just then.

After lunch, Norman Stimmel came to the stand to deny everything Shauna said. Yes, he had taken her to lunch at the country club because he had been aware of her work and was impressed with her. His firm was looking to recruit women and she would seem a natural if she was interested, and she was. He didn't wait until the trial was over (in retrospect, he admitted that would have been better), because he was afraid others might get to her first. He couldn't remember what, if anything, was mentioned about the Armstead case which she was working on for the other side, but most assuredly it was not a bribe for her inside information. As for the Armstead Foundation, who had allegedly funneled her the money, he didn't even know they existed.

His testimony was a model of doing something shady and covering your buns with vague syntax, then, if caught, explaining how everything really meant the opposite.

Would the jury buy it? Time would tell.

36

Bomber's opening speech to the jury was vintage Bomber. He worked all the emotional stops, but he hammered away at the facts and evidence. It was all carefully calculated and calibrated to climax in his rebuttal, which he would make after the defense gave their pitch.

One of my favorites from this speech was: "I'm sure you all remember the fun and furor we had about hiding the plaintiff's oxygen tank. No doubt the motivation was to protect your sensibilities, as well as to not give Mr. Zepf an undue emotional advantage to grab your sympathy or pity. I can tell you I have gotten to know Rich Zepf during this long and arduous process—which, all told, has been over a year in the making, and Rich Zepf is the last person who would ask for sympathy. He was pleased to oblige by keeping his oxygen tank out of sight. And he did keep it out of our sight so we wouldn't get shook up. But Rich Zepf isn't as lucky. He *can't* see it, but he has to depend on it to keep him alive."

Most lawyers could recount the facts and emphasize what it was that helped their case. But so many of them were not persuasive speakers. There were a surprising number of drones in a profession that called for flair. Bomber had the flair with more than a touch of flamboyance. In his elevator shoes, he had a commanding body language—it was the same body that he used to intimidate witnesses, only now he used to to make the jurors feel he was one of them.

Getting to the nitty-gritty with a jury—the discussion of bucks—was an art Bomber had mastered like no other. I have heard lawyers argue that part of the opponent's demand was reasonable when I thought it wasn't, and have the jury return zero after several hundred thousand had been conceded.

Other times, lawyers will ask too much and get less than they should have. Jury awards are not a mathematical science. Instead, they are like most decisions made by people, emotionally-based. And the emotions were Bomber's forte.

I could almost predict what he was going to say to this jury. In time, it got so I could write his speeches. That was only part of the battle, however, and nobody realized that better than I did. The big part was the delivery, the timing—the pauses, the emphasis, the body language. I was so aware of timing because of my music—and I could express my sense of timing in musical notes with confidence and competence. Talking was an entirely different matter. It all happened so fast. There had to be the words at your command, stored in the mind for release at just the right moment—not too soon or too late, not too fast or slow. And that is an art apart.

Bomber took a headlong frontal attack on the matter of money with this jury.

"Now for the size of the award," he said. "It is all up to you, of course, but there are certain numbers in my heart and I would appreciate you giving me the liberty to share them with you. It is not a scientific business, of course. It is no easier for me than it is for you. But I have arrived at a sum. How did I do it? There are twelve adorable girls in this family, and a lovelier band of young women I've never seen. I'm sure you've noticed, we never once had to wait for them to begin in the morning. Never once did the judge have to discipline them. Twelve! A dozen young women, ladies and gentlemen, and their future is in your hands.

"Now a million is a nice round number. There are a dozen girls all told, and a million each would seem a nice, manageable sum. A hundred thousand each would not cut any real mustard with a multi-billion dollar addiction business. Ten million each, while I certainly don't feel that would be out of line with the evidence, might doctor the girls' lives more than could be good for them."

This was one of my favorite of Bomber's ploys—talk about bigger numbers as though you think they would be excessive, adding to your credibility with the smaller numbers, which were large enough.

"Then, of course, there is the victim himself. You have heard him say his time is running out and he only wants to see his girls taken care of. You may take him at his word—because nobody's word is better—or you may just want to make that part of the award a baker's-dozen million."

So clever the way he dropped in "That part of the award." Then he moved on.

"What is to be said about Mrs. Rich Zepf? Languishing in an insane asylum, a woman—if I know anything at all about people—that is perhaps saner than I am. You heard the defense attorneys try to belittle her, and you saw how she held her ground. They made no inroads on that pure soul, ladies and gentlemen, not a dent.

"I say, let's bring her home where she belongs. I'm thinking not only the costs of home care for the full, rich and long life she so richly deserves" (I *loved* the way he pronounced "*richly*"—strung it out and let it hang on the air like a trial balloon) "but also some atonement for how the T. S. Armstead Company was responsible for destroying this model family. Let's let them put the pieces back together before it's too late, before they are all gone from the homestead that succored these adorable children—the last two years of which they suffered without their beloved mom."

"You heard them tell of how they scrimped and saved, how they were forced by their poverty to eat only potatoes, day after day. Now it's up to you. You can send them back to their potato trough, or you can put a little meat on their plates now and then. It's up to you. Often I tell juries, I don't envy them their difficult decision. This time I do feel some envy for you and your ability to make this very special family whole once more. What a nice position to be in. I hope you make the most of it."

That's what set Bomber apart from his fellows.

"So with the twelve for the twelve girls and another two for the magnificent and much maligned mother, perhaps another one for dad, just so as not to forget the man who suffered through all of this, and don't think it was easy for any of them. There are enormous pressures on all the parties in lawsuits. A multi-billion-dollar corporation can spend billions to deflect that pressure, but the potato-eating Zepfs have no such resources, so they feel all the blows personally."

"So, I say fifteen million—twenty if you are feeling generous. Personally, I might go higher, that's up to you. We don't want to appear greedy. But if you want to send a message about the abuse of the innocents by the tobacco giants, you may well want to consider a higher number. *That* I leave up to you."

By the time Bomber finished, I thought we had won. But that's not unusual. Feeling is bound to be positive before you've heard the other side tear you to shreds.

Norman Stimmel addressed the jury first for the defendant. He spoke of his long service to the community (but not about the piles of money the community served on him) and how he was so jealous of his reputation that he would never, ever dream of bribing anyone—and if you were going to be so foolish, why chance it in a high profile case like this one?

"Ladies and gentlemen of the jury, I have thought long and hard about this case and the strange way it unfolded at the end. Became unhinged, some might say. I know I have never in my life bribed anyone. I know I had nothing to do with a million dollars going into Shauna McKinley's bank account somewhere in the Caribbean. But I am reminded of the Reichstag fire the Nazis set and blamed on their enemies. It served their purpose. It got them sympathy and swept them into office.

"Could the plaintiff have taken a page out of the same deceptive book? After I took her to lunch, and no matter how the plaintiff's attorney paints it, it *was* an act grounded in the best intentions—why, I think he got the idea he could fake a bribe, tie it to me, and win sympathy from you jurors with a last-minute grandstand play.

"I don't mean to talk long. I leave that to others. I have had my say. I didn't mean to address the jury, but my good name has been dragged through the mud and I could not in good conscience remain silent."

Next we were treated to a rambling folksy message from the mayor of Cedarberg. I swear all the time he spoke, that corny smile never left his face. It was a mishmash of Chamber of Commerce pep talk and a rambling character witnessing for the tobacco moguls.

"I never played golf with a finer man than Ed Jones. All's you have to do is spend ten minutes with that man and you know he couldn't do anything bad."

I think it was a great relief for both sides when he finally sat down.

After lunch, it was time for the big gun himself, Harrison J. Hinkle.

"Ladies and gentlemen of the jury, I too thank you for your service here. Reasonable people differ in their view of things. Mr. Hanson would have you believe that is not so. The way he talks, the tobacco industry—made up of hundreds of thousands of people just like you and me—those companies of human beings are unmitigated evil. I know those people, I work for those people, and I can tell you unequivocally that is not so.

"You have seen tobacco people on the stand. Did you see any horns on them? Fire coming out of their nostrils? I'm thankful you got to see them for, if you had only Mr. Hanson's picture to rely on for truth and justice, you would have a hard go of it.

"You saw Ed Jones, the president of the company. Have you ever seen a man so important with less pretension? He is the kind of man you could sit down with for a game of gin rummy, and you'd never guess he was one of the highest-paid men in the world. And you could be sure he wouldn't cheat you. What did Ed Jones say on the witness stand? He said the tobacco industry was a service industry. They make cigarettes because people want to buy them. It is all well and good to say we make cigarettes because we want to make money, but we wouldn't make a dime if no one wanted to buy our product. Can anyone argue with that? Sure, reasonable people can differ, but can they argue the supply-and-demand hypothesis?

"And certainly you realize how tough the politicians continue to make it for the tobacco industry, an industry responsible for putting billions of tax dollars into the government coffers each year. Smokers have been relegated to the status of second-class citizens; they are sneered at, reviled and ostracized.

"But no matter how unreasonable it all seems to the smokers, no matter how bad they are made to feel by their fellows, they still want to smoke.

"We can't force our product on people who don't want it, any more than General Motors can force you to buy their cars. Tobacco companies are in business to meet a demand. And they *stay* in business *because* they *meet* that demand. And I don't care what Mr. Hanson says, every single manufacturing company in the United States of America who wants to stay in business attempts to create a demand for their products. But no one, NO ONE can make people buy something they don't want. And I'm sorry, but I don't see a tobacco company trying to sell its products as a sinister force in our society.

"A lot of people depend on cigarettes—on both sides of the counter. The tobacco industry is an enormous industry. The tax dollars they make possible are among the greatest of any industry going. The number of jobs is astonishing. You talk about recession, just shut down the tobacco industry and you will see unprecedented recession. And if that day ever comes, heaven forbid, I pray that the resources of this government of ours can sustain the bloated welfare rolls that will result just as surely as I am standing before you.

"Now, it is the contention of the plaintiff that the tobacco company has caused his troubles. There sometimes seems to be a great need in this country to fix blame on others for our own actions. If we walk into a wall, the person who put the wall there is to blame. Similarly, if we contract a disease, someone else must be to blame.

"Ladies and gentlemen, when are we going to stand on our own two feet and say, 'I am the master of my soul? I will take responsibility for what I do?'

"This is a case, if there ever was one, about taking responsibility for our own actions. I am not happy to see Mr. Zepf in this condition. Nobody could be. Mr. Zepf smoked four packs of cigarettes a day. Eighty cigarettes. He would have us believe he couldn't help himself. It was us who made him do it—by some magic and sinister formulation of our manufacturing process. But, ladies and gentlemen, do *you* smoke four packs of cigarettes a day? Why not? The evil tobacco company is making you do it, so they will get rich, rich, RICH! Nasty, selfish company.

"Would you consider holding the manufacturers of alcoholic beverages responsible for the twenty-some thousand automobile deaths a year caused by drunk drivers? Would any of us deny alcohol can be habit forming? Cigarettes can be habit forming. Tens of millions of drinkers do so in moderation without any ill effects. Likewise, tens of millions of smokers smoke in moderation and derive great pleasure from it, without contracting terminal diseases.

"Should we punish the moderates for the sake of a few extremists who can't help themselves? Sacrifice the normal for the abnormal?

"Now, I do sympathize with Rich Zepf and his twelve lovely daughters. But we are given choices in life and we are defined by our choices. It is a choice to have twelve children, and I can imagine the multiple blessings that provides him. It is a choice to smoke cigarettes in moderation and to derive considerable pleasure therefrom. And it is a choice to abuse a privilege—to smoke eighty cigarettes a day. T. S. Armstead didn't make him do that. Budweiser beer doesn't cause drunk driving, irresponsibility does. Is it right and just to punish the moderates for the sake of the extremists? I think not. I hope you agree.

"Yes, we can make cigarettes with no nicotine. We tried it. Nobody bought them, nobody wanted to smoke them. What would you do if it were *your* company? If you were responsible to your customers and your employees and your stockholders? Would you say take it or leave it? Some people can't smoke in moderation so, if you don't want to smoke straw, we will close our doors and put hundreds of thousands of people out of work, steal pleasure from tens of millions? All because of a few unfortunate and pitiful people like our unhappy plaintiff? Well, would you? Would you take the billions of dollars in tax dollars from our overstrained government whose budget has been out of whack for years?

"That is exactly what the plaintiff is asking you to do. He is saying I cannot smoke in moderation, therefore I don't want anyone to smoke at all. My misery should rob you of your pleasure. We must all act and think alike, there is no room for difference of opinion. I don't want to take responsibility for my own actions. I don't want you to either, even if you are better able to do so than I.

"Is that the vision we have for our country? I hope not.

"Those are the main points of our case. I am forced, against my will, to address the peripheral points that the counsel for the plaintiff has hammered away at so mercilessly.

"The first is his turncoat employee, who seems to have acted as something of a double-agent in this case. Her surprise, last-minute testimony for the plaintiff was one of the more bizarre aspects of the case, which I fear could easily become known for its bizarre aspects.

"Ask yourselves, what does Shauna McKinley bring to the fund of knowledge in this case? She was given a million dollars in her personal account on the Grand Cayman Island, a tax haven she ran to to escape paying her taxes. Wouldn't we all prefer not to pay taxes?

"Then she points to the coincidence that Don Powell was arrested a few days after she sold information about his coming testimony. She and Mr. Hanson want you to believe the company trumped up the charges against him. But that ninety-eight thousand dollar check was in his personal account. You saw the controller of the company and Mr. Powell's secretary both testify for the defense. Neither was shaken by Mr. Hanson's intimidating questioning. Naturally Mr. Powell says he didn't do it. You don't find many confessions among jail birds.

"Mr. Powell said we added nicotine. Mr. Powell was not too happy with T. S. Armstead, putting him in jail like that. And speaking of bribes, wouldn't that have been the perfect opportunity for a bribe? Mr. Powell, we will drop all charges if you refuse to testify. Did it happen? No. The facts are these: The defense received a list of witnesses from the plaintiff. We are bound to exchange our witness lists before trial. Don Powell's name *was not on it!* Don Powell was not offered as a witness until *after*—I repeat, AFTER—he was arrested. They can weasel all they want out of that one, those are the verifiable, and testified-to, facts.

"You saw the president of the company testify he never asked anyone to add nicotine to the product. You heard him, you judge him. Is this a man who got where he is by telling lies? I don't see it. Balance the president against a distraught man whose wife died, he says, as a result of her smoking. Is that a frame of mind that would endear the company to him? And then, perhaps to get back at Armstead, he tries to embezzle almost two-hundred thousand dollars, and makes up a cocka-mamie story about adding nicotine besides. Notice the plaintiff produced no corroborating witnesses on that; no, Mr. Powell spoke alone. And not from the witness stand, but from jail.

"You are allowed to weigh the character of a person by viewing their testimony. Don't lose sight of this testimony and the fact it comes from jail. We have an incarcerated man speaking for the plaintiff, and two respected, blemishless employees speaking for the company. You decide who is telling the truth."

There was more, but that was the most devastating of it. Harrison Hinkle was no slouch as a trial attorney. I wondered if

Bomber had underrated him. It was like so many cases—biases hidden in jurors could cause them to latch on to the merest straw to vote against you.

Harrison Hinkle had provided a lot of straw.

37

Fortunately, Bomber got another shot at it—the plaintiff gets the opportunity to answer points brought up by the defendant.

"Oh, ladies and gentlemen," he began after a break. "What a wonderful speaker is Harrison J. Hinkle. Oh, those mellifluous tones rolled off his tongue like the sweetest lullaby. And he is a handsome man. Watching him give his speech, so polished, so smooth, I could not help but feel envy in my heart. Were only poor Rich Zepf able to have a silver-tongued advocate such as Mr. Hinkle on his side, I should rest easier.

"For I could not help but feel, as I watched this suave New York lawyer, that the world was his oyster, that no lawyer joke would ever stick to him. And, next to him, how I really was a poor, country bumpkin with little going for me or the poor, wonderful Zepf family but my fervent belief in the justness of their cause. But you know and I know, my beliefs, no matter how deep they take hold of my soul, are not enough to move you to the side of the angels, and the side of the plaintiff. No, my convictions in this case are dross *unless* I can bring you to share them with me.

"As I listened to Mr. Hinkle, I found myself nodding within—saying to myself yes, yes, that sounds right. And, of course, that is cause for great alarm—for when I look below the surface I soon realize that deep down, his whole case is superficial. Just like the diet of the loving Zepf family—there is no meat there.

"Sure our star witness, Don Powell, the vice-president in charge of manufacturing cigarettes for the T. S. Armstead

Company testified from jail. And who put him there? And when? Literally the day before he was to get on a plane and come up here to blow the case wide apart. And then the great state of T. S. Armstead, excuse me, North Carolina, refused to let Mr. Powell appear here in court like a human being. I leave you to decide if that man was capable of hitting his guard over the head and chewing off his handcuffs so he could escape.

"I am interested to hear Mr. Hinkle say if they were going to bribe anyone, why not Mr. Powell? But why? They had so effectively destroyed him with the phony charge—he was finished—finished with the company he had served so well for twenty-odd years and finished as a witness with their foolproof, concocted story about this spotless man—this moral, upright man with a twenty-odd year blemishless record trying to take what amounted to about thirty percent of his annual salary. Why? Because he was mad at the company for what? For providing the cigarettes that he thought killed his wife. Well, we *know* they killed her, but the company doesn't want to admit that—okay—so this man, drawing over six-hundred thousand a year in salary, plus bonuses, from the company that killed his wife—the company that takes in billions of dollars a year—he is going to punish that company by stealing a paltry two-hundred thousand? Yet, I sat here and watched the smooth, suave Mr. Hinkle present that to you as though it were some kind of gospel truth.

"Really? I know better. You know better. This man, this beleaguered Don Powell never took a dime that didn't belong to him. There *are* people like that in this weary world. I suspect you are people like that. Don Powell is a person like that.

"Mr. Hinkle says this is a case about responsibility, and I wish they would take some responsibility for their actions. The people want to buy poison, they say in effect—we only give them what they want. I have another word for what this case is about and that word is cynicism.

"The defense in this case has put on one of the most cynical defenses I have seen in all my years of practice. And I am still practicing. I will have to practice a long time until I am half as polished as Mr. Hinkle. But we must, in fairness to the loving Zepfs, look beneath the glitter of the polish.

"I would love to have just a nickel for every time I hear about the poor stockholders. Mr. Hinkle has gone us better than that here today. We are not only asked to look out for the stockholders, but the employees, the farmers and the United States Government as well. That's quite a burden.

"But what do we get when we ask *them* to look out for *us? Nothing!* They tell us that people love nicotine. They won't buy cigarettes without it. But we have proof—of the nicotine they take out, then return—with an extra kick, that hooks millions of smokers. Sure, some people can lick the habit. Sure, some people smoke less than Mr. Zepf did. I don't doubt we can find people who smoke more—so what? This case is about the Zepf family—and Mr. Zepf *couldn't kick it.* They put too much nicotine in their cigarettes to allow Mr. Zepf and millions like him, to kick the fatal habit. Is *that* being *responsible?*

"So why not take their argument a step further? Why not double or triple the amount of nicotine they add? They could claim *more* people like that because now almost everyone would be addicted and unable to kick the habit.

"Perhaps the biggest fantasy in their fairy story is that spun by Mr. Stimmel. If I understand him correctly—and, believe me, I'm not at all sure I understand him at all—I don't see how you could follow his spinning that fantastic yarn about the nefarious, double, or is it triple, plot which he seems to be saying was engineered by us.

"He says *we* directed Shauna McKinley to betray us. Who invited her out to lunch? A highly questionable act in the first place, I don't care what he says about it being no big deal. You do not invite an opposing associate counsel out to lunch to pump them for information—to offer them jobs—in the middle of the case! The very idea that someone else in Cedarberg might get to her first and offer her sixty-thousand dollars a year is so preposterous I'm embarrassed to talk to you about it.

"But my favorite part of Mr. Stimmel's recitation is the part where he speculates that *we* set it all up. He doesn't explain how we were able to trick him into inviting Shauna McKinley out to lunch. He then says, we sent a mystery man to do the bribing—with a *million dollars* wired to her bank account from a secret Swiss account."

Bomber raised his eyebrow in his most exaggerated aren't-they-nutso manner. "A million dollars, ladies and gentlemen; maybe Mr. Hummel has that kind of money lying around, I wouldn't be surprised if a man of Mr. Hinkle's consummate skill and polish wouldn't have a little nest egg where he could spare that kind of change. I know that would be peanuts to the T. S. Armstead Company. But to Bomber Hanson? I'm going to get a million bucks into a Swiss bank account? Where am I going to get it? From the Zepfs? Hardly. I will confess I could probably rustle up a million if I sold everything I had. But with the real estate market what it is in California today, that is problematical. Even if I could, it would take years! But I wouldn't have the faintest idea how to do the Swiss bank account trick. I am a simple, hard-working American, and I put my money in American banks.

"But I wouldn't be surprised if the boys and girls at T. S. Armstead Company whose revenues are up in the billions annually knew a thing or two about Swiss banking—and it wouldn't surprise me if Stimmel and Hinkle did too.

"It's another riddle for you to figure out. I don't suppose it will give you much trouble. You saw Shauna McKinley testify. You saw attorney Stimmel. You decide. That girl has ruined herself in all this mess. I would no longer let a young girl ruin herself then I would paddle a canoe to the moon. She disappeared. We thought we'd lost it. She got to feeling guilty. She came back. Do you think Mr. Stimmel and his august firm of Bortz, Hillegas, Stimmel and Klerx will hire her now? Her sixty-thousand promise is out the window. Of course, I don't know that Mr. Hummel would have honored that agreement after she had done the dirty work. He might have figured that a girl who will sell out for you might someday sell out against you. I don't know, but I hope you will think about it. And think about the sacrifices Shauna McKinley made to tell her story. They are trying to ignore that story with a smoke screen, but you'll remember it. We are playing in the big leagues when we sue big tobacco. They have endless resources and they use them. We all must use what we have. They have more money than any of us can imagine. Just remember a billion dollars is a *thousand million*! Every year they make many times that, selling their own special products of death.

"Ladies and gentlemen, it's been a long road. I will forever cherish your attention and service in this case and I shall love you forever for it. You have an opportunity to make a statement that will resonate throughout the world, if you find for the plaintiff in a sum large enough to attract some attention. Believe me, you can't render a verdict in an amount the T. S. Armstead Company will miss. It just isn't possible, they are so rich.

"Please look at the plaintiff in this case, Mr. Rich Zepf, one more time before you go to deliberate." Bomber went to stand behind the plaintiff and put his hands on his shoulders. "Cigarettes have done this to him. Mr. Hinkle has talked about his precious stockholders and all the taxes they pay. Then look at Rich Zepf's lovely daughters." Bomber moved over to put the girls in view roughly between him and the jury. "Remember these girls, please, in your deliberations, and after. I don't know if you've ever known such a well-behaved, loving family—and no one was in a better position than you to observe them throughout this long and painful trial. Try to put yourselves in their place. It won't be easy, but try to imagine the pain they must feel seeing their father being taken from them by corporate greed. Listening intently as they have, and as you have, to the slanders the defense has hurled at their father and mother.

"Don't forget these children. You can assure their future. You can bring their mother back to them. If we can't save their father, we can give them something to remember him by. You can give David a victory in his battle with Goliath.

"Let's not let big tobacco confuse us about right and wrong. Killing people is wrong, I don't care how you do it. Never in my career have I seen a clearer-cut case of good and evil. You have on the one hand, a multi-billion-dollar conglomerate and the likes of corporate raider Jerry Horowitz running roughshod over innocent decent people like Rich Zepf. Can anyone wonder who *is* evil and who is good?

"Ladies and gentlemen, smoking cigarettes kills an estimated three-million people a year. That is the equivalent of the crashing of twenty-two jumbo jets a day, completely full with one-hundred-percent casualties. And that suave Mr. Hinkle has the nerve to compare it to a couple Budweiser beers.

"Send a message. Send it loud enough so it will be heard.

"God bless you, and God love you all."

*   *   *

When we got word that the jury had reached their verdict, we all scurried back into the courtroom. The first thing I saw when I came down the aisle was Bomber, Easy Willie, and Rich Zepf at the plaintiff table. Then I saw Shauna sitting in the front row with the Zepf girls. Curiously, there was an empty seat beside her.

I took it. "Where did you disappear to?" I asked Shauna, who was being treated like royalty with all the attentions of the Zepf girls.

"I hid out," she said. "I couldn't stand the suspense. I realized I might have cost you the case and I came to my senses too late. I also realized I couldn't ever expect you to trust me again."

"What about *Suite: Love?*" I blurted and I had trouble myself understanding what I meant.

"Your love was sweet, but you loved a sour apple."

I attempted several paltry arguments, but they fell as flat as a stomped-out cigarette butt.

"Do you mean you don't want to see me again?" I gulped.

"I mean you shouldn't want to see me again."

"I don't have any say? What if we win? Then, it will be because of you? Then, will we see each other?"

"You in California, me in the Grand Caymans?"

"Something could be arranged."

She stared at the judge's bench as though she needed to look away lest her resolve waver. Then I noticed she wasn't looking at the bench, but at Easy Willie, who was smiling at her. She was smiling too. "Tell you what," she said, looking back at the girls.

"What?" I asked eagerly.

"If we win, I'll spend some of my ill-gotten-gains on tickets to bring you and the Zepfs to the islands."

The Zepf girls squealed as the court crier began. I made a move to return to the plaintiff's table, then I looked at the girls and, after a moment's hesitation, when I was sort of frozen in a half-crouch trying to get up—I sat down again. All the girls smiled.

"Oyez, oyez, oyez! All manner of persons…"

When the jury was seated, I tried to read their faces. They had been out only a little more than two hours and I wasn't sure what that meant, other than pretty general agreement. But which way, I couldn't tell. They hadn't looked at anyone on the way in. That was supposed to be an indication. If they looked at the plaintiff, they probably found for him.

But I suspect so many jurors had heard that tale that they made an effort to be noncommittal to prolong the suspense if nothing else.

Judge Druckenmiller spoke. "Ladies and gentlemen of the jury, have you reached a verdict?"

"We have," spoke the forelady with a face that had weathered a lot of storms.

"Hand it to the tipstaff, please." The envelope was passed from the forelady to the tipstaff who took it to the clerk, a middle-aged woman of Pennsylvania Dutch proportions. She tore open the envelope and passed the contents to the judge. He looked at it and returned to to her for reading.

She read: "We find for the plaintiff in the amount of twenty-five million dollars. Our verdict was unanimous."

There was a lot of hugging and crying all around. Bomber and Rich Zepf—Easy Willie and Rich Zepf, then Easy Willie and Bomber—they all came to us in front where the Zepf girls were all over us like a swarm of bees, cheering in the most unruly manner, totally inappropriate for a courtroom. Easy Willie hugged Shauna in a familiar manner, I thought went beyond friendship. Then Bomber gave Shauna a bone-crushing hug, and I lost it.

Judge Druckenmiller reached for his gavel and raised it to pound it on the marble block. Then it was as though an invisible angel stopped his hand in midair, his mouth dropped in surprise, and he laid down the gavel and quickly left the courtroom.

Though no one believes me to this day, I swear I saw in the great Buddha's unpatched eye, a tear.